12
2

NEVERLIGHT

NEVERLIGHT

Donald Pfarrer

Seaview Books
New York

The people and events described or depicted in this novel are fictitious and any resemblance to actual incidents or individuals is unintended and coincidental.

The quoted lines on page 278 are from E. F. Watling's translation of Sophocles, published by the Penguin Classics and reprinted with permission.

Copyright © 1982 by Donald Pfarrer.

Manufactured in the United States of America.

FIRST EDITION.

Seaview Books/A Division of PEI Books, Inc.

Library of Congress Cataloging in Publication Data

Pfarrer, Donald.
    Neverlight.

    I. Title.
PS3566.F3N4   813'.54   81–84777
ISBN 0–87223–773–7   AACR2

Designed by Scott A. Young

NEVERLIGHT

I

Richard Vail had never wanted to be a marine and was not now a marine, yet here he sat, beside a trail with a shotgun across his lap, and the hood of his poncho thrown back because rain on the hood deafens you—deafens "you," the man in ambush—to small sounds. If a figure should appear before him out of the dark it was an open question whether he'd fire.

He was in fact one of three people authorized to fire the opening shot. This was both amusing and reckless. The whole arrangement was reckless and unnecessary. The patrol had two missions and two only—first, to reconnoiter two valleys (that was tomorrow), and second, to move to a hill and dig in by Day Three so that Vail, a Navy officer, a specialist, could conduct several naval gunfire attacks by radio.

The rain, the darkness, the dim glow of the trail, the knowledge that silent men were on either side of him, all seemed like the living out of a boyhood fantasy.

Ten men were ranged at intervals along the uphill side of the trail. Half were asleep. Two more were posted in the rice paddies across the trail and some twenty-five meters to the right, where two dikes intersected. The idea was that if an enemy column came along, the ten would blow it off the trail into the paddies. The enemy survivors would then, presumably, take shelter behind the dike and start returning the marines' fire across the trail. But at this point the marine outpost on what would then be the enemy's exposed left would open up, and the night's recreational program would be complete.

Vail didn't think it would work, but neither did he think he was going to die that night. He was infected by the general recklessness. If the plan was too simple, so what?

The other two men who could spring it were Gunnery Sergeant Zander and the patrol leader, a reconnaissance lieutenant several years younger than Vail. Vail liked Gunnery Sergeant Zander because the gunny had come safely through what he called "the big war," World War II, and the Korean War, and was now worried about losing his penis and his pension to "this big inconvenience." That was what Gunnery Sergeant Zander called the present war. Vail liked the lieutenant because he had included Vail in the select number who could open fire. He had been impressed by Vail's civilian profession. Vail was, or had been, a traverse leader. He led scientific parties in the polar regions for the National Science Foundation. Since you can't be a traverse leader all your life, and since Vail had a master's but not a doctorate, it was all but inevitable that he would end up working for an oil company, if he went for money, or teaching geology in a small college. In short, the future looked like a problem.

Vail felt a tap on his shoulder. He slithered back a few yards, hoping to find the place where Bishop had been lying. It would be dry and still warm. Bishop was Vail's radio operator, and Vail had been scheduled to wake him up, but had let him sleep on. Bishop had awakened and come forward to take his turn. Thus the tap. Vail had not heard him coming.

There wouldn't be ten weapons in the opening volley, if half the patrol were asleep, but only five. It wasn't going to work.

Vail groped around with his hands on the wet ground. No luck. He lay on his side, pulled the hood up, brought the shotgun inside the poncho, and drew his feet up under cover as quietly as he could. He closed his eyes. It was no darker than before. He opened his eyes and thought he could see a gleam where Bishop was, as if the rain were more intense there. Bishop was thoughtful, conscientious, quiet. He was not the picture of a marine. Vail's picture, at least, had always been: Kill, fuck, drink, masturbate. But Bishop couldn't be stereotyped. It would be reassuring to say that none of them could, but it would also be false. Vail did occasionally run into marines who were trying to live the myth, and some were succeeding.

His marine brother-in-law had said, on the basis of zero combat experience, that there are only two categories of men—the unfinished and the complete, those who have not fought and those who have. His brother-in-law was a jerk, but jerks can be right. And at naval gunfire school, which Vail attended at Coronado after he was transferred from an icebreaker to the Marine Expeditionary Force, an instructor had said: "You can learn a lot in two minutes, believe me, if they're the right two minutes." Which sounded like a truth, and was humbler. Vail knew that after only three weeks, and no such two minutes, he felt experienced. He also understood that this very feeling was deceptive and a sign of his inexperience. He kept catching himself feeling capable because of his little three weeks. He didn't like it.

Katherine wasn't there with him in the poncho. He didn't know why. With the hood up, and the enveloping all-obliterating sound of the rain, with his slow gain against the cold, with his slow slide toward sleep, she should have been there. He had the shotgun instead of Katherine. And he had this perfect myth, of which he was half aware—that he was one of twelve men cut off from all aid, lying in the rain beside a trail nobody could see. He slid along, upon a darkling plain, without Kit.

When Bishop woke him up everything was silent, and he saw daylight. So there would be no ambush, no ringing in his ears, no shock waves, no yellow flashes, sick terror, blood on the men's clothing, and eyeballs in the dirt. That was what he thought a short-range firefight would be. The two troopers from the outpost were already in, sitting in the stubble by the hedgerow looking at their feet. They were white and shriveled, but both men were telling the platoon leader, without speaking, that they could march. The platoon leader held up five fingers. The remaining troopers appeared one by one, and each man looked for a place where he could sit without flattening a pile of water buffalo dung. Vail folded his poncho, strapped his pack, checked his weapon, and solicited a sign of readiness from Bishop. He saw that he had crawled all around here last night and missed all the buffalo pies. The gunny sent a silent greeting, which he returned. The platoon leader asked, "Are you ready?" and he said he was. When they left, Vail looked at the place as though he'd spent a year there. The grass chewed off by the buffalo, the hedgerow, the trail showing tan through the thicket, the ripening paddies; and now the sun shone, and the blue of the sky lighted up all the colors. He saw the night identity and the day identity of the place, and as the column climbed a hill he began to see it from above; and it moved, it insinuated itself into his memory as a place where nothing had happened; where nobody had opened up, and he had missed the buffalo pies.

At the summit they stopped for a meal, and Bishop showed Vail a pepper bush. "Look here, Lieutenant," Bishop said. He was lanky, concave, almost chinless, and he was afflicted with the tropical pallor. His blue eyes stood out. He seemed to be rather gently interested in everything in the world. He introduced his hand slowly into a bush, rolled his eyes, and came out with a little legume. They sat down to eat. Vail would have taken cold rations, as he nearly always did, but Bishop lit a heat tab and contrived to balance his own and Vail's "heavies" on the grill he had fashioned from wires, which he carried in his shirt pocket and reshaped at every meal. He chopped up the legume and added some to each heavy, and mixed them with his knife; and he smiled at Vail. Vail thought: "What can I do for him?"

In a few minutes smoke rose from the bush where the gunny sat. Others lit up, and the smoke hung in the still air. Then the patrol leader stood, and then everybody did. One man dug a hole, and every man dropped his cans in it, and he filled it; then another man covered over the fresh earth. The men stood waiting, waist deep in the bushes that had concealed them while they ate, and then the patrol leader looked at the gunny, who moved the muzzle of his grease gun, and the point man started off.

There was brush at their thighs and a canopy about fifty feet up, and as the hill grew steeper, as they went down the other side, more sunlight reached them through the canopy. Looking back, Vail could see Gunnery Sergeant Zander at the end of the column, wading down in uneven strides, and ahead of the gunny a submachine gunner; ahead of him a man with an M-79 grenade launcher, then a rifleman, then another grenadier, then a mix of weapons up to Bishop and himself; and ahead of him a submachine gunner; the platoon leader, who also had a submachine gun, a Thompson; and the point man, who had a rifle.

The point disappeared into a wall of close-set little trees, and then the patrol leader. Each man felt better as he went into the trees. The hill steepened, and from down below came the blowing sound of a fast stream. Vail couldn't see the stream, but the column stopped, and two men from somewhere behind him collected canteens.

It was darker here. The soil was exposed, churned with humus, and black. The tree trunks were black, and there were nearly as many vines as trunks. When he got his canteens back Vail put a purification pill and a piece of cinnamon bark in each (to kill the taste of the pill), and gave some bark to Bishop.

When they reached the split point in the early afternoon Vail's hands were trembling and his stomach and bowels were warning that he wasn't used to the heat; but he believed a little rest and a little more water were all he needed.

The column stopped and the word came whispering back: "Gunny up. Gunsmoke up." The gunny and Vail went forward and knelt with the patrol leader in some dark ivy, and the lieutenant spread out his map. His hands were trembling too.

He said to the gunny: "I'll meet you there"—trying to plant his finger on a point on the map.

"Aye aye, sir."

"At, say, 1800?"

"Yes, sir," said Gunnery Sergeant Zander, checking his watch.

"Do the valley any way you like," the patrol leader continued. "You better get some water; we'll be on high ground tonight."

"Yes, sir. I will." The gunny had been dealing with young lieutenants for a long time.

There was an interval of map study, which Vail brought to an end by saying: "I can't hit any of this."

"OK, we're on our own," said the patrol leader, and he started to fold his map.

"Now, Lieutenant," said the gunny.

"Yes, Guns."

"That platoon we saw yesterday."

"Yes, I want your opinion on that," the patrol leader said.

"Well, sir. They heard our birds for sure."

"I agree."

It was college agreeing with experience.

"And let's figure they're Main Force—or Local Force with a smart cadre."

"All right."

"And let's figure the cadre's rehearsing. They're always rehearsing. So he might break into four units, depending on how many automatic weapons he's got, and set four ambushes—or however so many he chooses. But he'll set up where he can set up again another day, for the rehearsal value of it. Do you see what I mean, Lieutenant? He'll set up in certain places, so he can send his people back to the same place some other time."

Gunnery Sergeant Zander's bashed, crinkled face crinkled more, and he caught the lieutenant's eye and asked: "Do you see what I mean? It'll be a natural place. An obvious place. And there is one place," continued the gunny, "right around here, where we'll be on a hike today, that helicopters can land. Right here." Zander placed his finger on the map. "I don't see any others, do you?"

"I can't tell for sure, just from the map."

"No, sir, but I been all over this terrain on my belly. There's just this one spot." He marked it for the lieutenant. "It's a marsh or a bog down in a kind of a bowl, just before you start up your side of the ridge. It's so boggy the big trees don't take root. It's open. Our birds have touched there a couple times."

"Maybe the VC have booby-trapped it, then."

"Yes, sir, maybe. If you have any trouble, Lieutenant, this'll be your place, just because it's so fucking obvious—right here, a hundred or two hundred meters around the bog."

"I'll watch it."

"Yes, sir. I would. Or else this stream, like so, downstream of the bog." He followed the course of the stream with his pencil. "I can't be sure, Lieutenant—you might have to walk the stream for a ways. But look out around the bog, sir, a couple or three hundred meters anywhere around the bog."

"OK, Guns. Got your radio?"

"Yes, sir."

"Good luck to you, then."

"Semper fi, Lieutenant."

Vail went with the lieutenant, to stay out of the gunny's way. The lieutenant took the point. Then came Corporal Jameson, a black, or Negro as they were then called, from Los Angeles, who had a rifle. Budzinski, a grenadier. Vail, carrying his shotgun and double rations because Bishop, who came next, was carrying the naval gunfire radio and spare battery, besides his rifle and 150 rounds of ammunition. It was the beginning of the war, and the Marine Corps didn't have the new lightweight rifles. Tyson, another grenadier. And his close friend Vanaus, with a submachine gun. Seven of them.

They were soon in the stream the gunny had followed with his pencil. It was a dry channel full of mammoth boulders splattered with lichen, smaller rocks the size of a human head, long washes of gravel and sand, holes half full of water, and black vines hanging in curves from the trees. The trees arched over the channel and formed a tunnel, and the sides of the stream were so high, about six feet, that the channel seemed to have sunk half in the earth.

A march releases the mind. Even a reconnaissance patrol, when stealth adds so many burdens, opens the cage. Vail saw himself crawling around in the dark, missing buffalo pies by inches. He scanned the banks sharply, and listened. He was as acute as he'd ever been, but suddenly Kit was there. Not her lips or shoulders or her laugh, or anything so tangible, but her quality, her signature as a woman. Then he saw himself again crawling among the cow pies as if an angel were guiding him.

He came to a place where the channel widened and had a bottom of smooth gravel. As he walked along he heard a crackle, as of dry leaves, which startled him, and he looked down. What he saw, bent under his boot, was a snakeskin four or five feet long, which jerked when he lifted his foot; its scaly transparency made it nearly invisible against the gravel, and two steps farther along when he looked back he couldn't see it. He glanced at Bishop, ten yards behind, and saw the man's tentative expression, which seemed to ask if he wanted the radio. Vail kept walking. He heard an alien sound, a snap or something.

He denied he had heard it. But he was looking at the right bank, and possibly he saw a man in the foliage. He raised the shotgun and rammed the butt into his shoulder, and something flickered denial again, flickered "Stop," but he released the safety and aimed where the man had been and fired. He felt no kick but saw the barrel buck up. He pumped in another round, and an awful despair invaded him.

"Christ, I've compromised the whole thing," he thought, in the ringing of his ears.

The frag order stated that in the event of compromise after noon on Day Two the patrol would be withdrawn.

The enormity of his mistake was just coming home to Vail when a noise like a whimper came from the place he'd fired at, and then the whole channel exploded along its length in fire. Vail felt a concussion on his face; he fired his second shot at the same target and felt another whip, like a firecracker going off in front of his eyes. He was dropping to the gravel, and he felt his whole body and all his veins beaten at a stroke as a grenade exploded somewhere. There were richochets all over the place. He thought of Bishop and turned, and there a few yards back lay Bishop on his side. His hat was turning red. Vail found himself running toward Bishop, bent low, but he was hit from behind as if by a hammer in his upper left leg, and he went down rolling. He was furious with frustration. He had been in the gravel just a few seconds earlier, then he was running, and now he was down again, with gravel and sand in his face, and lying in the center of the channel, conscious of the burning of his leg and of a terrible solidity, as if the impact had lodged in his thighbone. He didn't understand yet that he'd been shot, because that was too incredibly unlikely; the chances were one in hundreds, in thousands.

And he didn't understand what was happening to Bishop. He saw the man's hand, the way it was bent at the wrist, and the way one leg was thrown forward, and concluded: "He's dead." But he saw the body jerk, then jerk again, and again, until he finally understood that an enemy rifleman was destroying the radio on Bishop's back. No sooner did he understand this than he realized the same rifleman could as easily direct fire at himself, and soon would. At about this time he began to see what was happening up and down the channel. He crawled and rolled over his burning leg to the left wall of the creek and fired twice into the brush above and opposite. He fired again and began reloading, knowing he had very little time.

He loaded and chambered a shell, then loaded the tubular magazine, which took several seconds. The ricochets were worse than the shots. After a quick glance upstream, where he observed a muzzle flash, he freed his knife and cut loose two of the grenades taped to his suspenders. He yanked and threw, yanked and threw, and he was already on his elbows and belly-worming upstream before the grenades, with two rather swishing reports, went off in the brush on the opposite bank. He told himself that he'd saved his life with these two grenades. He was drunk with exhilaration because his mind still worked. He wanted to scream with happiness that his mind was working. He seemed to gather facts as he crawled. The VC were firing down the axis of the creek from positions upstream, and into it from positions along the opposite bank. If he had not neutralized the closest of these latter positions with his grenades he would probably never reach the haven of boulders toward which he now heaved himself, using his right knee and his bleeding elbows. His left leg didn't hurt, but it wouldn't work. He tried to make it work. He was about ten yards from the boulders. All this heaving and worming reminded him of playing football with an injury. Then it flashed through his mind: "GSW T&T, left thigh." He had seen that sort of thing in casualty messages: gunshot wound through and through.

He thought of his two grenades as possessing a continuous effect, like radiation. He heard a shout from the rear. "On the point, on the point!" Tyson hollered. "Grenade!" And Vail thought: "He's going to kill me," and in the same instant came the *chunk* of Tyson's 40-millimeter grenade launcher, and Vail put his face in the stones, and his back and anus curdled while he imagined the blunt little tumor flying over him to burst upstream. He heard it detonate and resumed his reptilian advance upon his bloody elbows. Tyson let fly again, and Vail despaired. Half a degree too high and the thing would burst overhead, but again Vail heard in the chaos a detonation upstream that could be Tyson's, and Vail thought, "See, it's all right." He reached the boulders, and he thought, "I made it." These simple statements were enough to convince him for the moment that no further harm would come to him.

He was sure that Tyson was overshooting his target and wanted to tell him so, but he could see nobody and there was no point in shouting. Somebody was shooting at Vail as he pulled his feet into his refuge, and he soon realized it. He cut loose another grenade and arced it toward the hostile bank, and fired four times into the trees and reloaded, and wondered what to do next.

He said: "I'm sure to be killed here."

And it was really an unsatisfactory place. It had looked good only because he'd been exposed out there on the gravel. He tried to figure out what was going on, but to his inexperienced ear it was all chaos. He didn't want to stay and he didn't dare move. Again that hideous concussion, and a bullet lifted the gravel at his hand and shot chips of rock into his face; and he rolled onto his back thinking, "He's in a tree," and fired blindly upward, pumped the gun and fired again.

But the man who was after Vail was not so easily put off. From his high point of vantage upstream he saw the gravel leap to his shot and saw the American roll and fire, and saw as clearly that he himself was still unseen, so he drew careful aim on the center of Vail's body with his carbine and squeezed one off.

Vail didn't believe it. He did *not* believe it. At the same time, he was injected with a horror that meant it was true. He fired again, or intended to fire, but at what? "Where are you?" he asked. Vail still didn't believe he would die, but he was finally persuaded that something extremely bad was happening.

Jameson, who survived upstream, had located the VC in the tree by the flash of his last shot, the one that went through Vail's belly. Jameson took him out with an aimed shot.

In the rear Tyson passed his grenade launcher and bandoliers to his friend Vanaus, who crouched at his side in the rocks touching off an economical burst now and again and chewing the inside of his cheek violently. Tyson dropped his pack. He ran his .45 pistol through recoil and counterrecoil, set the safety, and jammed the useless antique in its holster. Then with a word to his friend he was up and over.

Vail saw him coming. In an interval of quiet he could even hear him running in the gravel and breathing hard. As he ran half doubled over he held out his right hand, and instantly Vanaus sent a burst of tommy-gun fire to do his bidding on the right bank.

Tyson had been seen, not only by Vail, and now a fusillade of rifle and carbine fire choked the channel, and he dived. He bellied into the boulders on the left. Vanaus's fire went whistling up the channel and shut up the VC, and Tyson was back on his feet. He was a fine, quick athlete—as Vail observed with something like a spectator's appreciation.

But what was the point? Nobody could move Vail—certainly not Vail himself; not even this athletic Tyson. For Vail was spiked to the earth by a huge fat spike which shed leaves of rust, but at its core it was hard; and when his body should rot or be consumed by the Asian vermin and birds the spike would stand there still in the rock.

Yet Vail saw this half-real man-boy coming on, and heard the M-79 speak its entire vocabulary again in a single witless syllable, and then a *chuff* when the grenade detonated, pretty close by, it seemed, and another concussive string from Vanaus's overheated Thompson. By that time Tyson was in, landing on his chest.

"It's Corporal Tyson, sir. Lift your arms up, Lieutenant."

Evidently Tyson was going to tear him off the spike and drag him away, and Vail didn't know what he thought of that.

"Wait a second," he said. "Did you see Bishop?"

"Yes, sir. Lift your arms up, Lieutenant."

Vail replied, "Ah—" and passed into a moment when he didn't care, and said clearly: "Ah—shit."

"Yes, sir. You got it," said Tyson. "That's the word."

As Tyson crawled around behind, Vail did as he'd been told. The man passed his arms under Vail's shoulders and grasped the shotgun in both hands. With a sudden and shocking movement he lifted Vail half up and began to drag. The shotgun gripped in the two red hands made a crushing pressure on Vail's chest, and he could hardly breathe. He watched his out-turned feet and saw his heels dragging through the gravel. Vanaus delivered his fire in short hot bursts, but there was no answer from the VC positions upstream, and those on the bank were likewise silent.

The first thing Vail noticed was the quiet, and how Vanaus kept breaking it with his Thompson; and Tyson's breath in his ear; and then the face of Lance Corporal Bishop. As he went lurching past, Vail looked at this face and thought: "Now he's a stereotype."

They laid Vail in a sheltered spot among the rocks, from which he could gaze up through the branches to the white sky. He lay still for a time, accepting the gradual return of some small fraction of his strength. Vanaus tore off a burst, and then there was quiet while he inserted a fresh magazine in the Thompson, and this quiet continued past the click of the magazine into its slot. The smoke spread through the vines and trees, and the blue in it was accentuated by the sun.

Gunnery Sergeant Zander, approaching from somewhere near the point, saw two VC in gray uniforms stripping the patrol leader's body of its weapon, ammo, and pack. They ignored the boots but took the utility belt and canteens. They had trouble with the catch on the watch strap, and they worked at a ring. Zander stopped his people and looked around hastily in search of other VC. Seeing none, he greased these two.

Then came a frantic racket in the brush, and Zander and everybody but the medical corpsman spent a full thirty seconds shredding the vegetation, and then Zander sent two men to look.

The medical corpsman checked the patrol leader's body and

moved immediately to Corporal Jameson, who was turning gray but said: "Hi, Doc."

Budzinski, a few yards downstream, was displayed like a starfish. This unnerved the gunny, who suddenly thought what a misfortune it would be if he were hit by a marine.

He dropped to one knee beside the remains of Budzinski and called out: "Recon!" And Tyson answered out of the smoke and dust: "Watch it, Gunny."

And for several minutes everybody watched it, and sweated, and listened.

The gunny radioed for a medivac bird. He told his superiors that he was compromised. He put out security and set two men to work making stretchers out of ponchos and saplings. And understanding as he did the needs of upper echelons, he made a body count and collected VC documents and weapons. There seemed to be five VC dead. There were three American. Tyson told the gunny that but for Vail's first shot he and Vanaus would have been waxed for sure. The gunny sent Tyson to the place where Vail had aimed, and he found blood and drag marks.

Vail was listening for the helicopters.

II

As Katherine Vail hung up the telephone she decided not to tell Terry yet. "Two more days," she said to herself. The voice of caution, the voice of discipline, the voice of severity. Her throat played a strange trick on her. It let out a sound that was not quite human speech. It made her straighten up and stare at the wall in surprise. She turned off the bedside lamp and went into the lighted hall. She could tell Ella. Ella was in the kitchen—or had been. John was out looking for the cat. But instead of going to the kitchen, Katherine went left, opened the door to Terry's room, and followed the shaft of light in. Terry's bed was a menagerie of dogs, cats, bears, horses, dwarfs, frogs, snakes, seals, ducks—and in their midst the little girl lay asleep.

Where was her face? Which way was she lying?

Katherine moved some animals and lay down on her side and moved the strands of hair to uncover the child's face, and looked at it with the addictive fixity of a parent.

Katherine whispered: "Daddy's going to be all right."

The girl slept on.

"Don't tell her," thought Katherine. "Wait till it's certain."

But she whispered again: "Daddy's going to be all right."

The girl slept.

"Terry, turkey, do you hear?"

The eyes opened.

Katherine repeated her message.

Terry turned her face, and Katherine said: "He's coming home."

And the child thought: "Coming home. Coming home."

"I just talked to the doctor," Katherine said.

"Is-is-is-is-is-is—" The child looked at her mother and finally said: "Is the doctor here?"

"No. I talked to him on the telephone."

"In-in-in Hawaii?"

"Yes, in Hawaii."

Terry had never lost contact with her father. When she was in a building, such as this apartment building in Washington, D.C., the bricks ran right down to the ground. The ground ran all the way to California, and from California it went under the ocean, across to the other shore. This she knew. On the other shore it ran right to wherever her father was, to the top of a mountain if necessary. Thus they were in contact all the time, except when he was in an airplane. While he was flying to the hospital in Hawaii they were separated. But as soon as he landed they were in contact again, the connection running right up through the legs of his bed, just as at this moment it ran down the legs of her own.

"Will-will he come in the morning?" Terry asked.

"No. In two or three weeks. In fourteen or twenty-one days."

Terry nodded. Her eyes all but glowed with interest.

Katherine said: "You can have some chocolate milk if you like. Aunt Ella and I will be in the kitchen. Or you can go back to sleep. Whichever you like. I'll leave your door open a crack."

Katherine kissed her.

The girl felt the kiss on her forehead, closed her eyes, and felt kisses on her nose and lips, and when the bed lurched she opened her eyes. She saw Aunt Ella standing in the doorway behind her mother.

Katherine stared down at the child and couldn't resist dipping down for another kiss.

Terry saw that Aunt Ella had come into the room. She felt a kiss and then another, and smelled her mother's closeness, and felt her mother's hair on her cheek, and saw Aunt Ella beside the bed.

Katherine turned. Ella started to say, "Was it the doctor?" but Katherine was already embracing her.

That was a surprise—and Ella didn't know if it was good news or bad. So Ella held herself somewhat stiff, uncertain, and pressed on Katherine's back, contributing to the pressure of the embrace in a hesitant way, and allowing herself to be moved from side to side.

Katherine noticed Ella's stiffness and said: "He's going to be all right. He's coming home." Then Katherine felt herself squeezed with an unbelievable eagerness. Terry was thinking, "Coming home. Coming home."

Katherine started sobbing, but she tried to hold back. "No, no, stop," she told herself. She had wanted, for Terry's sake, rather for the sake of being certain, to wait two more days, till she had talked to the doctor again—and talked to Richard, possibly. But she didn't care now. When Ella too began to cry, it was more than she could stand, and she let go.

The moment she released them, her joy and relief rushed out convulsively in long, regular waves. Nothing that had ever happened to her had felt so good, or lasted so long.

Part of the goodness was the way Ella's joy mingled with her own, and the way she suddenly felt amid her joy how valuable Ella was. Ella, who had always been lovely, slick, and remote, had been for the last ten days extraordinarily sensitive, and now was overjoyed with Katherine.

Both women felt the child hugging them, and they reached down and half lifted her, and she half climbed, up into their arms, and the sobbing turned to laughter.

"I want to know every detail, every syllable," Ella said as they untangled themselves.

They went into the bathroom, all three of them, and the women wiped their faces while Terry watched, as if witnessing a stupendous breach of adult decorum.

Katherine and Ella looked at each other, and each was such a mess that they couldn't stop another outburst of laughter. Katherine sat on the toilet seat, rocking, laughing, crying, hugging Terry, grasping Ella's hand—but in the middle of all this she also experienced a moment of pure silence, when her face was buried in her hands, and in this dark second several things happened, one after another. She abandoned those bitter fantasies of a solitary life, which she had not been capable of suppressing. She thought: "Terry will have a father." She understood that the good and the bad of life with Richard would continue. She felt the burden of this. She ached to embrace, to envelop, to comfort him.

"Are you ever going to tell me what he said?" Ella demanded.

They were at the kitchen table. Katherine was stirring the chocolate into Terry's milk and Ella was pouring two glasses of wine. Terry
was looking calmly up at Aunt Ella from beneath her black bangs.

"He told me to call back on Thursday," said Katherine. "He said
he'd be more certain then. He said I could probably talk to Richard
on Thursday." She looked at the child, who said:

"When-when-when—"

"The day after tomorrow," Katherine said.

The girl nodded, and listened for more.

"And he said, these were his exact words: 'The surgeons at Chu
Lai seem to have done an excellent job.' And he said there appeared
to be no infection, and there is probably no permanent nerve damage, and he said: 'I really think he'll be all right.' "

Terry drank her chocolate milk, and Katherine wondered
whether she should make the child brush her teeth again.

"And he's coming home," she said.

"Yes—how did that happen?" Ella asked.

"I said, 'Doctor—' "

"You talked him into it!" said Ella.

"Well, I don't know. I said, 'Doctor, once he can travel, is there
any reason why he couldn't convalesce at Bethesda?' And he said,
'Do you live near Bethesda?' And I said, 'Oh, about ten minutes
away.' And he said that it might be possible. And I said my daughter
and I—I said we—Terry—wanted to see her father—I wanted to see
—I wasn't acting, I just spontaneously became utterly incoherent,
and he said in this firm, manly, I-can-handle-it voice: 'I'll make sure
he's transferred to Bethesda as soon as he can travel comfortably.' "

Katherine rubbed the back of her daughter's neck, up under the
onyx hair, and said: "This man is going to wrestle the entire military-
naval-medical bureaucracy to the ground and send my husband
home to me."

She kissed her daughter, and got chocolate milk on her lips, and
smacked them at Terry.

They heard a key sliding into the lock of the back, kitchen door.

Knowing this would be Uncle John, Terry hastily put her glass
down, spilling milk on the table, shoved her chair back, and rushed
to greet him. John, Katherine's brother, came in from the landing,
squinting against the light, carrying the limp, unprotesting Crackpot,
Terry's cat, who had been missing for three days, and whose look

of satiety and indifference underwent no change as Terry took him from her uncle's hands and began stroking and communing with him.

"Let him eat, dear," said Katherine.

The girl released the cat and said to her uncle: "Daddy's coming home."

"What?" said John, and he looked at his sister.

Katherine began to cry again, with a terrible, irresistible convulsion that hurt her throat, and somehow she knew she was rocking like a stricken widow. She had no desire to do this, and tried to stop, but it seemed to go on. She covered her face, and heard Terry say quite clearly:

"He's going to be all right."

It didn't feel good anymore, and Katherine had no illusion that she was letting it happen. She tried to speak, but the result was unintelligible. Then there was no sound except her own. She could hear that as plainly as anybody else. In an interval she heard Crackpot calmly crunching his food. She knew she was in Ella's embrace and that she was soaking the shoulder of Ella's blouse with tears, mucus, and saliva.

She blinked, her focus cleared, and she saw John's polished shoes.

To John Ashley it wasn't altogether clear how anybody could be so unendurably precious to anybody else, but he regarded his sister with a sympathy based on understanding; he did understand that people acted this way.

He said: "So he's got a ticket home."

John Ashley was a marine lieutenant, who would be going over in a few months himself. He was no taller than his sister (but Katherine was a tall woman) and he was built for contact sports. He was blond, suntanned, and had crystalline blue "keep back" eyes. He did not have to earn the respect of his men; he had it the moment they saw him. It was his to lose, and he did not lose it.

"Three weeks over there," said John Ashley, "and he's got a ticket home."

Neither woman was deceived. Both knew Ashley would rather die than get such a "ticket home."

Terry went to sleep against her uncle's chest.

Katherine drank more than enough wine, slept soundly, and was restored to herself the next morning.

She didn't need to lecture herself about how lucky she was. Her mother's example was constantly in her mind, because her mother had not been so lucky.

Katherine's father had come home from World War II an unchanged man. He still couldn't see the point of business. He might have been changed in that now he could see it even less than before. He couldn't face a life of business after assisting in the destruction of Nazism, and after helping to liberate the camps. He bought a farm in New Hampshire cheap. It was exactly what he wanted. He loved the woods, the snow, the mud, the hunting, and the isolation, and his daughter learned this love from him. He probably couldn't have stayed there, because after all he needed action, which was why business had seemed so ludicrous. So he was probably heading into a contradiction, but as it happened he never had to face the decision whether to stay in the boondocks or go someplace where he could make a career.

His crop of apples in 1950 (it was an apple farm; no milk cows) was good, and he did well selling it by fractions in the autumn and winter, and into the spring of '51. Then he went to Korea as an overaged captain in the infantry.

His widow's name was Anna Yankowski. She was told she was a widow by a fat Army major in a uniform decorated, it seemed to her, with patches, decals, cartoons, and ribbons.

The major accepted coffee. She watched him closely as they sat at her kitchen table—and he suddenly produced a large brown envelope from his briefcase and placed it before him. Her eyes fastened on it, but meanwhile all her plans were careering through her mind. They would leave the farm and go back to Chicago and live near her relatives. She would get a job somewhere and pile up money for Katherine's education. (In those days prudence made sense.) She would keep the farm and its value would surely rise, and when John came of college age she would sell it and put him through school, and he needn't work.

Her mind wheeled over the whole American economy like a hawk over a henhouse, but she could see nothing for her. She was an educated woman but not a trained one. She was, in fact, the first woman in her family to go to college. Surely if she dropped down and searched she would find somewhere in this vast organism, this mammoth conglomerated process of gluttony and excretion, a small use for her talents, whatever they were.

"Mrs. Ashley," began the major.

"Yes, yes, yes, Major—I understand."

Late that night when the boy, John, came across the cold boards into his mother's room, because the sound of his sister's sobbing had driven him from his own, he found her lying on the bed wrapped in her winter coat, staring up. Her large eyes, which the boy clearly saw in the moonlight, were blank.

A few weeks later she moved with John and her teenage daughter, Katherine, the elder, to a Polish neighborhood in Chicago, where she rented a poor apartment as part of her fanatical campaign of saving for Katherine's college expenses. She and the girl shared the bedroom and John had a corner of the living room, an arrangement that meant Katherine's friends couldn't stay past nine o'clock at night, for which Katherine sometimes held the boy responsible and criticized him. Mrs. Ashley's rules of thrift were monastic. She bought clothing for Katherine at a placed they called "the junkie," and the daughter and mother often quarreled. Katherine at seventeen was a brilliant, willowy girl who had been her father's darling and had obeyed only him, and now would obey nobody. She read Keats and Sappho. She was irresponsible with money, and she found her mother's economies grotesque.

Must she go to school with elbow patches? In used shoes? In a Navy pea coat? After a while the pea coat set a trend in the school, but the rest of her clothing was "crappy." This indelicate word infuriated her mother.

The strain was eased when Mrs. Ashley got a job translating articles from the Polish press for an institute on a university campus. The articles were deadly but the pay was good, and this, together with her Army benefits, built up the college fund. They moved to a better apartment, and in the fall, sixteen months after her father's death, Katherine went to college.

Mrs. Ashley attracted men, and men interested her, in general. She matured to a new handsomeness that was perhaps an exquisitely transient form of beauty under the subtle attentions she now received.

John grew. He was more or less smart in school. From the age of thirteen he always had a job of some sort, and now he took jobs requiring physical exertion. By high school he didn't sleep well at night unless he'd done hard physical work or played in a game of football or some other rough sport during the day. Mrs. Ashley thought he was more intelligent than his marks showed, but exactly where his gifts lay and how they might serve him she couldn't guess. She thought perhaps he'd make a lawyer. She sold the farm, as she had anticipated, for an amount that would carry John through college if he chose to ride on it, but he accepted only a little help, to please his mother.

With John in college and Katherine married (Katherine married Richard Vail), Mrs. Ashley herself would perhaps have married, a professor six years her junior who had shared her table often and her bed sometimes, but while she was contemplating this at her leisure, even with a touch of complacency, she discovered herself ill with cancer. She who had considered a second marriage now regarded death. It was a progression which by the calendar, as such things go, was short, but measured in the waste and suffering of a woman was long. She grew less intellectual about it as she grew weaker. In it she perceived no order, no God, no rationale.

In the early stages she felt vindicated by God's absence. She had always known he wouldn't be there when she needed him, and he wasn't. She had been reared a Catholic, but she had never felt guilty for not understanding the paradox of human suffering. What the nuns seemed to be saying was that such calamities as cancer were prepared by God as opportunities to exercise his mercy by putting an end to them. Now that she had cancer all paradox and mystery disappeared from it. It was simply an evil power, and it was killing her. That was what it did, effectively denying her right to deny the goodness of God.

With her mother's history before her, then, as the true standard of war experience, Katherine felt as if the harshest of all laws had been relaxed for her sake. She tried not to say "I'm lucky." She could stop the words but not the idea. She was intoxicated with her luck.

But her self-control was far stronger than it had been the night before. When during breakfast John and Ella discussed whether they should return to Camp LeJeune that day (John was on emergency leave), Katherine noticed that the discussion revolved around a single fact: that if John signed in at his battalion office before midnight, today would count as a day of duty. This meant John and Ella would have an extra day of leave to spend together before he went over, in two or three months. Katherine said: "Go back today—really—please." Ella wanted that day, and Katherine wanted her to have it.

They packed. John descended the stairs with a suitcase in either hand and Terry clinging to his back. When the car was loaded and they stood beside it to say good-bye, Terry held John's hand and looked up at him.

Ella and Katherine kissed.

John's crystalline eyes fixed upon Katherine, and he said: "Say hi to Dick for me."

Katherine felt something slip, and she replied, not altogether reasonably: "I'm not counting on anything. I'm not assuming anything. I'm—nothing—nothing—until I hear his voice." She feared the membrane would break again, but it didn't.

"Well, OK, fine, *if* you talk to him," said her brother, "tell him I said hi—and congratulations."

"My beloved Beloved," she wrote that night. "John sends congratulations! In fact, 'Hi and congratulations.' My muscular brother running true to form. When he said this I thought it was like saying hi to somebody whose clothes and eyelashes have been burned off in an atomic blast, who crawls out of the blast zone and you greet him with: 'Congratulations.' But then I thought: John at least is assuming Richard is strong. And then I realized I too think you're strong—and in that spirit I report that while you lie there, my beloved, suffering what pain I know not, your brother-in-law-with-the-shoulders says congratulations.

"I wonder if you realize how unjust the world is. I'm not sure you think in those terms. What I mean is this.—I couldn't write this if I hadn't already written you a letter a night ever since the telegram, telling how I love you, and if I hadn't heard the doctor say last night that you will be well.—What I mean is that you, flesh of my flesh, have been shot, shocked, bled, cut open and sewn up, drugged, transported, and, I have no doubt, terrified and, I wouldn't be surprised, intimidated and thoroughly daunted.

"And what is the *result* of all this terror, pain, anxiety, fear, and hurt? The—or I should say *a*—result is that the one who loves you, the one who quivers like a taut wire each time your heart beats, this

lover, this adorer, this woman, this wife, shudders with relief and
joy. What a result!"

The next morning Katherine realized she had reached two decisions
while she slept. First, she would quit looking for a job. What a relief
that was. Relief and release seemed to have adopted her. But to be
rational, what was the point of looking for a job now?

For one thing, she didn't know what kind of job. Seven years ago
in Madison she had worked as the Competent Person at an electrical
supply firm while Richard wintered over at the South Pole. She was
newly married and pregnant. When he came back she quit the job,
and gave birth to Terry. Richard was then on the staff of the Geo-
physical and Polar Research Center at the University of Wisconsin.
He usually spent the summers in Greenland and the winters working
at the Center and taking courses. Next he got a job as a traverse
leader and they went to Dartmouth, where the project was being
organized. Thus she returned to New Hampshire, to her own
ground. She was surprised how good it felt.

Loneliness here was loneliness she could endure and profit from.
She had a card from the college library, a car, and enough money,
and she had Terry. She put Terry in a carrier and climbed the same
hills, in the same woods, as she'd climbed with her father. Richard
spent the austral summer of 1961–62 in Antarctica. Katherine was
again pregnant, but she miscarried. There—in this—was a kind of
loneliness that might have knocked her off balance, except that she
had Terry. Indeed, when Richard came back in March he seemed
more depressed by the miscarriage than she. To him, they had lost
a child; to her, a pregnancy. She reflected that it would seem more
natural the other way around. He wanted to make her pregnant
again right away, but she asked if they couldn't wait. Perhaps after
all she was more hurt than he. When she hesitated he felt the guilt
of having rushed her. She saw his guilt and felt an access of tenderness toward him, bordering on adoration; and he, seeing that the
miscarriage had hurt more than he'd guessed, took care for the first
time in their marriage to modulate his love. He made certain it
always reached her and that it was steady, and that she knew she
could have whatever privacy she needed. That spring they spent days
on end walking in the woods, on loggers' trails, in the open mow-

ings, and climbing in the White Mountains, nearly always with Terry.

Then Richard faced a fallow period, in which the logical thing was to resume the course work for his doctorate. Instead he accepted a job offer from the National Science Foundation in Washington, and they moved, and settled in, and discovered that he hated the job. He was expected to be a bureaucrat. He had hoped to influence the direction of the research by influencing the flow of grant money, and this still seemed possible, but at unbearable personal cost. One day he came home happy and astounded her by declaring he wanted to join the Navy. Seeing her expression, he said: "I always intended to do my military service." And it was true, but that was years ago. She set herself a minimal objective: to force him to see what he was really doing, which was abandoning a career. She did not oppose him; in fact in this she agreed with him, because what he was abandoning was a young man's career, like baseball. He was twenty-nine, and he must either get firmly into the academic track or get out. She saw the Navy as a benign interval. But she wanted Richard to understand what he was doing. She was no more a careerist than he was, but she knew that a man needed a career. Richard, on the contrary, said it was the quality of the experience that mattered. He signed up with the Navy in April 1964, four months before the Gulf of Tonkin Resolution passed Congress.

He spent part of his first Navy year in Washington, as a bureaucrat in the Pentagon oceanography office, and part on an icebreaker in the Antarctic seas. Then they sent him to naval gunfire school in California, and in August 1965 to Vietnam.

It was at that point Katherine thought about a job. She was looking at a solid year alone. But what the hell does one do to earn money —especially money one doesn't need? It was a vexing question.

But when she woke up Thursday, the day after Ella and John left, it was also an answered question. She wouldn't get a job at all. Not with Richard hurt, not with his convalescence lying before them, not with the uncertainty about where they'd be sent after he returned to duty. She had forgotten this question of a job when she received the telegram about Richard, and it was pleasant to remember it and settle it in the same stroke.

Her second decision was that Richard should convalesce in New Hampshire. There was no question he'd want to. He hated everything about Washington except the architecture, and was as addicted to the woods as she. But would the Navy let him? She awoke scheming, and her bare feet hit the floor with a slap. Not only her feet were bare. She crossed the bedroom clothed only in her idea, imagining a medical captain or rear admiral at Bethesda Naval Hospital who might be flexible enough, reasonable enough, accessible enough to be persuaded to let Richard go. After all, why not? Once they had examined him and put a few check marks in a few boxes, why not? She wrapped herself in her summer robe and went down the hall to look at Terry, saw that the child still was sleeping, and went into the bathroom.

She relieved herself, but there was scarcely anything because she had had one of those dreams that drenched the sheets with her sweat. Then into the shower, and she used enormous quantities of water fantasizing her encounters with the medical captain or rear admiral. "Will he even talk to me?" she asked—but she went thundering ahead with her argument, whether he would talk to her or not. If admirals didn't talk to the wives of badly wounded men, they should. Her argument was that letting Richard go to New Hampshire was a medically sound procedure. Once the doctors and hospital had played their role, Richard would benefit spiritually and physically from a few weeks of rest, moderate exercise, and clean air in the place he loved best, at the season he loved best. So when Katherine reached down to shut off the water she was seeing the soft maples turning red, the sugar maples orange, the poplars yellow—and Richard walking down a logging trail with the leaves flying at his feet, and Terry perched on his shoulders with her fingers laced across his forehead and her feet tucked behind his back.

The sheet of water across her chest broke and resolved itself into a hundred drops. The streams continued down her back as she pressed the water through her hair from the hairline to the nape of her neck. She resembled her well-formed mother except that she was taller and had more figure, and was hippier, and had elliptical, not rounded eyes. Her mother's eyes had been skeptical. Katherine's were unpredictable. There were streaks of gray in her hair, although she was only thirty.

She dressed, woke Terry and made breakfast, fed the cat, and called Mr. Willoughby in New Hampshire. Mr. Willoughby was a farmer who had been her father's neighbor and hunting partner. He was distressed to hear about Richard, and he agreed to rent the Vails his camp.

That night Katherine called Tripler Army Hospital in Hawaii. The doctor confirmed his early prognosis, set a tentative date for Richard's transfer to Bethesda, and then said: "Just a minute now and I'll put somebody on the line."

Katherine motioned Terry to her, and they put their ears together and cocked the phone so both could hear. Maybe for that reason, the voice Katherine heard was alarmingly thin. "Hello, Kit," it said. It was a voice she almost couldn't recognize, but it had to be Richard's because nobody else called her Kit.

"Terry, sweetheart—you know, you won't be able to do your circus jump."

"Why-why-why-why-why . . . Why not? Won't Daddy want to?"

"He'll want to, but you know where Daddy has been hurt, right here in the belly, and here in the leg. What if you jumped and your foot kicked his hurt leg or your knees bumped his belly?"

Katherine watched the child's eyes—large dark eyes full of the sight of just such an accident.

"Will we be able to hug him?" Terry asked.

"Yes. We'll hug him carefully and kiss him, and he'll kiss us—but we aren't sure we'll see him tonight, remember. We may just see his plane tonight."

"You can't see them if they're in the airplane," Terry surmised aloud, and formed a picture of a huge jet with lighted windows moving through the night sky, out of contact.

She said to her mother: "But we *might* see him."

"Yes—and we might not."

"But we might!" Terry repeated, and she began jumping up and down and saying, "Boing! Boing! Boing!" She jumped her way into her closet and continued jumping among the clothes, singing: "We might! We might! We might!"

"Clean 'em up—and get dressed," said Katherine, raising her voice simply to be heard.

Katherine went to her own room and surveyed her wardrobe, which was slapdash but had a few good things in it. "I'll know him," she thought, "at any distance, no matter how he may have changed."

His voice in recent conversations had been stronger, and she expected that Richard would be much thinner, and perhaps a little stooped until the abdominal surgery had completely healed—a rangy man six feet three inches tall, bent, walking slowly with the aid of a cane or crutch, with a decided limp (but not a crippling one) —alert receptive eyes, the pattern of Terry's—heavy black eyebrows, a prominent jaw, a nose that dives straight down—a wide, creased, scored forehead—hair "as black as a crow's wing," as Richard's father was supposed to have said once of Richard's mother's hair. Richard had a body like Abraham Lincoln's—big-shouldered, bony, with big extremities—a rail-splitter's body—a primitive, ungainly gift; a powerful inconvenience that worked.

"Terry," she called, "are you dressing?"

"Yes," answered the girl.

"What are you going to wear?"

No answer to this.

Katherine could dress for Richard, in which case she'd wear her russet shift because he liked the fit of it, or she could dress for the Military Police, doctors, nurses, and other authority figures who might try to keep her behind some fence while Richard and the other men were being transferred from the jet to the helicopters.

This part of the evening was in doubt. Richard had called to say he would be leaving Tripler on a jet that would make one stop in California to leave some sick and wounded men at Oak Knoll Naval Hospital, and then come on to Andrews Air Force Base, ten miles from where Katherine now stood. At Andrews the wounded men would be put into helicopters and taken across Washington to Bethesda Naval Hospital—and the only certainty was that their families could see them at Bethesda tomorrow morning. Katherine had called a friend of Richard's at the NSF, and he had called a friend at the Department of the Navy, who called a friend at the Military Air Transport Service, who obtained the Tripler plane's estimated time of arrival at Andrews. So Katherine had that.

She chose an austere linen suit with slash pockets, a silk blouse, and her best shoes. The suit was tan, the blouse was charcoal brown, and the shoes were an alligator pair that Richard had brought home from a duty-free port. They didn't quite fit. She also chose her best underwear.

She heard a bark. She turned and saw Terry coming along the hall on all fours, barking. The child had a knee sock stuck in her belt for a tail, and she wore a stocking cap with two mittens pinned to it for ears.

"See-see-see-see-see, I'm Gray-Eyes the ski dog, and I have a brown tail and black ears, and I'm black except for one white paw," declared the girl as she advanced toward her mother, "and I have a horrible scar on my muzzle and I have a limp, a really bad limp. You call me Gray-Eyes. You say, 'Hi, Gray-Eyes.' You say, 'Gray-Eyes, Dick is waiting to see you. Dick wants to see you.'"

"Well, hi, Gray-Eyes. What a terrible scar you have on your muzzle. Dick does want to see you. He's waiting to see you."

"But I limp away," said Terry, doing so. "My limp is so bad, my tail is so low it drags," and she shuffled down the hall into her room, where a murmuring monologue or dialogue continued as Katherine began to dress.

Katherine let a couple of minutes go by, and then she called, as if the visit of Gray-Eyes had not occurred: "Terry, you better get dressed."

Terry replied, "OK," and Katherine began thinking. She could see herself inciting a crowd of women, children, teenagers, and old men as it overwhelmed a cordon of MPs and streamed onto the runway. "Down, you drone, you mad wretch, do you expect me to stand here like a tree? I'm going to touch that man's face. I'm going to pull his hand to my breast. I'm going to look—see his eyes!" She thought the image of the tree was especially good—of herself in motion, yet powerless to move—and she shot out a series of epithets: "You incredible moron, you militarist, you martinet!" Realizing they all started with *m,* she looked for others. "You muddah! Milquetoast! Monkey! You insufferable mouse! Down! Back! Out of my way, you turd standing upright!" She drew on her stockings, and buttoned her blouse while looking in the mirror. She made no appraisal of her looks; in fact, she didn't really see herself.

On came Gray-Eyes with a different pair of mittens pinned to her hat, saying: "My ears are speckled—no—n-n-n-n-no, Mommy, don't worry. I promise I won't change 'em again. And my tail is all brown and my body is jet black—and my chest has a big white blaze. S-s-s-see, I have one white paw, and this is the injured one, and I still have my horrible scar from fighting the other ski dogs, and such a limp—and Dick says: 'Gray-Eyes, old friend, that's really a bad limp,

old dog.' N-n-n-now you say, 'Yes, Dick, old Gray-Eyes here was
crushed.' Now you say it, Mommy.''

"All right, dear, I'll say it. 'Yes, Dick, old Gray-Eyes here was
crushed.' ''

The girl barked and wheeled, rather too much like a horse, and
limped down the hall to her room, whence came more murmurings
and an occasional bark and growl.

Katherine sat motionless on the bed in her stockings and blouse,
feeling uncertain. She gave Terry a few minutes and then called:
"Terry, baby, what are you going to wear?"

To which she received no answer but the cessation of the child's
murmuring. And Katherine could see Richard walking in the half
dark between the planes, bent, slow and tentative, and then his eyes
quite close to her own.

"Terry, dear, are you dressing?"

"Yes," answered the girl.

"What are you wearing?"

But Gray-Eyes the ski dog came thumping into the hallway with
yet another set of mittens pinned to the stocking cap and a different
knee sock, issuing fresh descriptions and directives.

Katherine stopped these with her kisses, drawing the child to a
standing position and taking the beloved face in her hands, kissing
the girl's cheeks, lips, and forehead, trying to bite her ear, and
setting off a struggle. Katherine looked into Terry's eyes, which after
a few moments' evasion settled upon the mother's—their deep
brown, almost black irises standing in perfect contrast to Katherine's
daylight blue.

"Terry, dearest, Daddy wants to see you so much it hurts him. He
loves you, dearest, with all his heart. He is hoping—he wants very
badly, very badly, dear, to see us tonight. Do you remember what
he told you?"

The girl gave a low growl and a bark.

"Terry, please don't be Gray-Eyes now. Please."

Katherine took Terry to her room and helped her straighten her
closet. Terry cleared a place on the bed, moving stuffed animals and
half a dozen books on deer, dogs, and horses, sat down, and began
to unpin the mittens from her stocking cap.

A few minutes later they were on the Capital Beltway, beginning
a half circle of the city, and Terry said:

"Maybe we won't see him tonight, remember."

Katherine responded: "But maybe we will."

They cried almost in unison: "We might! We might!"

During the ride Terry looked at Katherine with brimming eyes and reported that she was having a "bad thinking," but refused to discuss it. Her spirit slowly recovered, and when they were approaching the gate at Andrews the girl said:

"OK now, Mommy, you do it."

And Katherine said: "Oh—boo—we might not see him tonight."

And they sang out together: "We might! We might!"

The sentry took Katherine's name and the number of the Pentagon sticker on her front bumper; he tore a map of the base off a tablet and made an X on it with a red crayon, and said, "The aircraft from Tripler is coming in here, at this X," and he drew a box with his crayon and explained that there were six sets of directions printed on the map and she was to follow the set he had enclosed in the box. He waved her through, and Katherine drove down the road a short way, then stopped to consult the map. The light was beginning to fail but she could read the directions, and she could see the X.

They parked in a vast and nearly empty lot and went down a pedestrian lane between two red-brick buildings. They were holding hands.

"I hear Daddy's plane," said Terry, and stopped.

Katherine expressed the view that with so many planes in the air, and likely to be in the air, how could they tell which was Daddy's?

Terry had no answer, only faith. "It's coming closer," she affirmed. She listened. She did not look up.

·There was indeed an increasing thudding noise, but Katherine said: "That's not a jet."

Nonetheless they stood listening as the throb grew within the roar, as the roar became more portentous. The thudding seemed to be struggling to get out of the roar.

They ran to the end of the lane, and as they escaped the confined space between the buildings they saw first one, then two, then six helicopters low in the sky before them, heading in from the left, showing belly and suspended wheels, looking very heavy and as if they were hanging from invisible cables.

One by one the six turned some imaginary corner and revealed on their sides the word NAVY, and they seemed to swing with a

greater momentum and to lift their bellies even more as they lowered themselves beyond a row of buildings. The sound was baffled,
and soon cut off. Terry and Katherine hurried down the street and
into one of the buildings, in obedience to their printed directions,
and found themselves in something like an ordinary terminal, but a
virtually empty one.

They went straight through and out the opposite doors, and here
was a low chain link fence with forty or fifty people spread along it.
Beyond the fence lay a cement apron, where the six helicopters
squatted, and beyond there was the airfield, whose other side was
lost in the smog and dusk.

In the door of one chopper a crewman sat swinging his feet and
listening to headphones; another strolled toward the fence; a pilot
in a khaki jumpsuit talked over the fence with a man in his early old
age, and Katherine heard the older man ask, "What keeps 'em up?"
and the pilot answer, "It's all a big mistake." A little boy her own
age confronted Terry and said, "My daddy's wounded," and Terry
sent him a censorious look. She studied the helicopters through the
fence, and even to her they seemed more like a problem than a
solution. To Katherine they didn't even look like insects. She wished
they did. "I must be weakening," she thought. "They're only machines." Ingenious, useful machines too. She conversed with an old
woman who had come for a glimpse of her grandson. The grandson
had guessed the time of arrival but had guessed three hours too
early, and the woman had been waiting since. "I don't mind. We're
lucky," she said. Terry roamed, and proved impervious to other
advances from the little boy, and came back to Katherine's side every
two or three minutes. Katherine could see a man in one of the
helicopters lying on his side with his knees drawn up and his head
pillowed on his arm. He made her think of the way Homer contrasts
metal and human muscle. Then she had a flash of the *Iliad,* of the
combat under the walls of Troy and the butchery of the Greeks and
Trojans. She felt the way the *Iliad* made her feel. An officer came
from the terminal building and told the families the plane was five
minutes out. He asked that they stay behind the fence until the pilot
had shut down his engines and lowered his ramp, and that they not
impede the transfer of the men to the helicopters because there were
seriously wounded aboard. And he said the helicopters could not
start their engines till the families had cleared the apron. Katherine
squeezed Terry's shoulders and bent down and whispered: "I think

we're going to see Daddy." Terry took Katherine's hand, and Katherine pulled her against her hip. The old woman, battered, balding, and encumbered with flesh, said to Katherine: "We can wait five more minutes, can't we." Floodlights came on, and it was night. Katherine saw pain and ruin in the old woman's face, saw the face as a mere register of adversity, and said to herself again, "I must be weakening." She looked again but could not eradicate the impression. The aged woman saw Katherine looking at her, and sensed without comprehending Katherine's distress, and took Katherine's hand. The hands of the very old, like those of the very young, have a special power of communication, so this blotched, blunted, arthritic hand transmitted to Katherine a subtle confidence. "There it is," said somebody; and down the line a man asked the officer from the terminal whether that was it, and he said: "Could be."

Two white lights had appeared in the sky, distant and seemingly motionless. There was a zone of blue light beyond them. They began to drift and slant toward the base, and Katherine heard the officer say it was the right kind of bird arriving at the right time, and when it landed it raised her expectations further by its slow stiff prehistoric turn in the right direction. It faced her and came whining toward her with its body bulging, and its wings drooping from their apex on the body. It showed its dim intelligence by whining and wheeling in response to the signalman who stood on the apron holding aloft two yellow wands of light, and as it wheeled one of its sagging wingtips described an arc that all but touched the closest of the helicopters. It presented its high erect tail to them. The signalman gave it the cut sign. The whine was set free and died. And a ramp began unhinging under the tail, and touched the pavement.

The toe of one of her alligator shoes touched the ramp as she leaned to peer into the plane. The light inside was weaker than she had expected, and her view was partially obscured by a big metal box with a red cross on it, but beyond this she saw several nurses, men in dungarees, cots, and a few men in light-blue robes who were looking out. She did not see Richard. Four men in blue dungarees and white sailor hats came along an aisle and down the ramp, carrying a stretcher, and the people opened a way. The man on the stretcher was blanketed and strapped down; he was not conscious. They took him by Katherine. He had a tube in his nose. She resumed her search of the plane.

Then came another four sailors carrying another stretcher care-

fully down the ramp, trying to hold it level, and this man was mostly
bandages. She thought: "How will his family recognize him?" and
thought of the possibility that a family could see its son go by, or a
wife her husband, so close she could touch him, and never know
who he was.

The next man seemed well, even embarrassed, and a woman said
his name and walked beside him holding his hand.

Katherine searched the dim interior and saw a lot of activity, but
not Richard.

The next man's stretcher was rigged with a little jostling mast and
a bottle of fluid, and both his arms were upright from the elbows and
taped to splints, and it seemed to Katherine at first that there was far
less under the blanket than there should have been. As the man
passed she saw that it was true and that he knew it.

The next stretcher had a mast and a full set of straps, and an
unconscious burden. The one after had a man who looked directly
at Katherine, and he seemed quite all right, but when he met his
family a moment later he said absolutely nothing. They sent signs of
love and gladness, they kissed and touched him, they walked beside
him. Katherine remembered his eyes—they had a flat, meaningless
look. Then came another with too little under the blanket, a man
with an intelligent, expectant face. A woman cried out.

Suddenly Katherine noticed that Terry was gone, and she was
smitten with fear. She turned away from the ramp as another man
was being brought down, and swept her gaze across all the choppers
looking for Terry, and searched the crowd again, and looked inside
the plane, and everywhere, including along the fence, and could not
see her.

Then came Richard walking very deliberately toward her, staring
at her with such intense love that she felt the opening of a new depth
in her own love. For a second just seeing him was all she could stand.
He came slowly nearer, limping, carrying Terry in his right arm, and
Terry held his cane and looked triumphantly at her mother with dark
eyes like Richard's.

Katherine ran and flung herself upon him, and the whole interval
of his absence and all her pain were obliterated in his familiar odor,
his familiar texture, the circling of his arm around her back, the
familiar taste of his kiss. As she kissed him she also tasted salt and
felt how hot his cheeks and lips were, almost too hot to be touched

for long, and once she opened her eyes and saw his great dark eyes so close they nearly merged, and she drew back so she could see him, but only for an instant. He was the same—the same—but his love was more forward. She was like a deprived addict who has sought not ecstasy but only peace, who finds an ecstatic peace. She kissed him, and murmured, and declared herself to him, and heard his declarations, and held her face still from time to time for his kisses, and then she kissed Terry and there was a minute or so of three-way kissing and Terry said: "Double smooches!"—a sort of code word between her and Richard. Katherine pulled back abruptly and exclaimed:

"My God, have I hurt you?"

"No, no, no," he said, and pulled her to his chest with something close to his old strength, and Terry said: "He's carrying me," which cut through Katherine in a way she never fully comprehended. She said: "Yes, baby, yes, sweetheart," and kissed the child with a desperate hunger, all the while seeing the child's face as it had been in that first moment as she held her father's cane.

"Let's get the hell out of here," Richard said.

"Yes, I'll show you my den," the girl said.

Katherine looked at him carefully and asked: "Don't you have to—" and she made a gesture toward the helicopters.

Richard said: "No. I can check in tomorrow."

"I'm going to faint," said Katherine.

They began to act rational. Terry got down and gave Richard his cane and they went forward to get his ditty bag, which he'd left on the ground where Terry had met him.

"Is this where you came from?" Katherine asked.

"Yes—the ambulatory exit. Also called the front door."

"Let me carry it," she suggested.

"No, thanks, I can handle it," and after he had taken a few of his rather difficult steps he halted and turned to her—in a place where the light was less good—and they looked into each other's eyes, and smiled. Richard broke the moment by saying to Terry: "I'm sorry I can't carry you on my shoulders, turkey," and she said that was OK, but then he hesitated, and handed his cane and ditty bag to Katherine, and lifted the child to his shoulders, and they moved toward the gate.

III

"I'm going to scream—I have a right to scream—damn him, where is that accursed *cat?*"

Richard leaned forward and said confidentially: "It's OK, Terry, don't be upset. Mother is having a fit."

"Crackpot, you miserable oversexed beast, you slave," she apostrophized, and turned to Richard and said: "He's not our pet, he's not our friend, he's the servant of his appetites."

"Well, he's—"

"I'll have him fixed. I'll simply remove his appetite. He'll never know the difference, and we'll feed him till he can't move. Crackpot, damn you! We'll miss the color," she added.

"No, no," said Richard, "we won't miss the color. We'll be delayed another day or two at the most and we'll see the color at its peak."

"Why are you so reasonable about this and so irrational about everything else?" she demanded.

"I'm irrational about everything else?"

"You're reasonable about little things and irrational about big things, yes."

"So, this is a little thing? Then why are you—"

"I will fix that cat with my own hands. Here, kitty-kitty-kitty, wherever you are, come to momma."

"Can I go to Julie's?" Terry asked. Her friend Julie O'Connor had come that morning to say good-bye. It was now late afternoon, and their bags still stood in a row by the living room door.

Terry conferred by telephone with her friend, and from what Katherine could hear she deduced that they had a school for mice. As Terry prepared to leave she put a toy mouse in her pocket, and a book the size of a postage stamp.

"I'll walk her," said Richard, and they started to leave, but Terry stopped and said:

"Pre-pre-pre-pre-pre-pre-pre-pretend I'm a bad girl, and you say, 'Go to Julie's!' but I'm bad and I won't obey you, y'see, and you have to kick me there."

"Kick you there," repeated Richard.

"A kid who won't obey *is a bad girl,*" she explained, "and I ... *pretend* I'm very bad, now, and I won't go—but first you tell me." She ran a few steps ahead, stopped, looked back, and presented her blue denim rear end.

"Now *tell* me, Daddy."

"OK, you brat, you beanbag, go! Git! Scram! Beat it! Shoo!" said Richard, lifting a Dickensian finger. "Go, you raggedy no-good *bad girl,* or I'll kick you there."

"Nee-o, nee-o, I won't, I disobey you."

He tapped her fanny with the side of his shoe, and Terry squealed and darted ahead, soon reassuming her position and looking over her shoulder with delighted eyes, watching his approach.

"I won't go," she declared. "I'm still bad. I don't obey you."

Her black bangs concealed her heavy black brows, and her eyes shone with an exquisite tension that was eased only by frequent squeals and tremblings.

"Now, Daddy, you have to kick me *hard,* because I'm *real* bad."

"You'll go, you disobedient brat. Here comes a kick that'll knock you into the middle of next week. Look out, Miss Bad Girl, here comes."

"Now, Daddy—not too hard—*pretend* hard—but I'm a real, real bad girl, and you tell me—"

He gave a judicious kick, which brought forth a squeal and sent her darting forward again. In this fashion they crossed the living room, but suddenly the child turned a meditative circle, came up beside her father and delivered her hand into his, and asked as they reached the door:

"D-d-did you do your ferapy today?"

"Well no, I didn't."

"Did you yesterday?"

"Yes."

"Did you run in the shallow pool?"

"Yes."

"OK," said Terry, and they went out the door.

When Richard came back twenty minutes later Katherine asked: "Did you see Sexpot?"

"No. Will you really have him fixed?"

"I won't *have* him fixed, I'll fix him with my bare hands. Do you object? What's so wonderful about two little balls?"

"I don't know about wonderful, but they're his, not ours."

"He is ours, so his balls must be ours," said Katherine.

"Well, we feed him and so forth—and he sleeps with Terry some nights, and you cuddle him when he wants to be cuddled—but most of the time he's out."

"That's exactly my point, he's not really a pet because he's always cruising."

"All right, if he's not really a pet," said Richard, "how is he 'ours'?"

"He is *ours,"* she said, "because we are sitting here instead of driving to New Hampshire because he's cruising."

"So then, if I understand you, you'll cut off his balls because he's delaying our trip."

"Richard, you're clever, but you're only a man. Your behavior is every bit as instinctive as Crackpot's. You are defending Crackpot's balls. That's in the first place. But unconsciously you are also defending the Platonic Idea of Balls, which men always do. That's in the second place. And in the third place you feel a vague threat to your own balls and so you're defending them too. But, sweetheart, nobody is going to take them from you. Certainly I'm not."

"What's so wonderful about two little balls?" he said.

"Little?" she asked, moving toward him.

"No you don't—"

"Dearest, just—"

"Leave 'em alone," he said. "I feel a vague threat—"

"Is that all you feel?"

"Absolutely. What's for dinner?"

"Good heavens, it's only five o'clock," she protested.

"I'm hungry. My belly doesn't know what time it is."

"Richard," she said, embracing him and putting her face against his throat, "how is your belly?"

"It's fine. I hardly notice it. Look."

He put his arm around her shoulders, stood on his right foot and lifted his wounded leg, held it out at an angle, and lifted the foot. One of the complications of the leg wound was that the foot tended to hang. Now he could lift it about halfway up. Seeing the gradual return of this function over the past three weeks had been a joyful, somehow tranquilizing experience for Katherine. She remembered when, it seemed to her, the foot simply hung at the end of Richard's leg. She remembered the day he turned in the cane. She went to the pool to watch him run—but only once, because of the other men she saw there. She went to the weight-lifting room with him—but only once. She took long walks with him, which grew longer almost by the day. She did not regret having seen the other men at the pool and the weight-lifting room. Seeing them, whatever else it did to her, left her gratitude undisturbed, and left untouched the strange peace she felt.

Richard said, standing on both feet: "I don't suppose there's any food in the house."

"No, nothing to make dinner of, except canned stuff."

Katherine thought: "I'm glad I saw those men. I needed to see them."

"Let's go to the store," Richard proposed, "and get dinner and breakfast. We won't leave tonight even if he does come back, will we?"

"I'll get my purse," she said.

"And we can pick up Terry on the way back."

"All right. And we'll get a bottle of wine."

They hurried through the shopping because now they were both hungry. They bought frozen pizza, lettuce, spinach, scallions, a pepper and a tomato, hard rolls, eggs, bacon, bread, milk, wine, and three apples. Richard bought popsicles for Terry and a can of Kitty Snicker. They picked up Terry, drove around the neighborhood for a while looking for Crackpot, and went home to make dinner.

"Damn him!" said Katherine, letting a sack of groceries crash on the table for emphasis.

"Right," said Richard. "Did you break the eggs?"

"Oh my god," she exclaimed, and carefully opened the box,

examined the contents, and reported "OK" for each of twelve eggs.

Richard uncorked the wine, poured it, and said: "Listen to that."

There was a series of small scrapes and crashes from the hall, which meant Terry was rummaging through the toys and things in her "den," an area under the hall table walled off by a hanging blanket.

They clicked glasses, and Katherine said:

"I'm glad you're so big."

"My balls, you mean."

"I mean your shoulders, your arms, your features—I mean the width of you."

"Wide-balled," he said.

"I-I-I-I-I-I—*I'm* the baby," Terry began while still in the hall; and spreading her hands, she explained: "This is the boa constrictor place. N-n-now, Daddy, you're the boa constrictor and you eat babies."

"I *squeeze* babies," he said, and grabbed her, but she wiggled and protested and admonished him so much he set her free, and she continued:

"Now this is the place where you eat me. Now you begin to eat me."

He snatched her arm and growled and began chewing, saying, "Gnaw, gnaw."

"Now I turn into Bat Man," she announced stunningly.

"Aaaah!"

"And I struggle with you."

She struggled in a stylized way and took a flashlight from her belt and declared: "This is the death thing and it kills you. First I kill you in the eye—"

"Aaaah! Pain! Death!"

"Now I kill you—"

She aimed it at his chest, and he clapped his hands on the assaulted place and made a gurgling noise.

"N-n-n-now I turn on the radio to hear Roger Mudd CBS News to find out what to do," and so saying, she punched some nonexistent buttons and listened. "This is the mercy ray, and I have to kill you more," she determined, and opened and closed the door of a cabinet.

"Mercy," protested Richard, "is when you're good to somebody who was bad to you."

"Well, pretend it means when you have to kill them. Now we struggle."

She approached cautiously and began a slow movement by which she appeared to be pulling a long fragile thread from his belly.

"Gads! You're killing and murdering and defeating me," he moaned, and whimpered.

"*Daddy*—it's just a game. N-n-now we go searching for the cave."

"No we don't. Now we make the salad."

Suddenly Terry's expression changed, and Katherine almost intervened. She held herself back with the utmost difficulty.

The child stood still, her face disfigured with grief or despair. She looked up at her father and once again raised the flashlight slowly. The flashlight didn't work, but she pushed the switch as if it did. She aimed it at his belly wound, and told him in a quavering voice, "This is the real mercy ray, the good one," and shone it on his wound for many seconds. She lowered the beam to his leg wound and let the rays pour into it—then she looked up, and seeing his face she lost control, and began sobbing. She doubled up, and Richard swept her up against his chest. To Katherine it seemed that Terry was all limbs and sobs as Richard gathered her into his arms, and she shook with sobs as if some terrible device had been implanted in her body.

As Katherine came near she heard and felt a grinding of glass under the soles of her shoes, and she looked down and saw that Richard's glass lay shattered on the floor in a pool of wine.

Richard was rocking Terry from side to side, making no attempt to break into her sobbing. He stopped to let Katherine kiss her, then rocked her slowly, telling her that he was all right, that she was all right, that everything was really all right. But he let her play it all out, rocking, holding her against his chest, and speaking softly to her, asking if she knew that her mother was right here, saying to Katherine, "Kiss Terry, Kit, she is ready to be kissed." And after several minutes of silent rocking Richard said the word "Pizza," whispering it to Terry, and rocked her gently, then whispered the word again, and rocked her. Katherine set the oven on preheat, unwrapped the pizza, and set the table while Richard and Terry remained in the middle of the kitchen and the crying gradually changed to sniffles and a staccato sigh.

"Terry, babe," said Katherine, "will you get the foxtail and dust-pan?"

Terry nodded. Richard let her slide to the floor.

"I'm sorry. I didn't realize I'd dropped it," said Richard.

"Of course you didn't," Katherine replied.

She sopped up the wine and the smaller chips of glass with paper towels. Terry put down her flashlight and swept the bigger pieces into the dustpan. Richard got more paper towels and handed them down to Katherine. He couldn't squat without pain, and she ordered him not to try. Terry worked without speaking. The last sigh rippled through her body.

They went to bed early to read. It was a warm but not a hot night, and the windows were all open and the curtains billowed in softly with the breeze. They lay all three on the bed, uncovered, Katherine reading Plato, Terry looking at *Peter Rabbit,* and Richard reading *Newsweek.* Terry got up from time to time to get a different book or a stuffed animal from her room, and Katherine saw that each time she did she stole a look at Richard's leg scar. The belly scar was under the waistband of his shorts.

Richard lowered his magazine and said to his wife: "Have you come to the Idea of Balls yet?"

"I have come to Socrates putting ordinary men down by walking barefoot in the snow," said Katherine, "and holding off attackers merely by stalking like a pelican and rolling his eyes, and yes, I'd say that's a good approximation of the Idea of Balls."

"Nobody attacked him just because he walked like a pelican?"

"Yes, Richard, exactly, and rolled his eyes."

"I'll have to learn to do that," he said. After a while he asked: "Why are you reading about war?"

"Actually this is a dialogue about love," she replied. "War insinuated its disgusting presence, I don't quite know how."

Terry scrambled down and off the end of the bed, went to her room, and returned with another book. She looked again furtively at the scar.

Katherine sat up abruptly and said: "Just a minute, baby. Here, walk over here," and she directed the child to stand on her father's side of the bed.

"This is where a bullet went into Daddy's leg," said Katherine, and put her finger on the hole.

"I-I-I-I know it."

"I know you know it, sweetheart."

Katherine moved her fingertip slowly back and forth, looked at

Terry and then at Richard, and said: "A bullet is simply a hard little stone going fast. It went right through Daddy's leg. That's how fast it was going."

Katherine kissed the scar, looked her daughter full in the eyes, and moved her finger gently over the scar. She said: "It hurt Daddy very much."

Richard took Terry's hand, and smiled, and said: "It doesn't hurt much now. And it hurts a lot less since you—" His smile got bigger.

"The mercy ray," Terry said.

"Yes, babe."

"But, Daddy, that's pretend."

"It feels better anyway," Richard said, smiling at the girl.

Katherine slipped her fingers under Richard's waistband and exposed the bullet scar and the rather long and uglier surgical scar just below it.

"The other bullet went in Daddy here," she said. "This is the good scar, where the doctor cut Daddy open to sew up the places the bullet tore."

"You're tickling me," Richard said.

"When Daddy's better, turkey, we'll *really* tickle him. Now, Dick —roll over, please."

He did so, and Katherine took Terry's finger tentatively, and moved it very gently and slowly to the exit hole in the back of the leg, and lightly touched the scar with the girl's fingertip.

"But this is the truly dangerous one," she said calmly, and a new solemnity and a deeper fascination were evident in Terry's eyes. Katherine took the girl's fingertip and traced the outline of the exit hole in Richard's back, which was three times as big as the hole in front. "This one," she said, nearly in a whisper.

She bent down and kissed the wound.

"Had this one been here," she continued, touching the closest point on his spine, about three inches away, "Daddy would have been very badly hurt."

"Killed?"

"No, but hurt forever."

She looked directly at Terry and said: "Daddy was hurt, and he was afraid."

And Richard, who was supporting himself on his elbows and couldn't see either of them, nodded his confirmation of these statements. Katherine saw how muscular his back and shoulders were and reflected that she seldom saw him from this angle. She put her hand on one shoulder and said, "Isn't he warm, and strong?"

And Terry, without touching him, said, "Yes." Terry yearned to touch him, and didn't dare. But her mother took her hand and drew it toward the center of her father's back, and spread it flat, and pressed it firmly on his back and held it down firmly.

"Feel how warm he is?"

He was much warmer than Terry had expected. She could feel herself smiling.

Seeing this smile, Katherine laughed and said, "Let's hug Daddy!" and they seized him as well as they could in the circumstances and hugged him and kissed his back and shoulders, and Katherine surreptitiously pinched his buttocks, which made him yell and spiral over. After a moment's struggle Richard ended up on his back with an arm around each of them.

They put Terry in her own bed, a place she did not by any means want to be, and spent another hour reading. Katherine now had a volume of Graham Greene's stories. When Richard had finished his magazine and the Washington *Star* he asked her to show him the passage about Socrates keeping off the attackers.

He read for a few minutes and then exclamations started to escape him, and he turned and said to her: "Jesus, Kit, do you call this philosophy?"

He went back to the beginning of the dialogue, and she heard nothing more from him. She closed her book and fell asleep—her mind moved about in the wild verbal zone—and then she realized he'd turned off the light and was embracing her, saying:

"I like the part about lovers being the separated halves of a single beast, who find each other."

"Yes," she said, "cloven, they cleave to one another."

The question in the morning was the Crackpot question, and it was soon answered. The cat was still gone. Katherine and Richard showered together. Richard said, "This is life too, you know," to which Katherine answered, "Of course. Missing the color is that form of life called deprivation. Seeing the color is that form called fulfillment. Fuck that cat. I will emasculate, eviscerate, torture, and destroy him."

"Pull his claws," suggested Richard. He was stepping out of the shower, a hazardous maneuver for him still. "I suppose Plato wrote a dialogue on fucking cats?"

Watching him, Katherine said: "Why should bodies be so important?"

They looked at each other for a long time, perhaps a minute, and she alternated between willingness to be seen and the desire and happiness of seeing.

"Well," said Richard at length, "you're not a sugar maple but you're all right."

"*Why* will you have to learn to walk like a pelican?" she asked.

"What?"

"I mean, surely they wouldn't try to send you *back.*"

"It beats me," he said.

She asked: "When do you get your new orders?"

"When I'm certified fit."

"And do we have to come back to Washington for that?"

"I don't know. The orders I've already got say I have to report in at Chelsea."

The orders he'd been issued two days before gave him leave for a month but required him to report for examination at Chelsea Naval Hospital in Boston once a week. The orders had been issued by Richard's doctor at Bethesda.

"But what's the policy?" insisted Katherine.

"I don't know, babe. I don't even know if there is a policy."

"But do men who've been as badly hurt as you have to go back?"

"I don't know, Kit," he said—and she heard a note of patience in his voice.

They woke Terry and started making breakfast. Terry went through her morning ablutions with the usual rapidity, then went down to the courtyard at the front of their building. When breakfast was ready Katherine looked out the living room window to call Terry, and saw her daughter down in the courtyard coming through a patch of sunlight carrying Crackpot, who lay cuddled, bottom up, in the girl's arms. As Terry approached, Katherine could hear her talking to the cat. Crackpot lolled his head back and took an upside-down look at the world, and then batted at Terry's hair.

"Where did you find him?" she asked when Terry came in.

"By the swing. Daddy! I found him!"

Katherine stroked his head, pushing his ears back, and put her ear to his side to listen for the start of the purring. She stroked it forth and said to the girl: "Can you hear it?"

They had breakfast, washed the dishes, and cleaned the kitchen, and everybody went to the bathroom. Richard began carrying the baggage down the stairs, and Terry told him how she had ridden down on Uncle John's back. So Richard invited her to climb on his back, and he took extra care. Katherine, alone in the apartment, checked the appliances and the windows, turned on the lights in the hall and bathroom, locked the back door, and left by the front door carrying Crackpot, with his leash wrapped twice around her hand.

As they drove away Terry burrowed into the den she had on the floor in the back of the car, and Katherine could hear her chanting softly: "Warm and strong, warm and strong, warm and strong."

To reach the Willoughbys' place, which was four miles in from the paved road, they drove up a gravel road through a valley flanked by high wooded ridges. The valley itself was hilly and the stream on their left shallow and jagged. Occasionally a flat hayfield spread itself out between the stream and the ridge, and at this season the herds had been let into the hayfields and allowed to graze the aftermath in the cornfields.

As the Vails reached the head of the valley the road turned left and back upon itself, crossed the creek, and began climbing at a slant up the ridge. On reaching what turned out to be a saddle it crossed the summit over a ledge of naked rock, the road itself turning to pure rock for a few yards, and then descended into a hillier, higher valley.

This was the place where Katherine had spent four years of her girlhood before her mother moved the family to Chicago, and soon they reached the fences on either side of the road that marked what had been her father's property. They rounded a curve where the somewhat narrower road ran through a sugarbush and could see the house, gray, weathered, unoccupied, on the right; and on the left, with its doorway opening into the road, the barn. The apple orchards were behind the barn, running up to the edges of the woods.

"Do you want to stop?" Richard asked.

"No," she said.

But he slowed, and Katherine looked into the empty barn as they passed.

"No," she repeated. "I'll come back."

There was a notch leading to a wider valley, but the road ignored it, kept left, and found the saddle of a second ridge, then led to an opening of high flat land.

Now the road was dirt and just wide enough for the milk truck, which made a run to Willoughby's every two days.

Katherine felt Richard's hand on her knee, and saw that he was smiling at her.

"What were you looking for?" he asked.

"You mean in the barn?"

"Of course."

"You're much too observant," Katherine said.

"Come on," he insisted.

"Listen, this is just your way of proving you can see into my soul," she said. "You don't have to prove it."

"But I can't see into your soul."

"Liar."

"I can only see—I love you." He kissed his thumb, and placed it in the center of her forehead.

"I was looking for his tractor," Katherine said as she opened her eyes. "It's been there every other time I've come back, in the same place. It isn't there."

"Does it work? Could somebody be using it?"

"Oh no, it was just a pile of rust."

They were passing through fields and pastures overgrown with hardhack, sumac, and juniper bushes, and came to another barn, this one bulging with baled hay, and to a cellar hole asprout with poplars. Then they were in a beech woods, then out again.

Then the road leaped up a few yards to a shelf of good flat land where Willoughby's farm began. Willoughby's Holsteins and Ayrshires, the dry and the lactating mixed up together, grazed in a long narrow cornfield at the foot of a ridge.

The road went through the Willoughbys' dooryard and diminished to two ruts, and proceeded through tall trees until after numerous curves it led sharply up a rocky scrabble. At the top of the scrabble a grassy lane went off to the left through the short pines.

Two hundred yards up the lane a high knoll lifted up a brilliant grove of white birches. Among the birches stood the "camp," an A-frame cabin with a steep shingled roof, a stone chimney, and wooden ends painted red.

From the porch of the A-frame one overlooked the dark pines, and the hayfields where a tinge of green survived, and the sere pastures where a few sugar maples blazed out in orange isolation, toward the ridge perhaps a half mile away. On the side and on the summit of the ridge each species was clearly marked out by its color —birches yellow, and losing pigment; beeches, elms, and poplars brown, the poplars having gone by their peak color long since; soft maples crimson and a little beyond, a little dimmer and darker, not so saturated as Katherine knew they must have been two or three days ago; and the dominant and noblest species, the rock or sugar maples, holding red and yellow pigments in a perfect balance that gave off a luminous orange.

They arrived in the late afternoon, just as the sun was deepening all the dark tones and lighting up the bright ones.

They had stopped in the dooryard to get the key and greet Mr. and Mrs. Willoughby, and had been invited for dinner. So now, having awakened Terry, who had been asleep on the back seat, and having put their bags and the cat in the cabin, they went down the stairway from the porch and down the footpath through the birches, intending to walk to the Willoughbys' and help with the evening milking before dinner.

They descended the path. Coming to the bottom of the path where it met the grassy lane, where their car was parked, they turned and looked back up at the knoll. The cabin stood angling up amid the yellow leaves of the birches, against a royal sky.

Richard had been feeling strong, and had told Katherine so. Now, looking at the sun-suffused birch leaves, he imagined that he saw Bishop's hat turning red.

He took Katherine's hand, and they went along the grassy lane through the short pines.

Terry did what dogs do on a walk. She stayed well ahead, pausing only to look around to be certain they were still following. There was only one path, and she grew more confident as it came out of the short pines and merged with the two-rut road leading down the scrabble.

When she went too far ahead Richard whistled and she let out a whoop in response.

As they went down the scrabble they passed from birches into maples. The rock maples held great quantities of intense orange light. The soft maples, in the late afternoon sun, seemed to repel light with their deep crimson leaves.

When Katherine felt her husband trailing she assumed it was because he found it impossible to walk at a normal pace in colors so sublime as this. That was how she felt. It was a cathedral. The two dirt ruts ran through an arch of colors as contrasting as stained glass. What awed her and what she had not remembered, not in a way to do it justice, was the antilight of the crimson maples, and the barely suppressed source of colorless light in the rock maples.

Richard had stopped, and his hand was uncommunicative. Katherine saw that he was indeed under the influence of the color. His face was stark. He looked as if he couldn't speak.

So they stood there for a minute in the streaming, contrasting light of this cathedral, in the blaze of the lucent orange; in the antilight of the dark crimson.

She put her arm around his waist, and only then did she guess he might be in a different world. His eyes were focused a few yards ahead, hard. Then it was she who saw into his soul—though he had never said a single word about the ambush.

"Richard—dearest." She touched his face, and watched to see if his eyes would change.

"It isn't anything awful," he said, turning to her.

Their eyes met, and she searched his large eyes, which she could never look at without thinking of Terry, to see if she could find any hint of just how awful it was.

"It really doesn't have any—emotion to it," he said. "It's just— a signal. It just flashes every once in a while like a signal. I keep seeing Bishop's hat."

She asked, "Who is Bishop?"

"He was carrying my radio."

"And why do you see his hat?"

"He was lying in the sand and his hat started turning red. Not exactly red. It was a green hat, and when soaked with blood it wasn't really red, it was some other color, a three-dimensional color, but it was obviously blood."

Katherine hoped he would say more. She waited, and for the first time heard the breeze in the leaves. Richard said:

"Then when I saw his face a few minutes later it was characterless. He wasn't there anymore. His face was untouched, I don't mean *that*. But it was . . . Ah, to hell with it."

"A face of the dead."

"Yes. It really isn't a big deal. I don't mean his death, but the hat and face and so forth. It's just that I keep seeing it. I see the whole thing, for that matter, from front to back. But it's odd—it's not horrible, it's not scary, it doesn't seem to have any profound meaning. It's just so clear."

"I should think it would remain just that clear—forever."

"For as long as I live."

"Yes, and as long as I live."

They went on down the road in their walking embrace. Richard's limp was almost gone.

Having no front teeth, Terry put the peanut shell far back in her mouth and crushed it with her molars. She extricated it and began to separate the peanuts from the shell. There were pigeons on both her arms, a pigeon on her shoulder, and some fifty in a fan on the ground before her. As she let the shells fall the nearest members of the company thrashed at them industriously, and didn't seem disappointed when they found no nuts. It was as if they hadn't been looking for nuts at all, but only wanted to peck and discard the shells. Terry cleared her palm and put the two precious nuggets in it, closed her hand, and lowered it slowly to the ground. The birds understood this routine and flocked around with much commotion and noise; the ones on her arms flapped down; the one on her shoulder stayed, as if unwilling to give up its advantage. Terry opened her hand and spoke softly, and felt a vague unpleasantness when none of her favorites won out. She had named three: Rainbow, Dry Toe, and Two Toe. The rest were an undifferentiated mob, interesting chiefly for their susceptibility to quick movements of her hand, and for the noises they made, which reminded Terry of farts in a bathtub. (She had learned the word *fart* from her father.)

She crunched another shell. She wished she had no shirt or coat on, so she could feel the toes gripping her shoulder.

When she lifted a nut the shoulder bird danced anxiously, pecked, and knocked it to the ground. A competition broke out, and the winner jerked away with the prize in its beak, casting panicky glances to each side without turning its head. Terry lowered the remaining nut under the very bill of Dry Toe, but this dolt let an anonymous fat-ass (another of Dick's words) get there first. Terry did not close her hand against the anonymous one because she was being fair.

Katherine was exercising self-command. She asked herself what that was. Self-command was not mere self-restraint. Self-restraint would have been the simple business of not eating the sandwiches. Rather, it would have been two things together, wanting them and not eating them.

But self-command was more. It was a passage, a progress, starting at self-restraint and moving through indifference to satisfaction; from denial through a vacuum to a reward. From wanting the damned sandwiches in the sack beside her (not to mention the pickles), to not wanting them, to a state of gladness that she didn't have them. Of the three stations in this passage, the last was interesting. It was like going for a long swim when you're expiring from hunger; you find your strength immediately and lose the hunger. It was making something good out of nothing.

Jesus exorcised devils with the words "Casting out I cast out." He threw them out by throwing them out. It was as if he said, "Don't ask me how I do this."

Then she thought: "No, no, he would say that he did it through the power of the Holy Spirit."

But it was true her hunger was gone. She had arrived at the condition which succeeds hunger, known as satiety, by not eating the damned sandwiches, and the pickles and the potato chips, and by not drinking the coffee, which was cold now.

"Damnation, where's your father!" she burst out, and she must have made a sudden movement because pigeons went scattering everywhere in fear and indignation, and Terry said:

"M-M-Mommy, you scared the pizzens."

"Well, so what? I'm starving."

"You didn't have to scare 'em. Now don't. C-c-come on, Dry Toe, come on, Two Toe, c-c-come on, Rainbow. Mommy, the one stayed on my shoulder."

"Ah—a good, good bird." She searched the various paths across the Common toward Tremont Street and saw any number of hominids, but not Blackstone. This was their second trip to Boston. On their first the doctor had simply said Richard was doing well and should return in two weeks.

So—how curious this obscure memory turned out to be; this trace, perhaps, of a sermon from her early childhood, from one of those few times her mother took her to church (her father never did).

Jesus, in saying "Casting out I cast out," claimed a self-sufficient power, a power originating in himself. He spoke politically, concealing that he was simply an agent of the Holy Spirit. He should have said: "By the power of the Holy Spirit I cast out." You had to know the rest of his story to know that he himself said he derived his power from another source.

"Casting out I cast out this bilge!"

She scanned the paths, rose from the bench, and strolled, keeping Terry and the pigeons—and the lunch bag—in sight.

Yet people do make their own power by expending their energy. She moved tentatively toward this odd conviction. Richard had his power because he had it and used it. He used it because he couldn't use it up. She was sure he didn't think these things. She was sure he was unaware, mostly, of his power.

By his power she meant that quality which was fixed in him by her love. She didn't mean his strength, his knowledge, his capacity to reason and argue, or to influence men and women, or to make things happen or to stay their happening. She meant precisely that kind and extent of power that he would lose if she ceased to love him. This power had just the same contours, it might even be the same thing, as the power to hurt her.

She had a feeling of discovery. Her discovery was: The power she spoke of was not Richard's own. It was something she had entrusted to him. "Not that I intended to," she added.

"M-M-M-Mommy! Rainbow got a nut!"

"Good," she called. "I'm glad."

She was suddenly rather excited. She used the disciplined instrument of language to explore her sensation of discovery. "If his power—this single power, not the others—if this power is in him only because I entrust it to him. One. But, two, if I never intended to give it. Then, three, I can't control it. So, four—what in the hell is it! And, five, who does control it? Or is it wild?"

Richard was coming toward her. No limp at all. He was wearing Levi's and a Marine Corps field jacket and no hat or gloves. He waved and smiled to her while still a good distance off, and let out the whooping "Ho!" he employed to communicate with Terry in the woods.

Terry's usual response was a wolf's howl, but now she raised an admonitory hand and said as loudly as she dared: "N-n-n-now, Daddy, don't scare the pizzens."

"Don't scare the pizzens," Richard repeated, and kissed Katherine and said: "I'm fit for duty."

Hunger, "self-command," and all that nonsense were utterly cast out. "What?" she said.

"And I have two more weeks."

"Tell me what you mean."

"And I want my lunch."

He more or less led her to the bench, sat down, and opened the sack. "Has Terry already eaten?" he asked, rummaging in the sack and finding less than he'd expected.

"Terry ate a long time ago. What do you mean 'fit for duty'?"

"He said I'm as fit now as before I was hit."

"Meaning exactly what?"

"Oh, I don't know. He doesn't know. I asked him your question, is there a policy? And he said, 'I'm a doctor, not a politician.' I said, 'I'm not asking for a favor, I just wondered if you knew.' I didn't say my wife asked me to ask."

"Aren't you curious yourself?"

"I must be, because next I called the detail desk."

He took a bite of his sandwich. Katherine held her food on her lap and watched him, and waited for him to speak. He took a second bite, and Katherine said:

"What is the detail desk?"

Richard took a drink of coffee.

"Cold coffee really isn't so bad," he said. "The detail desk is the people in Washington who make assignments."

"Richard, do you know there is something boyish about you when you talk about these things? Something perverse?"

"No, I didn't know that. There is a policy. I told the guy down there who I was, and he knew me. He's the guy that assigns naval gunfire types. I said, 'For Christ's sake, how do you know me? There must be hundreds of naval gunfire types.' And he said no, not really. He said he was in charge of naval gunfire assignments and he knew me because he had reviewed my file and sent an inquiry when my unit asked for a replacement. He said—this is the policy—that if you're sent to convalesce in CONUS—he called it CONUS, Continental United States—they replace you. That's the policy, and I've been replaced."

"Does that mean you won't have to go back?"

"Yes. And I get two more weeks. The doctor said he could certify me now but if I wanted two more weeks he could wait. I said, 'I thought you were a doctor and not a politician,' and he said, 'Do you want the fucking two weeks or don't you?' and I said, 'Do you think I'm some kind of nut?' So we've got two more weeks, babe."

"And you've been replaced."

"Yes. Eat, babe."

Richard ate, and Katherine sat with her food in her lap and watched him.

"That means," she said slowly, "that your old unit—"

She was now an actress. She realized with a thrill of fear that she was acting.

"—that your old unit—and Bishop's old unit—doesn't need you anymore, since you've been replaced."

And Richard drank more coffee and said, "Yes."

A few nights later a cold rain stripped away all the remaining leaves, and the next morning the sun reached clear through the stark branches, clear through the woods. There was frost that night and a bright sun the next day. The sunlight spread everywhere, on every side, and came down through the trees to the leaf-covered ground. The tractor wheels brought up the leaves and described two dark wet paths along the lane leading from the barnyard toward the cabin. Richard was driving. He held Terry on his knee. Terry looked back from time to time at her mother, sitting on the back edge of the trailer beside Mr. Willoughby, dangling her legs; and Katherine from time to time looked over her shoulder and smiled at Terry, and watched how Richard controlled the tractor with seemingly effortless motions of his left hand, and confined Terry in the loose half circle of his right arm.

When they reached the scrabble Richard stopped to shift gears. Tractor and trailer lurched, and the engine leaned into its work, and the rear of the trailer dipped down as the tractor began its climb. Mr. Willoughby's feet, hanging over the back next to Katherine's, dragged along the ground, and he watched them bump along. Katherine at first lifted hers; but then, seeing Mr. Willoughby dragging his feet, she did the same, and she thought that when he first rode through this dip and up the scrabble he would have been too little for his feet to reach the ground. Then for a couple of years he would have dragged his heels through the leaves as he was doing now. Then for all the rest of the intervening years until this very morning he would have been up front driving. So it was possible that he was dragging his heels through the leaves at this particular place for the first time in sixty or sixty-five years.

Willoughby said the horses had never liked the scrabble. Katherine saw the horses straining against their collars.

It was a rough ride up, and Katherine wondered how his old bones stood the jiggling. His boots, swinging now and just touching the leaves, were fairly new, and their laces were still dark from the hosing he'd given them after morning milking.

Richard stopped at the top and shifted, and at its new pitch the thudding of the engine found its way into Katherine's chest. She turned around. Terry's arm was around Richard's neck and they were pressing their ears together and "zipping" brains. This meant they put their ears together so the knowledge of each could zip into the brain of the other.

The engine ran rapidly but the wheels turned slowly as Richard proceeded in a low gear up the track that went straight into the high woods from the top of the scrabble, where the lane went left to the cabin. Katherine and Willoughby swung their legs, and as they passed the turnoff both of them looked down it, through the short pines to where the lane turned out of sight.

Had Willoughby been a woman, or another kind of man, Katherine would have said, "I love that lane."

Willoughby said, "God—them pines!"

She replied: "Yes—you mean they're so green?" She meant, now that fall is over.

"They grew right up. Pfft!"

From over her shoulder, through the noise of the engine, Katherine heard Terry say to her father: "Now your mind is saying we have to duck," and Richard reply:

"And your mind is saying, 'I'm a mugwump.' "

"No! No! Your mind is saying, 'I'm a pug dog with a pig's tail.' "

"Duck," said Richard, and they huddled over the wheel as a branch rattled over the exhaust stack and clawed its way along their shoulders and backs.

Richard explained that beech trees had hard, pointed buds, like spears, that could hurt your eyes.

Terry said: "I knew that because you knew it."

"Then you must also know that I like to tell my girl the stuff my dad told me," Richard said.

"And you must know—that I want a dog! Your mind knows th-th-that you had a dog when you were a boy, and now I want one."

"Fee fie fo fum," Richard said, to Terry's disgust, and Willoughby confided softly to Katherine:

"I *know* a dog."

"Oh—I don't think we'd better."

"Trained," added the old man in a whisper.

"At least until we know where we'll be living," said Katherine.

"Well, if you ever," concluded Willoughby.

"Thank you," said Katherine, and the old man added:

"A mongrel mutt. Brown. Ears stand up and droop down. Female. Runs deer. The owner's going to—says he's going to shoot her."

Katherine thought: "Damn. Damn. Damn."

Mr. Willoughby's hand gripping the trailer edge reminded her of the hands of the grandmother at Andrews Air Force Base. She was thinking: "How can a woman I knew so intensely—well, all right! I didn't know her thoroughly, I didn't learn her history—she *could* be terrible. But the way she said, 'We're lucky,' and the way she took my hand—how could she simply vanish from my life?"

She asked: "Will he really shoot the dog?"

"Him? He could."

When they reached their destination, a part of the woods that had been thinned by loggers the previous autumn and littered with slash and tops, Richard swung the rig in a big loop and cut the engine. Katherine stuffed cotton in Terry's ears, commanding her to stand still and be still, and then tentatively approached Mr. Willoughby.

Mr. Willoughby had splotches on his face, and scarcely any eyebrows, but such as he still had he now raised as far as he could, while he looked down at the balls of cotton. Katherine took one and stuffed it into his right ear. Willoughby put on a patient, understanding expression, but stopped her when she began on his other ear. "No use," he said.

Katherine approached Richard and methodically stuffed his ears, staring at him with mild defiance.

Richard said: "Henry's unbalanced."

"Oh shut up. Now is that going to stay?"

"How can he walk like that? He's already starting to tip."

And Mr. Willoughby was indeed listing gently to the right, looking perplexed.

Katherine put a cotton ball in the left side-pocket of his old plaid coat, and he straightened up and said: "Now the bubble's in the middle, Dick."

And as Katherine walked away, following the track leading through the woods toward her father's valley, she heard the two men laughing, and Terry too, and wondered why Terry should laugh. Then the chainsaws started roaring like lions in a furious show of aggression. But for these, Katherine would have run back to kiss all three. She had wanted to kiss Mr. Willoughby for years. She walked quickly, ducking branches when she had to, loosening her scarf and putting her hat in her pocket. She heard Richard shouting over the saws. She did not believe her father had opened this trail, but she knew he had used it. She was on his land now, having stepped over a strand of wire, and in a woods that hadn't been logged since he logged it. This woods was less rational, less useful. There was more vault to it. It was higher and wilder, and had hemlocks scattered throughout, darkening it. The trail descended, and she stretched out her steps. She was going down into her father's orchard. She couldn't see it yet but knew it was down there all across her front, still a good distance down. Except for the hemlocks here and there, she could have seen it by now.

"Damn," she thought, "I like those tulip ears," thinking of the brown dog whose ears stood up and drooped from the top. So she imagined them. Should a dog be saved for its cute ears? Should the question of its life or death be subordinated, to put it bluntly, to the question of whether its ears were genuine tulip ears or simply Mr. Willoughby's vague idea of ears that "stand up and droop"?

The trail steepened, and she plunged on down. The branches, leafless as they were, closed over the top of the trail and impinged upon it from the sides, and Katherine thought of the ambush, and realized that for the rest of his life Richard, in some part of his mind, would walk along every trail such as this as if into an ambush. He had told her how the stream bed was like a tunnel through the trees. "I see it—even if we haven't zipped brains." This was a game she did not play with Richard. When Terry proposed that they all three line up their heads and zip brains she said no, and walked away. Now she saw Bishop's hat turning red. She saw little chips of plastic flying off his radio.

Now she saw the orchard, wider than she expected, still heavy with frosted apples and clogged with trampled June grass, timothy, orchard grass, and hardhack. She paused before her final descent through the last band of hemlocks, and thought that nothing looked older than an old apple tree. Down she strode, and slid on leaves riding on a subsurface of mud, and broke into the pure sunshine and the smell of apples the deer had crushed in their browsing that morning, and walked among the ancient rows.

Her scarf was too long to put into her pocket, so she tied it around her waist, and opened her jacket. She was thinking of the grandmother at the air base when she suddenly felt like a young girl again, in her father's orchard. She felt as if her mother must be in the house across the creek and the road. Just as quickly she came back to herself —a mature woman exploring the ruin of the orchard.

She heard the chain saws—far off but distinct. She knew how loud, powerful, dangerous, and unwieldy they were, and how heavy, and she could see Mr. Willoughby with the trimming saw moving carefully and using every degree of leverage he could contrive, and Richard swinging the big saw like an extension of his body. The right cut, the right angle, the right pressure, the right velocity of the chain, and he would cut through fifty years in a few seconds, and enjoy it.

Her father had not been a sentimentalist and had not named his trees, but there was one Katherine had called Shipwreck Doris, trying to be clever. It was an eccentric tree and it adopted the name. She now stopped before it; it was one of the few Baldwins in the orchard and now a wreck truly, but still bearing fruit. Its branches were low and the deer could browse it; the ground all around was tramped and rich with dung. In the spring the grass here would grow higher and mingle with the knurled branches.

"If Mr. Willoughby tells Richard about the dog," she thought, "that'll be it. He won't let a dog be shot for chasing deer. The great defender of Crackpot's balls—yet he doesn't much like dogs or cats, that I can see. He has no particular affection for them. He seems to believe they have rights. He hates obsequious dogs."

Passing through a sag in the fence, she left the orchard and went down into a pasture cut by a creek. Her father had kept five or six beef cattle here. He abhorred dairy cows. He had said: "I'm a city man. I come from Springfield, Mass., if you call that a city. I have a bachelor's degree in history and a master's in business administration, and I do not know how to milk a cow."

The pasture was choked with juniper and was hard going. She jumped the creek—she could not utter the word *brook* after having lived in Chicago—and climbed the bluff to the barn, and then she saw the tractor.

"There it is!" she exclaimed.

A heap of rust indeed. A heap of rods and angles and curved sheets of rusty steel, lacking a steering wheel and a seat, lacking tires. But the name "Case" stood out in dignified block type on the faded orange hood. She heard her father say that a dairy farmer was a human being who belonged to a herd of tumid cows. Then for the first time Katherine wondered what he had done all winter. He read a lot and brooded a lot, and went out all day on snowshoes. He brooded about the war, presumably.

"Richard sees—recognizes—let's see . . . It's part of Richard's *mind* to believe there is a gulf around every soul. He wouldn't say soul. I don't know if this gulf exists. Maybe it's just a fashion to say it does, but Richard isn't fashionable—that's for sure!"

She entered the barn at its lower level, going through the open place on the south-facing side where the cattle had sheltered in the winter. She climbed over a board partition and up a ladder that went through a hole in the hay. She emerged on the main floor, at road level, and stood where the tractor had always been parked, and looked out onto the sunlit road.

For a second she identified Richard as the man who had fathered her child, but this seemed surprisingly unimportant if the question was, what makes him him?

She strolled toward the wide-open doorway, toward the sunlight, kicking hay.

"He affects me! He brings me out. He fuses my body and my soul."

Richard was the man who made this fusion—a very satisfying idea. She wondered why. Did it mean that Richard up to now had frustrated her understanding? And that now suddenly she "understood" him? Just because of this lucky metaphor of the fusion of her body and soul?

"Casting out I cast out this metaphor!"

But she didn't cast it out. She felt that for the first time she knew what happened, sometimes, when she and Richard made love.

She stayed some distance from the house. She didn't know who the present owners were, except that they lived in New York, and she had no desire to look in the windows at the signs of their proprietorship.

She climbed the bare hill behind the house and arrived at the top winded and carrying her jacket. She was now on a level with the woods across the valley where Richard, Mr. Willoughby, and Terry were working, and the discord of the chainsaws came across clearly. She was high enough to see the crests of several ranges between herself and the White Mountains, whose top line was indeed white. Yet here she stood looking at a goldfinch, who should have flown south weeks ago. He was twittering and leaping in a birch tree. She had seen a thrush and a catbird earlier. The goldfinch was full of energy and light, all but incandescent.

It was, she guessed, nearly noon when she reached the stream at a point well below the orchard. She lay down and drank. The bottom was flecked with chips of mica the color of the goldfinch. She had seen this "gold" in her girlhood. She crossed a hayfield and began climbing the wooded side of a ridge—listening to the far-off ring of the splitting hammer. There was no other sound except the wind in the branches overhead and the noise she made in the newly fallen leaves, and her breathing. The hammer rang with a short, sharp flash and she knew who was making it ring. She knew the force of the blow. She had seen the steel wedges with their tops deformed like mushrooms, after a few hundred of these blows, and she had seen a wedge go lengthwise through a birch log at a single stroke.

She looked for other goldfinches and thought: "How dead the woods is," and saw a skinny red squirrel the next instant.

She was on the same hill now as the three workers, and perhaps a half mile from them, straight through the woods.

Having seen the deadness of the woods, she searched for evidence of life, and found it all around and all along her meandering course. She saw squirrels, woodpecker debris, sparrows, mouse or shrew tunnels, leaves disturbed by the deer, the droppings of a fox, and a porcupine's devastation of a young maple.

At some point she deciphered the message of the ringing steel. It was that Richard was swinging the maul all but incessantly. She thought of his scars, of how he must be stretching his newly healed abdominal muscles.

Now there was a definite pattern because now she was close enough to hear the two or three light taps that came before each series of two, three, or four cracks of the eight-pound hammerhead against the embedded wedge. She was going directly toward the sound. She ducked and dodged through the dead branches of some close-set pines, and heard the thud of a thrown log hitting the side of the trailer.

Then came a period of silence, and she kept to her course, and in another minute she could see the tractor, then Terry laboring to carry a split log to Mr. Willoughby, who stood by the trailer—and Richard lightly rotating a log until he found a stable setting for it. He poised it on a huge stump. When it finally stood still, poised and upright, he stared at it as if it were alive, and set his grip at the end of the handle, and swung the maul slowly almost along the ground —it almost skimmed the leaves—and lifted it in a simple circle, with a slight widening of his eyes at the top, and brought it straight down with invisible speed, which speed was perfectly cancelled by the log as it divided to form a V that lasted long enough to notice, then fell in two pieces off the stump.

Richard had used the sharp end of the maul, which was like a very dull and very heavy ax, for this stroke.

Terry rushed in and dragged away one of the halves while Richard set up another log. That had been a little piece of ash, no more than eight inches across; this was a much bigger piece, and the irregularities in its bark indicated a crookedness of the grain inside, so Richard would need to use the hammerhead and a splitting wedge. He picked up a wedge out of the leaves and placed it experimentally on the cut surface. He lifted the maul in his right hand, holding the wedge in place with his left, and struck the wedge a controlled blow with the hammerhead of the maul.

Richard had taken off his shirt. He was sweating. His hair was blacker than ever and his face was flushed and abstracted. He did not seem to notice Terry or Mr. Willoughby. He looked as good as he had ever looked; he looked unscathed. He took a complete but easy swing to set the wedge deeper, and then he paused, as if to let the wedge cool, and then his body dipped and lifted as the hammer

traced a full circle from the wedge down along the leaves and over
his shoulder to an arc several feet above his head, and down to the
wedge, where the hammerhead leaped and rang.

Willoughby grunted, the hammer rang again, and Willoughby
and Terry stood in silence to see if the next blow would split the
problem open; and Richard, with a more intense ferocity, swung the
hammer a third time, producing a crackling sound as the wedge
burst the cross grains of the log. Richard pried it in two with his foot,
and split each half with a single blow of the maul. Terry darted in,
and Richard paused to throw some pieces in the direction of the
trailer, then picked up a heavy, bulging section of elm. His muscles
defined themselves set by set as he slowly carried, dropped, and
rotated the elm on the stump, and as he pounded in the wedge.

"It'll be a bastard," said Mr. Willoughby, pronouncing the last
word in his own way.

Richard didn't answer. He set the wedge deeper with a careful
blow, then struck it two hard blows in succession. He rotated the
piece of elm, and placed a second wedge. Swinging the hammer
rather high with one hand, he set it, then drove it deeper, and then
stepped back for a second or two.

He held the hammer out in a way he hadn't done before, finding
his distance, then dipped and extended his body to its limit and
struck a hard, ringing blow, then another, then another, and then a
series of blows.

He set yet another wedge and drove it in with a clear, carefully
aimed stroke. He glared at it. The sweat was running down his face,
and his chest was rising and falling. He struck it again.

Willoughby said: "Some elm don't split, Dick."

Richard let fly another full-circle blow, and the hammerhead
bounced with a sharp ring. He struck again, and again, and again.
With each blow his torso twisted. His arm, shoulder, abdominal
muscles stood out. And at the top of each circle his eyes widened a
little just before he brought down the hammer with a force bordering on fury.

IV

"Richard, let me just ask one question. I'll continue to respect your silence in general, but—"

"What silence?"

"*What silence?* The silence you've been filling this house with, and the woods and everywhere else. Dearest, I honestly do respect it. I won't intrude very far. But you know you've uttered exactly one word. You said 'Yes' when I asked you the other afternoon in the Boston Common if you'd been replaced. Now I want to ask a different kind of question. What you've told me is that the Navy and Marine Corps have a policy that a man who comes close to giving everything will not be asked to give any more. Am I right?"

"Apparently. That's what the detailer said."

"My question is, do you think that policy is just?"

"Yes. Do you want your blue jacket or your parka?"

"My blue jacket, please."

He held it and she slipped into it, and turned again to face him.

"All right," she said, "thank you."

They left the cabin and walked through the twilight, following the same path as on the day he'd told her about Bishop's hat. They took the path down through the birches to the turnaround at the end of the lane, where their car was gathering a fleece of frost, and went left along the curving lane through the short pines to the top of the scrabble. It was darker here, and Katherine stumbled going down the scrabble, and they took a grip on each other and followed the two-rut road along a row of great ancient maples.

Richard said: "Why did you ask?"

"Oh—out of a suspicion, out of a certain anxiety."

"What suspicion?"

"I'd rather not put it into words."

"And you'd rather that I 'respect your silence'?"

"In fact, yes."

"Clever, clever woman."

"I'm not *being* clever."

"Simple, humble, meek, sincere—spontaneous."

"None of those," she said, "and not clever either. I wanted to ask one question, and you have answered me."

The barnyard mud was impregnated with frost. Every step they took was a calamity for the crystals underfoot. Katherine bent down in the light of a window, examining the strange, striving complexes, and went back to one of the first walks they had ever taken—and thence to the first time he had said he loved her. She had been behind him in that; she hadn't felt it so early.

The barn wasn't really very bright but it seemed to be, and the milk and manure and cow sweat were pungent because it was always summer in the barn. As Richard shut the door Terry rushed and jumped, and he caught her in midair and said, "Mugwump, mugwump!" and she said, "Pug dog!" He was the perfect opposite of a pug, with his dive-down nose and sharp forehead and sensitive, confident dark eyes.

Terry was always on her good behavior in the barn, and she would not have jumped had they been near the milkers. But Richard and Katherine had entered through the calf stable. Mr. Willoughby had told the girl on her first visit to the barn that a strange dog could set all the cows to moving their bowels just by trotting through the place, without giving a single bark, and he had lifted his hand in a slow, steady gesture, indicating all the cows, and from Terry's eyes it was obvious she was seeing an awesome series of bovine defecations. But if you cozy the beasts they give more milk; and if you win their liking they give more still. So said Mr. Willoughby, and Terry had affirmed all this ever since. She was sure the cows liked her. Mr. Willoughby said they gave more in the evenings, when she was there helping him.

Katherine went to the sawdust bin and began filling the wheelbarrow, and Richard started carrying milk buckets.

On his second trip to the cooling room he found Terry waiting inside with her cat bowls. Richard poured most of the contents of one bucket into the cooler, then stooped down and filled the two bowls, brimful, then held the door as Terry, with excruciating care, walked out the door into a mewing, meowing, stalking, circling bunch of kittens and cats. With eyes shifting from one bowl to another, and murmuring to the cats, the child moved with careful steps to Cat Corner, next to the calving pen, and deposited the bowls amid the hungry cats—selecting favorites, as she had among the pigeons, and urging them forward, but never going so far as to remove one cat to make way for another. Sometimes Crackpot attended these feeds. He was here tonight, shouldering his way in.

The Vails had dinner with Mr. and Mrs. Willoughby and then returned along the lanes through the woods without benefit of flashlight, moon, or stars. Terry averred that with a dog it would have been easy. Richard said dogs could do surprising things in the dark but guiding people home wasn't one of them.

"How do dogs run through the woods in the dark?" Katherine asked.

"That's what I'd like to know," said Vail.

"They put down their nose," said Terry, "and slip through."

Richard read to Terry and tucked her into bed while Katherine laid a fire.

"I want snow," said Katherine.

Vail continued staring into the flames.

" 'They put down their nose,' " said Vail, " 'and slip through.' " His head went back and he laughed, and drew Katherine closer to him, and squeezed her shoulders and kissed her cheek. "Do you want a brandy?"

"Yes, I do. I'll get it."

"No, I'll get it."

"No, no," she said, and they had a little contest, which Vail won.

He returned with two brandies and sat beside her. They were sitting on a sheepskin barely big enough for two.

"Closer," said Richard.

They scooted the skin closer to the fire, took off their boots, and put their feet on the warm hearthstones.

"Are you ready?" he asked. "I'm about to make a sensible declaration."

"God no! I am not and never will be ready for anything sensible from you. Don't do it—it'll hurt us both."

"Cut the shit, woman."

"No! No! The pain, the incongruity!"

"Pain is right. I have decided to recognize the stinking—the sickening—the *deforming* necessity to earn money."

"What?" she asked. "Giving up already? Only thirty and you're caving in already? Richard, is this you? Is this my lover?" She insinuated her hand under his shirt and ran it up to his chest and said, "Yes, yes, 'tis the hairy one, the wide-balled traverse leader."

"You better take your hand back—you know about my chest."

She removed her hand—smiling and looking into the fire. "It was the talk about my dad, wasn't it?" she said after a moment.

"Yes. When Willoughby was telling about your dad trying to cross the stream in his jeep—well, everything he said. These are old thoughts, but he called them back."

"My mother believed that Dad was about ready to get a real job or start a business—not willingly."

"I'd like to go on on this track," said Vail. "I like it. I'll never do anything, any work I mean, that's better than charting the Beardmore Glacier or tracking the coal seam in the Transantarctic Range."

"Perhaps not, but there are other kinds of work that are good. What are you thinking about?"

"I haven't gotten that far yet."

"Ah, no? Just a recognition of the abstract need to earn money?"

"Just that."

"Are you actually thinking about the future?"

They looked at each other, with a look that might have contained their whole past, and kissed: a chaste, comprehending kiss.

When they had finished their brandy, and in accordance with a subtle exchange neither was conscious of having initiated, Richard went to the porch for firewood and Katherine went into the loft to look at the sleeping child and to strip their bed of its blankets. She spread these before the fire, with the sheepskin in the center, while Richard built up a huge blaze.

She undressed, leaving one garment for Richard. He undressed and left nothing.

"Till it burns," she said, urging him closer to the flames.

They sat holding hands, with their feet and legs more or less entangled, and Katherine asked:

"You didn't mean a *lot* of money, did you?"

"No—enough."

"A lot would be dangerous."

"A lot would be nice, but we'll never have it," he said. "It's not the money itself that's dangerous, I don't think, but the process of getting it. You melt yourself down."

She listened to the timbre of his voice—not exactly a "wide-balled" voice, perhaps, but one with dimensions, subtleties, an ample reserve.

"I think that's true," she said.

"I'm not going to give my life for money."

"You mustn't *give* your life for anything, my beloved," Katherine said. "You must live it."

She was happy, and the kiss she gave him was a happy, light kiss. He was letting go his illusions without letting go his ideals. And he admitted that the policy on the severely wounded was just. If this was so, there could be nothing dishonorable in allowing the Pentagon to apply it to him.

When Katherine aroused him she never knew what she was arousing. When she took the lead, she always knew he would follow but didn't know who he would be.

She took the lead tonight by looking into his eyes, dark in the firelight, and he responded to the love in her eyes by going quite still and forgetting everything in the world except her.

Now for quite some time he lay across her lap, almost passive, while she told him repeatedly in the plainest words that she loved him, and in a quiet, honest voice he said those same simple words back. All the while by her kisses and by the loving touch of her hands she was changing him, but as yet she couldn't see the direction of the changes. They mystified and thrilled her. They could signify the coming of the man neither of them knew or could control, the man who had no idea what he was doing until he had done it. Or she might be bringing forth another man altogether—the disciplined, perfectly selfless hero, as she called him. This "hero" was capable of performing miracles of invention, variety, and endurance for her sake. She would have to accept—it was always her wish to accept—whichever man came forth.

Then there would be a drama, perhaps a rather long one, with a beginning and an end, but the middle would be unknown to her. The center would be oblivion.

The man who came to her that night out of these changes was the disciplined, all-knowing man. He knew her body, soul, and psyche with a knowledge so thorough that she wondered where it came from, since it exceeded her own. Late—when the drama was over and he had covered them both with blankets—she hugged him and laughed and started to praise him: "My hero, my Iron Man—" But he quickly kissed her lips because he wasn't ready yet to see the funny side of their final paroxysm.

And during the drama she herself had been a long way from laughing.

At the beginning he had spoken to her devoutly. He described her beauty; he told her she was vital, passionate, and open, and she listened as if her name had been called from out of the sky. He said it was a joy to him that she had chosen him. He parted her legs, as if his doing so proved that she wanted him.

He addressed her at times as if she were a child, telling her not to hurry, because they had no destination. He said, "We are where we're going." At other times he spoke as if to a goddess—he exclaimed, "Goddess!" He said as if amazed, "I love you, Kit!" and it seemed he would cry. She saw his face distort and turn aside.

But he didn't break, and he didn't try to break her. He carried her into the oblivious center, where the mystical and the physical are the same. Here, even here, from time to time she heard him say, "I love you, Kit," and looking up, she could see the joy in his eyes. There was something of triumph in his joy, and she would have smiled had she been able.

" *'You know why'*—spoken in that solemn tone of voice. *'You know why'*—in that calm, resonant, weight-of-the-world voice. Well, god damn it," she thought, "I do not know why, and neither do you. *'I'm just thinking about it'*—in a pig's ass, Richard. *'I haven't decided'*—and you haven't got the right to decide, either, in your god damn moral dilemma weight-of-the-world—bullshit!"

She slapped her stick against an ironwood tree and it broke, leaving her with the stub. She beat at the tree again as she passed. She was skidding down the side of a hill, which was almost a ravine, and she threw away the stick to grab a tree, and swung down from tree to tree. "Me ape!" she said aloud.

At the bottom she walked beside the stream, looking for another stick, and as soon as she found one she began punching holes in the ice.

" 'She's lucky to have a father like you.' When did I say that—on what occasion? He did something so considerate, so kind, without even knowing it, something that showed he understood how frightened she was. Oh yes, yes, riding her bike. Well—she'll have to be even luckier to keep him."

Katherine hadn't noticed it was snowing, but when she came out of the woods into an open pasture the snow was falling so heavily she could scarcely see the trees across the way, and could not see the stone fence at all.

"Yipes, no hat. And my ears are cold. Did I really slam out with no hat? Did I break the window? Is that what I heard?

"So then—I have snow in my hair, no doubt. Richard likes that. We must do what Richard likes. My ears are freezing. 'Yes the policy is just. Do you want your blue jacket?' Yes I want my blue jacket and I want you to come to your senses. 'You see—flash, flash—a red hat.' Don't hand me that red hat business, and don't try to take the argument where you think I can't follow, because everybody lives with something. Do you follow that? What? Can't come along? I have never been ambushed, thank god, and you, thank god, have never had a miscarriage at five months. So don't try it, Dick. Don't even think about it.

"There. Now I see it. That's exactly what 'You know why' really means. It means 'You can't possibly understand.' The unscrupulous, ruthless bastard. I wonder if he knows how fucking ruthless he is. 'Kit, babe, I really *hate* to hear you use words like that.' Do you, fucker? Do you, shithead? Do you—expunge that word! That seems to be the worst word they can imagine, yet they all want—stop, stop. *Some* discretion, please."

She was striding across the open field, and the trees didn't seem to be getting any closer. The flakes were big and thick, and they descended straight down.

"Wow, am I lucky there's no wind," she said. "I wonder if I could put these mittens on my ears." She believed the light was fading. She was climbing a hillside through beeches, maples, birches, elms, and ironwoods, and she wasn't sure where she was. Maybe it wasn't the coming of dusk but only the snowfall that dimmed the ridge. "So

—let it get dark," she thought. "I'll just put my nose down to the ground and skim through." But she started going hastily along the ridge. From spacious sugarbush it soon changed to a rapidly descending spine. She took it down and came unexpectedly to a neatly crafted, square stone foundation, with several mature hardwoods inside it. She stared at it incredulously, half suspecting she knew it, and turned and looked back up the spine as far as she could see, and tried to penetrate the heavy silent storm to the right and left. She thought she must be on a saddle, and a fairly high one, and that this must be a sugarhouse she had seen once before, the old Rowell sugarhouse, which she and her father had happened upon; which meant she was twice as far from home as she'd thought. "You bastard," she hissed, and started down a gentle slope through a hemlock woods, where hardly any snow had got in.

"You see, my poor little cunt, *it's not my fault.* It's the mystique of combat. How can I explain it to you?

"Well, try, try. Maybe I could grasp one little part of it.

"I doubt it, since you're nothing but a girl. A female. In the brief intervals between being depressed because of your period, you stupid little shit, and being nervous because you're ovulating, there's hardly any time for you to learn anything about the world, is there?

"Ow!" she cried, and stopped short. She had ducked one branch and driven another into her cheek. It was so dark among the hemlocks she could hardly see her way.

" 'I'm *thinking* about it, Kit, only thinking about it. I haven't decided anything.' The question is, in the name of God, why think about it? Jesus! That he could look at me with *charity* in his eyes, with sympathy, with love, with *pity,* god damn it! and say he was thinking about it.

"I've got to be careful through here," she said as she passed from the hemlocks into a grove of young beeches with their light brown leaves still clinging, "or I'll go home with a sore eye and get a lesson about how beeches have these little spearlike buds. That would be the limit. 'Well, Kate, my dad told me and I told you, but you went out and stabbed yourself anyhow.' " She grabbed a branch and took off her mitten and touched one of the points with her fingertip. "He's right," she said. "A little needle. 'You know why, you know

why, you know why.' Sure I do. He means the red hat. He means
Bishop, whoever this poor Bishop was. God bless his mother. He
means everything and everybody but Terry and me. Sure, Dick, I
know why. Ugly! Ugly!"

The question now was whether she would reach a road before
total darkness reached her. She marched on steadily, coming to an
open gate where she had expected to have to climb a fence, and felt
a jolt of gladness. She passed through and went along a tractor lane
beside a hayfield. As she rounded a curve the yellow lights of a house
came into view, and beside these a long, low row of lights in a
milking barn.

The snowfall was abating, she was still warm, and easy walking lay
ahead if she didn't have to face a mean dog. She stopped and
shouted: "Dog! Beast!" She covered half the distance to the barn
and shouted again, and the farmstead was glowingly silent in the
falling snow. Then she set her course and strode boldly toward the
barnyard, and passed through it to the road unchallenged. This was
like a second open gate, and she all but skipped up the road, thinking: "Whose dog that was I do not know. He didn't come out, so
ho ho ho." She pulled down her jeans and squatted, raising a thin
cloud of steam. She could just see it as she looked back at the lighted
house and barn. "The unmet dog who didn't bark—cheers me
homeward through the dark.

"O Doggie dear, when you come this way, you'll sniff the pee of
—of the Lady K? O Doggie dear, if tonight you roam—O Doggie
—O dog unmet, from a lady grateful—accept this pee for your
evening plateful. O dog unmet, I salute your fangs—

"O dog alive with fangs of steel, is it you or I who's really real?
—Lord, it must be three or four miles by road, but I can't go
cross-country. I could, but . . . There's the swamp," she said as she
passed its cedars. The road loomed vague and white. "If this were
daylight and hard winter I could walk right through the swamp.
Hunger, hunger. Richard, make dinner. Spaghetti, green salad,
beer. No, no. Steak, broccoli, and hard rolls. The steak is on the
bottom shelf. The broccoli is in the freezer and the rolls are in the
breadbox.

"O dog alive with fangs of steel,
Is it you or I who's really real?

I'd say I think, and so must be;
But it was you who frightened me."

"Kate, I'm not sure I like this," said Vail.
"Not *sure* you like it. You mean you don't like it at all."
"I don't much like this Socratic technique of yours, no."
"So—you'd rather not answer my questions. All right then, as Socrates always did, I'll be happy to answer yours."
"I don't want to ask any, babe. I haven't got any to ask."
"You mean my opinions are of no interest to you?"
"Oh Jesus," Vail groaned, and covered his eyes with one of his big, bony hands. When next she saw his eyes they were large and somewhat shining, and as always she saw Terry in those eyes. Richard said: "Does the cut hurt?"
"Richard, do you know what would please me? The cut does not hurt," she said, putting her hand to her burning cheek. "It would please me if you would say a sentence of ten words or more. An outpouring, a torrent of words."
He was leaning back in his chair, which he had propped against the windowsill. The snow was beating against the pane all around his head—the flakes smaller and harder now and coming down faster. He had folded his arms across his chest and he was smiling at her.
"You love me," Katherine said. "I see that, and I want you to know I see it."
"I do," he said. "I'm glad it shows."
"But you have already decided," she added calmly.
"I have decided nothing," Vail said.
"Yes. You probably don't know it yourself, but everything's settled. All that remains is for you to walk down to the Willoughbys' and pick up the telephone and call your friend in Washington, if you haven't done so already."
"I have not done so. I have not decided."
"I didn't see it at first," Katherine said. "Although when you spoke of the red hat as a 'signal' I should have guessed. I thought you meant the mere residue of a trauma."
"And he's not my friend," added Vail.
"No, but you'll soon be his. When you tell him you're willing to go as a replacement for somebody who's been—oh—blown up. Let's say blown up."

"Let's not."

"But the signal was meant for me. It wasn't you, it was I who missed the signal. And then when you tried to drive that wedge through the center of the earth the other day I thought: A titanic struggle is going on in my beloved's soul. But that was silly. You were just pissed. You were afraid I was going to make a fuss, cry or something. But what's the point, if you've already decided?"

"I have *not* decided," said Vail.

"You haven't?" she asked. "You're maintaining *an open mind?*"

"I don't like this, Kit," he said.

"And we can discuss it rationally?"

"Of course. But what is there to discuss?"

"Oh—your life."

"Kit, please, for Christ's sake."

"Please what? Please don't be melodramatic? Please don't allude to your wounds, or to that space of three whole inches between the scar in your back and your spinal cord?"

"That is exactly what I mean," he said. "Please don't refer to that."

"Does it make you nervous?"

"Yes."

"Then why think about going back? Do you want to be nervous for a year?"

"No. It wouldn't be a year."

"Well, whatever's left of a year."

"No," said Vail.

"Do you see this red hat?" she said. "It doesn't necessarily mean what you think it means. It could mean: Stay away. It could mean—"

"Stop it, Kit."

"It could mean: Here is blood and death and gore and violence."

She got up and went around the table to him. He was staring just as if at the red hat, or at that ghastly chipping away of Bishop's radio which he had told her about. She took his face in her hands, and held his head against her body, and kissed his forehead and nose and his dry, inert lips. When they had looked into each other's eyes for a few seconds, she smiled—he did not. In his eyes she saw a mixing of wretchedness and love.

She took their coffee cups to the stove, and asked: "Brandy in your coffee?" He said no. She filled the cups, taking no brandy herself either, listening to the silence from the loft. Richard had left his chair and was down before the fire, goading it. He deftly placed a new log, and came back to the kitchen and sat once again with his back to the window. Katherine said:

"You're wrong about the Socratic technique. I'm not using any technique. That's what I decided today. I decided that technique, artfulness, strategy, drama, all would be worse than useless. I am saying exactly what comes into my head. I tried strategy yesterday when I coaxed you into an admission that the policy on the severely wounded was just. What good did it do? So now I speak straight out, Richard, as well as I can. What I say may be distorted by fear, by horror, by shock that you would contemplate leaving us when you don't have to, but it won't be distorted by art. I am your wife, and I want you with me, and I do not see any legitimate reason why you shouldn't be."

Then they were silent for a long time, looking at each other, but without tension. Katherine was thinking of his spinal cord and of the night she told Terry he would be all right. She also tried to find a rhyme for "right-of-way." She wanted a verse to commemorate her voiding in the middle of the road. Richard thought of his loathing of machine guns. Smaller weapons and larger weapons he could stand, but machine guns gave him a headache.

Katherine said: "Thank you for cleaning up the window glass."

He smiled at her and replied: "We'll have to replace it."

"Yes, tomorrow. Was there any other damage?"

"No, unless you count my nervous system."

"I do not, of course."

"You are either a great actress," he said, "or a—"

"I was not acting. But what were you about to say? I've cheated myself by interrupting. A great actress or a what?"

Vail smiled and said, after a long pause: "Sorry."

"And you are either a great bastard or a great son of a bitch. If you were to go," she said a moment later, "to prove you weren't a coward, I would hate your motive but I would at least understand it."

"No, no," he said, "I'm not afraid."

"That's all too obvious. If you went for glory, to become a hero, I would say you were confusing values, but at least I would understand."

"No," he said.

"I know. If you went because of a philosophical compulsion—to live life—I would think it a twisted motive, but it would be one I could understand."

"No," said Vail.

"Of course not. You wouldn't trifle with us in that way."

"I wouldn't trifle with you—"

"Yes, yes, I know. 'In any way.' I meant no accusation, honestly. If you went because of patriotism I would say you were immoderate, intemperate, but I would understand."

"It's not that—exactly."

"No, not exactly," Katherine took him up, "yet there is a certain . . ."

"I do have a country," Vail said.

"Yes," she agreed cautiously, "and so do those 'Asian boys' President Johnson talked about during the campaign, who should be fighting their own war."

"They are fighting it," said Vail.

"Yes, but if you speak of patriotism, if you say you have a country, mustn't you also take the next step and acknowledge that it's their country, not ours, which is threatened?"

He said nothing, and after the lapse of a few seconds Katherine went on, more cautiously still: "If patriotism is love of country, what does it have to do with going over there to fight for somebody else's country?"

"If I go back, babe, it won't be from love of country."

"Oh no? Then from what? What's left? Not to finish your tour," she said, "your year. The Navy and Marine Corps have absolved you of any such obligation. They have said you have no duty to go back."

"I'll decide that," Vail said, "not the Navy and Marine Corps."

"The *country* decides who has a duty, and it has decided you don't."

He said quietly: "I'll decide that."

"All right, but how? If you went, for whom would you go? For those little military gangsters who run South Vietnam? For the United States Government? For your family? For yourself?"

"For myself," he said, almost before she finished speaking.

"Now it's you who's being clever, Richard. Now it's you who's arguing for victory."

"No, babe. I know it may seem that way. You have too much faith in the mind, babe, in words."

"But it has to come to words in the end, doesn't it? What words, for example, will you use to explain it to Terry if you go?"

"I'll tell her I'm going back to finish the year I started."

"And what if she asks, 'Do you have to go?'"

"I'll say yes."

"Then you'll deceive her. Forgive me, Dick."

"No, I won't deceive her."

"You've decided, haven't you."

"No."

"You've taken this above me, above Terry, and you've made your decision according to some unknown standards that have nothing to do with us, however much we love you and want you. It's as simple as that, Richard. Our love and whether we need you is irrelevant to you. You've taken the question into some other court. I don't know which one."

"If I go—" he began.

"Oh stop it! Stop this pretense."

"If I go," repeated Vail, staring hard at her, speaking almost as if he hadn't heard her, "it'll be because I think I should."

"Empty, Richard, utterly empty. You have just said exactly nothing."

She got up and threw her coffee into the sink and poured a hot cup, and stood drinking with her back to her husband.

"Do you know what this is," she asked, "this war?" She turned and faced him, and found his expression quite closed.

"To the Vietnamese," she said, "it's a civil war. By definition it's none of our business. But to the so-called great powers and to the so-called statesmen of the world it is simply the arena where the struggle is being carried on today—for a few months or a few years, it doesn't matter which. Someday it'll end. It will be like the Korean War. Thousands, hundreds of thousands of people will die, and when it's over everything will be as it was. It is a great, monstrous game."

Vail said: "That's not what it is to me."

"Then in God's name will you say it? Will you speak a complete sentence for once and not force me constantly to ask you questions? If it's not a great monstrous game to you, what is it?"

"I don't want to try to define it," he said tonelessly.

"You are!" she exclaimed. "You're arguing for victory instead of exploring all this honestly. You're staying clear of what the war *is,* because you believe that if we discussed it your motive for going back would evaporate. It is not your fight," she said, barely controlling her voice.

"I know what the war is," Vail said quietly. She noted that his color was up. "It is, in a general way—I mean I understand it, in a general way, as the thing you said it was—the struggle of powers, communism versus the West."

"The South Vietnamese gangsters are the West? Christ, Richard."

"The struggle to stop communism."

"Kill a commie for Christ?" she mocked.

"But if I go back," he continued, with that same intensity that suggested he hadn't paid any attention to her last comment, "it won't be because of that."

"It won't be a crusade," Katherine interposed. "It won't be for a glorious cause—to save the gangsters. It won't be to give your little drop of blood for the survival of the West—I hope!"

"No," said Vail.

"Good, wonderful, fine."

"It'll be because I think I should. Just—to finish my tour."

"My god, Richard, do you love us?"

"Yes," he said.

That night she might have despaired, had Richard not come to her in just the way he did. He began as the disciplined man, as the master of both their responses, and she could not have borne that. But he faltered early, and lost himself. The universe in which he lost himself was Katherine. For a few moments he was like a blind man being stoned. She was undecided whether to calm him or deepen his confusion. There was nothing mystical about her state, for she was in full possession of herself, or about his, for he seemed to be half mad. She let it continue like this for quite a long time, giving her breast, her hands, her mouth, and every other place and consolation he needed, together with the assurances of her love that he kept asking for. It occurred to her that in this rather dark way she was making love to him, prolonging his frenzy with acts of consolation.

Terry's sorrow came a few hours at a time. When it would smite her she would be all but helpless. When it would leave her alone she would be the same brat or angel her parents might otherwise expect. She clung to Richard, sometimes even riding on his back as he moved around the cabin tending the fire and packing his bag. He possessed little; he was to be reoutfitted at Camp Pendleton on his way over. Terry collected his toilet articles from the bathroom, and brought them, and he packed them in his bag, even though he'd have to remove them next morning when he shaved. He put his hands on her shoulders, and they seemed to be very small shoulders; he caught her eye and smiled gently. Her lack of response was less a reproach than a revelation of how stunned she was.

Yet when they left the cabin late that afternoon on their last expedition she shot down the slippery path and was bouncing up and down at the turnaround before Richard and Katherine had descended the porch steps.

At the turnaround Vail motioned her to him. "You have to be very quiet, Terry," he whispered, bending down.

Getting this solemn admonition and her father's hand on her back at one and the same time turned the girl stiff with attention—her large dark eyes staring fixedly past him.

"Not a sound—don't step on any sticks—quiet, quiet, quiet," he whispered.

They started off down the lane through the short pines, with the child far in the lead.

From the top of the scrabble to the barnyard was about a quarter of a mile, maybe a little more. Having walked half this distance, they turned off to the left, passing through a sugarbush and into a dark stand of old hemlocks where it was easy to go quietly over the damp snow—but Vail saw that Terry was about to pop right out into the open field beyond. He pursued her, ducking the dead branches, and crouched beside her with a silencing motion of his hand until Katherine came up.

Katherine went a pace or two forward and knelt. Her eyes, blue and youthfully limpid from a sufficiency of sleep, roved over the field. Mr. Willoughby had described a widow's peak jutting from the woods into the hayfield and a single wild apple tree standing there.

She searched, but her view across the field was blocked. She whispered: "We'll have to go closer."

They crept through the hemlocks to a place where some younger trees grew up more bushily than their elders, throwing out their heavy green branches laden with short flat needles and little cones to the very edge of the hay. They waited under these trees, exposed, actually, to the hayfield but, because of the darkness of their place and the overhang, very inconspicuous.

Mr. Willoughby had left the rowen uncut; and the snow was shallow and melting. The sun was already down and all the colors were dark—dark green, near-black in the hemlocks, the dark gray of the deciduous woods that rose on the hill beyond the hayfield.

But the apples hung by the score on the naked tree, red, orange, and brown. It was part of Mr. Willoughby's lore that the deer preferred frozen to ripe apples because they were sweeter.

Shortly Terry began squirming, and got a stern look from her mother. The child shifted, making some slight noise, and settled onto one hip, propping herself with a stiff arm. To her father she directed a grotesque expression, bunching her nose into a "snoot" and exposing her lower teeth down to the gums. Vail ignored her. She shifted again, more noisily, looking from one parent to the other, and started bobbing her head up and down and posing with her hands and shoulders in gruesome crippled attitudes.

"If you make any noise," he whispered menacingly, "and if you *move* anymore . . ." He didn't say what he'd do, because he didn't know.

After sitting still for a time and gathering cones in her chilled hands the girl began staring woundedly out from under the canopy of her projected brows. Vail couldn't get used to the bold black dominance of her eyebrows, now that her bangs had been cut—to him they seemed unbelievably beautiful. The girl cracked a twig with her heel, and by a glance Vail delivered her over to her mother. Katherine shook the child by the arm and, yanking her closer, poured dire whisperings in her ear, after which the girl retreated into utter misery and cold.

The long johns Katherine was wearing under her Levi's were now soaked at the knees. Terry's snow pants looked warm enough. Richard as usual looked as vulnerable as a husky.

Katherine's knees and back ached, and she rested on her heels.

She continued her watch with a rambling sort of attention that was not quite systematic but neither was it a daydream. The stripped old tree suspended its incongruous fruit over the snow, and the deer were bound to come.

It is easy to see a deer in the open. It is not so easy to see a deer in the act of leaving shelter. Katherine, who had lived here for years, had never seen it.

And she didn't see it now. With a little catch of wonder she saw a big doe feeding on the rowen several paces into the hayfield, in a place where her glance had glided only a few seconds earlier.

The doe dragged a hoof lightly back and forth through the snow, and dipped into the grass with gentle plunging strokes of her neck, while her ears twitched as if at the bidding of a different brain.

Katherine searched the tree line, trying not to dwell on the sleek and gentle doe, whose head was now halfway lifted, her big scooping ears attuned to the Vails' hiding place. The doe now raised neck, shoulders, and head to full height and let her ears blare wide open toward the Vails. Katherine forced herself to keep searching the tree line. The doe returned to her browsing and took a sedate step toward the apple tree. Katherine saw a smaller deer, hardly bigger than a fawn but without spots, standing tautly in the woods. It came forward a step and browsed at the edge of the woods, then lifted its babyish countenance and pointed its slender muzzle straight at the Vails' place, cupping its ears, and remained in this scrutinizing posture for fully a minute, while Katherine returned the scrutiny and kept utterly still. The young deer then walked freely into the open with soft, reaching strides, and made Katherine a happy woman.

In the light of the fire her breast was golden and her nipple cast a long, tremulous shadow. To see her better he lifted his torso, and she raised her hands blindly and followed his face upward with her caress. Her face was noble and at peace, the features rendered somewhat austere by her supine attitude and the slight lift of her chin. She looked at him once through half-opened eyes, and her lower body slowly began the oceanic movement that affirmed her complete freedom.

For Richard this was the source of relief and happiness, because his only desire was to sustain her in this freedom and be the instru-

ment of her going deeper into it. If he shivered her body in the end
that would be fine; and now he knew he would; but that wasn't what
he really wanted. That was as nothing compared to their time in this
sublime freedom of the oceanic movement, when he could devote
his body and his concentrated will entirely to her.

Richard understood that a man who seeks his reward will not get
it. A man who riots will be pacified with a spasm, and will get
nothing but a spasm.

But if he denied himself he might accumulate a mystical power to
take Katherine to a plane she could reach by no other means. And
if he did this, then he would experience everything his self-denial
made possible for her.

It wasn't easy to concentrate his will. He began to feel as a distrac-
tion the heat she gave him. But he saw her face in the unsteady
firelight, and her descending arms, her half-opened eyes, and
through a supreme act of will he kept his restraint perfect—for a long
time.

Wanting nothing, truly nothing, for himself, with the muscles of
his calves hardening and his back arching and his mind focused, he
gradually liberated Katherine. He saw her face transforming and
was overjoyed. But he also felt the intrusion of a greater force. Her
warmth also enveloped him and penetrated deeper than before—
and now he was both invading and invaded.

He felt her breast against his, her hands on his sides, her breath
on his cheek. But these and all other signs of separateness were soon
obliterated. He still felt her breasts, but as if they, and she, were
contained in him. Her smooth lower lip was a sensation on his
tongue, and a part of his identity. The sound of her breathing was
the only sound in his mind. And her loins encompassed his. Her
cries, at length, stood for his own; and her storm sucked the fluid
from his spine.

They lay still until Katherine began to notice a vague oppression,
and then realized that he was heavy.

She straightened the blankets and sheepskin and then lay on her
side with her back to the fire. Tossing back her head, she slipped a
hand under her hair up against her temple, and she stared at him
with quiet, selfless eyes. With her free hand she reached out and
passed her fingertips slowly over his chest and up to his throat. Her
reaching out rounded her shoulder. Vail saw this roundness almost

with amazement, it was so clean an arc. Likewise the height of her uplifted hip, as she lay on her side, amazed him. The fire behind her traced a soft mantle of light over her body. Her breast, her navel and loins were shadowed, and her face seemed nearly as unearthly to him in its present quietude as in its former ecstasy.

He thought: "Why am I leaving her? Good god, am I really going to leave her?" Her belly continued its gentle swelling and lifting as she breathed.

"I must be out of my mind," Vail exclaimed aloud. "I must be the biggest fool in the whole country."

"No, no," she reproved him softly. "You're gentle, and kind—you're a fine man. You're so gentle—so strong in your gentleness, Dick."

"Jesus, I'm a lunatic."

"No, Dick, my love." She stroked his chest again, and Vail saw with the same captivated wonder her abdominal muscles taking form as she moved her arm.

She said, "I can feel the fire all the way down to my heels."

Vail was preoccupied with his stupidity and her loveliness.

Katherine observed, with a glance down his body: "You are looking quite humble all of a sudden."

Vail saw that it was true but didn't reply. He was still gazing at her as if she were a wondrous contrivance for which he had just discovered the use.

"I can hardly believe I'm such a frigging idiot," he said in amazement.

"My dearest, dearest love, stop it," she insisted. Taking his hand, she kissed the great red knuckles, her brown hair with its streaks of premature gray falling around her face and touching his wrist, and her kisses reinforcing his opinion.

"Gads," he groaned, "good Christ!"

"Dick, dearest, you'll have to stop that talk eventually."

"I will," he replied, "eventually, I suppose."

"It's an impurity, you know."

"What the hell do you mean by that?"

"Well—an impurity in your—I mean that since you insist on being 'a good and strong man' you must not doubt yourself. That would be the impurity. Anyway, it's too late."

He had said to Terry that if he were a good and strong man he would go back.

She still held his hand, which in hers felt stiff as a board, and he still stared at her—looking into her eyes as if he were determined never to let her see anything else but his eyes. She shook his stare and rose to her knees, then backed rather awkwardly toward the fire, saying: "Dick, the heat is wonderful. Can we sleep right here?"

"Sure, but the fire won't last."

"You'll have to get wood. No clothes! Naked to the woodpile."

He replied with a crooked expression, dragged on his trousers, and went to the porch. The cold covered his upper body like a second skin. He loaded his left arm, which he held curved like a big hook, with logs of black birch and elm. Katherine was now attired in a flannel nightgown and knelt facing the fire, and watched the sparks rising as her husband threw on the logs and raked the embers. She objected to the elm because burning elm stinks. Vail justified it because it gives high heat. Vail brought cognac, and drank his at one take, while Katherine stared into the fire, holding the glass idly in her lap. They slept on the blanket for several hours, until Vail was awakened by the cold, and saw the fire had gone out. Then he took her hand and woke her and they went up to the loft in the peak of the house and got into a bed that was just as cold, at first, as the hearth had been.

They breakfasted early. The child begged to be allowed to run down the road to meet Mr. Willoughby, who was coming when he finished morning chores. It had seemed to Katherine that Willoughby wanted to do the Vails a favor, and since Katherine had dreaded the drive to the airport, and worse the return, it was arranged that Willoughby would take Vail the thirty miles to a town where he would catch a light plane to a connecting point for his flight to Washington, where he must stop before going on to Pendleton. The only thing wrong with this arrangement was that Mr. Willoughby had taken Katherine's father on a similar ride in the spring of 1951.

Vail told the child she could go, and she leaped up with a clap of her hands, cheering, "Yea! Yea!"—for the snoot maker of yesterday was gone, and into her body and blue jeans had slipped a simple, gay child.

"Have you had enough breakfast?" Vail asked, catching her, and she replied:

"Can I have an apple?" as if this were a favor he might grant her by unusual good luck.

"Good lord," thought Vail, "she doesn't want a Coke or a Hershey bar, she wants an apple."

He gave her one, and she worked it around to the corner of her mouth and crunched at it sloppily.

"What's the matter?" he asked. "Are your teeth too loose?"

She had just dictated the following missive: "Dear Tooth Fairy: Please leave more than twenty-five cents. I am bored of twenty-five cents."

She experimented with a tooth, and removing a glistening finger from her mouth pronounced it "very, very loose," swallowing the *l*. Vail took the mutilated apple and cut it in quarters and sliced out the core, then returned it. Terry put on her mittens and balanced two of the quarters precariously in each hand and stood tentatively, even shyly at the door, wondering if someone would open it, which Vail did, and she went carefully off down the lane looking from her right hand to her left, as if she were carrying two frogs. Where the lane joined the road she sat down in the snow in the middle of the road, looking down the scrabble, and with lips open, providing her own musical accompaniment, she ground up the apple in her jaws. This done, she thought of returning to the house, then of making a sanctuary among the pines—but she remembered Mr. Willoughby's barn. And with images of swaying udders, bluish veins, dripping teats, cascades of splattering urine, and giant circular anuses driving out large quantities of dung—with these images dancing in her mind she hurried down the road toward Mr. Willoughby's barn.

The child was hardly out of the house when Katherine heard Willoughby's car approaching. At every moment she kept hearing the car and then realizing that she hadn't heard it. She cleared the table and went to stand on the porch in the sun, and as Vail mounted to the loft to put the last things in his bag he saw her old green sweater whiten across her back as she folded her arms. She was wearing the sweater over a white blouse, and a full, pleated green plaid skirt, and heavy socks. Returning from the loft down the rather strange stairway, which was built of halved pine logs and was like a ladder, Vail asked her whether Willoughby had built the cabin himself. Katherine found the house dim after the sunlight and initially she couldn't quite see Richard. "I don't know," she answered. "I suppose perhaps he did."

Vail remembered that his shaving kit was in the bathroom, and he got it and packed it, and felt brutal. Katherine seemed far off, and indurate, and he began to realize that she had said her farewell last night when she embraced him in their cold bed in the loft.

"I have an idea," she said. "I mean, rather, an idea is *examining* me. You know how awful it can be, don't you, Richard, to be *examined* by an idea. I can feel its antennae." With a plain glint of fear in her eyes she looked at him, then looked down at her hand, which she was slowly lifting. "The idea thinks I am unworthy, and it must see whether my hand is shaking—which, as you can see, it is not."

She folded her arms, smiling, and asked: "What would you think if we lived here while you're gone? Do you think this house'll keep out the winter? Will the pipes freeze? Do you think, perhaps, it would be—oh—rather lonely?"

"Yes," he said.

"Yes the pipes would freeze?"

"You'd be lonely, Kate."

"And you don't give a damn about the pipes?"

"I think you'd be lonely, Kate."

"Ah, yes, yes, I certainly would. Do you think more so here than in Washington?"

"In Washington," said Vail, apprehensive that Katherine had unleashed her Socratic technique, "you would have friends, like the O'Connors, the—"

"I could attend their parties as the forlorn war wife, while they suspended all talk of the ghastliness of the war, in deference to me, and I could sit in a corner dressed in a clinging jersey and the men could speculate or fantasize about how sex-starved I must be."

"I doubt that people would think that way, babe."

"No, you're right of course, that was wishful thinking. But really, Dick, don't you think I'd be an impediment to the free flow of conversation among liberals?"

Vail knew now that he should shut up.

"Do you—don't you?"

She suddenly broke into a smile that displayed her perfect, manly teeth, as white as a child's, a smile that reshaped her nose and set laughter lines stretching off from her eyes; which greatly relieved her husband but didn't quite induce him to answer. She said:

"Speak, counselor. Speak, brain. Please do speak, governor,

leader, husband, dearest Richard—eponymous archon of the family, suzerain, deacon, swordsman." Vail smiled, and Katherine added meekly: "You have to help me decide."

"No," he said, "you've *already decided.*"

"You see, Dick, I can go back and live in Rapeville in the heat and traffic, amid all the urban amenities like being a prisoner in your apartment after sundown, just you and your air conditioner and TV —hating or fearing or envying everybody around me—or I can live in paradise. I've talked to Mr. Willoughby, and he seemed pleased that I might stay. He's very kind to Terry. Have you noticed?"

"Of course."

Katherine's eyes attempted to assess her husband. "He said the town will plow the road," she continued. "They ordinarily never plow beyond his dooryard because nobody uses the road, but with somebody living here year round they will have to, it's a town road, you see. And he will plow the lane himself with his tractor. Do you know, Dick, he wanted me to say here free, but I insisted on a fair rent—and we finally agreed on—well, is fifty dollars fair, do you think?"

Vail shrugged.

"Well, that doesn't matter so much. You know, in the spring the bluets and daisies and black-eyed Susans grow all over the pastures. The bluets are so tiny, dearest, you can gather and gather and hardly fill a teacup."

"Katherine, is there a decent school around here?"

"Oh heavens, of course there is. I went to this school for five years and didn't get mugged or extorted even once."

"That's not what I meant."

"Of course not. Well, it wouldn't surprise me if the school were as good as the one in Washington. If it isn't, she's only in the first grade, after all, and I could help her with reading and arithmetic and so forth, and 'modern math,' whatever that is. I've already enrolled her. She starts tomorrow."

Vail looked at her half in exasperation and half in approval, and she said:

"Really, it's not so bad, Doc. Four rooms, eight grades, four teachers. They've got some of the best teachers down there for four or five miles around. Look at my brother and me. John's a marine. What's wrong with that? Semper fi! More for the Corps! And I turned out all right too. I managed the office of the Badger Electric Supply Company error-free. It was so stated by the owner. If they gave medals for that I'd have one. My other distinction is that I'm married to a big wonderful sperm factory who's made only one insane decision in his life."

"May I go to the bathroom?"

"Why—sure—sir."

When Vail came out she was pouring coffee at the kitchen table. Thinking he heard a car, he went to the front windows.

"That's only the wind in the peak of the house," Katherine said. "Are you so anxious to go?"

Vail took the coffee, which he didn't want, and stood in silence for a moment before admitting: "I wish I were gone."

"Yes, dearest, you nearly are. I'll write you letters from paradise. You write me letters from hell."

She thought: "Our grandchildren can read our correspondence in a concentration camp." And immediately she detested herself for this stupid flippancy. Why should she think of a concentration camp? Why had she made that idiot remark about the teachers? Must she always be smart? "God," she thought in amazement, "this is self-pity."

She composed herself. She buttoned her sweater clear to the throat, distinctly remembering the day her mother had bought it at the "junkie's" in Chicago, during the year of self-imposed poverty.

"I'd like it if you would tell me everything in your letters, Dick. If you write false and happy letters that are incomplete then I'll have to worry about what you're not writing, but if you promise to tell me everything it'll be easier."

He said, "OK," in a choking voice, and she looked up to see what she hadn't expected, that his eyes were bright with tears. He was such a big, rangy, hard man, and he looked, this morning as always, slightly tortured in a business suit, like a lumberjack at a dance.

"I hear the car," she said, and Vail nodded, put down his untouched coffee, and picked up his bag and stood there scowling.

"Oh good grief!" Katherine cried. "You were going to tell me about the car—I mean our car. You were going to give me a list. You didn't give it to me, did you?" She stood up in consternation, and repeated, "You didn't make out the list, did you?" and Vail shook his head, scowling more darkly and plainly irritated.

"I'll write you a letter from Pendleton," he said.

But she ran to the little desk at the front and began rummaging around. Not finding any paper, she snatched up her purse and brought it to the table, producing a black notebook, and she took a pen from her husband's inside coat pocket herself, uncapped it, and presented it to him.

Vail took the pen almost with a growl and sank down at the table to make the list she demanded—that their car should be tuned up every six months, that the oil should be changed and the chassis greased every 1500 miles, the tires checked, and a new battery installed.

"Is that all?" she asked, hovering at his shoulder.

"Yes. I said there was nothing to it, god damn it."

"Why, what a relief. I thought I had to read the complete works of James Watt, or Henry Ford, or whoever he was. Don't scowl at me like that, Richard. I know you're not so tough. I saw your tears."

Terry appeared at the door and announced that "we," she and "Mr. Wiwlby," had arrived. Katherine dismissed her.

Katherine kissed Vail's palm, then his lips, and drew his hand to her breast. Still pressing his hand greedily and perhaps bitterly to her breast, she stood up on her toes and kissed his lips again, and accepted his kiss.

When they came out on the porch into the sun, Mr. Willoughby insisted on carrying Vail's bag, and after awkwardly nodding to Katherine he carried his burden down the steps, and Vail and his wife followed.

Seeing Willoughby's car, which was only a year or two old, Katherine thought: "Thank goodness, at least it isn't the same car."

It was parked at the turnaround at the foot of the knoll, about thirty yards from the cabin, where some poplars lifted their pale green trunks among the birches. The sun was bright and the snow was nearly gone.

Vail lifted his daughter, who looked at him as she rose, uncomprehendingly, and kissed and embraced her, astonished at the small circumference of her chest. Thinking that he was going to tickle, the child began struggling and kicking, and got him in the kneecap. His knee was swollen and stiff for a week.

As he rode away he looked through the back window and saw his daughter running down the lane after the car, and his wife standing by a white birch, with her sweater buttoned up to the throat and her hand lifted in farewell.

Presently the child returned and Katherine proposed: "Shall we go to the house and you can help me?"

"OK," the girl panted. "Mommy?"

"Yes?"

"Can we go see Mr. Wiwlby milk?"

"Why, he's finished milking, sweetheart."

"N-n-n-n-n-n-*no*, Mommy, they're going to fill up all over again, and he's going to milk 'em again."

"This evening, yes. We can if you like."

"Mommy, I don't want to go to the house. Can't I go to the creek?"

"What for, dear?" she asked. She wasn't paying enough attention.

"I want some rocks."

"All right," she consented, "but when you've gotten your rocks you must come back to the house."

The girl raced off, and Katherine began climbing the path through the birches. After a few steps she halted and paused uncertainly, then descended to the turnaround and stood listening, hearing the wind in the "trembly aspen." And nothing more. She shivered and got her blue jacket and set off through the woods in the direction of the creek.

V

Becahe was free to send somebody else, Vail had to send himself. He walked in an aura. He was the guy who'd been shot up on a recon patrol. Navy officers scarcely ever went on recon patrols, and to be shot T&T twice without buying the farm was something. So the marines had their eye on Vail, particularly the thirty-five or forty marines, plus the two other naval officers, in the naval gunfire section.

He didn't have to be a hero but he did have to authenticate himself. So when this job came up, being the section head and free to assign whomever he chose, he had to choose himself. Had anybody else been the boss, somebody else might have gone.

Vail wasn't scared, just reluctant. He wasn't quite ready in his mind. Judging from the trembling of his hands, he wasn't quite ready in his body either.

He was trying to load seven fat cartridges into a pistol magazine. "It's the god damn heat," he thought. "I wish they'd fight their god damn war in Greenland." Instead they were fighting in a truly green land. In the sun the heat was extreme; in the tent it was unnatural. He got the seventh shell in and turned the magazine base down and slapped it hard against the heel of his hand—to align the rounds or seat the rounds or some damned thing that Gunnery Sergeant Zander had taught him. Then he rummaged in his footlocker for another magazine. The plywood deck around his cot and footlocker was stained with big dark drops of sweat. He found a magazine, his fourth, and loaded it, thinking: "It'll be cool in the chopper," and he could hardly wait.

He heard somebody call his name, and a trooper came in carrying a case of C rations, which he pitched to the floor. Taking pliers from his pocket, he snapped the wire, yanked off the cardboard jacket, and tore the case open with quick and almost vengeful movements.

"I don't need a whole case," said Vail.

"The gunny said bring a case, sir."

Vail took five rations and said: "Thanks. You can take the rest back."

"Sir, the gunny don't want it back."

"Take it back, please, or take it somewhere."

"Yes, sir."

The man gathered the wire and the cardboard scraps and carried out the carton, scattering his own drops of sweat on the sandy deck.

"Now, don't tell me I'm ready. Here's a weapon, shells, compass, canteens, salt pills, iodine pills, bandage, knife, binoculars . . . food —have I got a John Wayne?—all right." He continued his inventory, a peculiarly childish process on completion of which he could have reported that he had everything but his galoshes.

He looked around the tent as a departing guest looks around a hotel room. It was a pyramidal tent with a parachute draped overhead to cut the heat, and a bare light bulb hanging on the center post. There were six cots, all of them covered with mosquito netting except Vail's. And there was sand, and balls of human hair on the deck. Somebody was shedding like a Saint Bernard.

He slung his pack over one shoulder and went out into the sun, which stabbed into his eyes as it had when he was a boy coming out of the Saturday matinee. A little more so. He walked a sandy trail running along the base of a dune, with the regimental command post on his right, and then the sea, and the ammunition dump over the dune on his left. He went to the Operations tent, which had two fans, and dropped his pack and helmet in the corner of the tent that was his office. This was the FSCC, the Fire Support Coordination Center, where the men who ran the three "supporting arms" of aircraft, artillery, and naval gunfire coordinated their efforts, more or less. He said hello to everybody and then walked down the bouncy plywood flooring to talk with the Two, at the other end of the tent.

"Hello, Two. May I get a map?"

"What—are you going yourself?" exclaimed the Two with truculence.

"Yes."

"By god, you feeling aggressive? Why don't you send somebody?"

"I'm sending myself."

"Did you know they stepped in it down there?"

"No," said Vail. "No, I didn't know that."

"*Yes,* man, they're in deep shit—the reaction platoon is. The
Three is sending down another company. At first he said you'd be
enough with your floating popgun, but now he's cranking up India
Company."

"That's fine. May I have a map?"

"Fine your ass. Corporal Holloway, *don't,* for Christ's sakes, *don't*
give it to him that way."

A corporal who had proferred two map sheets withdrew in cha-
grin and sat down to trim the edges with scissors and glue the sheets
together. Vail went on to the Three section, the Operations section.

The Three Alfa watched him coming. This man, known as the
Swedish Meatball, was a captain who had commanded a line company before being assigned his present job as assistant operations
officer. He remarked how Vail's belt and canvas suspenders seemed
to magnify him; he remarked Vail's tropical pallor. "The Big Two
Six," he said, and Vail replied, "Hi, Skipper."

"OK, this is Mo Duc," the Three Alfa said, putting his pencil on
a map board, "and this is Duc Pho. Here's where the bird went
down. She's lying right there. And here"—indicating a tiny blue arc
—"is the reaction force." The Swedish Meatball turned to his boss,
a major, but the latter was busy on the telephone cranking up India
Company. "The company will go in right here, at about the same
time you do—as soon as we get the birds. We're sending you down
on a medivac bird."

"OK. How many VC are there?"

"Better ask the Two. Didn't he tell you?"

"Are you going to stop with a company or send in more?"

The Three Alfa shrugged. He observed the interest, the life in
Vail's eyes, and said: "There's no artillery, but we're trying to get
air."

The Two came out of his corner and gave Vail a map, now
consolidated into a single sheet and folded in a clear plastic envelope.

"I'm giving you my own personal see-through map case," he said.

"You can fold it, see? and put it in your side pocket"—he so placed it—"and take it right out, and she unfolds, and you're ready for war. Got your grease pencil?—your most deadly weapon. You make a dot with your grease pencil, the dot of death"—he made a dot, then erased it—"and you can erase it with your thumb if you want, or leave it there. Fold, unfold; never slip; dot always same place."

He parted with it, and Vail put it in his side pocket.

"Whatever you do, don't lose it," said the Two. "I couldn't fight without it."

"Thanks. I won't lose it."

"It's waterproof, too."

"That's good."

"It's not the Holy Bible. It won't stop a bullet."

"How many VC are down there, do you know?"

"Ain't I the Two? Of course I know. A shit-potful. A small pot, a large pot, a shit pot."

Vail smiled, a smile of amusement, of curiosity, and faint affection.

The Two added, "If you were a general I couldn't do better. That's my whole briefing on the enemy situation, but don't worry, you'll soon have more data than you can assimilate."

"Janeway," said Vail to the FSCC operator, who sat in a canvas chair by a fan, "would you please make certain Griffin is on his way to the landing zone?" Griffin was Vail's radioman.

Janeway cranked up the telephone, and Vail picked up his pack and helmet. Slinging the pack over his shoulder, he was starting to leave when the doorway was filled, or one-sixteenth filled, by the ectomorphic rags of a naval lieutenant. The man's uniform was like cloth on pipes.

He almost bumped Vail, but caught the canvas flap and clung to it, apparently for balance, and asked in astonishment: "Where the hell are you going?" He had been in his tent all morning packing and throwing away and giving away his possessions. He was Vail's predecessor as head of the naval gunfire section, and he was leaving the country that night.

Vail said where he was going, and a wave of nausea passed through his predecessor's insubstantial body, curling his lips. He listened with revulsion, which changed slowly to a kind of sickly contempt, as Vail said that a helicopter had been shot down and the reaction force sent to secure it wasn't adequate, and now a company was being sent.

"Mo Duc," the man repeated. "Fucking Mo fucking Duc. Why the fuck are you going?"

"I have to get going," said Vail, moving past him.

The man stepped back into the sunlight and walked beside Vail on the way to the landing zone.

"Do you have a destroyer?"

"Yes," Vail said, "Hickory," using the ship's call sign.

"Oh, that putrid bitch. Did she say she's coming at flank speed? She never goes anywhere at other than flank speed. Her captain has the shizzling drifts of the mouth. That ship'll plead with you to shoot her whether you have a target or not."

As they walked along he occasionally took Vail's arm in his elongated fingers, the better to communicate his bitterness and nausea.

"When you fly over Mo Duc you'll see this tin-roofed thing on the hill, with a trench all around—that trench is a dream, I can tell you, the Arvin have made it so nobody would have the stomach to jump in it even to save his life. It's a laterite hill—bare, no grass, no anything—four howitzers; you'll see it. Then look inland. You'll see this nice little green, flat-bottomed valley ending up against the mountain on the west. There are six or seven vills in the valley—you look, you'll see the vills."

They strode along at a good pace through the sand, where the going was hard. The trail led over the dune separating the command post from the ammunition dump.

"In that valley," Vail's predecessor continued, panting, "starting about two kilometers from the tin roof and going west to the end of the valley—all among the vills in there, you'll see . . . I did that. That's the sort of thing . . . I didn't do it *for nothing,* but I did it. Not with Hickory, thank god; I can't stand that fucking ship. With some other ship; I think it was . . . Oh hell, I forget."

As they crossed the helipad the man kept his fingers insistently attached to Vail's arm, and Vail looked about with some concern for Griffin.

"You'll never get home tonight. Maybe not even this week. Once you're in Mo Duc you could be a thousand miles away. You don't have any artillery support, do you? You're not going to try using the Arvin artillery? It's not safe. Don't. The crazy fuckers'll kill you."

"It's out of their reach," Vail declared laconically.

"Oh! Near Thac Tru, towards Duc Pho. Nice—wonderful. What a nice place. They'll give you some air."

"So they said."

"Air is no good," the man said categorically. "The planes are never on station, and when they are they can stay only a few minutes. When they're there you have to use them whether you want to or not. They're excellent at blowing holes in the ground exactly where the enemy was located ten minutes before. They're too fast—they fly so fast it's not practical. They go bellowing off like idiotic bulls twenty miles in one direction and then come charging down on the target making this incredible fucking noise. It's always possible there are some VC in wheelchairs or in flagrante delectissimo who can't get away quickly enough, so we . . . Did you see that story in the paper about the 'surgical precision' of our air? Listen, I went through a village one day after an air strike and the casualties were gruesome. I vomited. I wasn't the only one. There were water buffalo makings all over the vill. You know, Dick, that's the telephone."

Vail cursed and looked around in bewilderment for the telephone.

"It's over here," said his predecessor, and he walked into some bushes to a short post where a field telephone was ringing. He pulled out the handset, which looked huge in his hand.

"God, aren't there any snakes around here?" Vail thought as he pushed through the bushes. Since his arrival he'd seen a bamboo viper and something locally called a cobra, and here was the telephone stuck back in the bushes just where a snake might be cooling itself in the shade. "It wouldn't bite *that* skinny bastard first. There's a reason for putting the phone in here, I just wish I knew what it was. God damn it, where's Griffin?"

"Hello. Yes, sir, this is Mr. Vail."

"Hey, Big Two Six, this is your friendly One Four. I can't hear you. Can you hear me? Your bird just left Ky Ha."

"Thank you, Major."

"Good luck, buddy. We'll send you some air. Listen, I hear your bird. Do you hear it?"

"Yes, sir, I hear it."

"Wait a second," the major added, "here's the Three Zulu."

But the approach of the helicopter made it very difficult to understand the Swedish Meatball, who now took the phone. Vail shouted, the Three Alfa repeated himself, and the noise of the descending helicopter, both thunderous and metallic, increased so that listening on the telephone was pointless. A storm of sand ripped across the pad, and Vail turned his back and crouched in the bushes, his face stinging, having no thought whatever of snakes. As the helicopter settled to the ground it throttled down, and Vail thought he could try again.

"I can hear you now. Go ahead."

"Dick," came a dogged shout, barely understandable, "the first lift of India Company is on the way—and the platoon is all cut up. *Dick,*" the Three Alfa shouted, *"can you hear me?"*

"Yes—yes. What is it?"

"The first lift of India Company is on its way. Did you hear that?"

"Yes. Go ahead."

"The platoon is all cut up."

"All right, I heard that."

Then the Three Alfa began repeating himself again, and Vail's assurances that he had heard made no difference. He looked at the telephone as one might look at a puppy who has fouled the rug, and hung up, and strode out of the bushes and across the pad toward the helicopter.

Griffin was running toward it from the other direction, his face twisted with anxiety. Vail paused and motioned Griffin in, then climbed in himself, and the thing wound up its drenching, shattering thunder and began to shake, and was airborne with a distended lurch, tilting forward, darting at a strange angle and with exhilarating speed over the stacks of projectiles and bombs below.

The helicopter rose in a spiral of lengthening radius till it entered the cool air. It made its rendezvous with the chase bird, and the two planes began their deafening progress south over the sand dunes and brush hills and bulldozed laterite of bunkered Chu Lai; along the cut lines of the little toy French-made railway and the little toy French-made highway to the shallow Song Tra Bong, whose bridges all lay on the water; over the crooked alleys and shamble huts of Binh Son and south to the fortified ridge of Nui Vo; over hills standing up like islands in the green sea of rice land, rectangles dry and wet and all shades of green; over the green and comely town of Son Tinh and flat-headed Buddha Mountain, by My Lai, a name not then known to every American; to the meandering Song Tra Khuc and to Quang Ngai, the city of the half-built cathedral; toward Nui Vong and the bending Song Ve, and toward fucking Mo fucking Duc, the lagoon of blood.

Vail sat cross-legged on the floor by the open doorway on the right or inland side, and opened his notebook, holding its pages against the wind. He located the entry on Hickory, learning her name and class and the number and caliber of her guns. He replaced the notebook in his breast pocket and buttoned the pocket. Observing the gunner making signs to him, he got to his knees and moved close. The gunner shouted through the hail of noise that the pilot wanted to speak to him, so Vail took the man's helmet with its associated wires and devices and pulled it down over his head.

The gunner's hand guided Vail's to a switch. Press to talk. "What do I call him?"

"Hello, pilot, this is your passenger," Vail said.

"Hi there—you the Navy gunshot?"

"Yes."

"I'll tell you, they say it's a pretty hot zone. I'm talking to a man on the ground and he asked if you were on the way and I said you were, then he said did you have a ship. Is that your ship out there?"

Vail made his way rather staggeringly over the ammunition boxes on the deck to the window on the left side, out which he saw on the dark sea a glistening ship of pearl gray that lay like a sword, with a wake of white nearly her own length, which she seemed to be stretching even while seeming to be motionless.

"That's mine," he said—and she was at flank speed.

On the left were the placid sea and the steady ship and on the right the placid land. Twelve gnatlike helicopters far behind bore the second lift of infantry, while close behind and slightly upward the chase bird wavered imperfectly in her station, looking with her bulbous, pipe-pierced snout and her dangling wheels as if she'd escaped from a science museum.

Below was Nui Vong with its black hole. The helicopter drifted left over the disappearing lake and straightened its course with the coast, driving south over Mo Duc District halfway between seacoast and highway. Vail's eye followed the highway with its microscopic foot traffic and blown bridges, until he could discern the bare hill with its great trench and its tin roof. He looked westward to the valley and the green stands that concealed the villages. He saw the extensive paddies and a brown road entering the valley and a Christian steeple, but he did not see any of the "work" of his predecessor, through he looked for it. He thought of the man's starved little hand holding out the telephone, of the breakable little wrist.

The air was blessedly cool and the earth very open in the visibility of her details, yet also quite divorced from him, because, perhaps, of the force of the wind and the inhuman noise. He seemed to act and to think in this special envelopment as if by memory alone, by the residual influence of prior thought. He again went to the left side and looked back for the ship and found her less distant than he expected, which of course seemed good. He motioned to Private First Class Griffin, and they both looked at the ship.

In the west there was white smoke. The aircraft fell away in a steep falling turn rightward, dropping (not slanting) downward even as it curved right toward the highway, over which it soon passed at an altitude no longer immune from small-arms fire or the earth's heat. The foot traffic had become people. Those pushing bicycles were most probably men and those carrying shoulder poles women. None looked up, all were hastening. The plane briefly followed a level course, and in the stability of level flight the smoke ahead appeared to rise whiter.

Unexpectedly, and with lurid results in Vail's stomach, the chopper heaved up and tried to climb. And only gradually and after a strain did it resume its feminine, rising spiral of gentle acclivity and great radius, ascending until it reached the cool air again. Vail could see the downed helicopter lying like a bent and moldy tusk. He could not see any troops around it. His plane orbited, and from the south a helicopter of vindictive, trim, and lethal design, not like the truck Vail was riding but a flawless-seeming weapon, worthy of Jules Verne, came skimming along the very brow of the land obliquely toward the white smoke. The smoke poured out of the trees, and from the hamlet the trees sheltered. The attacking helicopter ran on, and presently thin stuttering puffs of dun-colored smoke trailed out its side.

Three such runs and Vail's craft descended its spiral again, the suddenness of the event catching Vail unready because he had been watching the helicopter attacks almost as he'd recently watched them on television at home; but this unreadiness, in which there was a measure of protest, quickly passed. First he felt ready, then he felt willing.

As the helicopter dropped in curves his keenness of appreciation and praise increased for the colors and character of the earth, for this sight of humane order and fecundity, this expanse of green fields of waving rice, a bending creek, and scattered villages. But the craft continued its turning and he was faced again with the roiling smoke, which was brown now; and on this pass he was low enough to see clusters of brown coconuts in the trees, and narrow trails, roofs of grass, mud walls, a well with paving stones still wet, and the blackened bamboo frame of a house by another house that was burning. The ground was swift and close, and the wind was hot. There was a series of bangs like beatings on a snare drum, and another quick *rap,* and a stream of silver fluid shot across the interior of the helicopter and blew in the wind, wetting Vail's neck with tepid drops. The gunner half jumped up and sat down again. Griffin looked uncertain. Vail soon realized the plane had been hit but simultaneously noticed it was still flying. The fluid on his neck and ears was of a suspicious temperature. Was it blood? It was not.

The gunner started firing, and the hot brass ejecting from his gun came flying against Vail's chest and face, bouncing off his helmet, as he sat with legs dangling out the door. It didn't seem to matter. One of the hot shells hit his cheek and he scarcely noticed. He checked his chin strap and suspenders and touched the map in his side pocket; it was all like football. He looked at Griffin—no smiles in that direction. The gunner ceased. The plane bellied up and tailed down, and the rice began violently bending in the prop wash. Vail went out on the step and leaned out and jumped, landing in the gray mud at the same moment the helicopter landed joltingly, sinking its wheels, and also at the same moment the gunner began throwing out the ammunition cases. The first case struck Vail from behind in the thighs and knocked him down, both arms and knees sinking into the mud. His arms went in nearly to the elbows, but the surprise was not how the mud yielded but how it burned. And it was no cooler at elbow depth than on the surface. As, without much effort, he pulled one arm out of this hot pie, the other sank deeper, but he got himself out, more or less in abrogation of the laws of physics. The wounded were coming, four men carrying a fifth on a poncho, two men supporting a third between them, and a man struggling through the mud, a distressed man, who looked at Vail. Vail searched for an antenna and saw three some two hundred yards away, and assumed this to be the location of the company commander. He started walking, or rather pulling, through the ooze. More wounded came. Griffin called. There was a terrific cacophony of fire, which was rich in information but to his unlearned ear a mere muddle, but as he and Griffin advanced through the ooze he began to take notice. Some of the shots were different; were like the shots in the ambush. What made him so alert were those shots distinguished by a certain sharpness, and by a shock, a concussion in the sound of preceding it. And having noted this distinction in the first few seconds, he was alive to it thereafter, and he began to be aware, dimly at first, of the thrill of being missed.

They rested against a low dike, and Vail listened. He saw that Griffin was also listening. When both felt stronger they went on through the ooze and noise, the sunlight and heat and orange dragonflies and the rotten shitty odor and the concussive shocks of those particular shots—each of which strengthened Vail's half-conscious conviction that he was a whole man. Being missed isn't simply a thrill. It restructures the atoms of personality. Vail hurried as well as he could through the mud, which made his boots unbelievably heavy, looking back now and again at Griffin, who kept following, openmouthed and glancing sidelong.

What Griffin saw was Vail's bent back and slightly cocked helmet, his long swinging arms and gawky elbows, and the water splashing to his hips as he kept up a pace that was making the younger man desperate—but of course the lieutenant wasn't carrying a radio either; but then he was carrying the C rats for both; maybe it was about even—and he saw an absolutely fearless man.

They were still going parallel to the dike and approaching the flank of a line of troops deployed behind this same dike. From ahead the squad sergeant raised his hairy-chested voice in obscene and prolix command—something about laying down a base of fire which initially Vail didn't understand, but soon understood. He nearly jumped. The line was touched off by the sergeant's words in an explosion of suppressive fire, under whose protection Vail and Griffin advanced twenty or more yards on their arduous course.

They took refuge behind the dike, half lying in the rice and half leaning against the low wall.

"Hey, Sergeant!" Vail shouted.

From a few yards down the dike the squad sergeant replied: "Sir!"

"Thank you. That was nice. I could go anywhere with cover like that."

"That was nothing, sir. We'll do it again when you leave. Are you looking for the skipper?"

"Yes. Is he over there?" indicating the direction.

"Yes, sir. The antenna farm over there. Are you the Navy gunsmoke?"

"Yes."

"Are you going to take out that vill?"

Vail stretched a little to look over the wall, and seeing the beaten path on the top of the wall a dozen inches from his eyes, he thought how easy the walking would be if one could only walk on the path; and seeing the thinning smoke and the single visible hut among the trees, he thought of the paving stones around the well.

"Is that where they are?"

"Yes, sir. You see the brown spot there, the hooch?"

"Yes."

"To the left about fifty meters is a machine gun. He hasn't moved since I got here. To the left farther there's a bunch more Charlies, then you go to the right of the hooch and you see that pole there? You see where the moat sort of comes this way . . . ?"

The company commander was a thin blond man about twenty-five, with a thin blond mustache and sun-bleached eyebrows. He had removed his helmet. He lay in the rice and water and mud with his head toward the dike, leaning on an elbow and sometimes, while he talked, resting his head briefly against the wall as if the mud were good for a headache.

He spoke with a civilized diction, quietly, permitting noise to interrupt him rather than raising his voice. "The simplest way I can explain it to you is to say we're surrounded. We have about fifteen dead and ten or so ineffective from wounds, and since your helicopter was hit on its approach I'm informed the air would prefer not to land any more troops until the zone is cooled. The bird . . . you notice the VC haven't destroyed the downed bird. There it sits. They could zap the bird if they wanted, but they'd rather use it as a magnet and zap us." He leaned his head against the mud wall and smoothed the plastic of his map, which he turned for Vail's convenience. "I have a platoon in the creek . . ." He looked toward the creek as if hoping to see some of his men, but it was only a brushy line sinuating across the open space; then he looked back at the map, with raised brows. ". . . This creek. You see? That platoon, which is the reaction platoon, the first one inserted and the one with the heaviest casualties, is pinned down by enemy in the village to the south—on which we conducted an air strike just before you touched down. I asked for nape, but all they had were rockets and bombs, so I got rockets and bombs, and my people are still pinned down. We needed the nape. I want more air and have requested it, but the FAC says it could be some time in coming.

"Then," he went on, again resting his evidently tender head against the mud wall and shutting his eyes briefly, "then . . . next . . . that was the south. On the west it's not so bad, just a sniper or two somewhere over by the railroad. On the east there are enemy in these two vills and they've done it for the squad I put here, along the trail. I sent a squad out from the trail before I knew what was in the vills. Uh . . . As for the north, there it is." He gestured over the wall without lifting his head. "I haven't any idea what started the fire, unless it was a tracer round, but it's just about out now, isn't it? Can you see? I haven't put anything much in there. I had a helicopter gunship, but the result was squat. As things are now . . . Excuse me, I have a slight headache. As things are now, the air can neither reinforce me with troops nor lift out the crippled bird, so we have to cool the zone. You know, I think it's the sun. I thought I was accustomed to the sun, but maybe I've been spending too much time in my tent."

Vail asked: "Why don't you keep your helmet on?"

"It hurts too much. I haven't felt so—sick—since I was a kid. Do you know what? When the reaction platoon came here they found a big pile of human crap in the downed bird. There was a period of not more than fifteen minutes from the time the crew took the guns and left the bird in their chase plane until the reaction platoon came, and in that period the VC somehow managed to get five or six people, at least, to shit on Uncle's property. Can you picture our regimental operations section writing an order directing a company to go out and find something belonging to Ho Chi Minh and shit all over it?"

Vail went down the wall to the place where he'd left Griffin, not wanting to add his own antenna to the absurdly conspicuous concentration around the company commander. In returning to Griffin he had to pass for the second time a thing he hadn't forgotten.

Reaching it, he felt the same compulsion to look at it as before, and when at last he looked it was less to examine than to surrender. He examined the "thing," yes, but the "thing" tested him. His soul opened in fraternal, or perhaps paternal, love. And though he could endure the sight for only a few seconds and resumed his crawling course down the wall in postures alternating between an ape's and a dog's, still this "thing" seemed to displace his soul.

He reached Griffin. The radioman was huddled and leaning sideways against the wall.

"How's everything, Griffin?"

"Fine, sir."

"You're all right?"

"Yes, sir, I'm fine."

Griffin was about eighteen, he had buckteeth and blue eyes, and he was one of those who join the Marine Corps for the obscurest of reasons. He was sitting with one leg outstretched and all his subnavel apparatus immersed in the Asian mud, a price he seemed willing to pay to keep his head below the level of the wall.

Vail took the radio handset.

"Hickory, this is Winter Wheat, over."

"Winter Wheat, Hickory, over."

"This is Winter Wheat. Where are you?"

"Wait."

Vail knelt. He propped the map between his knees and the dike wall, unsnapped a small green pouch on his belt, opened his compass, and laid it on the top of the wall with sights raised. He leaned forward and rotated the compass until it was directed at the center of the high barrier of vegetation that masked the village—a barrier which, had he not seen it from above, he might have mistaken for an island of jungle amid the open paddies. He studied it, and under close scrutiny its orderliness emerged—the regularly set palms, the moat and thick fence of brush and crossed bamboo and the swatches of brown, the brown of thatch, and an earthen trail entering.

The ship said: "Winter Wheat, this is Hickory. Stand by to write. My position: shackle: Bravo Delta, X-ray Charlie, Golf Juliet: unshackle. Over."

"Roger. Wait . . . Can you break a shackle?" Vail asked, turning to Griffin, and the man's expression was sufficient answer. "OK, watch. It's easy. If a kid got anything this simple from *Captain Midnight* he'd feel cheated." Vail unfolded a booklet that he'd taken from his shirt pocket. "He sent us these letters, you see? in sets of two. You turn to the page having the same number as today's date —but you have to know whether he's using local time or Zulu time —except that right now it's the same time both local and Zulu, so it doesn't matter—all right, encode, decode; we want the decode side—run down the list . . ." Vail broke the cipher and plotted the ship's position on his map, finding, as he glanced up, an expression of fenced vulnerability. "We'll do another one later, and I promise it'll be the easiest thing you ever learned. Here—you keep the shackle sheets"; which Griffin accepted as he might an apple that he suspected of worms.

"Hickory," said Vail, "this is Winter Wheat. I roger your position and request you move south about a thousand meters and report when on station and ready for call for fire."

"Which fuze?" Vail thought. "Damn—I don't know much. How thick are the treetops? Now wait—if I use a time fuze . . . Oh, wake up—mass, mass, mass, speed." He saw the trembling foliage and faint smoke. "By god! That's the machine gun, and he's moved, or else he has a partner. Is he firing at me? No, he's trying to get that squad sergeant again. OK, bastard."

"Hickory," said Vail, "this is Winter Wheat. Are you moving south?"

"This is Hickory. Affirmative."

"Thank you. I should tell you my unit is in contact with Victor Charlie on all sides."

"Ah—roger."

Vail said: "Let me give you the mission now and you could report ready when you reach station. Maybe we could save a few seconds."

"This is Hickory. Send your traffic."

"Target number—"

These are pregnant words. They mean not only "I am going to assign a number." They are a warning order and the formal start of a mission.

Vail was astonished by a thudding on the dike—Griffin rolled up and fired his rifle three times and rolled back down with a stunned look, and Vail said: "What happened?"

"They were shooting at us."

It was a machine gun.

"You keep your head down, Griffin, and run the god damn radio. Hold it up out of the mud."

"Yes, sir," said Griffin. "Didn't you hear the bullets hit the wall?"

The ship called: "Winter Wheat, this is Hickory, over."

Vail: "Hickory, Winter Wheat—*target number,* five dash one; *bearing,* three five five degrees magnetic; *coordinates,* seven six seven, four three eight; *height,* five meters; active machine gun; *danger close,* south, three hundred; two guns, main armament; high explosive; fuse quick; will adjust. Over."

There was silence on the radio for some moments before the ship read back the mission, then added: "First salvo at: north, two hundred. Break. Delay two. Over."

"Good god," he thought, "two minutes."

"Hickory, Winter Wheat. Roger your delay. I request first salvo on target instead of two hundred yards north. We'll keep our heads down."

"Wait."

"Now the captain is there," thought Vail. "They're asking the captain. Lucky man, he gets to decide whether he can rely on someone he's never met."

"Oh . . . Winter Wheat, this is Hickory," came a different voice from the ship, undoubtedly the captain himself. "All right . . . I'll —a—put it on target."

"Thank you."

"I'm maneuvering . . . wait."

There was a small, mud-glutted explosion and flying water.

Vail looked toward the company commander, who still lay on his side and was watching.

"Hi! Skipper!"

The skipper jerked his chin upward.

"About a minute."

The skipper waved and turned to his radioman.

"Keep your head down, Griffin."

"Yes, sir. You too, Lieutenant."

"By god, he wants me to keep my head down. What do you make of that?" said Vail to himself. "Adjust along the bearing, please, the bearing, not the line of sight to the fall of shot. Will you please remember that?"

The ship: "Winter Wheat, Hickory. I am on station. All guns bearing. Break. *Gun target line:* two seven one degrees true; *ready* five four. Over."

"Roger, gun-target line two seven one, ready five four. Break. Fire."

"Fire, out." And a moment later: "Shot."

"Hi! Skipper!" Vail shouted. "Fifty-four seconds."

The skipper's hand (Vail could see) deliberately rose, slowly, and pressed his forehead; the squad sergeant kept firing, but conservatively, while his men were down and huddling, looking neither here nor there, like cattle in a heavy rain.

"Stand by," from the ship, ". . . out"; and the time from this "out" to the impact should be five seconds.

On hearing this word Vail gave the handset to Griffin and made himself small, and the two men exchanged a brief, rather tentative glance. Their faces were twelve inches apart.

There came two meshed reports of perceptible duration (there was no shaking of the earth), followed soon by the *blat* sound of large high-velocity guns when they are pointed toward you. After a hesitation, during which he knew perfectly well what to do but didn't do it, Vail looked over the dike.

His face was clean, cleansed by sweat, and his eyes were vivid. His hands, on the dike, and his arms vibrated with a motor excitation visible even on his shirt.

He found everything exactly as before, which could mean only that the rounds had struck deep in the vill where he couldn't see, leaving him one choice: to draw the fire closer to himself till it should break into the open fields before him, after which he could step it back with one adjustment to the target. He took shelter under the wall and said, "Drop one hundred," to Griffin, who radioed the adjustment to Hickory.

All seemed well. He studied Griffin and regretted the buckteeth, which he assumed poor parents had neglected to straighten.

"Shot," Griffin said, repeating what he got from the ship, and Vail waited, and Griffin gave the five-second warning.

Vail counted three and stood up. He met the same evidence, much magnified, with the addition of a shock in the face and inside the helmet, and returning to his sanctuary (seeing unexpectedly the "thing" down the wall) he said again: "Drop one hundred."

This message given to the ship led in swift train to a gigantic black eruption in the paddies just before him, and a whiplike wave and a splattering of earth. Where the other round hit Vail couldn't see, nor did he waste time on finer adjustment.

"Add seven five—four guns, five salvos, fire for effect."

Like great flowers, like poisonous flowers, quick-blooming, they rose repetitiously in blacks and browns from the paddies and the village floor—raising a chaos of earth, trees, mud, water, and possibly a little blood.

The exploding projectiles made a predictable, stunning kind of noise. But there was nothing predictable about the *blat, blat, blat* of the ship's high-velocity guns pointed toward Vail, and nothing natural. And crouching in the ooze, looking at the "thing," Vail listened to the *blat, blat, blat.*

The blond skipper looked down the wall at Vail and tried to get his attention, to thank him, but Vail's eyes were fixed on the corpse. The skipper held his ears, but this did no good; he pressed the heels of his hands against his eye sockets, and leaned and crouched against the wall. The more the blatting and thundering continued, the safer he was; but he wished they would stop. He looked again at Vail, but Vail was still looking at the corpse. The skipper wished that would stop too.

VI

"See-see-see-see-see-see, *you're* Mr. Wiwlby—and I'm the deer, and—"

"No, Terry," said Katherine. "I don't want to pretend that."

Mr. Willoughby had shot a deer that morning. He never hunted during the season, because it was too dangerous. He hunted between the season and the time when the deer started yarding up for the winter. If you waited longer, he said, the meat was no good and you would freeze your feet.

"Oh *please,* Mommy," the child pleaded, and she was already on hands and knees, crawling at extraordinary speed through the snow, Katherine observing with distress how the snow got into her mittens and reddened her wrists.

"No, Terry. Please, dear, let's not"—but where was her resolution? Where was her assertion? The child wanted to play, the mother did not, and they were playing.

Katherine found herself going down on one knee behind an imaginary bush and raising her imaginary rifle toward the alert and sniffling deer, who even as it searched for danger issued a stream of directions.

"N-n-n-now I sniff. I have a big rack of horns and I raise my noble head and sniff, and you see me, but you don't shoot. You wait. You think, 'My, what a noble stag. What a great big rack of horns.'"

"Antlers," said Katherine.

"I'm all reddish brown, and I lift my flag because I have a mate and a fawn in the woods. I tell them not to come into the meadow yet." She placed a hand at her rear and lifted the flag. "Now I see you, and I know the danger." The stag perceived its danger. "And I . . . see-see, I tell my mate to run that way deep in the woods, but I run this way . . . so-so-so-so . . ."

"So that I don't see your mate and your fawn."

"I tricked you. I run."

"And I shoot," said Katherine, *"kah . . . kah . . .* but I miss."

"But you have one bullet left."

"And I fire it . . . *kah* . . . and miss."

"No-n-*no,* Mommy, you hit me." The stag halted, it swayed, its legs weakened, its eyes rolled skyward. "And I fall—and I . . ." The mouth and eyes of the stag opened in death, but after a moment the instructions continued. "N-n-n-now you have to gut me."

"No," replied Katherine.

"Yes, Mommy. You take out your hunting knife to gut me."

"No," said the mother. "I put you on the sled to haul you home." And so saying, Katherine rolled the limp body onto the sled and began pulling it toward the cabin.

"Remember," the girl persisted, "you have to show me to the town clerk, and weigh me and put on my tag."

"Yes, OK, stag. We'll stop at the town clerk's on the way to the laundromat." And she added to herself, appreciating Willoughby more than ever: "But the town clerk will never see Mr. Willoughby's deer."

"Aw, Mommy, please," the child protested, sitting up. "Do we have to go to the laundromat? I hate the laundromat."

"I do too. Get off and walk now, it's uphill."

"Mommy, I don't want to go. It stinks in there."

"Well, we're going."

"Oh, Mommy . . ."

"We're going, dear. I'm sorry." And she was truly sorry, because there was something squalid and fishy about the laundromat.

Katherine stood the sled against the woodpile on the porch and they went inside, took off their outdoor clothing except for their boots, and began sorting the laundry, the child working beside the mother according to a routine. The little girl enjoyed the sorting. She was in her own home with her cat and her mother close by, doing a job for which she'd be thanked, handling familiar things.

Katherine worked dully, slipping down already into the influence of the smell of bleach, the fluorescent lights and whirling rags and wasted time.

They were delayed as they left the house by Crackpot, who came to the door and stood exactly so Katherine could not shut it, and surveyed exterior conditions, the diminishing light and tightening cold. There wasn't much doubt what he'd choose, and as Katherine slowly swung the door he slowly backed away and sat on the rug, placing his forepaws twice, and watched his mistresses depart.

They went down the path through the lifeless birches. The sun had shone during the day, and together with the wind had glazed the top of the snow, which was freezing hard in the gaunt light of evening. Their steps were like the felling of trees. Katherine carried a basket squeaking on her hip, and Terry, like an elf, dragged a sack.

"Uncle John won't like this snow," said Katherine.

"But I like snow."

"Yes, so do I, and so does Uncle John, but this is getting a crust, you see." Squatting with the basket still upon her hip, she spread her hand on the crust and pressed till it broke through, with a sound that both crackled and resonated.

"Y-you mean he'll slip? He'll fall?"

"He might. It's not good skiing snow."

But Terry, as she resumed dragging her sack down the path, spoke in a fascinated undertone: "See-see, there's a deer in the woods, and he's listening . . ."

At the laundromat, sitting in a chrome chair and watching television, in a corner full of limp and ugly magazines, hog-tied in her poverty fat and toothless because it had been arranged in that era that false teeth should cost three hundred dollars—an amount of money equal to a month's wages at the poultry factory or to the value of three unregistered yearling Hereford heifers, four tons of grain, 1500 pounds of milk replacer, or half a year's purchase of bob calves for her veal business—in her little chrome chair sat a dame of the hills upon her swollen legs like two congresses of the milk veins on the underbelly of a Holstein cow.

Now and then she looked from the television to her whirling clothes. When the door opened, admitting Katherine and Terry, she honked a greeting. Katherine was pleased, and she put her basket on a worktable and came along the row of machines to talk to this woman, whom she didn't know as well as she thought; and Mrs. Sutton was pleased to see Katherine Ashley, Harry Ashley's daughter, so young, comely, and "slick," leading around an illegitimate child.

"I heard your husband has quit shipping milk," said Katherine.

"Oh yes, honey, that was years ago."

"Why?"

The state had come out with a book of regulations about milking machines and bulk tanks, and being unable to buy the new equipment or get credit, the Suttons had quit milking. Now Mrs. Sutton kept heifers, which were all right, and veal calves, which were scouring, and a few pigs; and her husband had been laid off at the mill.

"What do you feed the pigs?" Katherine asked.

Mrs. Sutton responded, not very responsively: "You should keep a pig, honey."

Katherine seemed to show that she might consider it.

"You'll need two. One gets lonely. Two, then you sell one and eat the other, and the one pays the bills." Piglets cost fifteen dollars; they were recently ten. Mrs. Sutton had a few to sell.

Katherine pondered where she might put a pig.

"What's your name?" the woman asked Terry, and the child answered.

"Oh," said the lady, "Terry what?"

"Terry Vail."

"Oh, *Vail* is it?"

The girl asked: "Do your pigs bite?"

"Pigs ate my grandma," said Mrs. Sutton.

"Was she fat too?"

The woman's pale eyes flickered. She looked up at Katherine and said: "I came from a good family. I came from New York State, but I married Ed and came up here and I've been a hillbilly ever since."

Katherine forced the child to apologize, then she asked further questions about Mrs. Sutton's animals, and after ten more minutes' conversation about the dysentery and pneumonia of the calves Katherine faced her work, and Mrs. Sutton returned her attention to the black-and-white television on a shelf just above a worktable.

Every so often Katherine would glance over and find Mrs. Sutton staring at her, a stare that was averted whenever caught but shameless anyway, and shifted sometimes with intensified contempt to

Terry, who sat reading a book of Charlie Brown cartoons. Katherine became uneasy. She felt the woman's derision and surmised it came from Mrs. Sutton's poverty and her own easy life. Katherine worked two days a week keeping the accounts of a ski lodge, but that was only because she wanted to, and she kept her house, her A-frame, exceedingly neat. She had changed in these brief weeks from sloppy-intellectual (a delineable type of housekeeper in her reckoning) to orderly.

"I have an easy life—a regular life—I love the woods—I feel . . ."

She felt serene. The woman's envy stung less because it was so deserved.

There was also the money that Mrs. Sutton's husband had borrowed from Katherine's father and never repaid, a debt of something less than a hundred dollars. It was for a grain bill, Katherine thought. "I remember his coming. If Dad had refused she would hate me now just as she does because he lent the money. Well then, don't just stand here, run right down and buy a piglet from her."

She flung the last of the laundry into a machine, slammed the door, and set it going with a coin.

She felt peace in her life, patience, yet she was slightly off her poise.

Now, discovering her purse short of the proper coins, she had to approach Mrs. Sutton.

"Mrs. Sutton, I've run out of dimes."

The woman moved, jiggling her legs, and brought out her purse, but found no change for "honey." As Katherine looked at the upturned face of Mrs. Sutton she saw the skull implicit in the face. Mrs. Sutton's head was massive and her face was fat, but the jaw outreached the nose, the forehead was cornered and the cheekbones padded, the skull within. Katherine imagined the shape, the cave, the orifices of her own skull.

She had enough dimes to dry the sheets. Were John and Ella not coming she would have taken the other laundry home to dry on a rack before the fire, but she didn't want Ella to think she lived like a Kallikak.

She took Terry by the hand and went out the door and along the walk past the dark windows of the barbershop, the grocery and dry-goods store, and the hardware store, where a clock glowed with

a weak yellow light. All this was on her left. On her right was a long
row of cars with Connecticut, Massachusetts, and New York license
plates. She grew nervous as she approached the Wrong Branch.

"At least they aren't hunters," she thought. So they must be skiers,
and that couldn't be too bad, but she entered the tavern as if it were
hostile territory.

She knew there was a sign on the door that said, WE DON'T MAKE
CHANGE, but she averted her eyes and pushed the door open. The
place was a converted restaurant. The bar was an old lunch counter.
In she came—a tall woman holding her girl's hand, expressing pride,
wearing shapely black pants disappearing into her boots, with a red
and black checkered shirt and a dark red beret knit of thick yarn. She
held her daughter's hand tightly. Some of the local men spoke and
the out-of-staters were silent, mostly, for a moment, and then even
though the conversation in the room continued she was certain her
voice was audible at every booth and table. The barman made her
change just as if there were no sign, and she thanked him with the
consciousness of an immense, welling, ridiculous gratitude.

She fed more dimes to the dryer, sat down with a magazine, and
discovered that she wished Mrs. Sutton hadn't left, for the woman's
departure now seemed the end of an opportunity for a kindness, or
for the uplifting in some way of herself; at least for talk; and the
woman's hostility troubled Katherine with the feeling of having
inflicted some injury which now she couldn't heal.

She lived in anticipation her reunion with Ella. She was sitting in
one of the chrome and plastic chairs in the middle of the empty
laundromat, much as Mrs. Sutton had been sitting a half hour before,
with her laundry spinning ten feet from her eyes and her daughter's
legs rhythmically swinging from the chair at her right. She got up
and turned the television off. She was in a tank, an aquarium of
bluish fluorescent light with chrome and white machinery all about;
but it affected her less now than when she had been sorting the
laundry at home.

She wanted to see her sister-in-law, to greet her, to show her
through the cabin and take her walking in the woods, to introduce
her to Mr. and Mrs. Willoughby, to protest to her that the snow
presently on the ground was nothing to what would soon come, to
listen to her—to sit over coffee at the table in the kitchen and hear
her speaking of her life and her tastes—to tell her that solitude here

was quite bearable—to listen, contradict, and agree—to laugh or smile and to fetch more coffee for this too perfectly beautiful sister-in-law.

"But what about the winter, Katherine? My god, it'll be incredibly cold."

"Oh, it'll be cold, yes, it is already, but it isn't so awful as you imagine" (with a gentle voice, more reticent, and softer, than the voice Richard elicited from her). "If you're active and you enjoy the storms and you always have a warm place to go—and if you wear long johns and a T-shirt and good turtleneck jersey—it's fine. I wear hunting boots outdoors and these Indian boots or whatever they are indoors" (raising her foot awkwardly and humorously to the table and displaying an indoor boot of calf height, made of sheepskin and red and yellow beads). "If we get cold, truly cold, we're not loggers after all, we needn't stay outside all day when there's a fireplace inside.

"The plays of Aeschylus and Sophocles, the histories of Thucydides and Xenophon, and I enjoy histories of ancient Greece written by modern men, especially Englishmen, and a little of Plato, and some of the lines of Sappho —and the sonnets of Shakespeare, and I love The Tempest. *You haven't read that, have you? You're simpler."* (Meaning that anyone so beautiful as Ella could doubtless exist on her beauty alone, without reading The Tempest or anything else. "A half-baked idea," Katherine thought later.)

"Solitude in this place isn't the loneliness of the city. Of course I'm lonely, but not because I'm isolated. Rather because of one fact and one alone. Richard. It would be harder in Washington. Solitude here is . . . woven in.

"I write two or three times a week and could write oftener, even though my life is uneventful, but if I wrote every day I'd spoil it. It's my chief pleasure —it's my intercourse and reflection. I don't write erotic letters. I think erotic thoughts.

"I would want the first hours to be pure. The first hours I'd want us to be like a brother and sister, or, let's say, as if one of us were weakened by illness and so we were going to be pure. Not all day but for a time. If he arrived, say, at eight in the morning without breakfast I'd make breakfast, and possibly he'd take a shower and shave while I cooked our breakfast. Then a long conversation. I could listen to that voice. I would want a kiss, certainly. Then I'd want him to come with Terry and me to her sliding hill. He could see how she goes down the whole hill. Then he'd have gifts for us, we'd see the Willoughbys, and I'd want him to see how the winter has changed the place where we waited for the deer. Would you like it if I showed

*you that place? It's an open mowing with woods all around where the deer
come to browse. I think you'd enjoy it. May I take you?"*

"Yes, please do."

*"I've thought of our going there. I know you so little, really, yet ever since
that night in Washington I can imagine your entire—personality, all your
tastes, and know in advance what you'll enjoy."*

"And you think I would enjoy this place?"

"Oh yes."

"Then let's go."

"It's under snow now."

*"Certainly, but I could picture it in all the seasons, and you could show
me where the deer come out and where they browse, and I'm sure I'll be able
to see it all very clearly, if you'll take me."*

"I will, nothing could delight me more, but you'll be cold."

*"If you think I'll be cold . . . you're so generous, Katherine, will you lend
me your coat?"*

"Yes, I have another, wear mine."

"May I also wear your gloves?"

"Yes."

"May I take your beret?"

"Take it, please, you'll make it look good."

*"The coat is large but it feels warm, and your gloves are also large for
me but there's a lovely lining. Is it rabbit?"*

"Yes, dear Ella. The beret looks very gay on you."

*"You're so thoughtful—will you be warm now that you've lent me your
things?"*

"Yes, very, don't give it a thought—very."

"You're kind, I love your kindness, Katherine."

"Mommy, do you still have the list?"

Katherine, who was folding the laundry and putting it up in warm,
fresh stacks, paused to unbutton her shirt pocket and produce a
talismanic scrap of paper, which she showed to Terry, thereby passing a test. But this time Terry surprised her by asking for the list and
a pencil, which her mother got from her purse. She watched while
the child with first-grade labor made two additions to the list, which
was a roster of significant personages. Katherine appeared therein as
"Kit," the Willoughbys were there, grievously misspelled, as were
many schoolfellows, besides Crackpot and the imaginary "ski dogs,"

meaning sled dogs, Super Pass and Star Passer. Their real dog, Yuk, wasn't there.

The names now added were those of Katherine's brother, John, and his wife, Ella. When this list had been entrusted to her a week ago Katherine had asked why Daddy wasn't on it. The child's reply was that she had forgotten, and that he did not "belong" on the list. Whether Richard was segregated as a traitor or a treasure Katherine didn't know, but she did know that since Richard's departure Terry had never made a reference to him except in response to one of Katherine's.

"Shall I still keep it?"

"Yes, Mommy."

Katherine returned the list to her breast pocket.

"Put your chin up," she said, and wedged a stack of bedding between the girl's outstretched hands and her chin. The child took the load outside and returned from the darkness a moment later with a slightly vindictive assertion:

"Mommy, there *is* something wrong with our house."

"No there's not."

"Oh yes there is. I have to stand on a stool to brush my teeth and you have to stoop way down to brush your teeth."

"Well, good heavens, so what?"

"Well . . ."

"That doesn't count as anything wrong with the house. Now here —chin up."

When next she returned, the child was even more certain.

"There *must* be a hole in the roof, Mommy, because I saw the string come down."

"No dear," answered the mother quietly, "there is no hole and you didn't see a string coming down. Maybe you imagined that you did. If there were a hole in the roof, rain would leak in on your bed."

"It could be a hole too little for the rain but it could let the string in."

"If it were so little, dear, how could the bad men take you out?"

"I don't know," said the girl, "but *they* know."

Katherine had confounded the child without comforting her. Terry evaded her eyes, and Katherine very nearly made the concession that was constantly sought of her, that mother and daughter should sleep in the same bed.

"Terry—dear . . ."

"Will Uncle John sleep with me?"

"No, dear, he'll sleep with Aunt Ella."

"Will you sleep with me?"

"No, dear. You may have Crackpot if he isn't running down to the barn—and Super Pass and Star Passer."

Terry replied with disgust, "Oh, Mommy, they aren't real."

"Neither is the string, dear."

This too was more logic than comfort, but Katherine didn't know where to turn after logic except to the concession she so distrusted.

"Mommy."

"Yes, dear?"

The dark wayward eyes of the girl roved about the laundromat with its steel tables, its chrome, plastic, tubes, and white machines.

"See-see-see, I'm a ski dog," she said, "and my name is Brambo. See-see, I'm all gray except for one black paw and the end of my tail, and that's black, and my tail curls over my back. My ears stand up, and see-see, I have a very bad limp but I'm the leader of the team anyway—see-see . . ."

While Katherine listened to the whole description of "Brambo," her eyes sought the child's with wretched, unrequited patience.

"Terry, dearest," she began, bending to the animated face of the child.

"N-n-n-*no*, Mommy, I'm Brambo, and see-see, you're the Eskimo, and you say: 'Brambo, old boy . . .' "

Katherine was hungry, and while she was loading the laundry into the car she had to pause and lean on the fender through a spell of dizziness.

Later she gave her hand into the arthritic hand of Mr. Willoughby and allowed him to lead her through the dark while she in turn led her daughter. Her booted feet were uncertain of the bumpy, frozen earth floor, and her eyes were incredulously dilated in the darkness. She kept searching for a flaw in the darkness but found none.

"He's here," said the old man. "You wait," and the thick stiff hand left hers, so she drew her daughter closer to her side.

"Mommy? Where is he?"

"Right here, darling, somewhere."

Mr. Willoughby was gone, and neither his steps nor his breathing, which was never of the best, could be heard. Katherine stood with senses agape and at length heard a cow shifting in her stanchion in the adjoining barn. The darkness, rather than fading, seemed more visible and pure the more she searched it.

There came a click, illuminating the place with amber, and she saw Willoughby turning from the switch. Turning likewise, she saw split logs stacked clear to the roof, and turning more, she saw, just at her shoulder, an eviscerated buck hanging head downward.

Terry gave a cry, left her mother's side, and stroked the plunging face of the buck, imparting to the suspended body a nearly invisible rotation so, as Katherine stared, his abdominal chamber came around to her, a smooth opening of monstrous depth into which she gazed against her will, beholding its size, emptiness, and silken walls. Besides the dominant brown there was some black and some white in his coat, and his cloven forehooves had a dark enamel luster. There was a shaft of sapling sharpened at one end and driven horizontally through his hind legs at the soft spot by the hock. He hung suspended from this bar, from a hook on a chain going up to a rafter. Just as this rusted chain went up, so did his pointing legs go down, and his muzzle and his tilted rack of antlers. His silence and his stillness were an embodiment of motion, as sculpture is.

Slowly Katherine removed her mitten, and reaching out to his coat she found it all icy spicules; then she felt his ear in her whole hand, as a farmer feels the ear of a sick calf, and she found it frozen hard. She realized that a hideous impulse was gathering in her to feel his tongue, which hung long and slack between his frosty jaws.

Willoughby was about to tell how he'd shot him, and although in such poor light as this his vision was rather general, he could see, by reason of her slow feeling of the body, what effect the buck was having on Katherine; nor was this the first time he had seen such a wondrous hypnosis. He said nothing. He observed her deliberate, gentle, complete examination of the tongue.

Katherine felt guilt for wanting to do it, but nonetheless she took the tongue in her bare hand, and found it was not at all slack, as it looked, but frozen through, with a surface rather rough and greaseless, and at length taking away her hand—going from the tongue to the rather modest rack of antlers—she so powerfully comprehended his identity, his wildness, that she could not bear to look at his eyes. Terry was looking at his eyes and her lips were moving. Katherine returned her hand, which was beginning to hurt from the cold, to the brittle coat, and ran it contrary to the growth until to her dismay she found she'd gone over the entrance hole, on the left side. And then her curiosity prompted her to examine the right shoulder, and she discovered with a small measure of pride in her knowledge of these matters, being her father's daughter still, that the shoulder was broken, as she thought it might be, and the right foreleg very slightly out of line.

Her hand being painfully cold now, she drew her mitten back on (these were not her rabbit-lined gloves but an old pair of knit mittens with worn leather palms), and she glanced at Willoughby.

"It went through his heart," the old man said, pronouncing the last word like a Yankee.

"Yes, sir, I see."

"Don't say sir."

She looked at him in surprise, and the corners of her lips deepened.

"Why don't you say Will?"

Katherine smiled and seemed to consent, and Willoughby thought her the handsomest woman he'd seen in fifty years.

"Nan's got it in the kitchen. It'll make good sandwiches if you slice it thin, it'll taste like good beef. It's got a hole you could drop a stone through."

"That's excellent shooting," she said.

"Naw," replied Willoughby scornfully, "it wasn't any kind of shooting, it was the third shot hit him. The first two was practice."

"My dad said the first two were to warm the barrel."

"Maybe, but your dad never took those two."

"Oh," she replied, quite pleased, "sometimes he did."

"I wonder, did you ever hear the name of Jim Fifield? I went to his place when I was an infant of about forty years of age because I heard he was selling his stock. I hent seen him in years. He was just struggling down off his pawch when I got there, and I asked if he was Jim Fifield. He said, 'I used to be.' That's how I feel"—the old man smiled, jumbling the colors of his eroded face—"but when I knock down a buck like that I feel pretty good."

"I shot one when I was fourteen," said Katherine. "Dad dragged it out of the woods for me and he told me"—she gestured as her father had—"'Now gut him.' I said I didn't know how. I wasn't afraid, or squeamish, but I thought it would be . . . too much of a job."

"I know, you was squeamish too."

"But Dad said a girl who could shoot a deer could gut him."

"Sho-ah."

"He said he would show me how."

"I *know* how he'd show you, your dad."

"He put in the knife here"—she indicated the place on her own body—"and took my hand and put it around the handle and told me to cut downward and not to punch in, so I did as he told me and was surprised at how easily the knife went."

"Yeah, it don't take much."

"I finished the slit all the way down and then he said, 'Now cut a circle around his bum,' which I did, then he parted the slit from the breastbone on down and opened it for me to see. And I was . . . well . . ."

"Confused."

"Perhaps—at the sight of so much . . ."

"Complication."

"Yes."

"It's complicated as hell if you look close."

"I turned to Dad and asked what I should do next, and he said, 'Now, Kit, here is the complicated part of it.' "

"I know what he said. I'll bet he said, 'Now, little girl, you just reach in there and pull it all out.' "

"Yes, sir, that's what he said."

Willoughby grinned at the memory of Katherine's father, and Katherine smiled. But she also sought a way to express an idea that had come to her when she had "pulled it all out," an idea she hadn't expressed to her father but hoped she might present to Mr. Willoughby now. But surely it was too personal, too childish, too obvious, and if exposed to the light too pale; whereas in the dark of her mind it had kept its luminosity all her life since.

Willoughby offered to give her the heart. She declined with thanks, and his response was to insist she take not only the heart but that portion of the liver which he and his wife had not already consumed at dinner, which was most of it, and said he'd give her more meat when the animal was butchered. When Katherine redoubled her protests the old man construed it as a gift to her brother as well. So when they continued their homeward drive a few minutes later Katherine and Terry carried not only their laundry and the hunger, which revisited Katherine and made her dizzy, which made the child sleepy, but the organs of the buck.

"Dad," she thought, "I felt that I shouldn't have taken all this out because I didn't understand it, I could never replace it—I never appreciated how intricate it was."

John Ashley, a strong man, shorter by an inch than his tall sister, crouched at the fire and opened an air passage in the coals and asked questions.

"So he's *resigned* to the necessity of making money," said Ashley.

"Yes," Kit replied. "He says he is."

"How resigned?"

"Why, I don't know. How resigned must he be?"

"In his case . . ."

Ashley threw in two birch logs, whose peeling white bark instantly blazed up.

Katherine said, "In his case what?"

"He's a career evader," said Ashley, settling the fire with a poker. "That's not bad, and it's not good. It's what he is. You know that."

"Do I? What is a career evader?"

"It's not somebody who makes a career of evasion. Don't get the wrong idea. It's somebody who evades a career."

Ashley, who was on his haunches, reached up with both hands to grip the mantelpiece and lifted himself like a gymnast. He brushed his hands and looked at his sister. She saw those quartz-blue eyes.

"I'd say there's room for doubt. I'd say he may not know his own mind," Ashley declared.

Katherine was sitting in an ancient leather chair that had been Willoughby's good chair for decades before it was relegated to the cabin. Her legs were extended on another, wooden chair, and crossed at the ankles. She held a glass of Scotch, her first alcohol in weeks. She took no offense whatever, for she felt rather neat and composed, and half amused.

Ella, wearing a sweater with a green and white snowflake pattern, and green ski pants, was sitting on Katherine's desk with her legs toward the fire. At long intervals she sipped beer from a clear glass mug. In her right hand a small, black, twisted, rum-soaked cigar burned pungently and slowly, and she stared into the fire with brows slightly lifted, listening to their conversation, saying nothing herself. Her hair was freshly brushed.

"By 'room for doubt,' " said Katherine, "you mean he may not be *totally* committed to money-grubbing?"

"You're caricaturing my argument, which suggests a reluctance to deal with it. I haven't said anything about money-grubbing."

"All right then, I'll be as solemn as you, even though I used to wipe your little red bottom."

"She never did," he said, turning to his wife. Ashley was leaning against the desk beside Ella, and at some invisible sign she gave him her cigar. He took two puffs, the first to heat the cigar and the second for the taste, and gave it back. These two, now John and Ella Ashley, had been known to their college classmates as "the unbelievable couple." He had been a wrestler and she a diver. Their children, if any, would be little gods.

"And while we're being so damned serious," said Katherine, "somebody should point out that you haven't really made an argument. You've simply called my husband a name, and I assume a nasty name."

"No," Ashley replied, "not at all. As I said, it's neither good nor bad. And here's the argument. I don't know him very well, only as an in-law. But I do know who picked him."

Ella spoke for the first time, without taking her eyes off the fire: "What about me? Look who I picked."

"Dick wants it big," Ashley said, taking no notice. "None of your little piddly shit for him. Right?"

Katherine observed the face of her brother—the blond, almost white hair, which would have been curly were it not cut so short; and what she called the "bounce-back" eyes, and the clear, small features; the finely formed, small nose with its flared nostrils, and the rather wide mouth. With his muscles and with this face, she believed, he could have been an actor, in or out of his clothes.

"He wants it deep," Ashley went on, "but money is shallow. And money is little. Am I right? The one thing he can't do is make a shallow commitment. It's against his nature. But: He equates an ordinary career with money. So he evades a career decision because a career is money, and money is shallow and small."

"That's an argument all right, but it's circular," Katherine objected, not quite certain it was. She later decided it wasn't circular but was untrue.

"No, it's simply the circle he has drawn around himself," Ashley said. "The whole thing is, he wants what's big. Explore the poles. Search the unknown. What do you do after that?"

Katherine sought the eyes of her sister-in-law and found them rather luminously receptive.

"So," concluded Ashley, "when he tells you he's ready to make money—"

"I'll say: 'You're a liar!' "

"Exactly," said Ashley.

"But he didn't mean," said Ella, "that he was going to devote his whole life to it, did he?"

"Obviously not," Ashley said, addressing Katherine, "but you don't make money without that commitment. You make wages. Dick'll make wages. I'd bet money on it."

Katherine thought about this while she assembled a platter of bread, salt, mayonnaise, lettuce, and the heart. They made sandwiches at her desk, Ashley commenting with a grunt on the bullet channel in the heart as his knife laid it open.

Ella spoke again: "You call it evading a career, but is that bad? All you're really saying is that other things are more important to him than money."

"For the third time, no. I'll bet Dick likes Beethoven. Does he, Kate?" Still holding a sandwich in one hand, Ashley spread his arms and walked around with bent legs like a gorilla and said: "Big! Big!"

A few moments later Ashley was saying: "You have to be suspicious of Beethoven. There is no joy in the 'Hymn to Joy.' Some of the things he wrote are sinister. Sure he's a great artist. Sure he deepens life. But we deepen his life. That's the sinister part. I was listening to a sonata just the other day—I don't know music, but then you can't read Greek—so? And it happens I have an ear for patterns —a mathematical sense.

"Early in the piece he sets up a firm expectation of a pattern to delight the ear and comfort the soul. For the remainder of the piece he teases and manipulates you, constantly arouses your expectations, and never, never brings the pattern to full realization. Never. He

toys with his listeners. And that was his purpose in writing that piece
—to manipulate and disappoint gullible, stupid human beings who
are hungry for beauty.''

"What John means is that he doesn't like Germans,'' said Ella,
who was one quarter German.

"My kraut-head wife—''

"I am not a kraut-head. I had one German grandparent.''

"But your German quarter starts at the neck,'' Ashley said. "And
anyway I don't have racial prejudices. They are an admission that
you can't cope with life as it is.''

"Well then, John, I gather,'' said Katherine, "that you have no
weaknesses.''

"No, no. One.''

The women looked at each other, and Katherine said: "Don't
embarrass us with your sexual history.''

"My weakness is that I refuse to discuss my weaknesses,'' he said.

"But do you have a weakness,'' Katherine said, and paused—"for
money?''

"Probably not. And not for Beethoven either.''

"So in a couple of days,'' said Katherine, "you'll start driving
across the country, and you'll go to Travis Air Force Base, as I'm
told, and get in a plane and fly to Vietnam, and fight. But not for
any big motive like saving Western Civilization, I presume.''

"Well, I've already said people don't always know their own
minds.''

"But you know what's in your consciousness.''

"Yes, in that insignificant fraction of my mind, you're right. I
don't find anything like a duty to help defend Western Civilization
against the forces of the dark. I leave that sort of thing to the
religious, the fanatic, and the simple.''

"And in that insignificant fraction, what do you find? What's
there?''

"As I say, Kate, nothing like that.''

"Then what?''

"Oh—that I signed up for three years in the Crotch, that they sent
me written orders, and that obeying the orders feels like the natural
thing to do.''

"You mean feels good,'' said Katherine.

"Well, they say it isn't much of a war but it's the only one we've got. It's like anything else, I suppose. If you look at it and see what it actually is, instead of what you wish it was—if you break it down and spread the components out—there's not all that much to it."

"What do you mean by that?" Katherine demanded.

Ella was still looking at the fire.

"But for Ella now," said Ashley, "hey, that's another story. For her it's the biggest thing that's happened since we got married. Am I right, El?"

Ella's brows rose, almost imperceptibly, and her face assumed a fixed, isolated expression.

"I mean for *her,* holy shit, what an opportunity. A whole year, right? The new horizons, the adventures, and plenty of material everywhere, marine and civilian—the experiments, the convolutions, the novelties—god, it's really awesome. It staggers the imagination—doesn't it, El?"

Ella's eyes were steady on the fire. Her hand trembled a little as she took a puff from her cigar. She said absolutely nothing.

Katherine didn't know what to do.

"I'm faithful," Ella said.

Katherine nodded. Katherine's eyes were stinging.

"And he knows it," Ella continued. "When he says something like that you never know what's happening. You have to—"

Ella fell silent, and took a careful sip of her hot chocolate, which was steaming.

The two women were sitting at a table in the lodge, near the two-story glass wall, whence they could see much of the slope and the benign and gentle motion of the descending skiers. There was a light snow falling but they could see even the minute figures near the top of the center run. And because Terry was wearing her bright red parka and blue cap Katherine could, from time to time, recognize her among the scores of others skiing or tumbling down the beginners' hill, on the extreme right of their view.

John had hit ice and taken a fall in the morning, and had arrived at the bottom pale. Katherine was amazed to see he was frightened, or something like it. But Ella had explained: "He's afraid of showing up at Travis with a broken leg. How would he ever explain that?" And that of course was it. Now, in the late afternoon, he was over his scare and ripping down the mountain just as he had in the early morning.

"There he is," Ella said.

"Yes, I see him," Katherine replied. "I slept badly last night. I kept trying to figure out whether that—remark—was cruel or simply trivial."

"With John there's no difference," Ella said.

They watched him for a moment, then lost him as he made a turn on a side trail.

Ella said: "I'm not sophisticated like John. I never know where it's coming from, or why. I didn't sleep either. It took me half the night to figure it out. The 'remark.' He was arranging it so that if I'm faithful I get no credit, not that I'd want any, and if I'm not, I'm the slut he said I am. There he is again."

Ashley now reappeared in the center run about two thirds of the way down, tacking gently from side to side. He was easy to spot because he wasn't wearing fancy ski clothes, just khaki pants (over long johns) and a black windbreaker.

"He'll sprint in," Ella predicted, and on his next tack he turned sharply down, and made a line straight down. When next they saw him he was at the top of the beginners' hill with Terry.

"I do want—what he calls novelty," Ella declared. She looked guiltily at Katherine and half smiled and asked: "Novelty? Do you remember the word?"

"So what?" said Katherine.

"Well, I may be very—alive. Who knows? How could I ever tell? I mean as compared to anybody else. But John keeps sending me messages, 'Are you sure you want this?' And yet all I want is him. I don't even think about faithful or unfaithful."

In the beginning Katherine had disliked Ella intensely and called her "Suppleton." Thinking back on such cheap and stupid terms as this, she was always surprised Richard hadn't brought her up short. One explanation was that he had thought she was jealous. This possibility chagrined and reduced her even more. There was something to be jealous of.

Ella in those days had been diving in AAU competition, and John, Richard, and Katherine had gone to three or four meets, two in Madison, as she remembered, and one or two in Chicago. Ella would stand poised on the balls of her feet on a high board or higher tower, with her back to the water and the hushed multitudes, and raise her arms in a dramatic V, and just be there, for twice as long as necessary. Then, as if something in Nature had changed, a change no one but she could perceive, she would let the miracle happen. A thing either of unutterable beauty or unbelievable difficulty then happened before their eyes, and a few seconds later Ella would emerge from the water with her head thrown a little back, so her passage to the surface sculpted her hair.

The hard part was, she scarcely ever spoke to Katherine and never smiled at her. She was animated enough with everybody else. When Katherine complained Richard said: "She admires you," and tried to go on, but Katherine hooted him down.

Katherine hardened in the conviction that Ella was a stupid egotist and that her younger brother had engaged himself to marry a diving body. She expostulated to Richard on "the power of pussy," and actually got angry. She suggested that she was tempted to "save" John, and Richard simply looked at her as if she were touched.

Then one day the four of them were taking a walk on a railroad track and two roaming dogs joined them for a few minutes. Katherine commented that a human being had to adjust his stride each time to land on a tie, and that this was done consciously. But the dogs, she said, with four feet to worry about instead of two, landed on a tie with each step and seemed to do so without trying. John then objected: "But for all you know it's a conscious act for the dog too." And then Ella came to life, it seemed, and acknowledged Katherine's existence for the first time. "That's not the point," Ella said. "The point is, they simply do it. Trot, trot, trot."

The two women began to talk, and lagged behind the men. Katherine said a diver must have a special kind of knowledge. She needed to know the distances, speeds, angles, and forces, and the relations of each of these to all the others. Yet, Katherine said, one couldn't believe that the diver's mind registered all this data and solved the problems of geometry and physics consciously. And the skill surely lay beyond instinct.

Ella said she was right, and that it frightened her to look into the mystery because she knew it could ruin her. "Doesn't it make you feel good?" Ella asked, meaning the "mystery," and Katherine looked at her in surprise and said: "I think it does." And they watched the two strays trotting up the ties.

"How would you like . . ." Katherine began, looking up from her hot chocolate, and hesitated, and was astonished to hear Ella say:
"How would I like to come back here after John goes over?"
"Yes. My god."
"I'd like to come for a while, if you want me—for a little while."
"You could live with me the whole time, if you like. There's room."
"Yes, I noticed. I was surprised, I thought you were in some little old log cabin. But I think I'll stay in California, at least in the beginning. I'll live with my parents out there for a few months, but then my father's retiring in the spring and I couldn't stand to be around the house after that. I thought I might come here then, if you're still here, and if you want me."
"Of course I want you."
"I'll come for a while. But I was wondering, maybe Dick will be due home by that time."
"Dick isn't coming home till next fall," said Katherine.
Ella repeated, "Next fall. How do you stand it?"
"Why, how will you?"
"It isn't the same. You know that."
"John loves you," said Katherine, regretting her brevity.
"I can't argue with that, since I don't know the definition. But he certainly utilizes me. That's one of their Marine Corps terms—utilize. Maybe it is love. He doesn't understand me, though." She stopped. "That sounds so disgusting," she observed, "that I doubt it's what I really mean. I utilize him, for that matter. I really don't care if he understands me or not, now that I think about it. What I meant to say was . . .
"What I object to," Ella continued, "and really, 'object' is the lamest possible way of expressing it, is that he doesn't react to me. He acts like I'm not there—like he's pretending I'm not there. But he's not pretending."
"He doesn't perceive you," said Katherine.
Ella glanced again at her sister-in-law and seemed to accept the phrase. "If I'm with you," she said, "or even your little six-year-old girl, or my father or mother or practically any man I know, I can tell that they are aware of me. They're aware of something about me. I don't mean anything wonderfully marvelous, I just mean aware. They don't act, if we're in a room together, as though they were

alone in the room. But if John and I are together, even if we're arguing, I sometimes feel that he hasn't noticed me yet—like those executives in the movies who keep working when some poor guy comes into their office."

Ella looked at her watch and at the sky and said she wanted to take one more run. She put on her dark green jacket and zipped it, and put on her black beaver cap, which shone against her shining hair, and they went outside.

Katherine and her daughter took a run down the beginners' hill, and neither fell down. They caught the rope tow to the top, and Katherine stopped and scanned the chair lift as far up the mountain as she could follow it, and did not see John and Ella. She surmised they were out of her sight at the top of the mountain, and she wondered if the snowfall up there were heavier. Terry helped her search, and they watched everything they could see, the side runs and the main, central run, which was split halfway down by a long ellipse of birches. There were fewer skiers on the mountain now, and the light was imperfect.

They came gliding into view as if airborne, into the center run from an opening high up in the woods. They were skiing very close together in the gray light, and seemed at times to merge to a single figure; then they'd part, and merge, and float along so close they might have touched. They crossed, and tacked gently down, and crossed again and disappeared into the woods.

"Th-th-th-th-they—"

"Yes, babe, they'll be coming out right by the split," said Katherine, referring to the only place they could go now.

And three or four minutes later they reappeared, still proceeding at a glide, a float, till they parted and John seemed to shoot across the open belt and to cut back just as sharply. Then Ella crossed and recrossed while John hesitated, and they intersected in the center and came sinuating down together.

Everyone stripped off skis and boots, and Katherine and Terry, being renters, turned in their equipment. While they stood in line John bought a hot chocolate for Terry, and she looked up at him as she drank, dark devoted eyes absorbing him.

The atmosphere outside was frigid now, locked, and dark. There was a line of lights set at wide intervals along the path to the parking lot. Ashley started out carrying his skis and Ella's on his left shoulder,

and felt his right hand joined by Terry's. He saw her looking up at
him with such an expression of unconscious fealty that he lifted her
and perched her on his arm and made her jiggle as they went down
a flight of wooden stairs through a grove of pines.

Katherine and Ella were a few steps above him. Ella made a
comment in a soft voice and Katherine laughed, a long melodious
ribbon of laughter which sounded to Ashley almost supernatural, it
was so like their mother's. Halfway down the stairs he again heard
Katherine's laughter behind him, and when he reached his car and
opened the door, and the two women entered, he could see their
faces in the interior light, flushed and happy. Katherine glanced up
at him and took her daughter from his arms, calling her "Monkey"
and "Tulip" and "Slop Chops," wiping chocolate from her lips with
a handkerchief and saying, "OK, captain, home!"

On going to bed that night Katherine rearranged her daughter's
blankets and drew the satin edge up to the girl's chin, and looked
at her face. She saw the serene and simple beauty of the child. The
simplicity and vulnerability of the child entered her, and displaced
everything else; all that remained was the knowledge, like a piercing
desire, of how precious the child was.

As she tucked in the blankets her fingertips hit something hard
under the mattress, and she pulled out two books belonging to the
school library. They were large illustrated editions of *Bambi* and
Bambi's Children, and Katherine bent at her lamp and turned the
pages. Here were colored pictures of Bambi's mother licking the
newborn fawn, of the "old stag" in majesty on a cliff, of Bambi
fleeing the meadow where his mother lay shot, of courtship combat
among bucks, and love between Bambi and Faline. Katherine slid
the books back under the mattress.

"I have said nothing to her," Katherine wrote, "because what if she
thinks I'm part of the conspiracy? It must be obvious to her that *all
adults* shoot deer and cut them open, or congratulate those who do.
How believable would I be, then, if I claimed sympathy with the
animals? Particularly after retelling the story of 'my' deer. An adult
for a mother may be bad enough, but a hypocrite? So my mouth is
closed, and she may look at her Bambi books in secret for as long
as she likes."

Katherine wrote with too much tension, so that her hand tired quickly, and she would lay down her pen and sprawl in the chair like a teenage boy, staring at the fire or up at the stone chimney or into the darkness of the loft, where Terry, for a certainty, was not sleeping; or at the fifty or sixty books neatly stowed in this her solitude corner, where she read nearly every night the books she had wanted to read for two years—not only books about Greece but works of Tolstoy, Turgenev, Flaubert, Hemingway, Kazantzakis, O'Neill, and the Brontë sisters. Her heap of books on Vietnam and the war policy she kept in another place and read, like journalism, in the kitchen, over a meal, in the morning, in the bathroom, or wherever. It was all getting redundant, but she bought every new title printed on the subject and read the stuff till she was numb.

Her writing paper was tinted an orange so pale it was almost white. Over the top of each sheet there was a row of six small dark red owls and at the bottom right-hand corner a single wing of the same color. Across these sheets she wrote swiftly and rather large, stretching out long slanting lines of an unbridled script that was legible, at best, to herself and her husband.

She wrote in ink with a black pen that had belonged first to her father and then to her mother, and the ink glistened behind her pen point.

"I wrote Ella last week and my only offering was a pitiful commonplace—that marriage is complex. An honest woman would have said —well, I guess I couldn't really say my own brother is a son of a bitch. But *I wish he were not my brother*. And why burden her with my honesty? If it's impossible to wish you had other parents, as children often do, I suppose it's equally impossible to wish somebody were not your brother, or I suppose it's the same as wishing he'd never been born. And who am I to wish that? You're pushed right up against that dismal and tedious question: Am I so much better? What a maze! John is a shit!"

She sprawled again in her chair, smiling, and shook her right hand. When she sprawled like a teenage boy it was all the more obvious she was no such thing.

"I forgot to tell you John is 'suspicious' of Beethoven. Can Beethoven's reputation survive this? Actually I can't knock John, since I'm suspicious of Plato. Aristotle by contrast makes him seem like a snake-oil salesman—but we must have an ideal, we can't live without the ideal. Plato surely believed that. So why does he let Socrates get away with such shabby arguments? Another maze! I long, I long, I long for the straight line, and your magnificent body."

Her pen stopped. She put it down and bowed her head, rubbing her temples with a slow, bobbing motion, loosening with this massage several thick strands of her hair, which swung to her cheeks.

She wanted to speak no more of bodies, yet she knew the skin below her navel was smooth, smoother than silk, slick paper, or the shell of an egg, nearly as smooth as the lining of an egg. She went to the window, but she could see only her very dark and unfinished reflection. Opening the door, she stepped outside and stood on the porch listening and watching. The dog tried to follow, but Katherine kept her inside. The night was chill and dark; there was a steady wind, and half a moon. The thermometer by the window showed eight degrees above zero. Turning her back to the windows and the light and leaning with bare hands on the porch rail, Katherine looked down the hill, down the path through the birches toward the turnaround, where her newly acquired rust- and rattle-infested jeep station wagon was parked. The darkness and the cold formed an element in which she habitually immersed herself in the evening, because it refreshed her. She listened keenly, her body bent as she leaned over the rail, and in the dark her eyes dilated with the same earnestness of searching, a reaction almost of hope, as in Willoughby's woodshed the night she saw the deer. She made a cradle of her left arm and stacked it with the small logs of white birch, wild cherry, beech, ash, and elm that Willoughby and Richard had split, and reentered the house.

She fed and tended the fire (which markedly changed her eyes) and went up to check Terry.

She paused and asked the shadows, "Do you have to go to the bathroom?" and they said no; "Are you warm?" and they said yes. She bent down to kiss these loved shadows. Two thin, tense arms circled her neck and pulled her down, and she toppled forward. Her arms were pinned by her own weight, and the two hard little arms circling her neck tightened painfully.

"Terry, you're hurting me."

The child whispered in her ear: "Mommy, I'm afraid."

"Terry, you hurt my ear. Good grief, will you let me go? You shouldn't whisper so loudly right in someone's ear." Katherine extricated her arms, but she could have freed her head only by wrestling. "Terry," she repeated in a stifled voice, "will you please let go of my neck?"

"Mommy," said the girl, holding on more tightly, "if only I hadn't seen those stones."

They had been to an old cemetery, where Katherine had made a tracing of a willow and urn, and the child had asked for help in reading the stones; and in this as in any old cemetery there were dead children everywhere.

"Terry, you have to let me go. I know you're afraid, but you can't hold my neck all night long, and besides it is *hurting* my neck, dear, so please let me go."

"If I let go will you stay?"

"Terry, I am not going to make a bargain. You let go because I told you to let go. Now let go."

The girl did, saying again, "Mommy, I'm afraid," and not only her plainly petrified voice but the poverty of her vocabulary conveyed her fear.

Katherine believed the fears of childhood were not equaled in later life. To her it made no difference that the more you know the more reason you have to be afraid. She herself knew nothing so affecting as the girl's vision of early death, or the "string." She turned the light on and lay across Terry's bed on her side, smiling, and reached out and caressed the girl's face and hair. The black hair was so silken and neat and the eyes were so full and brilliant, the shoulders of the nightgown and the pillowcase so fresh, that the girl must have been lying paralyzed and staring all these hours.

"Have you been to sleep?"

"*I* don't know."

"Well, then, probably you have, if you don't know."

"Is Uncle John here?"

"No, dear. You know he's not. Babe, there are medicines now that doctors give to children who become sick, so children don't die. Those children would not have died if they were born when you were born. If a child today gets the spotted fever—do you remember the one who had spotted fever?"

"Yes."

"Today that child would not even get the fever. If she did get it, by some chance, she would be cured. She'd have to stay home from school for a few days, but she'd soon be well again."

"One boy drownded."

"That's true. There is no medicine—"

"A kid could drown today."

"Yes."

"That boy was kidnapped in Boston. Y-y-y-y-y-y-you said . . . I-I-
I don't know if they have kidnappers *here,* but if we go to Boston
again . . ."

"There are kidnappers, but very, very few. In the whole country
there might be two or three children kidnapped in a year."

"In New Hampshire?"

"No, no, the country." She attempted to explain herself, but she
had not yet found a way to explain what a state was.

"And," Katherine continued, "all the daddy longlegs are dead.
All the insects of last summer are dead, because they can't live in the
snow, but there is *one* daddy longlegs still left." She leaped up on
the bed, startling and delighting the child, and began dancing on the
heaving mattress, drawing screams from the girl as she jumped up
and parted her legs at the last moment, straddling rather than tram-
pling the girl's body. *"I* am the daddy longlegs. See my long black
legs. Hop! Hop! Leap!" Her legs were indeed long, and their length
was stressed by the black pants, in which there was much tailoring
skill and no surplus material. "I'm the good daddy longlegs and I
won't crawl up your walking stick, I won't, I won't," she said, and
bounced with redoubled vigor, heedless of the mess she was making
of the bed.

"But what about the *string?"* the girl screamed in self-mockery.
"Blaa, blaa, bloo—blaaaa!"

"Just look here, there isn't any string, you goof. Who said there
was a string?" and Katherine swept her hand over the sloping boards
of the roof.

"Blaaaaa—bloo, bloo!" cried Terry.

"Your tongue will *not* blow up like a balloon and choke you. You
will *not* lose your thumb. You *will* be able to hold on to your milk
glass. I do *not* have three legs, as you dreamed I did, and I have not
been turned into a light bulb. Something else that isn't true is just
this, Missy—I tell you there are no lobster monsters, and if people
show such things on television it's only for fun. And furthermore,
Missy, you will not smother under the hay bales, but look out! The
daddy longlegs is going to *hop* right on *top* of your tubby belly. Look
out, here I come!"

Terry shrieked, and Katherine leaped to the floor, ordering immediate, deep, and dreamless sleep. Amid the girl's protests and new cries of fear she straightened the bed, shut off the light, and went downstairs.

She got more logs and stood them in an arc on the far edge of the hearth, and the snow adhering to them formed pools on the bricks while she wrote her "confession" to Richard.

"Terry as usual was dragging a pillowcase full of bedding, and I was at the *very door* of the place—I had turned to push it open with my rear—when I saw that the news was on television. I did not wish to see the news. I stood there holding my basket. Terry said, 'Why don't we go in?' and I put my basket down and watched through the window. It was a peace march and a clergyman was exhorting the marchers. Terry said she was cold. I said I was cold too but I wanted to wait just a minute. I could have opened the door to let her in, while I stayed outside to watch the meaningless lipping of the clergyman, but I did not. And the reason is that I didn't care to hear *a single word or phrase.*

"I have read whole forests of articles and books on the war, as you know, but there seemed to be passion in that man, and I refused to change a dumb show into a passionate argument by opening the door. This was a stupid thing to do—a silly act of trivial cowardice. I drove 40 miles the next day to get the *New York Times* and read what he had said. And—I enclose the article for you, because you are strong."

She blew gently on these final words, folded the letter, and sealed it.

VII

Richard Vail, lying in a ditch and trying to keep his feet out of the water, cocked his pistol. He peered over the road edge and let fly an entire magazine at the house across the way. He inserted a new magazine, and again he stitched the house from one end to the other at knee level, raising puffs from its mud wall. He slumped back down and reloaded the magazines from a box.

As he loaded he listened, distinguishing two M-60 machine guns and several M-14 rifles, automatic and semiautomatic, an M-79 grenade launcher, and two LAW rockets; all this friendly and outgoing. The incoming was much diminished.

"God damn it, Sergeant Hackman," said Vail.

"Yes, sir?"

"I know what these sons of bitches are doing."

The sergeant, to whom this officer's conduct of their mutual affairs was acceptable and sometimes better than acceptable, turned and bellowed with incredible rage at the sons of bitches in the ditch.

"Jensen!" shouted Sergeant Hackman. "You fucking civilian, what the hell are you shooting at?"

Lance Corporal Jensen said he was trying to cut off a bunch of bananas hanging in a tree by the house.

"Mush Head! You fucking Mush Head! What the hell are you shooting at?"

Mush Head said he had just blown up a water bottle by the well.

"OK, Sergeant Hackman, OK," Vail said quietly, and the sergeant strained to hear him. "Every man, every man, had better walk away from here with a full marching allowance of ammunition, or I start playing squad leader and you'll be the water boy.''

Sergeant Hackman hounded the team, and at the same moment a chicken came around the house and into the courtyard with the strut of a petty magistrate, as if it intended to restore order. Vail had no sooner seen this stiff and stupid bird than he realized to his amazement that he was going to shoot it. The chicken advanced with authoritative little jerks into the courtyard, and Vail drew the slide on his pistol. The chicken pecked the earth with a movement no less mechanical than the snapping forward of the slide, and it soon formed a white feathery ball atop the front post of the pistol sight. Vail focused on the chicken and the sights blurred; he focused on the sights and the chicken blurred.

Vail tracked the bird and watched its senatorial gestures; then he hardened the sights and softened the bird, and squeezed, and the pistol bucked.

Sergeant Hackman was less surprised to see the bird jump than was Vail to see it on the ground in a little shower of feathers. Hackman commented, "Rank has its privileges, Lieutenant," and Vail looked at the glob of feathers and blood as if it astounded him. He turned to Sergeant Hackman with eyes bloodshot from want of sleep and face somewhat gaunt and much exposed to the weather, and broke into mirthful, cathartic laughter.

Vail and his team of twelve marines were in a column of six hundred ascending the An Lao Valley, a place of beauty and hitherto of peace. Only one man had been killed in the past four days. All were hungry. The next echelon kept sending ammunition instead of food, so these men who had already begun eating less were given extra ammunition to carry. Vail and every man in his team carried, besides twice the usual quantity of ammunition for his own weapon, a smoke grenade and an 81-mm mortar round. Some of the men were also decorated with long macho belts of machine-gun ammunition. Sergeant Hackman had taken two such belts on himself and looked like Pancho Villa. The whole team and indeed the column moved with the agility of the Tin Man. But this condition was vastly relieved in the ambush or harassment to which the column had just been subjected. After five minutes of "fire superiority" over a mostly unseen enemy, the column re-formed on the road, having driven off its enemy and lightened its load.

The column began moving.

A loudmouthed trooper issued a foul-mouthed challenge to "Nimbus," who controls the rain, to "break it out," and another verbally spat upon Nimbus and said he didn't "have the balls." This Nimbus was desecrated by a whole line of troopers who invited him to take all manner of obscene and painful action upon himself. Likewise they abused "God," who controls the sun, for refusing to break it out, since they had been rained on by Nimbus in the morning and were still wet because God hadn't let out the sun. Thus insulting Nimbus and God, the troops proceeded utterly without caution, carrying two wounded marines to a place where the road curved in the village. There was a soccer field here. They waited till helicopters should come and take away the wounded.

In approaching this place Vail had to pass a row of houses built close by the road and lying, due to the curve, between him and the soccer field. The walls of these homes were of mud and the roofs of rice straw, and they were simple and poor, having neither courtyards nor porches, but they were not squalid. The first shots of the ambush or whatever it was had scattered the people, and even now, as Vail's part of the column came near the center of the village, there was nobody to be seen anywhere. As he passed the houses he looked inside and saw no one. He saw only, between two of the houses, a tricolored rooster, and he smelled the familiar odor compounded of excrement, both animal and human, urine, charcoal, and cooking. He heard a baby crying. The troopers were quieter at the center of the vill. The baby's was the only voice. The road had a greasy, muddy surface.

Passing the last two houses, he looked between them and saw the battalion surgeon, a naval officer like himself but, also like himself, outwardly indistinguishable from the marines. The doctor was in fact quite distinct on account of his voice and his pediatrician hands.

The doctor and a medical corpsman were lifting a bare-breasted woman onto a mat. Vail saw blood. Her head was toward him, her feet away; he saw the Oriental sheen of her black hair, her nose, breasts, and her slack feet. Her tight-bodiced black shirt was open and drawn partway down her arms, leaving her shoulders bare. Vail had a glimpse only. It wasn't the woman, however, that stunned him, but the baby. The baby was sitting on a flat stone in a tiny brown shirt and no pants, and crying in short enraged shrieks. There seemed to be no end to his shrieks. His face was contorted and

tear-streaked, but what Vail saw or imagined he saw were flecks of
bluish-white milk around the child's mouth and on his chin, and a
streak of the same bluish white on his cheek and neck. The streak
was partially washed away by tears. Vail had no sooner seen this than
he was past the house and could see no more.

As the column penetrated higher into the valley it came to a
tributary stream which had to be crossed the hard way, the bridge
having been dropped into the ravine by the VC. In most cases
enough remained or was restored to a blown bridge to accommodate
pedestrian and bicycle traffic, since the bridges were used in this way
by those who blew them up, but in this case the central span was
gone. The troopers descended the side of the ravine on a slant. The
stream was deep and full of force. Its color was green even so soon
as this after a rain, when it might have been brown. That a stream
of this color and depth should be found at the bottom of so precipi-
tous a gorge seemed unreal. As he unlooped his suspenders and
removed his utility belt with its weapon, magazines, compass, canteens, knife, and first-aid kit, and carried this mess together with his
pack over his head, Vail looked to his right, upstream, for rapids. He
could see only a short distance in the bent trees and saw no rapids
nor heard any. It was the same on the left: the felled span with its
incongruous guardrails, and the green stream soon disappearing in
the trees. He stepped slowly into the water, following as closely as
he could the route of the man ahead.

The water was tepid and the bottom uncertain, and the force
increased as the water rose on his body. He was in to his chest. He
watched the man ahead, who was in to his armpits. He thought:
"This is the end of my cigarettes." At the same moment he lurched
and raised a splash, some drops flying against his face, and these
tepid drops recalled to him with a cruel vividness the baby. Another
yard or two, after sinking deeper, and he began to emerge. Now he
was climbing. But when he had come out to knee depth he again
lurched on the rocks that he couldn't see, with the baby still shriek-
ing in his mind, and twisted his right ankle. This accident was going
to plague him, he knew it. He was surprised it hurt so—it opened
passages in his head. He limped out of the stream with pant legs
bulging with water, sloshing, lurching, and cursing.

The pace of the column was desultory but to Vail it seemed
relentless. The sun shone for a time. The An Lao glittered in her

wide bed, and the column throbbed at her side like an idea in the dim brain of a general.

A general came out of the sky in the late afternoon, as generals are wont to do, and talked persuasively for ten minutes with Lieutenant Colonel Clinton, the commander of the column. From a distance Vail could see the red-faced redheaded general gesticulating, rolling and unrolling his map, and finally laughing, looking brightly around with his infectiously cheerful red countenance. He was among the liveliest of men when speaking, but when he listened it was with a silent completeness that his subordinates often took for contempt. Vail liked him. Unfortunately, he was not the boss of all that was happening at that moment in Quang Ngai and Binh Dinh. Smiling, waving, invigorated no doubt by visions of whiskey and fresh meat, he went back to where he had come from. On the tail of his departing helicopter was stenciled: GIVE A SHIT. Vail thought: "Give us food."

When they halted in the evening he was assigned a cemetery; and although the arc of perimeter running through it was much too long to be defended by twelve men, still Vail and Sergeant Hackman were happy. With luck they wouldn't have to defend the damned thing anyway. The place was convenient and somehow hospitable, free of mud and brush, with the soil sandy and diggable. The graveyard was on flat ground and there was neither marker nor monument in its whole expanse, but only the mounds of the humble. Each grave had a low, circular earthen wall about a foot high. Inside the circle was a body-size mound. The walls could be for utility or beauty.

To imagine the mound without the circling wall was depressing; but when the mound was encircled by this simple low ring of earth the whole found serenity and a sense of completion. In some of the graves a small breach was left in the wall, perhaps so it couldn't fill with rainwater, and indeed the entire purpose of the walls might have been to keep away the water during heavy rains. Even if this were so the walls had grace and seemed to bestow a philosophy on the dead.

Vail couldn't get the boot off his twisted foot.

He lay down inside a grave ring to sleep, his body stretched out beside the mound and wrapped in a poncho and his mind entertained not with speculations on who lay nearby but with the problem of keeping warm. It was the same problem here as on the South

Polar Plateau except that in the latter place one must lie still in the sleeping bag until the body can heat the air surrounding it, while here the body must heat the water it lies in, which is not so easily done. The rain had been incessant since about seven P.M., and while Vail had chosen his grave carefully, there was no such thing as a dry place, so his poncho filled slowly from both beneath and above. He lay patiently and gave his dumb body the work of warming the water. It did its work slowly. The prospect was that soon after he was warm and asleep he would be wakened by Sergeant Hackman or Private First Class Richie Rood for his turn at watch; but this prospect was welcome. He felt no need of sleep, only of rest, warmth, and food. Knowing warmth to be impossible on insufficient food, and truly refreshing rest impossible in insufficient warmth, he lay in his poncho and puddle shivering but not miserable, listening to the rain on the poncho. Everything else had stopped. He was on his side, facing his host, with his eyes open. The mound was covered with leaves, which glowed dimly in the dark like radium. When Katherine lay this way, on her side in bed reading a book propped between herself and him, he could look over the book and see her face, her busily shifting eyes, which might or might not acknowledge him, and her pulse striking visibly on the right side of her throat. He had counted her pulse more than once when she refused to quit reading and turn out the light. He could have taken his own pulse now, if he chose, by the throbs in his ankle.

He thought it amusing how much importance was assumed in human affairs by mere feet. The suffering occasioned by frozen feet, trench foot, immersion foot, and similar ailments he found more unaccountable, or at least harder to rationalize, than other forms of suffering, because a phrase like "shot in the foot" had such an unserious sound. Yet he knew an Army lieutenant who was shot in the foot, and the number of small complicated bones and joints destroyed was, as it proved, too much, so the foot was amputated. Captain Lawrence Oates of Scott's second Antarctic expedition was surely one of the noblest heroes of the English race, the shadow of whose suffering was known through Captain Scott's diary, yet when Scott said of him that he tended to cold feet it sounded like ridicule. Once in Turkey an old man approached Vail barefoot over a beach carpeted with jagged stones, much to his admiration, and sold him a bottle of wine. Then the old man asked outright for his boots. Vail thought: "I must really look like a soft touch if he just up and asks for my boots." He didn't compare himself to Captain Oates or the hard old Turk. He reflected rather on how petty his pain was; likewise his hunger. He reflected next on how petty he was even to be aware of these. "This isn't so bad," he thought.

The steadiness of the rain, the way the rain applied all its force straight down, and the everlasting radium glow of the leaves displaced all anxiety. Had he lain at the edge of hell on such glowing leaves, in such a rain, he would have felt the same as he felt now.

Katherine nursed her baby in this posture, lying full length on her side, for two days while she was weak. He brought her the baby and she drew it to herself, presenting the breast, and when it was taken closing her eyes.

He slept for a time and awoke shivering. A man was cursing somewhere in the cemetery. He slept again, and was awakened by two words which he heard as plainly as if he'd been listening. The words were "Who's there?" and the voice was Sergeant Hackman's.

Hackman repeated his question in a voice so calm as to imply indifference, as if he didn't care whether he received a civilized answer or fired a burst from his weapon.

Then came the highly communicative sound of the bolt sliding on Hackman's rifle, and Vail thought: "Oh damnation."

A young voice suddenly said, "Jesus, Sergeant Hackman, it's me."

Vail fell asleep and was awakened by PFC Richie Rood, who spoke his name in a low tone like a great bell softly struck. Richie Rood, who had been admonished by NCOs never to touch those he was awakening in case they should slug or shoot him, never did touch them. Ever since the death of Griffin Richie Rood had been Vail's FM radio operator. During Regimental and larger operations when they were in a command post in a tent with ten or twenty radios of artillery, air, and naval gunfire, and the "radio war" was going on, Rood was reduced by sheer nervous conscientiousness to an incompetent. But alone like this with a single battalion in the boonies he was calm, effective.

Richie Rood was gentle. He shared his candy with Vietnamese children and was learning the Vietnamese language. He had a sensitive, unexpressive intelligence, and though he wasn't meek he was small and meek-looking, and was often joked about, especially by persons who hadn't seen him under fire. He had felt too much ridicule and was in danger of surrendering to an attitude of hostility to his fellow marines.

"Thank you, Rood," said Vail as he gave his pistol and took the man's rifle.

Rood replied in his peculiar, gentle way, "Oh, that's OK, Lieutenant," and said, "Well, good night, Lieutenant," when he lay down on the other side of the grave, speaking as he must have spoken for most of his life to his brothers and sisters.

Vail said, "Good night, Rood."

He stretched, tried his ankle, and went off to check posts.

The team had dug four positions, and if all was well one man would be on watch at each, the colonel having declared a one-third alert. Vail saw that it was so, exchanged a few words with the waking men, and went back to his mound, where he sat with one leg protruding from under the poncho, with his arms and rifle inside the poncho and the hood thrown back. The rain was merciful; still, he could hearing nothing but rain with the hood forward. So soft was the rain that he couldn't feel it on his hair, but if he turned up his face he found it.

Solitude was rare. It was rare that everything should stop this way. But his tranquility and images of Katherine were scattered by other images. Rather than Katherine giving suck he saw the woman being lifted by the doctor and corpsman. Rather than the baby he carried to Katherine's bed he saw the other baby.

The colonel summoned a meeting of his company commanders and staff.

Vail got up stiffly from his mound, went to Sergeant Hackman's place and awakened him, then went limping off through the cemetery. The graves seemed to rise out of the earth as the darkness faded into light.

He came to a small group of men standing around the colonel at the edge of a cultivated field.

This group included the officers who controlled artillery and air support, the doctor, the commanders of the three rifle companies present, and the colonel's battalion staff of One, Two, Three, and Four. Marine officers are so interchangeable they can be called by numbers, and if questioned or required to act each will answer and function according to his number. They are nevertheless so different from one another that their interchangeability is much less striking than their distinctness. Each is himself, and sometimes the self is developed to an extreme. Few are ciphers. Any group of them exhibits great riches of personality, which is startling chiefly because of the false impression given by their uniformity of dress, their mechanical reaction to certain recurring stimuli, and the fact that their jobs are called by numbers.

Lieutenant Colonel Clinton, the commanding officer and thus the Six, was a man of such mildness and charity that he was inefficient. This so excited his subordinates on his behalf that they scrambled to save him and his career from himself, with the result that his battalion wasn't half bad. His basic approach was his unconscious assumption that men were excellent. He already thought Richard Vail was excellent before there was any work for Vail to do. The column had up to now been outside the range of naval guns, but it would now move toward the sea.

The colonel said the general was pleased but he didn't say why. He said the march to the sea would take about three days, and he said: "I don't want any marines killed." He instructed his company commanders and then asked Vail if he could provide a naval gunfire spotting team with each company, and Vail said he could.

Vail broke his team into four parts, sending a spot team capable of calling for and adjusting fire to each of the three rifle companies and keeping four men with himself in the command group. He had, besides Rood, who carried the FM radio, Mush Head carrying the transmitter-receiver unit of the long-range radio, which alone weighed forty-seven pounds, and two other men carrying the spare batteries and the radio accessory pack.

Mush Head opened the straps of his packboard and swung it heavily up to his back, shouting "Holy—*by* the Jeez!"

In Sergeant Hackman's absence Mush Head was the senior man, and Vail approached him—limping, smiling, with his pack on one shoulder and helmet tilted, but appearing clean. Mush Head had always been impressed by Vail's cleanness when others looked like hogs kept in a corner.

The rain and the march continued. The troops said of Nimbus that he was unworthy to chew on a certain obscure anatomical attribute of Mush Head's grandmother. When the raid stopped and the sun appeared they thanked God and called him "decent," but as the sun heated up their gratitude cooled. The trail showed signs of turning dusty.

At noon Vail was sitting on his helmet eating his last ration with mixed appetite and nausea. There were troopers to his right and left along a bank, and now a lone corporal whom he didn't know knelt on the clay just in front and a little to his right and began preparing a meal. The corporal bent his brow nearly to the ground and lighted a heat tablet, which burned with invisible flame and sent its fumes toward Vail, burning his nostrils and eyes, so that he thought about moving. He didn't move because his ankle hurt.

In the soggy little cardboard box at Vail's feet the heavy was a can of ham and lima beans, the most odious of the government's concoctions, which he soon finished. He turned to the contribution of the American Bread Company of Nashville, Tennessee, then to the box's other delights, till only the cigarettes remained. These were damp but combustible. The food was rich and usually caused heartburn.

Points of pain—sharp burning points—like spattered bacon grease —covered his right forearm, and there was a rending noise in his right ear. He didn't want it to happen. But he was rising, picking up pack and helmet, unconscious of his ankle for the first time since morning. He saw the corporal, who had stood up, spiraling slowly down, looking worried, with one arm held out—shattered bone, blood, and sinew, bleeding. The man sat down with his arm out and looked at it.

Vail dropped his gear and grabbed the man under the arms and hauled him (as he had once been hauled). The man cried, "Ah!" and looked around at Vail with great eyes. There came another rending crack, and Vail pushed the corporal toward the dirt bank, where he fell, forcing Vail to lift him again and propel him up the bank with a knee in the rear. The man crawled and Vail pushed him by the rear as more of the shocking sounds pierced his ears and other invisible debris splattered his arms and face. He was half aware. He noticed the lethargy of his movements, rather the lethargy of his progress. Would the corporal ever reach the top? The corporal crawled like a hurt dog, and Vail pushed and kept saying unkindly, "Move! Move!" and at the top he pushed him face first through the thick bushes. At the same moment a storm of marine counterfire erupted with such thrilling effect that Vail went headlong through the bushes, which at any other time would have been impenetrable. Once in the brush, he forgot the corporal. He wormed around, fully realizing that his place was one of concealment but not cover, and saw his pack and helmet where he'd dropped them. A marine—Vail hoped it was not one of his naval gunfire team—cried in distress. Someone shouted exasperatedly, "For Christ's sake!" and at length an officer howled, "Cease fire—cease fire!" The firing stopped almost at once. Nevertheless, an 81 chuffed three times like a coughing pig and its dinky rounds exploded impotently in the jungle of a hillside four hundred yards away, doubtless giving the snipers a good laugh. After these reports all was silence for a time until a voice called for a medical corpsman. This brought Vail to his feet, and he shouted likewise, "Corpsman!" and turned and made his way with great difficulty through the brush to the place where the corporal had crawled.

He passed his hand under the injured arm just below the armpit and dug his fingers deep into the flesh, finding a grip which retarded the bleeding; then without releasing his hold he went awkwardly from a squatting to a kneeling posture, because his ankle couldn't stand the continued squatting. His old leg wound hurt, too. Turning his head, he shouted again for a corpsman, and would have lost his temper except there was no object for his anger.

The inside of the corporal's arm was smooth and even tender. The man himself was gross. However gross, however tough he was, this injury which was indeed terrible seemed to afflict his whole body. His mouth trembled, and Vail realized he was passing through a dark night. The flow of blood increased. Vail found a new, surer grip on the limp arm, and the flow subsided, revealing somewhat more of the wound in its depth and detail.

In another moment a corpsman and a squad leader had come, and Vail was striding in long slides down the dirt bank, his pants and his hands slick with blood, and though the corporal was truly in his soul, and bid fair to stay forever, Vail also wondered if his blood would draw flies.

He called out: "Corporal Knowlton!"

In response to this familiar summons Mush Head, with shaving cream clinging to his face, came sliding down the bank and on reaching level ground cradled his rifle and approached with a slow shuffling gait and a smile.

"They're all OK, Lieutenant."

"You too?"

"Yes, sir. What's all the blood?"

"It's not my blood," said Vail.

Mush Head, the only man in the team taller than Vail, stepped close—his customary odor smothered by menthol. He examined the motionless Vail and then raised his hand, and with painstaking slowness he pulled from the officer's face a stick of thorns about two inches long.

The column was pausing for resupply by helicopter, and it was for that reason alone that Vail had decided to eat his last ration. But when the helicopters arrived they brought ammunition, not food, except for three cases of oranges. When Vail received his orange it was still cold. Though he might have saved it for the hunger ahead, its coldness was so rare that he did not, for to save the orange was to waste the cold.

His fingers, still caked with the blood of the corporal, broke open the fruit. He crushed a section of the orange in his mouth as he watched the wounded corporal, supported by two corpsmen, being led with a paper tag fluttering from his shirt toward the waiting helicopter. As he made his slow way toward a different world the man looked around, looked over his shoulder, as if saying farewell or searching for someone, and Vail watched with intense interest as he was assisted, after pausing faintly, to the door of the helicopter. He was made to turn around and sit on the deck in the open doorway and then dragged inside by the gunner. Vail lifted a hand, but unseen.

The helicopters rose on their own dust. Then long cries were raised along the column: "Saddle up! Saddle up!" as if scores of men had reached a decision all at once; and laden with too much ammunition and too little food, the men struggled with their various straps, belts, and burdens and the column moved, and the trail smelled of oranges.

In the evening the column came under the guns of the Navy for the first time—a fact you could hardly grasp without unfolding a map, for the place seemed like the center of Africa. It was a high and extensive hillside affording a position for the whole battalion, and it was waist deep over its entirety in Johnson grass. A man had the feeling not of walking but of wading, and the way the grass swished, parted, reclosed, and bent in the breeze gave a sense of flux. The sun was setting in a yellow display, and the field was tilted toward the sunset.

Vail had had difficulty keeping the pace, and in keeping it had so favored his right ankle that the muscles in his left hip were now sore. He knelt, bent his E-tool at a right angle, and made a sort of hole, but it was not a proper hole, and he was aware that for two consecutive nights he had not dug in properly. The colonel wanted harassing fires all around the position that night, and Vail stayed up until two in the morning, first making up the plan for harassing and interdiction fires, then the night defensive fire plan, and then firing in the closer H&Is, many of which he had to adjust by sound. When he finally could get away from the radio and lie down beside his hole, deep in the grass, staring at the stars, he found that his appetite was gone and his hunger was manifest only in lassitude. He found too that he was indifferent about sleep. Doubtless he was starting to live on his reserves. He saw a satellite crossing the sky. There was a brief outbreak of firing on the other side of the position. The satellite pursued its path. Vail lay still, touching his pistol.

Sergeant Hackman had "liquid" brown eyes. Women fell for him like tenpins. That at least was his testimony on the subject, and it was plausible testimony. He was probably about twenty-four, and looked like an athlete a little past his prime, but when he took off his shirt to dig in for the night he revealed a strong, economical torso, shoulders, and arms. He smiled easily with a smile expressing an adulterated scorn. What the scorn was adulterated with was anybody's guess, but it wasn't pure and it didn't burn. Sergeant Hackman thought just about everything was shit. If he yelled at the troops everybody knew he was putting it on. In this life without women he lived to kill. The chance didn't come along every day, but Hackman had been raised poor and he knew how to be patient.

He said to Vail: "Did you see the infiltrator?"

"No. What infiltrator?"

"We had one in the lines last night. Didn't you hear that guy yell, 'I got a gook in my hole'?"

"I heard shooting over in this direction, is all."

"He's over here," said Hackman with his adulterated smile. "He's got no pants on. He's got a leaf."

Lieutenant Vail and Sergeant Hackman walked through the waist-high Johnson grass along a row of Alfa Company's fighting holes. A field of fire had been cleared in front of the line. A heap of earth flattened the grass by each hole. The infiltrator lay on one of these heaps.

He wore a black shirt and was barefoot and there was no leaf. His limbs described the letter X except that one leg was turned upward from a blackened knee. His genitals were relaxed, large, and darker than his body. There were drops of blood on his shirt. It was impossible to see any character in his face because of the bugs, but Vail could deduce that there was an opening in his forehead, also because of the bugs.

His hands were quiet and looked alive. He had been a laborer, fisherman, or farmer, probably a farmer. Therefore a farmer's son. The hands were mundane, a paradigm of daily labor, while the face was something out of science fiction.

"Somebody took the leaf," said Hackman.

"Why doesn't he have any pants?"

"I don't know, Lieutenant. There they are."

Vail hadn't noticed the shorts, sandals, and canteen in the hole, among the C-ration trash.

"Maybe they came off when they pulled him out of the hole—I don't know," Hackman repeated. "He's pretty well hung, would you say?"

"I would," agreed Vail.

Vail and Hackman were not conscious of how long they stood there staring, nor was either ashamed before the other on account of it. The body had no fat whatever, and though very small it was muscular. Vail observed the flat thick soles, the developed calves with their sharp ridges, the stretch of the shirt over the shoulders where the arms were thrown up. He didn't pause on the face. He looked again at the soles, and would have squatted for a closer look except that his ankle hurt so badly.

"Do you know what I'm thinking, Sergeant Hackman?"

"Maybe I do, Lieutenant."

"I'm thinking you and I have got a cruiser out there with six eight-inch 55s, and six hundred marines, and a battery of artillery somewhere, and this guy had what? A rifle? A carbine?"

"No, sir, just a pistol."

"Jesus Christ."

"That's true, Lieutenant, but a guy like this, you kill him first and respect him later."

For the rest of the day Vail turned that over in his mind.

The column approached a defile and the Six called a halt. Alfa Company was in the lead (Sergeant Hackman was with Alfa Company as its naval gunfire spotter), and the Six did not want this or any other company entering the defile naked. He hesitated for several minutes, standing with his command group on a col overlooking the defile, with Alfa Company spread out in front of him, ready to form a line if need be. The high ridges on either side of the trail ahead were covered with jungle. It was a question of what to do about these ridges, whether to send troops up or shell them or leave them alone. Vail and the artillery officer had already decided the artillery would take the left and the Navy the right. Both men had already sent preliminary messages to the firing units. Sergeant Hackman was ready to conduct the Navy's fire. Mush Head was setting up the long-range radio on the col in case Hackman's communication with the ship fell apart and he needed a relay. Neither Vail nor the artillery officer had any doubt what the Six would decide. He would want screening fires on the ridges while the lead company transited the defile.

"Say, Dick, can you hit that?" asked the Six.

"Yes, sir. It'd be easier if I could divide it up with the artillery."

"All right, OK, fine. Why don't you two gents take it?"

The explosions at first made no sound. They leaped with odd violence along the ridges, each starting in a vicious jerk and mellowing in a slow throwing of earth and brushy debris, making a pall of smoke and dust hanging by the hillsides. There seemed to be no relation between these jerking, fitful bursts of earth and the far-off sound of the guns—the yapping of the ship's guns from another world and the popping of the howitzers from another valley. It was even difficult to identify the brown bursts on the ridges with the much louder, three-dimensional sounds of the projectiles exploding. These sounds filled the defile and hove back and forth from ridge to ridge. It was this disconnection of the burst and the sound that made it seem as if the barrage were being fired straight up out of the center of the earth. There was a spasmodic and sudden quality to the parade of the bursts as Hackman and the artillery observer moved them down the ridges.

Alfa Company formed up and moved out, descending into the defile like a snake feeding itself to an alligator, and the conduct of the fire passed upward to Vail and the artillery officer.

That night as they worked on the plan of harassing and interdiction fires Vail looked up and said: "Have you noticed, Hackman? They send men and we send steel."

The infiltrator was still in his mind the next morning when helicopters resupplied the battalion with food. Vail's hunger was long past, and he ate simply because he knew he should. But he liked the way his belly felt after he ate. He threw his trash into a bonfire and tried to find the yellow in the flames, but the sun consumed it and left only the orange. Vail's ankle felt better. He decided to invest a cup of his precious water in a clean set of teeth. The water he used was half of what he had, but the course lay downhill, so he didn't worry about it.

They were in another belt of opulent grass, on a high massif. The sun shone on each blade, on each wave, as they walked a contour line around the massif. Now a pass lay below. They began descending through a vast field where water buffalo grazed in herds of ten and fifteen. The animals increased their distance as the battalion came down toward the pass. Green, irregular, windy, and low, the pass afforded easy access from the mountainous interior to the valleys giving on the coastal plain. For this reason it was the site of a relic of an ancient civilization.

Straight across its heaving fields, running in a true course regardless of the undulations of the earth, lay a fortification wall. It was disintegrating and splitting with trees and vines, but it was monstrous. Over the next hour, as he drew closer and then walked beside it, Vail imagined where these colossal stones had come from, by what means they had been brought here and lifted or ramped into their present configuration; by what gangs, by what hordes of human beings and water buffaloes this had been done. To imagine this was to feel the menace and regimentation of the society that built the wall.

"My god, Dick, do you think I'm mad? Do you think I defend this? I know exactly how long I'd last in such a society. I know what would happen to you. I know what would happen to Terry—to her spirit, to her intellect, to her chance to create herself."

Vail walked along in the shadow of the wall, not really wanting to argue. But there was one point he had to make before Katherine did.

"That infiltrator . . ." thought Vail.

"Yes, his face! Why did you show me?"

"He proves something we both have to recognize," Vail went on.

"That such societies don't crush mankind absolutely," Katherine supplied.

"I was going to say—"

"Something more limited, no doubt."

"I was going to say only this," Vail persisted. "That he proves men do not live by freedom alone."

When they rounded the flank of Mount Lo and came out on the coastal plain there was a stiff breeze blowing and threatening rain. They crossed the stretch of rice paddies between the hills and the railroad, and crossed the track by an overthrown locomotive. It lay on its side, impotent, with its ganglia exposed.

A convoy awaited them on the highway, and Vail observed its organization. There was an Ontos first—a steel bulbous bug with six rocket tubes. Then four trucks, then a machine-gun truck, then four trucks and another Ontos, and so on.

The marine walking in front of Vail had a narrow, rounded, and ugly back. His pack was also small, as if he had thrown away rather than carry his extra rations. His feet made sucking sounds in the mud, and Vail wished he weren't following him. "I wish he were not my brother!"

Vail climbed up a rear wheel and into a truck bed. It was littered with cargo and junk in complete disorder—ration cases, ammo, barbed-wire coils, and shovels. Vail walked over this treacherous junk to a place near the front, turned a ration case on end and sat on it, and beckoned to Richie Rood, who came and cleared a space and sat cross-legged, droning into his radio. The truck engines cannonaded and howled. From the rear of the line, coming on at treetop level, the scout bird came along with wonderful ease and precision, as if on a wire, flying the line. It passed in front of Vail a little above him, the pilot waving to the groundlings with the back of his hand, like Prince Philip.

The junk lurched, almost tipping Vail's seat over, and the convoy moved. The breeze doubled and trebled. The sky was not clear.

They were going south, with the railroad some two hundred yards to the right, and Vail could see the overturned locomotive. Also on the right and passing one by one was a row of utility poles of cast concrete, with dangling wires, and on the left rice paddies that seemed odd because they had no craters.

The road was cut in a hundred places but had been repaired and would remain open for as long as daylight lasted and not much longer.

Vail heard, over the engine noise and the noise of shifting cargo as the trucks crashed across the overfilled slits in the road, a sound. It was such a sound as a man hears and is certain he couldn't have heard but begins to act on anyway, as if he had heard it. Exactly as in the ambush.

Vail started to rise, and there was an outbreak, a quick series of other such sounds, and then the truck abruptly stopped, pitching him forward and landing him painfully on his shoulder. In front of his face was a cardboard box, and he read the printed legend: MEAL, COMBAT, INDIVIDUAL, as the shooting started and Mush Head gave a whoop of joy.

Vail discovered that his right hand was in barbed wire, extricated it quickly but carefully, and then as he began collecting his limbs from the mess he was in he saw the troopers, his own four and the fifteen or so others riding his vehicle, scrambling off the truck like turtles. The noise was awful and all but paralyzed his thoughts. There was a fucking machine gun.

He suddenly noticed he was alone on the truck and standing erect, and that certain invisible "events" were happening. He felt these concussions on his left, on his right, and directly in his face, and he heard slugs striking the next truck in line. His exhilaration was raised higher by another shrill and utterly joyful shout from Mush Head, under the truck.

Mush Head was one of those who are sure they can't be hit. Vail was one of those who are sure they can't be hit again.

He searched the paddies and found what had to be a machine gun, but too close for attack by naval gunfire. He was amazed how much he could see merely by standing up and looking. The invisible procession, the "events," the splitting of the air continued all around and above him. Even so, he heard from a different dimension his own voice calling out to the marine gunner on the road between trucks and giving the location of the enemy. But Vail knew he did this only to justify his standing up.

There was a sudden terrific increase in the concussions, a splitting from behind. This was the first thing that worried Vail. His soul taking the impress of the savage mechanical weapon behind him, he turned to see it. He couldn't immediately locate it. It kept on splitting. He thought perhaps it was behind the railway embankment, but he saw to his intense delight that it was the scout bird racing in, a deadly and undeflectable goiter and a tiny point of fire. The fire-string passed over him, and in another few seconds the helicopter itself did, and when it was gone the machine guns in the paddies threw it all at the convoy, and Vail still stood.

Vail looked down and saw Richie Rood crouching by a rear wheel, looking up at him with an expression of horror. Not fear. Rood was looking at Vail as he might have looked at a man falling from a tall building.

Vail dived and felt the water rush over him like a sliding sheath in a single cleansing motion. As he slanted down and swam along the bottom he felt a chill at his back. Like a frog—stroke and glide—he toured the bottom in that state of mental suspension peculiar to swimming. But it was cold down here, and he was so vulnerable that he was soon reliving last night, that part of the night when they were still riding in the trucks and it was dark and raining. Mush Head had unfolded a tarpaulin and several men got under it, including Vail, and this helped a little, but still the warmth communicated to him from Richie Rood on one side and Mush Head on the other was not enough. He was shaking, and he realized that the men on his sides were shaking also, not in waves but constantly, which seems to be the tropical style. He wasn't equal to it. The cold was like a fever, and somehow it isolated him even though his entire left side could sense the contiguity of Mush Head and his right the insubstantial, trembling Rood. He wished they could walk instead of riding. Walking in the rain was never this bad no matter how tired they might be. He would rather walk all night than sit and tremble.

He backed water, swung his feet forward, and launched himself off the sand into the sunlight. He saw fishing boats out at sea. He sank again, and once again with a dolphin's lack of purpose he fired himself off the bottom, glimpsed the fishing fleet, sank, and began a steady crawl to seaward, propelled at the rear by a geyser of foam and pulled by his long lazy strokes. This was the finest swim of his life. He was a strong swimmer. He admired his crawl but admitted it was tiring, and rolled over into a back crawl so powerful that his shoulders lifted and he could watch the beach, and he imagined he could see it receding. His team had been reunited last night and the whole bunch was now building a pyramid in the surf, with Richie Rood no doubt to be the apex.

All were stark naked, and even from this distance Vail could see their shining white asses. While he was backstroking he saw the pyramid go up and topple. He went through all his strokes, floated for a while with the sun in his face, closed his eyes, sank, hung in the water relaxed for as long as he could, and noticed for the first time since leaving garrison how full he was of semen. He swam farther seaward and watched the lateen-rigged fishing boats luffing, running free, tacking, seeming never to interfere with each other, though all were working the same area. He sniffed for the charcoal of their cook fires but he couldn't detect it, only ocean and perhaps fish. He tasted brine. He began swimming toward the beach, diving repeatedly in hopes of finding something unusual on the bottom, but it was all sand. The gradient was gentle, and he began walking while still a considerable distance out.

He was urged along by a big wave. The same wave, running ahead and gaining force, made the pyramid of naked men shake like jelly in slow motion, and a man at the top dropped like a slate. A foot slipped on a shoulder and another man disappeared down the center, followed by half the remaining structure, and in another moment nothing survived but the protesting, accusing, shouting men swimming and splashing around the four musclemen of the bottom tier. The thing was rebuilt as Vail advanced, with Richie Rood, who had a surprisingly hairy chest, standing with arms lifted above the waves while Sergeant Hackman and Mush Head faced each other in the bottom tier, absorbing jolts, the body of Hackman perfected through an iron plan and weight-lifting, and Mush Head's through involuntary servitude to father and farm. When three tiers were assembled Richie Rood began picking his path upward like a spider monkey. And so emboldened was he by the idea of being the apex that he kept shouting, "Hold still, damn you, Hyde—hold still— damn it—you're greasy—"

In the afternoon a dense, vertical rain was falling.

The troops had built a hooch by snapping together four ponchos and guying them with communications wire and sticks. Outside they had hung a piece of cardboard, soggy now and barely holding together, on which Vail thought he could identify the poetic wit of Corporal Michaelson: COMPARING ANY OTHER HOUSE TO THIS HOUSE IS LIKE COMPARING THE PUNY PENIS OF A FRENCH PRINCE TO THE RUSTY ROT OF A ROMAN GLADIATOR.

Vail, who had been making an inquiry at the Three's hole, arrived running in the hard rain, bent low, and crawled under the roof of this "house," to which he had contributed his poncho. The troops were used to his coming and going, and they made room for him without formalities, except that in the reshuffling one man was left no choice but to put his feet in a puddle. He declared that he felt the same whether his feet were in or out of it.

A man was filling canteens at a hole in the roof. So heavy was the rain that he could fill a canteen in five minutes; then another would be passed to him and he would accept it without complaint and hold it under the stream of water, apparently preferring this work to none. Vail, looking around, finding rest for his inconveniently long legs and feet, saw quite a difference between these cramped, soaked, and in some cases ragged men and those he'd seen that same morning swimming in the ocean and building a pyramid, with the sunlight casting silver planes and bright beads on their bodies.

"All right," said Sergeant Hackman quietly, in a voice that was not the voice of an angel, "Mr. Vail's here, and now we're going to have a fire."

"Hell, don't make a fire on my account."

"Yes, sir, we're going to have a fire and toast marshmallows."

There were no marshmallows, but apparently there was going to be a fire.

"All right," Sergeant Hackman asked, "who's got the dry paper?"

There was unanimous agreement, except from Corporal Michaelson, that today was Corporal Michaelson's day to produce the dry paper.

"I don't have any fucking dry paper," said Michaelson poetically.

Mush Head, who had recently been elevated to corporal himself, advised Michaelson to pull it out of his ear. The adamancy of Mush Head and Sergeant Hackman and the neutral attitude of the lieutenant brought the troops together against him. He brought out his toilet paper and showed how soggy and useless it was, but this only elicited from Hackman a soft-voiced suggestion that he bring out his skin book. This book, Michaelson's only source of beauty, in which he plunged himself during all free intervals ranging down to two minutes, recounted about three hundred repetitions of an act Michaelson had not performed for many months. Michaelson now told Sergeant Hackman that a fire would make everybody cough and nobody warm.

Vail was curious to see how Sergeant Hackman would get the book. He got it by the simplest of means. He was the sort of man a subordinate obeys and a superior respects—and this quality of his, whatever it might be, seemed to bear only the remotest relation and possibly no relation at all to his undemonstrative, perhaps unconscious courage during contact. He was the sort of man whose very obedience made an officer feel like a fool if obliged to give a foolish order, whom the troops regarded as both a superior and an equal. He simply stared at Michaelson and held out his hand. Michaelson looked at the hand.

Michaelson was a gymnast who could be seen on any afternoon (in garrison) just before evening chow doing feats on the parallel bars he had erected behind the squad tents in which the naval gunfire team lived during "peace." Vail could not watch him without admiration nor admire without liking him. The troopers trying to emulate him looked comical. Michaelson's cheeks had a tendency to break out in fatty-boy patches of red; they did so now. The sergeant's hand, and the eyes at which he didn't look, conquered him; and he got the book from his pack, unwrapped the plastic around it, and gave it to the sergeant. Sergeant Hackman told a certain "Jumper" Zapponi to make a fire.

Corporal Michaelson watched the delicate little fire grow—and these flames, so dearly bought, seemed to cheer him.

"When I get home," he said, "the first time I hear a backfire I'm jumping under a mailbox, and this beautiful slender toad with round hips is going to crawl under and tell me it's OK and I'll say, 'Oh, I can't come out,' and she'll say, 'Oh, you darling, you poor son of a bitch, I'm going to offer you the only comfort a poor girl can offer a god damn battle-scarred veteran,' and this poor little toad is unbuttoning her button . . ."

He was definitely cheering up. The color in his cheeks deepened, and he began bleating like a ship's alarm: "Clit call! Clit call!"

There was something disgusting about Michaelson's sex stories and imaginings, but this made it all the harder not to listen. A man suggested that he patronize Pussy Corner, a notorious crossroads near Chu Lai, and his all-American-boy features wrinkled as he replied with infinite revulsion, *"Germ pudding."* He proceeded with a tale about a prostitute and a string that was knotted at intervals of a few inches; the tale was short but led to another. Soon the smoke came Vail's way, and Vail put his face in his hands. Behind this curtain his thoughts roamed freely, but in a few minutes he was caught up by the voice of Richie Rood.

He looked up. The smoke had cleared, the man was still filling canteens, and Sergeant Hackman was slumped over his folded hands.

Richie Rood was saying with naive, intelligent inflections: "But what would you say—if you brought her the body in your poncho like he did—"

Someone had shot a boy. The boy had been carrying a stick and was two hundred yards away, and had been hit by a very good shot.

"—and laid him down at her feet . . ." Richie Rood looked around as if no one understood. There was silence in the "house" except for the rain on the taut ponchos and the splattering of the runoff water.

"Well," said Sergeant Hackman at length, reflectively, "you could say, 'May I have my poncho back?' "

Richie Rood rocked backward as if from a blow, and it seemed for the next few seconds that the blow had knocked out his hesitancy and prudence.

"Sergeant Hackman, let me see your dog tag," said Private First Class Richie Rood peremptorily.

The sergeant stared at him with no greater scorn than usual. "Why do you want my dog tag?"

"I just want to see if you've got the courage of your convictions."

Sergeant Hackman looked away as if he found the sight of the naive little Rood painful; but he slipped the chain over his head and gave his dog tag to Mush Head to pass to Rood.

Rood read the last line, which said "No preference," and returned it to Mush Head, confessing, "I was afraid it was going to say 'Disciple of Christ' or 'Catholic' or some other lie."

The thing was then passed around, most of the men never having seen a "No preference" dog tag, or even known such a curiosity to exist.

"They won't put 'atheist' on a dog tag," said Sergeant Hackman to Vail.

"Oh? Are you an atheist?"

The sergeant smiled and said, "I don't know what I am, Lieutenant, but I'm no Disciple of Christ."

"What about Jones?" It was Mush Head. He sounded accusatory.

After a moment in which no one responded, Vail asked: "Well—what about him? Do you mean was he an atheist?"

"Jones was a Catholic," Rood interjected.

"I mean," continued Mush Head tentatively, "what about the way they put out his eyes?"

The man filling canteens looked at Mush Head with large, expectant eyes, and the water ran down over his knuckles.

Someone said, "Yes."

"And slashed up his feet," said Mush Head.

Vail conjectured, "His feet could have been cut because they made him walk without his boots."

"Yes, sir. And broke his jaw."

Again a man said, "Yes."

The men waited. Jumper Zapponi continued slowling feeding twigs to the fire, and the top of the hooch trembled in the unabating rain.

"The collar . . ." said a man.

"And put that wire," resumed Mush Head hesitantly, "around his neck."

Vail replied, "I'm not sure I believe that."

"No, sir, maybe not. It was barb wire. His skin closed across it."

There was another, longer silence, in which the men glanced at each other through the thin, shifting smoke, until Vail said:

"I'm sorry, I can't swallow all that. I didn't see his body." Neither had any of the others. "Until I see a thing like that, I think I won't believe it. I can't deny it, and I don't deny it, but I'm not believing it either."

Vail did believe that an enemy who pursued a strategy of terror by killing teachers and petty bureaucrats, by blowing up buses, rocketing towns, and machine-gunning refugee camps, could put a barbed-wire collar on Jones. He said: "Jones's eyes might have been eaten out by insects after he was dead."

"Yes, sir. What about the collar?"

"I don't know about the collar anymore than you do."

"Well, sir, I don't know like seeing."

"That's all I say. I didn't see it. Nobody here saw it."

"All I say is, I bet it's true."

"His eyes was gone," said a man whose face Vail couldn't see. "His feet was slashed. His jaw was broke. He had that collar on—the skin growed right over the wire."

Someone added, "You forgot he was dead."

"I didn't forget it."

There was not a single man in the hooch who was afraid, at that moment, of dying, but more than one had thought of being maimed. Corporal Michaelson, the gymnast, said:

"I told my girlfriend I wasn't afraid of dying. I was afraid I'd get my balls blown off by a grenade, and she wrote and said: 'Oh don't worry about that, it'd take three or four grenades to blow those balls off.' "

Michaelson laughed, but no one else did.

A figure was approaching through the rain. It was a man shrouded in a poncho. The uneven sand imparted an uneven swing to his streaming garment. For a moment he disappeared, his path taking him behind some pines, and when he reappeared he was much closer, and the rain could be seen beating so heavily on him that it made a luminescent outline around his head and shoulders. Vail, recognizing the Six, crawled awkwardly out of the heap of men and into the dense tropical rain.

Richie Rood had also seen the figure approaching in its green, hooded robe, and he too recognized the colonel, from his way of wandering aimlessly about his own command post as if searching for someone who could explain something. The colonel's benign and helpless face deep in the hood, with the white light beating on his head and shoulders, held Rood; and he watched the two officers conversing, though he couldn't hear them for the rain.

The colonel talked slowly, without gestures. Vail looked down into his face intently. Vail, whose poncho was in the roof of the hooch, had been wet to start with, but while he stood listening to the colonel the darkness of his shirt turned to a silvery brilliance at the shoulders. The water went down his face and dripped from his ears and nose, and he blinked frequently.

The colonel's map appeared from inside his poncho, and immediately streams and streaks began running down its plastic cover. The two officers bent over it, with the colonel watching and the lieutenant talking, seeming to speak to the map—sweeping away the water with his flattened hand.

Then the colonel was turning. The lieutenant was coming toward the hooch. In another instant Rood could see only Lieutenant Vail's legs and boots.

Then Vail squatted down, wiping water from his eyes, and said: "Sergeant Hackman."

Not only the sergeant but every man turned.

"Yes, sir," said Hackman.

"War call."

"Yes, sir. All right, you fucking civilians, saddle up. Michaelson, put out the fucking fire."

VIII

L iving in the center of the winter, Katherine discovered the gaunt and subtle rewards of self-denial. She experimented with various forms of deprivation and found them always less harsh and more rewarding than seemed reasonable. Her companion was her daughter. She discovered how much companionship there was and how much loneliness in this constant association with the girl. She dressed more plainly. She ate less, slept less, read more, and took longer walks, preferring the worst weather. She had her hair cut very short, and the plainness of it seemed to radiate a dim excellence through her body.

But her true excellence was that she chose not to mitigate her hunger although she had the means. She gave it a place in her loins. She had read the phrase "the splendor of the body" and thought that if the soul could sustain hunger, so could the body, if this phrase were true. That the path to the end of her tension was always open was exhilarating so long as she didn't follow it, and she did not. She elected the other path. That was the result less of resolution than of election—her state was less resolute than elective. For she would wake in the morning with a consciousness not of some vow, but of her freedom. And would elect to simplify her life and make it rigorous. Of her hunger she said: "I will keep it." And if sometimes she recalled her daughter's characterizing Ella as "the lady who cries," she herself was the woman who said "I will keep it."

Therefore her life was full of pain and feeling. She discovered, which was not a surprise, that the less she allowed herself, the more she possessed; the more plainly she dressed, the more beautiful the fire seemed; the more she read herself into exhaustion and stupor at midnight or one or two o'clock, the clearer everything seemed when she arose at six or seven.

The snow was often faintly purple at daybreak. She would awake with the tension and fullness of hunger in her loins, and in the presence of her choice. She would arise, come downstairs and wash, shout up to her daughter, make breakfast, and send the girl off to school, sometimes walking with her to the Willoughbys' dooryard, where she met the school bus, and then walking back along the road accompanied by the dog.

She knelt on the bricks of the hearth, shoveling ashes into a bucket. There were coals in the ashes. Each, if she looked closely, was a universe. The shovelfuls landed in the bucket, filling its empty space with swirling gray ash and concealing the coals.

The heart of an ascetic nun is a coal plunged in ash—and she thought: "A nun could kneel on these bricks for an hour." And she could see a young nun with slack arms and closed eyes kneeling, growing paler. As her shovel scraped across the bricks, gathering less and less ash with each excursion, she saw herself kneeling in this way—even as her knees began to notice the bricks. She thought: "But it'd be so boring." For herself, not the nun, because the nun would have orison while she would have mere daydreams, and perhaps a demoralizing examination of her motive. It was too paltry. Yet if the pain in her knees was to be believed, it wouldn't be boring after all; she might even faint. She thought: "I could crack my head." And instead of orison, mere curiosity. Would that last an hour?

She beat the shovel on the side of the bucket and replaced it in its rack; and concluding with contempt and relief that the idea was barbaric, she got stiffly to her feet and carried the ashes outside.

The dog, Yuk, greeted her with immoderate enthusiasm, dancing at the end of her chain as if on hot metal, yipping her happiness at the prospect and the seeming assurance of a long walk along the white roads, or perhaps a delightful chase of a pregnant doe. She was a young bitch with a wolfish face, black, with a white-ticked chest and white feet and one brown leg. Katherine scattered the ashes in the snow, and a coal hissed. She spoke regretfully to the dog and without touching it went back inside to begin the housework. She could clean the whole place in a morning, not entirely without pleasure.

The phonograph played one after another the records she was beginning to tire of, while also enjoying them a little better with each
listening. She always intended to buy more records and always forgot until cleaning day. And besides, records were expensive.

By the time she finished the housework she had acquired a healthy
distaste for it. She shut her cleaning implements away in a closet and
went to the bathroom to wash her hands. She was struck again with
the shortness, the severity of her haircut.

She felt extremely hungry. Intending to prepare the lunch she'd
been mentally devouring for an hour, she was detained by a thought,
paused in the doorway, and next found herself in the living room.
She knelt on the hearth. She was acting like a person who is overwhelmed by a temptation—acting, that is, with curtailed consciousness; or like a man in battle whose deeds are, so far as he is
concerned, those of somebody else whom he's never met.

She balled up several sheets of newspaper and stuffed them under
the irons and then got up and went outside and selected a few sticks
of kindling. The sun was strong, but when she went under the eave
for the heavy wood she was shaded, and the chill astonished her.
There was elm on top, which she wanted no part of, so she spent
some time putting aside the top logs, as well as the next she reached,
which were birch, until finally she came to a lode of maple. How
affectionate, how childishly affectionate she felt toward maple. Inside, she shortened the sticks of kindling across her knee and laid
them this way and that on the fitfully expanding balls of paper; then
she laid the logs across the irons and touched two matches to the
paper; and as the paper began burning, sucking up the air through
the newly opened space under the andirons, she noticed again, even
as the lower bark blackened in the flames, the texture of the bricks.
Getting up hurriedly, she went to the laundry bag in the bathroom
and found a towel, folded it till it made a thick pad, and dropped
it on the hearth. The flaming kindling lapped at the logs. These were
impervious, settling, but the fire faithfully continued.

Katherine watched this process intently and not quite consciously
and dropped to her knees, crossed her wrists, and lifted off her
sweater. She felt no heat. She saw herself naked, walking through
a drift and sinking to her knees; keeping her balance with difficulty.
With the usual contortions she removed her brassiere. She went as
close to the fire as she dared, and when gradually the heat and rising

energy of the fire seemed mature enough she touched it with a poker, perfecting it, then ran to the bathroom, snatched her towel from the rod, and ran across the living room. With a final nervous glance at the fire, she went out the door.

The dog barked hysterically as she ran down the porch stairs with the towel caught around her shoulders, the sun's rays striking with surprising warmth on her neck and chest. The snow almost blinded her. She said, "Good grief, Yuk, I'm *not* going for a walk," but the dog knew otherwise and screamed her demands. Yuk lunged at the end of her chain. Katherine simply hoped the dog wouldn't choke herself.

Katherine ran precariously down the beaten path, sliding, because her sheepskin boots were never meant for a slippery surface. Halfway down the path she turned, saw how especially strong and lovely was the sunshine in a cluster of naked white birches, and went wading off the path. Under the top six inches of new snow was an old crust, which sometimes she broke through and sometimes walked upon with ease. When she crashed through, the snow was at the thigh of her Levi's. The jagged crust bruised her shin when she fell through again. She reached the center of the grove, where the sun was as brilliant on the bark as upon the snow, where the white shafts were thickest, and each seemed a source of sunlight. Her eyes still stung with the brightness of the whole earth; her shin was aching; but very soon the cold painted her with its swift brush from the waist up, except her scalp—she was aware of the sun's warmth on her hair. Her nipples stood up in amazement; her flesh contracted.

She heard an exclamation in her own voice which sounded as if she'd been stabbed. It set the dog off again. The barking passed through the trees like a wave through pilings. With a motion both hasty and flamboyant she swung the towel over a branch, at the same time sinking through the crust with her left foot. This appeared so convenient that she lifted her right and smashed the heel through; so she stood calf deep, trembling, reaching into the fresh snow, and, lifting an arm, began to wash herself.

Her skin found this application not too terrible. She washed first with one hand, then the other, because her hands quickly became cold. She cleansed—with such thoroughness, abrasion, dissolution— everything she could reach except her ears. She thought there might be something a little too gung-ho about stuffing snow in her ears. But her navel got a thorough abrasive treatment, as did her armpits. Her bath, her escapade, was nearly over when she began to realize how cold she was, that the cold she had forgotten was the superficial and the cold she now suspected was the basic.

With sufficient control still of her fingers to grasp the towel, she reached out, dragged it off the branch, and wrapped it around her shoulders, closing it at her neck. She began her torturous way to the path. If only she would break through with every step she'd have no trouble keeping her balance, but this never knowing, walking high at one moment and plunging the next, was exhausting. Her trembling, the tightness of her jaw, the scraping of her shins on the crust as she broke through, her strange general distress, all were unjustly, treacherously overpowering. They were so masterful. She felt almost as a little girl feels at the moment she gives up and cries for her mother. But Katherine had the fire in mind.

She reached the path without falling. Her boots were full of snow, but that was the least of it. Going slowly as if walking on pebbles, she went up the path bent with cold and determination, climbed the steps into the ceaseless joyous yaps of the dog, and without a sideward glance opened the door, freezing her hand on the knob, and approached the fire.

Her pad on the hearth was occupied by Crackpot, who lay stretched to the heat, and upon hearing her lifted his languid head, stretched forth his forelegs, and separated the toes; but in the midst of this delicious motion he was forced to the alert, his eyes widened, he gathered himself, and the next instant he fled to avoid the swinging toe of the sheepskin boot.

Kneeling, her towel falling, with an involuntary moan, she stretched out her hands, and soon came the pain of thawing, which far exceeded that of freezing. It was in the fingers particularly of her right hand and was not only horrible beyond her expectation but seemingly alien, like a swallowed and active poison. She hadn't wanted this.

With her body bent most humbly forward, her mouth open, eyes shining with the pain, breasts pendant, glistening and streaming all over with the melted snow, she bathed her hands in their fiery cure. Nor did the pain immediately subside. Weak little streams of water, hastened by her trembling and her breathing, streaked down her back, between her breasts, and down her arms, and a drop descended the long steep route of her nose and poised at the end, full of firelight, before falling; her eyebrows were heavy with water, and streaks were keeping in the creases of her belly. She turned her hands at the fire and looked at her palms and the fingertips, which except for a healthful color gave no outward sign of their pain; and as it subsided and the weakness of her legs and distress of her inner body likewise subsided, she seemed to observe, to see herself—kneeling, bent, half dressed, shorn, with her arms extended toward the fire and wrists curved back. A sense of strangeness made its way, although feebly, to her intellect.

When her hands felt warm she reached up to the mantelpiece, which was of maple, and clung to it, closing her eyes—blinking away some water and closing her eyes finally after the flames flashed at her with her blinking—and let herself relax, almost hang. Her back arched, her body sagged toward the flames, and for so long as she was able to hang in this way, she seemed to be in motion, breasting the almost intolerable waves of heat.

Sitting, she took off her wet boots, shook out the slush, and set them by the fire. She removed her socks, which were soaked, and something—the ordinary act of unclothing her feet—caught her attention. From this moment she was decided. She hadn't planned to bathe her other half, but now she said: "I didn't really mind the cold," and actually believed, being warm now, that she hadn't.

This part of the bath was more difficult than the first and her recovery took longer, but when she was fully recovered, warm, dressed once again in her husband's old Navy sweater with the high neck and the sleeves with tight wrists, a clean pair of Levi's, and clean wool socks and slippers, she felt the same:

"I didn't really mind the cold," she said, "all I minded was the thawing."

She pushed back her hair, which again fell forward over her brow. Her blue eyes were exceedingly bright in their appreciation of the fire, her complexion was flushed, and she was hungry for the lunch so long ago deferred, but she would not leave the fire. Crackpot came back and assumed a setting-hen posture under the tent of her legs; and he stared at the fire with great absent eyes.

"How can it be ascetic," she asked, "if it feels so good? But certainly it's harder than taking a shower. Certainly it's cleaner—I mean only that it's *different* from lying in a hot bath and feeling rapeable."

She stroked the cat, who offered no objection, nor did he alter his great-eyed expression.

" 'But, Judge, I rape so easy.' Where does that line come from? Oh yes, a woman has accused the fifth or sixth man of rape, and finally the judge says—and she says, 'I rape so easy.'

"But isn't it vigorous?" she asked. "Isn't it clean? Isn't it cold, painful—and glorious in the sun and yet natural—but if I were natural I'd do it all at once—but I couldn't. That would hurt too much and I might freeze something and the doctor would say—and I could answer, 'Well, Doctor, after all, I bathe in the snow, don't you?' I am so hungry I could die. I don't mean here, but here.

"If I were really natural my hair would be very long and no doubt tangled—I'd have few if any teeth—I'd have hair in great globs under my arms and long hairs on my legs like Mrs. Dilke—yet look at this leg."

She pulled up the cuff of her Levi's. It was so tight she could raise it only to her calf.

"So smooth, like marble," she observed, "and think of all the veins, the muscles—and I have a uterus, oviducts, yet the outer appearance is so like marble. I wish there were a better suggestion on the outside of what's within."

She looked at her hands, at their backs, as a model of what she meant. Then her hands dropped, hanging at the wrists, and she pulled her knees closer to her body, slightly discomfiting Crackpot, and thought:

"It isn't really the *cleanest* bath. There's no hexachlorophene or anything! Richard could tell me exactly what's in the snow. O Great Glaciologist, tell me, what's in the snow that makes me feel so good?"

On another day when the sun came out and shone blindingly on another new snowfall she was again tempted; but she didn't repeat her escapade. The snow was plentiful. There were heavier snowfalls than usual. But in February, even as the mornings were coldest, the days began noticeably lengthening. On a single day she read the coldest temperature of the winter in the early morning and saw lingering daylight in the afternoon, when formerly there was darkness at the same hour. In March even as the snow lay deepest there came a break in the weather, which could happen at any time and mean nothing, but during this break crows came, and although the cold returned, the crows stayed. She would see them on the manure piles and in the fields. She rejoiced to see these birds, realizing all at once how long it had been since she'd seen the earth; but also she felt uneasy.

On nights when the moon was full, even if the night was cold she could see a circle round the moon at a great distance, taking nearly half the sky, signifying palely what the crows signified in black. Daylight still lengthened. A single day of uninterrupted sunlight laid all the roads bare, except where they ran through woods, so in the daytime they were slick with mud and at night the ruts and splash patterns froze hard just as they were. There was thawing even in the woods. The snow, while not visibly melting, seemed to be settling, and the tops of fence posts seemed to be rising; and where there had been a single strand of barbed wire, the top strand, now there were two.

There was a day of rain and a night of freeze. This made a universal crust in which, on the succeeding day, long faults appeared. The crust divided and sank. Katherine saw, while walking one day in the middle of March, the pale impressions of snowshoes going up a hill, and she recognized these as tracks Willoughby had made around Christmastime, on the far side of the winter. Their reemergence now, even as the stones were rising taller in the cemeteries, made her think, as if logically, of her miscarriage. She visualized—rather, a picture filled her consciousness—a picture of her uterus and a child the size of her thumb; and the little white formaldehyde fingers of the child. She searched the side of the road for a footprint of hers or Terry's that might have been preserved in the mud since last fall, but she found none. Instead she thought of a picture in a magazine of a dead American soldier on a tank, and the crescent pattern of the tread of his boot. She didn't find this pattern in the mud either. On her walks she sometimes saw steam rising in clouds from the sugarhouses and she heard the engine-driven drills roaring in the woods as the sugarmakers tapped the trees. Along the roadside where the maples had been scarred by the blade of the snowplow there were icicles, and finding one of these well formed, she broke it off and ate the end for its sugar.

The weather blustered, the mud in the roads deepened (and on that account the mail was late), dun-colored grass appeared in patches in the steeper south-facing slopes, while on the opposite slopes the snow was still two or three feet deep, but settling always. The butternut trees budded before any others. The balm of Gilead budded, and she took clusters and smashed them in her hands and rolled the mash back and forth, then smelled the fragrance of her fingers. She had lived so long in cities that it smelled of a candy store in Chicago rather than the woods, at first.

For so many years the effects of spring had reached her through such a thickness of pollution as to be negligible upon her. She had forgotten the influence of spring. It is indirect. She now observed the coming of spring, but failed to observe herself, thinking she was no part of it except as one who loves to see it, and that it was no part of her.

But its most hesitant steps, by their delicacy, refined her perception. The hillsides of maple and birch that had been a dull brown flourished in gentle pastel colors under the influence of the lengthening light and turned rose, with a soft hue of purple. The colors were at first undetectable. This same hill in a hard rain became the color of rust, but was restored by the next day's sunshine to its faint outspread rose. Where the water ran in a ditch in the daytime under a shelf of overhanging ice she found green shoots. This green, growing under the ice, was the first she saw. On the south-facing hills the brown grass that had seemed so dead last autumn and seemed so sentient now was still spreading, and surrounding the snow; so in some fields it was now the snow that was surrounded and not the grass.

She went walking one day in April in her blue jacket, which was too light, wearing no hat and only a pair of thin leather gloves. She thought, after all, it was spring. She felt as if she were just conquering the effects of a brutal shaking. As she walked she repeatedly came to clear springs of water flowing up in the road. Less than a mile from where she lived she saw a junked car lying on its top in a pasture which she had walked past innumerable times. She had never seen it, and therefore could hardly believe she was seeing it now. But the thing had been there always—in summer and autumn muffled up in orchard grass, vetch and burdock and weeds, and in winter cloaked by a drift. Only in the spring did it stand out so plainly, a sign of the season in our country as surely as the barn swallow. She went close to this car, walking on the flattened weeds, and looked up and saw a decaying snowdrift on a wooded hillside, gray, mammoth, and dark.

The nights were lively with the noise of running water. On a cold night the stream she could hear from her bed was low and slow, but on a warm day it exceeded its banks by noon. The cat returned every day with a body flopping in his jaws. The dog caught a woodchuck dopey with hibernation, broke its spine with a shake, and chewed on its head as on an old bone, thoughtfully, and crushed the skull. On those hills blessed with sunlight green grass rose thinly through the brown; and when two inches of new snow fell upon this it looked even greener, rising through and outlasting the snow. The farmers put out the heifers and dry cows.

There was a place where a pony had wintered. It was gone now. A three-sided shelter, a stream, pony droppings, and the scatterings of its winter hay. Katherine saw its stranded white hairs where it had rubbed its neck against a tree trunk, higher above the ground than she could reach. She walked by the stream. It was very late afternoon, the sun was low and leaden, and she discovered a phenomenon of light. If she looked downstream, looking with the rays of the sun, the water chased itself along its course, brimming its banks, with a sweet curving swiftness. It was musical and vernal despite the dismal day. But if only she turned and looked against the leaden rays, looking upstream, and saw the water as coming down toward her, then its rolling serpentine action and its metal color menaced her soul, striking the color into her soul. She felt in her body perfectly safe, rationally, but the insinuation disturbed her as she forced herself to stand and see the transformation of this stream. She did see it; and twice she turned and looked downstream and down-sun at the brimming stream and up, at the cable-twist, leaden, coiling, spineless serpent that constantly lost its form over the banks; merely a phenomenon of light.

Her feet were wet. She was chilled as if she'd just swallowed ice water. She went up to the road and walked along the hardening mud.

About the coming of spring she was of two minds, for she had lived well in the center of the winter.

She expected Ella at any time, and now Ella came. She happened to arrive when Katherine was turning over the pages of a book at her desk, searching for a single line. She was certain it was near the bottom of the left page, but not certain this was the right book.

The search was pointless because she could amost quote the line anyway, and there was no elaboration. It was simply a statement in Herodotus, or Bury, or Hammond, that a quarry had existed in a certain place in Asia Minor near Halicarnassus. That was all. There was no list of temples or roads or walls that might have been built with the stones quarried there, nor any history or description of the quarry, which after all was one of many. Katherine hadn't read a word about ancient Greece for weeks. However, the books were still in a pile on her desk, and the fact of the quarry had surfaced in her mind after long incubation. Why?

Wherever she went, whatever she did, there were the footfalls of an idea dancing in her brain: that these people quarrying the stones were slaves. That these *slaves* were people essentially the same as John Keats and Fanny Braun, or Richard, and of course herself. Perhaps this quarry had gone into her mind at about the time Richard wrote of a fortification wall he had seen, whose stones amazed and depressed him. She didn't know. She didn't care. It was the slaves—without liberty, peace, rest . . .

An objection was respectfully raised that she knew nothing, really, of their life, that they might have had plenty of rest and some liberties, etc. etc., but she scorned it. No, they were brutalized. Neither personal liberty, peace, privacy, rest, or regard. An objection was raised: "Well, big deal, did you ever hear of the pyramids?" But this of course was no objection, only another and worse example.

She imagined the quarry could be seen from the sea and if she sailed by she would find it grown up with trees, a kerf like a blind canyon in the mountainside. She imagined she could wander among the trees at the bottom and look up the sheer bare walls, and see the path of a cutting tool in the stone. She didn't go quite so far as to imagine herself as a laundrywoman, cook, or harlot for the managers; for she was fixed on this idea: that each slave had endured until he died.

An objection was raised that this was half-baked, uncriticized, at best the nucleus of an idea. Without denying this she shrugged her shoulders as if she intended to continue her fascination with the thing and to hell with all such objections. No—half-baked or half-assed, inchoate, nuclear, naive—they were slaves. (And none had had recourse to ascetic "election.")

She slammed the book shut, said one of the words Richard hated to hear her say, and looked up and saw the headlights outside, and a thrill passed through her as she hurried down the dark path, once nearly falling, to help Ella with her bags.

But Ella had brought only one large suitcase and a leather toilet bag, from which it was evident she had not come "to live," as invited, but only for a visit. Katherine had to lecture herself against the unreasonable pain she felt at this. It was already late, and they stayed up talking till after three, and Katherine was up again at half past six getting Terry ready, and took her to the Willoughbys' door-yard. When she came back and silently closed the door, after admonishing the dog, she found Ella still asleep on the daybed. She was neat even in sleep, with the blankets drawn evenly over her shoulders, and beautiful even with her mouth open. Her beauty was partly in her color. Katherine had seen it last night.

Her hair was perfectly black and she had just brushed it (of course), perhaps consciously taking advantage of the firelight. Her eyes were brown and black and rather shining. Her complexion was perpetually suntanned, evidently. Her hands were suntanned, and she had a gold wedding band on her finger, and the gold was no smoother than the skin so neatly stretched across the back of her hand. Her smile and her teeth were bold, although she didn't smile much—and her physical condition was perfect; that is, her health. She was actually a rather large woman for a diver (not nearly as large as Katherine), and erect of carriage, and of a supernatural efficiency in motion. Her language was sometimes coarse—but her voice was usually soft, and she passed long, long silences. Then perhaps she was at her best.

Katherine imagined these stillnesses as having the same quality as the apex of one of Ella's dives. Ella could put stillness into a dive, and this would be the beauty of it. She still practiced, and was not averse to diving if people asked her.

Mounting the stairs, Katherine looked again at her sleeping sister. Katherine was rather cold and returned to her bed gratefully and soon slept. There was something missing. It was Ella's scorn, chiefly her comments on the Marine Corps and military language. During the whole night she hadn't made a single acerbic comment on the marines, and had even used the word *battalion* in the sense of battalion staff, plus *gook, slope,* meaning slopehead or Oriental, *crotch,* meaning the Marine Corps, and another word Katherine had forgotten because she didn't know its meaning. All this while telling of John's activities.

At noon they prepared a breakfast of two eggs and three strips of bacon each, and coffee. Ella was wiping the dishes without paying much attention while Katherine washed. Putting down her towel, she moved a little behind Katherine and looked over her shoulder out the window.

"Katherine—would you like to lie in the sun?"

Turning, with hands suspended over the dishwater, Katherine retorted: "What, in a raccoon coat?"

"In nothing," said Ella, "or practically nothing."

"Ella, where do you think we are? People around here don't take a sunbath in April."

"They could, on a day like this."

A minute later Ella called from the porch, "Come here," and Katherine, who was glad enough to leave the dishes, came.

"Feel it," Ella suggested.

"I hardly can."

"Oh no, it's a pretty good sun. Feel."

"I feel the wind," Katherine said, but she lifted her face to the sun, closed her eyes, and let the sun fall on her face and throat. She felt the wind on her wet hands and wrists. When she opened her eyes everything seemed closer, as trees do in a fog, and all the colors, including those of Ella's face, were suffused for a few seconds with blue. "It's warm," she admitted.

"Yes . . . it isn't high but the air is clear."

Neither woman spoke for a moment, as if silently enjoying the sun's effect. The suspense was too much for the dog, who finally began to lament.

"Oh, shut up, Yuk," Katherine said, and moved to pet her. Her coarse black coat was almost burning. "Ella," she said, "feel her coat," and Ella spread her hand on the dog's side and smiled. Yuk picked up and put down her forepaws, squirmed, laid back her ears

—still in a state of apprehension that she'd miss something—and washed her chops repeatedly.

Ella observed, "She's terribly nervous," moving her hand and sinking her fingers again in the thick coat.

"She is always."

Katherine sat on the painted rail of the porch. This too was warm, yet the breeze was sharp.

"I think we'd freeze to death in this wind."

"No—isn't there an open place in the woods, a clearing, where the sun could reach us and yet the woods would shelter us from the wind? Or a hollow—out in an open field somewhere. A small deep hollow is just like an oven."

"Good lord," said Katherine, "you're exactly like your husband. Now I know why you married him."

Ella had been moving her hand from place to place over the dog's body, calming the dog and plunging her fingers into the hot coat. She looked up with a rather twisted expression. "What do you mean by that?"

"I'm sorry. Nothing profound. I only meant you're so like him. Everything is all planned out in advance . . ."

Ella didn't respond, and Katherine added in embarrassment: "John would say, 'All right, I want a deep hollow, and no insects, and only so much wind, and no clouds are to pass over the sun, and *you* bring the beer, and *you* bring a blanket . . .' "

Ella stood up and said, "I'm going. May I take the dog?" looking squarely at Katherine.

"Why, no, except on a rope."

"Why must she be on a rope?"

"Well, she's a deer chaser. She'd be off after a deer."

"What's so awful about that?"

"Well, good heavens, she kills them."

Ella, to Katherine's surprise, seemed skeptical.

"She's killed three or four already. The man who owned her was going to shoot her because of it. If she's caught, she'll be shot by the game warden."

"You mean she's a fugitive?" said Ella, and she took the dog's muzzle, clamping the jaws shut, and shook it.

"No—I mean if she's caught again."

"I see." Ella released the black muzzle and gave a full white smile to the dog—who had suggested the release with an ominous gurgle in her throat. "Well then, Yuk, you'll come on a rope, won't you," and she entered the house, leaving Katherine thinking:

"What happened? Did we argue over the dog? Did I insult her? Did I insult John?"

As she wiped the last glass Katherine looked into the living room. Ella had unmade the daybed, stripped off the top blanket, and was remaking the bed.

"I'd like to go," she called, and saw Ella straighten up. And as that same bold, ambiguous smile was turned upon her Katherine thought: "She isn't angry." And Katherine felt a slight sense of loss that the woman who had said "I'm faithful" was not the woman folding the blanket.

They were in good spirits as they went down the path—Ella leading with the blanket under her left arm and the end of the dog's rope turned twice around her right hand, laughing and leaning backward against the ridiculous joy and eagerness of the dog; and Katherine following with hands pushed flat into the hip pockets of her Levi's, looking to the side with private pleasure at the grove of her snow bath. She cried, "This way," for they had gone by the turning, and Ella replied, "OK, if Yuk'll let me." And passing through the grove Katherine said, "You should follow me," and Ella again laughed, "OK, if Yuk'll let me," and the dog dragged her along at Katherine's heels.

Katherine couldn't go directly to the place she'd chosen without crossing through a deep drift that lay on their path like a stranded whale. She asked over her shoulder, "Should we go through it?" and Ella replied, "God no," with a mimetic display of shivers and consternation. So they went somewhat downhill to their left and crossed an old trampled fence and then the stream where Terry had garnered her precious rocks; and climbed the steep opposite bank and wound through an old pasture among scattered pines. They walked side by side in this open country, gliding through the broken dead grass of last summer.

"I thought we could lie here," said Katherine, and she took the end of the dog's rope, which had left a white streak across Ella's hand, and tied it deftly to the branch of a poplar.

"My god, you're a regular sailor," said Ella.

"Oh, that's just my horse knot. It's the only one I know."

They spread their blanket, but Ella looked up at the sun and decided the position of the blanket must be changed, so they spread it anew and smoothed it. It was a dark blue blanket, which Ella predicted would soon be as hot as Yuk's coat. The dog's ears were pricked and her tongue lolled as she sat by her tree and scrutinized these doings with whatever thoughts cause a dog to tilt its head. When at length she was satisfied they weren't deserting her, she leaned, and fell to her side with an old man's groan, and lay there panting as if it were summer.

The blanket was spread in a hollow. There was a ridge of rock on one side. Ella undressed to her underwear, sitting on the rock to unlace her shoes, then brushed off her rear where some of the lichen from the rock had been clinging. She put her socks inside her shoes, folded her slacks twice and placed her folded jersey on top of them, then took this remarkably compact bundle to a pine tree, lifted a bottom bough, and secreted it underneath. Seeing that Katherine was trying not to ask a question, she said, without a trace of self-defense in her voice: "They'll be cool when I dress."

Katherine turned away to conceal a smile. She strolled in the old grass. Enjoying the earth with her bare feet, having stripped to her underwear, she sought out the mosses, which were like carpet in a wealthy woman's bedroom, and the stiff lichen that was like beds of inch-deep coral, but collapsed to a gray powder under her weight. She walked along one of the ribs of rock and found it less warm on her soles than she expected, and upon a little study she could understand why. All the ribs were slightly canted at a northward angle and thus were poorly set to take the sun. She walked through the hardhack and found it was easy and didn't hurt; on the contrary, the branches brushed her calves. The breeze was chilling her shoulders.

Returning, she found her sister supine, arms above her head, so her wrists were off the blanket and her fingers were twined in the grass. She looked at her sister's closed eyes, at her fingers—and with incredulity at a perceptible silver glow on her neck. "Ella," said Katherine, "don't tell me you're warm."

Ella said remotely, "Yes I am."

"I'm cold."

As Katherine was lying down Ella said, with the same remoteness, "You'll be warm now."

Stretching her body on the dark blanket and closing her eyes,

Katherine passed from one world to another. The blanket made a sheet of radiant warmth for her back, for her buttocks, which were suddenly centers of emanating heat, for her calves and even her heels. Her cheeks burned, even her lips burned. There was a benign and spacious warmth on her shoulders, and strangely enough she could feel it, although weakly, on her hands. It seemed that her body was a region of balance, of equalization, between the heat of the blanket and of the sun; a region of peace. No peace so suddenly felt had ever seemed so deep.

Her vision was quite acute, of a red chaos playing against her black lids; and so was her hearing, of the wind, whether in the pines overhead or in the grass. Her sense of touch was incredibly ubiquitous. Of smell, nothing. She asked herself: "Can I smell Ella's breath?" for she remembered Ella's head was toward her; but she could neither smell nor hear Ella's breathing in spite of her alertness. She watched with fascination the dancing of the red, this evidence so far from the sun and so close to her brain of the solar fire.

Ella's voice was extremely close. "Well," said Ella, "what do you think?"

To open her lips with English, to break her "balance" and mutilate her meaning, was not what Katherine wanted: "I'm warm, as you said I'd be."

"Yes."

"Did you know I'd feel like this?"

"Well . . ." Ella hesitated. "How do you feel?"

"I feel perfect."

Ella laughed—she had a very pleasing, calm laugh. She said, "It's the next best thing to making love."

Katherine heard Ella stirring, but she herself didn't stir. But despite her stillness, the moment was passing—the "balance." Her tenderness was abating; and now the possibility that someday she might walk again or laugh, or that a swarm of insects could drive her from her place, wouldn't strike her as absurd. (These possibilities didn't cross her mind.) But she felt a little stronger; yet a fantasy stole upon her and she did not resist it, but drifted in it. She perceived, in this dream, Ella's breath, which was dark, and Ella's lips . . .

"I do not resist. I do not turn my head."

Her sister's dark lips blot out the red chaos.

"I do not turn away."

They touch hers.

"I open my lips—a little. Her tongue is sweet, to my taste and my heart."

The red chaos again dances.

"Suppose her hand—what a powerful thought—suppose her hand should be spread on my stomach and she should say, 'How warm,' and move her hand, and trace my ribs."

Katherine sat up so violently that the blood must have left her brain; she sat dizzily blinking in the sunlight, looking with shock at the bluish grass and a pine tree restrainedly waving in the wind. She thought: "What on earth am I thinking? Ella isn't like that."

"Did something bite you?"

She looked around. There was Ella, shielding her eyes, holding up her head and smiling.

"No—there aren't any bugs yet, thank heaven. In a week or two we couldn't stay here a minute without being eaten by ten thousand blackflies." She thought: "What in the world am I babbling about? I'm not like that either. Look at her. Even in that awkward position, with her head up, she has a pretty chin. How can a creature be so perfect?"

"Are you going somewhere?" Ella asked.

"Yes, I'll be back."

Ella relaxed, lay back her "perfect" head, the tendons disappearing in her neck, and closed her eyes. Up gently went her hand, and the fingers twined in the grass. Katherine looked at her—stared—for a minute almost dumbfounded, as if something had actually happened—"something."

She walked down to the stream. How joyous, how strangely joyous it was simply to walk in bare feet and bare legs through this stiff dead grass.

"And is it true," she asked, "that to do a thing 'in your heart,' as Jesus said, is the same as actually doing it?"

Coming to the borderline of the old pasture by the creek, she went somewhat carefully down the bank and received some scratches on her thighs from last year's berry canes.

"If it's true, I'll have to be electrocuted and sent to the penitentiary for a hundred years. And incidentally, you fraud," she addressed herself, "what has happened to the Solitary Ascetic?" She stepped in the icy mud by the stream.

"God, how cold," she thought. "Listen—I say *god* the way Ella does."

She squatted, joined her hands, and drank from the stream, which numbed her hands before she could get her fill; and she stood by the loquacious stream and looked around at the thickets of wild apple and cherry trees which clogged the stream bed in tortured attitudes, at the snow-tamped fern sticks splayed radially on the damp ground, at the willows and the little struggling ironwoods, poplars, and elm saplings. It was chill—it was a low place, the air was damp and the sunlight all broken up—and she decided to go back into the sun; she shivered, almost. But looking at the stream in a shallow place where the water streamed over the rocks without changing their color, she asked herself whether she shouldn't lie down in it.

She might lie down—slowly, on the uneven and jagged rocks— and let the water flow by her sides. That would be cold. She knelt in the mud.

"Wait," she said, "please. What is the difference between dreaming, in that way, that I opened my lips, and actually . . . If I've done it 'in my heart,' how do I differ from the woman I would be if I'd really done it?"

She put her hands again in the rushing water and drank, washed her knees, and climbed the muddy bank into the pasture. "Oh, I love the sun," she exclaimed, realizing again how long the winter had been. "I am different, I must be. In the one case it happens and in the other it doesn't. Isn't that enough? Of course the volition was hers—no, no, the imagined, the unreal volition was hers, and the real volition mine. Oh what the hell. I am different because had she done it I would probably have screamed. *Probably.* I heard that word."

Walking back uphill, she saw the pointed ears and face of Yuk protruding from the grass. She went to the dog, petted her, and talked with her. The dog was most articulate in the way of nervous affectionate dogs. "Yuk, dear girl, can't we just be friends?" Katherine asked, and wiped the dog's enthusiasm-love slobber on the dog's own coat.

Ella was naked. Two garments, destitute and white, lay in the grass halfway to the pine tree. Katherine picked these up and lifted the branch and put them with the rest of Ella's things.

"I've put your stuff under the tree," she said. "I wouldn't want to see you burned alive."

"Oh, it doesn't matter with white things," Ella replied without opening her eyes.

Katherine thought: "There's no end to it. She's so scientific."

Katherine didn't know whether to lie down or to dress and go back. She didn't look at Ella.

"The dog was whining for you," said Ella.

"Yes, I don't doubt it. I am loved of Yuk. Excuse me, I've been reading Shakespeare."

"Is that a Shakespearean haircut?"

Now Katherine looked down at her sister and couldn't help noticing that her breasts were as tan as all the rest.

"Don't you like my haircut?"

"I'm sorry, no. It makes you look sort of naked."

"Naked?" Katherine repeated.

Ella opened her eyes, shaded her eyes, looked at Katherine with sudden comprehension, and both women laughed.

"I hope I'm not embarrassing you . . . I didn't think you'd mind."

"Oh no," said Katherine. "You are embarrassing me and I don't mind."

Katherine still couldn't decide whether to go back; and without having decided, avoiding a decision altogether, she took off her last two garments. Seeing the first motions of this, Ella closed her eyes again—her arms were at her sides, her fingers extended on the blue cloth.

Katherine lay down on her back again, and at first she thought of Jesus. She argued that if, for example, a man plans and thoroughly fantasizes a murder, but stops short of committing it, think of the difference to the victim. And that's only one side of it. Think of the difference to him—to his kids, his wife, his mother. But she was distracted from this question—although she intended to pursue it with the whip of her logic—because involuntarily she was betraying herself; she was betraying, at least, the Solitary Ascetic. Where was "election" now? She saw what was taking place only gradually; she didn't want it but she was not "electing." She was in the very act of betrayal—not with Ella, for that was *impossible* and *unnatural* and even frightening; but with the sun. In astonishment she thought: "Oh lord, feel the sun."

She had been alone very long. She was a chaste woman emerging from the winter. The sun with the power of a dream spent its endless energy on those dark parts of her body it had seldom seen before. Her spirit was stunned at the behavior of her body, for it came forth to meet the sun with every manifestation of its meeting with a man.

In an ecstasy—as she lay in the first shock of the sun's strength—she felt the processes of greeting going forward within her. She felt the sun's energy seek the darker places and penetrate there. These were also the most secret and responding places. What excellent knowledge this seemed, and what a nice coincidence. She let free. She released herself, released her spirit—with her hands at her sides and her fingertips turning into her palms, and her whole body motionless and secretly in motion. It was during these moments that she realized, for the first time after all her months of ascetic self-denial and seeming self-knowledge, how deep and unexplored her hunger was.

Ella received a letter that day. Katherine thought this a good sign, showing as it did that John was thoughtful enough to anticipate his wife in her wanderings and send his letter ahead to meet her. If the letter pleased Ella she didn't show it.

In the evening Terry played hide-and-go-seek with the dog. Both women found this game hilarious because of the dog's ineptitude. Terry would command the dog to sit, which she had learned easily, being able to learn anything except to leave the deer alone; then Terry would hide somewhere under a bed or behind the chimney and call in a clear, transported voice, for she was completely absorbed in the game: "Here, Yuk! Here, Yuk!" And Yuk, who had been working her forepaws up and down on the kitchen floor, would come scrambling into the living room; and though she used her nose profusely, it was to no avail, apparently because there was such a confusion of scents. She would sometimes spin almost like a top while Ella cheered, "Find her, Yuk!" Even if Terry called a second time it did little good. The women at first couldn't believe it, but the dog couldn't tell the direction of a sound. Terry was calling from the loft and the dog went storming into the kitchen, then back through the living room—that was all there was on the ground floor, except the bathroom. When she saw Terry at the loft railing Yuk got a tidbit of bologna and praise, which keyed her up for the next round.

Late in the night Ella and Katherine were talking. Although it was nearly midnight, Katherine had just built up the fire again, and it gratefully filled its cave with flames and soft sound. Outside the weather was cold. The wind seemed like a November wind to two women who had lain naked in the sun that same afternoon. Looking through the flames at a split log, Katherine volunteered:

"Mr. Willoughby says it warms you six times. Did he say six? First when you cut it, then when you haul it home, then when you split it, then when you stack it, and then when you burn it. Is that six?"

Ella smiled and shifted her glance to Katherine for a moment—her rich, ambiguous eyes. What was perhaps most striking in Ella was not even her beauty but the perfect clarity of her eyes, of their three distinct and perfect parts, the clarity and color of her skin and hair, the suppleness, the tone of her body; in short, her physical state, her health; and what they would call in an animal it's "condition"; she was what stockmen call "slick." Within this perfection, like a knife introduced through a natural orifice so there's no bleeding, her ambiguity.

She was sitting on the edge of the desk with her knees toward the hearth, swinging her feet to and fro and letting her heels strike softly on the wood. She was wearing a many-colored plaid skirt and black knee-length socks, and her bare knees glistened in the light. For the past hour, since returning from a diddling expedition with Yuk, she had been wearing Richard's black Navy sweater.

She wasn't smoking. There was an empty cup beside her. In the pocket of her blouse under the Navy sweater she had her husband's letter, folded twice to fit in the little pocket.

Katherine listened to the soft beat of her heels and to the fire. Katherine said quietly, looking almost diffidently at her sister:

"I was stunned today. I don't think that's too strong a word."

"Oh—you were stunned by what?"

"Well . . . by the sun, really."

Ella smiled at that, and Katherine continued:

"I'd never done that before—to lie there just as I am . . . stretch marks and all," she added nervously.

"How did you get those scratches on your thighs?" Ella asked.

"They're nothing. Down by the creek."

"Yes," said Ella, "it's quite a feeling the first time, I agree."

"When you said 'it's quite a feeling'—that doesn't tell how it was."

"No?" Ella's brows lifted and there was a return, perhaps, of some of her irony.

"No—I discovered . . ."

Katherine knew precisely the words she wanted, but searched for others less intimate, and Ella waited with her almost indulgent smile, and her heels still striking the desk ever so gently.

"I discovered a reservoir—of sensuality."

"Well, good, fine. Lucky you."

"And I never before had a sense of the sun as something potent. It seems stupid to talk of the sun as something . . ."

"Something masculine?"

"Yes."

"But it just shows," said Ella, "that our bodies are more alive than we think. If the sun is masculine it must be because we feel so feminine at certain times. Today maybe you felt unusually feminine. You have a right to."

"Didn't you?"

"No, I didn't feel so very sensitive. It was just a pleasant warm half hour for me."

Katherine replied nothing to this, and both seemed to be listening to the fire.

Ella resumed: "Our bodies are alive to other things than men. Mine is sometimes very alive, when I'm nude I mean, to the wind. Didn't you feel it today? There are moments when I'd rather have the wind than your brother. Listen," she continued, without the slightest change of tone, "isn't there some way to break the dog of her habit of killing deer?"

"Yes, there are ways."

"Why don't you break her?"

"Well, it's so complicated," said Katherine. "One way is to put deer guts and what-have-you on an electric fence, and the dog comes along and—"

"Yes," Ella interrupted.

"The other way that I know is with a radio collar. You can buy a special collar with electrodes, and the idea is that you go out walking with the dog till she goes after a deer, then you push the button on this little radio gizmo and it shocks her."

"Lovely."

"I could try one of those but I haven't. I mean why should I? I'm not staying here—for all I know we're going back to Washington and I'll probably have to give up the dog anyway."

"Why should you?"

"Even if I don't, there'll be no deer in Rock Creek Park."

Katherine was suddenly depressed. She went to the kitchen and put on water for tea, and when she came back Ella confronted her with an unusual expression, the ends of her mouth turned down.

"It's all really nothing—it's all nothing—all this wind and sun, and anything you can do by yourself, you know."

"Yes, I suppose it is," Katherine felt compelled to answer.

"It's all no good. I don't mean *evil,* I just mean it's . . . well, it's shitty. It's no help. The more inventive you are, the less good it does."

Katherine turned without a word and went back to stand by the pot till it boiled, with "inventive" in her mind like a piece of ice. She returned with the tea, and Ella said:

"Your brother doesn't love me."

"He might, Ella. I think he does. But he's distracted."

"No."

"He sent you a letter. I know that that alone is nothing, but he was thoughtful, he took the trouble to send it ahead."

"Would you like to read it?"

"No thank you."

"Oh, but you should read it," Ella insisted, reaching up under her sweater and taking the letter out. It looked small, folded as it was. "It's not a request for a divorce or anything, it's just an ordinary letter, a standard letter from your brother. You could read it— there's nothing personal in it. It's two pages long, just like all his letters. He writes pretty often, you know, at least twice a week. The first page is always about what he's been doing, a sort of summary, and the second page is the part on politics, sort of variations on a theme, and the last three or four lines is when he tells me he loves me, how he misses me, how he can't stand being apart, how he'd like to squeeze my ass, all that sort of thing."

Katherine still wouldn't take the letter, and Ella, seeing that she wouldn't, returned it to her blouse pocket.

"My precious letter," she said, placing her hand over it. "There's more love in his letters to you, I'm sure, than to me, although he doesn't love you either, I'm sure."

"Sometimes when I'm writing to Dick," Katherine said, looking keenly at her sister, "I try to tell him how I feel, how I miss him, or something more difficult."

"How you love him," said Ella simply.

"Yes, and I really try. I really think each time all over again that there must be a way, and I always find if I read the last part of the letter there's an insignificant line at the bottom saying 'I miss you' right under something about an insurance bill or the dog or some other domestic thing, and it always strikes me that if he should read the letter at an ordinary speed he'd go right over it. It would seem like I just threw it in for an ending. How can I say I love him? He's been gone for months and I've written I'll bet over a hundred letters, so how can I say it in such a way as to . . ."

"To impress him?" Ella asked, almost cynically.

"No, just to tell him."

Ella declared as if Katherine hadn't spoken: "I'm a widow. No, a widow is one who has no husband. Then I'm the wife of a man who isn't married. It's one of those old-fashioned marriages where the wife is a housekeeper and a piece of meat."

Katherine didn't dare to deny this, fearing she might spur Ella to say, thus to crystallize, more.

Ella said a few seconds later, with her heels knocking, "I don't exist for your brother. I am an unnecessary person." Fully a minute later she said again the single word "Unnecessary," and took up her tea, stirring it with concentration and care, and shook the drops from the spoon.

In the morning Ella seemed rather cheerful. Katherine was in a rush after oversleeping and was hounding Terry relentlessly from one of her morning tasks to another—get up, come down, go to the bathroom, wash, dress, eat, lunch box, coat—and in the midst of this the girl said, as if announcing that today was her birthday: "Aunt Ella's going to take me in her car." Katherine looked and saw that the daybed was indeed empty, and a minute later Ella came out of the bathroom, smiled a rather thick morning smile of greeting to Katherine, and dressed hurriedly so she was ready and standing by the door while Terry was still fighting her rubber boots and listing, for her mother's benefit, the names of all the children who didn't wear them.

As the door closed Katherine went to the window and saw them going down the path through the fog, Ella extending her hand in its black glove and Terry delivering her own bare hand into her aunt's as they hurried into the fog and soon disappeared. On the porch the dog's "antenna ears" still showed Katherine where they were, until she could see the vague yellow headlights through the fog as Ella turned her car around.

By nine o'clock the fog contained so much sunlight it was painful to look out the window, and by midmorning it had thinned away, vanished, and the sky was blue, the air cleansed, and the earth rapidly drying. Ella proposed in the early afternoon that they go again to the old pasture. Katherine wanted to go, and her whole countenance was glowing with the excitement of her inner debate, until she said to Ella: "No—I think yesterday was enough for me"; a decision she found so severe that she could force it on herself only by a kind of violence. Ella turned, said, "OK," when already half across the room, took the blanket and the dog's rope, and left.

Katherine found things to do in the house for about fifteen minutes, but the day outside was far too glorious and her desire was far too strong. Gradually she came to resent even a single square inch of fabric on her body on such a day. She slammed the door of a cabinet, looked out a window again and cursed herself as "some kind of mushroom," and searched the house for an interesting job; but of course it was all housework.

With a release of gaiety that astounded her, she ran down the porch steps and even ran the first several yards down the path, until she came to the turning at the grove of white birches. She stopped in the grove and looked at the sun. It was nearly white, and the day being cloudless, it seemed motionless and therefore perhaps intenser. It was impossible to look at. She closed her eyes, and this white fireball floated and leaped and at once turned bright green against the black of her shut lids.

By the time the sun dots had faded from her retinas she was standing at the edge of the drift considering the "insane" idea of stripping and walking through it. This idea, whose images filled her mind and pleased it very much indeed, she decided to defer. It did seem crazy.

She went around it to the right rather than left, as yesterday, which took her uphill, so she crossed the stream above yesterday's place. Thus as she advanced through the scattered pines of the old pasture chewing on a dead stalk of timothy she was higher than Ella's "oven." This pasture with its pines was like a gigantic chessboard. The trees were separated so each got all the sun it wanted from every angle and thus they grew like huge bushes, both outward and upward; and though many were over twenty-five feet high, they were almost spherical.

She was going a little downhill, at a stroll, chewing the timothy. The top three buttons of her blouse were undone. Her hair, short as it was, felt the effect of the wind.

First she saw the dog at her former place by the poplar tree. On recognizing Katherine, the dog laid back her ears nervously and washed her chops, and showed every sign of having staked her hopes on the remote chance of being released. Katherine thought: "There must be a deer," and turned and quickly scanned all the country she could see behind her, but saw no deer. With another step she saw Ella. Instinctively she looked away, and her eyes fell on the knot on the dog's rope—it was tied in a bow. Katherine was ready to laugh aloud at this dainty knot with its drooping loops—but her laughter was checked by a certain feeling. What feeling? She looked at Ella.

It was fear and it stopped her. She understood slowly—as if registering one element at a time—what she was seeing. Ella's clothing was nowhere in sight. It must be under this or that other tree. She was on her back with her arms over her head, and the fingers of her hands were lightly interlaced and her legs were together, straight, and the feet were extended like a dancer's, and only after watching for a second did Katherine realize that her sister's body was rigid, except for the lightly joined fingers.

This picture of the laced fingers stayed in Katherine's brain wherever she looked, as the burn of the sun had stayed on her retinas. And with these laced fingers in her brain she saw the rest, the tanned rigid body, the gleaming black hair, the navel, the breasts made small and poignant by the attitude of the arms, the swelling thighs, and the black mons. Ella was rolling. The face Katherine had seen in profile was now coming full toward her—empty of expression, eyes closed—but perhaps there was a slight downward curve to the lips. Slowly the left breast was pressed to the blanket and crushed, and Katherine was miserable—not knowing whether to go back or to call out. Then Ella was lying on her stomach; and still the lightly laced fingers were in Katherine's brain as she heard a cry, like "Ah," like a small cry of pain; and the rotation of her sister's body was evidently continuing.

Katherine turned and began walking back, her only thought an urgent hope that Yuk wouldn't give her away. She didn't remember the stream or the birches or path or the porch steps. Only the prosaic interior of the kitchen revived her—the sink, the faucet which through habit she pushed to be sure it wouldn't drip—there was a carving knife and a roll of aluminum foil.

She couldn't escape the thought that she had witnessed something terrible. Yet she argued:

"Good heavens, I've done worse myself, and look at me, I'm all right. I kissed a tree—I put my breast against it—"

And she recalled how as an adolescent girl she had embraced a tree, kissed it, put her leg around it, and later lain on the ground and licked a stone. She remembered all this without shame, and would even have told Richard about it. She thought, going still further: "I might even do such a thing today."

But the idea that Ella's rolling was terrible, was desolate, had seized her imagination. The laced fingers kept turning in her brain.

She exclaimed: "Good lord! She was just making love to herself —she was just *thinking* to herself some . . . some damned thing!" Katherine concluded in anger. But this too was unavailing.

"She was consoling herself—what's so horrible? What's so tragic? Haven't I done worse?"

Yet Katherine seemed to hear Ella sobbing, and wished she could offer comfort.

"There's nothing I can do—I can't help her—I can't help you— dear god, Ella, please don't *roll* like that."

In the empty face, in the closed eyes—in the waxen face, like a face in a wax museum, Katherine no longer saw "ambiguity" but desolation.

"Dear god, she's desolate—and why shouldn't she cry? If she has any feeling left she'll surely cry."

And it seemed that Katherine took Ella's "perfect" head to her breast as Ella had taken Katherine's in Washington, and pleaded with her, patting her back and her shoulders awkwardly. "Don't cry, Ella, please."

To which the answer was "I am unnecessary."

IX

Ashley did the company commander's thinking for him. Besides being a platoon leader, Ashley was company executive officer, and as such he solved problems that Dip-Shit never knew he had.

After a "walk in the sun" in the morning the company came late in the afternoon to an old French fort at the bend of a river. As he started to lay out the position for the night Ashley found a dozen or so craters inside the perimeter, which accorded with expectation, since a marine company spending the previous night here had reported being attacked by mortars. But the craters didn't look as fresh as they should. This went unresolved into Ashley's mind.

He deployed the troops, walking with the other platoon leaders through the ankle-deep grass along the parapet, while the company commander established himself in the pillbox. The fort had but one, whose iron reinforcing rods were coming through and streaking the concrete with rust. Its position in the layout of the place seemed ill considered; that is to say, it was not placed for maximum effect in defense. But the French had been expert in fortification, so Ashley had two problems. Why had they put the pillbox where it was? Were the craters he had seen last night's craters?

He slightly revised his defense, placing an outpost at the edge of a grove outside the perimeter.

The trenches and parapets were overgrown. Amid their luxuriant green were thick dark clusters where deposits of manure from grazing animals had fertilized the grass. Two hundred yards outside the perimeter at the bottom of a slope there was a bridge, half in the river. The whole place was like a virgin archeological site.

By a stroke of imagination Ashley took away the thicket of young trees where he'd placed the outpost and saw that before these trees grew up the pillbox had overlooked the bridge, and thus had been situated both to defend the fort and to provide covering fire for the bridge guards. Solving this enigma was no great feat, but it didn't ruin his day either.

When the defense was arranged he returned, still curious, to the craters. On second look they seemed fresher. He had now to show the company commander the defense lines, which he did, and got approval; then he returned and stared into a crater as if perseverance would make it speak. He decided these couldn't be last night's craters. He collected three men who were cantoning themselves elaborately in an old strongpoint and set off in search of fresh craters.

They jumped over a trench, climbed a parapet, and went out in a line abreast into a field of blowing grass asprout with anti-helicopter poles six feet tall. On the first sweep across this field they located a new crater, and within fifteen minutes they had traced a fair outline of the beaten zone of last night's mortar attack. The craters in some cases were as perfect as textbook illustrations.

He went from one to another observing how little, how very little, they were disintegrated—and he looked around at the circling jungle, at the parapet, behind which he could hear the mutual abuse of the troopers, and at a high hill of jungle that rose to the north. The breeze and sun were benign.

He strode back to the fort, forgetting entirely about the three men who still waited upon him, shouted for his platoon sergeant even as he mounted the parapet, allowed the steepness of the inner slope to run him down inside the fort, and shouted again, something he was seldom inhibited about doing. The sergeant met him near the center and received these orders: to assemble about thirty men and to stand one man beside (not in) each of the craters in the two sets. The sergeant was slowly convinced that this order was literal and plain, and set about it.

Ashley put his foot in a firing port and climbed to the top of the pillbox, where he managed with difficulty to let the sergeant do the thing at his own speed, and neither shouted nor waved his arm at the sergeant but stood in silence with folded arms while the men were placed, while they shouted at one another, struck poses, slouched, and spat. Ashley took off his helmet, revealing drenched hair and a pale forehead. The rest of his face and the back of his neck were sunburned, the short blond hair on his neck was bleached by the sun, and his forearms and hands were nearly brown.

His eyes kept shifting from one group to the other. What he expected to find and did find, although it was constructed piece by piece, seemed to emerge all in a moment, as if a man who was color-blind in one eye were looking at a page of meaningless gray dots and upon opening his good eye found the numeral 7 stretching in red across the page.

What emerged was a similarity between the two beaten zones. If he disregarded three of the men in the group to his left, the older group (which men could represent adjusting rounds or erratics), the two groups had the same egg-shaped outline and approximately the same size and density; both had a concentration of rounds in the lower left quadrant, and both contained fourteen rounds.

He threw up his hands, shouting a dismissal to the sergeant, and jumped from the pillbox with a strange, sailing grace which made his pistol stand straight out at his side. He went to find Gunnery Sergeant Boyle. Ashley was never anything but courteous to experts. Gunnery Sergeant Boyle, the artillery FO, a man who did only what was necessary, accepted a thing as necessary either when it was or when a person of superior rank couldn't be convinced it wasn't. A short time later he was standing at one of the craters and appraising it, as if he were considering buying it. He sent his radioman to the woods to cut several long and short sticks, then asked Ashley:

"Is this the only one?"

Ashley showed him the others, at each of which the gunny paused, as in a used car lot, then glanced at the lieutenant. When he had seen all fourteen, he said, "They're 82s."

One of the three men Ashley had left behind came up with a tail-fin assembly he'd found in the grass. The gunny took it, looked at it for two seconds, and commented as if it were the most worthless piece of trash: "Made in the Gobi Desert by underpaid coolies."

He lay down on his chest with middle-aged reluctance and began rooting in the bottom of a crater with his hands. He reached back with a grunt for his sheath knife, which he began passing into the earth at an angle all over the bottom of the crater. Abandoning this effort, he got up stiffly, with a glance at Ashley, and went to another crater and did the same, this time producing from the hole a thing to which he seemed utterly indifferent, which he held up to Ashley without even looking at him. It was the fuse of an 82-mm mortar round.

The two men conversed in brief and infrequent phrases, squatting, with hands folded, scanning the wall of jungle some two hundred yards away, waiting for the gunny's radioman. Ashley asked the gunny if he could ascertain whether one or more tubes had done the firing, to which the gunny responded by asking what time frame had been involved, and when Ashley said he didn't know, the gunny confined himself to the observation that it was a tight pattern. When the radioman appeared Gunnery Sergeant Boyle went out to meet him, got the sticks, and went straight to a crater on the far side of the beaten zone, with Ashley following.

Gunnery Sergeant Boyle stood over the crater—watching as if it might try to escape. After nearly a minute, apparently making a careful choice, he squatted down and laid one of his long sticks in one of the radial grooves on the rim. These grooves—radials, striations, or splinter grooves, as they're called—had been cut in the ground by fragments of the exploding projectile, but their place of origin, the point of detonation, had been lost in the explosion. Choosing another of the sharpest grooves, Gunnery Sergeant Boyle laid another stick in it, and slowly pushed it toward the center until it crossed the first. He did this also with a third groove. Thus he reconstructed (by extending them backward) three rays, and found their origin, which was also the point of detonation, and not quite the center of the crater. He drove in a short stick as a marker here, cleared away the ray sticks, and went down on his belly.

With gentle hands he took away the loose dirt from the base of the upright stick, uncovering gradually a hardened and burned inner crater like a clay vessel; at the edge of which, after some probing, he found the fuse. He carefully removed this, keeping a finger in the fuse tunnel, and let it be known that he wanted another short stick, which the radioman would have picked up and handed him had not John Ashley done so first. The gunny drove this stick into the deepest part of the fuse tunnel, the fuse well, rose to his knees, and looked at his work with a poker face. He pulled at his nose, dirtying it, and looked at the two upright sticks for a few moments more, apparently less in inquiry than appreciation. He got up one leg at a time, with his customary glance at Lieutenant Ashley, and went to the other side of the crater, which in fact was its front, and with extraordinary carefulness took a compass reading of the line described by the two sticks. He wrote this in his notebook and then yanked up the sticks, obliterating the fuse well, and set off without a word for another crater, Ashley and the radioman following with the extra sticks.

The gunny did at the second crater what he'd done at the first, but a little faster, and proceeded to a third. Here, instead of locating the point of detonation and the fuse well, he simply took the longest of his sticks, circumnambulated and studied the crater, and laid it across. The stick was so placed as to divide the crater into halves; it ran from the front, which had a built-up and definitely undercut rim, to the back, which had a rather lowered rim, from which most of the radial grooves shot out. After a fine adjustment of the stick the gunny took its compass reading from front to back.

He did some arithmetic in his notebook, obtaining the average of his three compass readings, which was the average back azimuth of the lines of flight, and announced the result to Ashley, who scrawled huge hasty figures in red across his map: 6300. He also wrote the reciprocal: 3100.

The effect of these numbers on Ashley was such that his hands were trembling when five minutes later, with his map spread on the floor of the pillbox, the only smooth surface he could find, he placed the base of a protractor at the beaten zone and picked off the direction 6300. He was painfully aware of how much ground difference the slightest map error would mean. Each unit of map error in fact was multiplied by a factor of fifty thousand on the ground. After marking the angle once, therefore, with the redundancy that had often driven his sister wild he whittled the end of his grease pencil to as fine a point as it could take and again marked the angle (breaking the point), and checked everything again before aligning a straightedge and carefully pulling a faint red line from the beaten zone northward on a bearing of 6300 mils magnetic, for a distance somewhat exceeding the maximum range of an 82-mm mortar—that is, for a little more than three thousand meters.

The company commander asked, "What the hell are you doing?"

"I'm drawing a line . . ." replied Ashley as he drew it; and although his tone implied more to come, he said nothing further, but only bent over the map, a drop of his perspiration falling on its transparent cover.

The company commander knew that Ashley thought he was lazy. He knew Ashley called him Dip-Shit. He justified himself by saying to himself that all he intended or wanted to do was minimize casualties. He understood that General Westmoreland had been appointed because he had a general's jaw and a trial lawyer's eyebrows. He knew that he, Dip-Shit, did not understand the war, and knew that this was more than Westmoreland knew.

He went outside and screamed at someone about digging a 1-2-3 trench. He seemed to have to defecate more or less always. He came back in, sat cross-legged on the cement beside Ashley, and looked at the map, wondering what this prick was up to. He was a short-timer and thus inclined to be cautious, but he was also inclined to let Ashley have his way.

Ashley studied the map by the light of three candles. When he closed his eyes the red line of the mortar trajectory ran from the fort north over the two-peaked mountain, down its gentle northern slope and across a belt of low woody growth, and into a square kilometer of rice fields, where it ended without quite reaching the hamlet where Ashley assumed the mortarmen lived, or were based. His effort was first to memorize his route to the rice field by rote recitation of turnings and night landmarks, and second to print in his mind a representation of the map.

His plans assumed that the mortar crew were irregulars living in the hamlet, which was the only one nearby; that they were incompetently led; that once having fired-in the concentration they were still using the same data and aiming stakes; that their firing position was not very far up the mountainside, since they could reach their target from the bottom by firing over the mountain; and that their tube, baseplate, and bipod, and perhaps ammunition, were cached near the firing point. All this might be completely wrong, but none of it was outrageous.

He left the fort at midnight with a force of two rifle squads and a machine-gun section.

Twice as this force descended the trail toward the ruined bridge the word was passed from the point to the rear with perfect fidelity: "The lieutenant says quiet"; and as each man said these words over his shoulder there was a remarkable absence of mockery. As each man received and spoke this simple instruction he was bound by its unsuspected power to all the others, and the effect on all the men was a lessening of hunger, thirst, and selfishness.

At the bottom of the trail Ashley paused. The rapids of the river revealed themselves in the moonlight under the shining girders. He allowed time for readjustment of the interval in the column (he ordered a three-meter interval) and for the men to effect those corrections to their gear and clothing which often seem requisite after the start of a march. He took the turning to the left. This put him on a trail running generally north, with the river on his right, the trail going upstream.

It was a wide trail but not wide enough for a formation of two columns. It was quite dry, so it reflected moonlight. It made for easy walking, which could have been rapid as well, but Ashley was concerned less with speed than with quiet, and so instructed his scout. The river was the An Lao. He knew Vail had been in this valley and imagined he might now be walking where Vail had walked; not that he cared. The trail veered slowly away from the river, and having lost the river on his right, he now gained on his left the high dark dominance of the mountain. The pace was regular, the moonlight continued adequate, and Ashley was once again realizing a dream, realizing himself. The disfigured angel of "contact" was going to touch him. Maybe.

When he rested the troops he did not rest. He walked down the line with his thumb hooked in the sling of his rifle, looking slowly at each dim and quiet form. He talked with the squad leaders and the machine-gun crew chiefs and to several of the men, including the medical corpsman, whose lips were swollen with fever blisters. His lips in the darkness seemed all the larger to Ashley as he asked:

"Do you know we got a sick man, Lieutenant?"

"No. What are you talking about?"

"There's a man sick."

"Sick with what?"

The corpsman said, "Dysentery."

Ashley was enraged. He located the platoon sergeant. The corpsman, sergeant, and officer went to the place beside the trail where the sick man was lying on his back with his hands held over his chest, as if someone had just taken a book away from him.

"What in the hell is this?" said Ashley to the platoon sergeant.

"Oh, he'll be OK, sir, he's just—"

"How the hell do *you* know he'll be OK?"

"Well, he's just got the shits."

Ashley crouched beside the man and perceived with disgust that he had shat himself, and asked: "Did you skip any malaria pills?"

"No, sir." The voice was long in coming and hardly audible.

"How do you feel?"

"Bad, sir," said the man.

Ashley stayed crouched in silence for a moment, cursing the platoon sergeant for including the sick man in the patrol.

"Can you keep walking?"

"Well, I don't know, sir . . ."

Ashley said, "You don't have any choice. Get up." And standing up himself, he said to the corpsman, "Give him a pill or something, Doc," and to the platoon sergeant: "If he can't walk, Sergeant, you carry him."

Ashley's intention, which he achieved while there were still two and a half hours of darkness remaining, was to throw the line of his force across the line of the mortar trajectory, making a figure T, with the trajectory forming the vertical and his troopline the horizontal member.

If the mortar crew fired during the last moments of darkness and then sought to return to the hamlet they would have to cross Ashley's line. If they fired shortly after daylight and then sought to disperse among the laborers from the hamlet, who would have filled the fields by then, they would still have to cross the line. And if there had been no firing by about seven o'clock Ashley could sweep the trajectory line and perhaps by luck find their cache.

In fact, Ashley had very little hope. He could easily have slept. But the night passed with that rapidity which teaches us what a profound value our minds place on such nights, as on few others; the rapidity of precious time. So when the idea of sleeping finally occurred to him it already seemed pointless.

He was near the center of his formation, exactly on the line of the mortar trajectory as drawn on his map; but when he arranged a poncho and ducked under it to shine his flashlight on the map, the line was invisible, because the red light of the flashlight (which is less damaging to night vision than white light) obliterated all the red marks on the map. He knew where the line was anyway; and the next time he consulted the map he had no need of a flashlight.

The wind was favorable. It was blowing lightly in his face from the direction of the mountain. Behind him in the open the sunlight had begun its soft painting of the rice fields, and beyond these the smoke of morning was lifting through the treetops of the village. On either side of him the lines of his force extended out like exaggerated arms. The laborers were already coming into the fields. Ashley sent a man crawling to the left, who returned presently with the information that the sick man was no better and his squad leader didn't know whether he could walk or not. When the laborers had entered the fields in numbers and their voices could be heard coming faintly up the wind, Ashley gave the order to prepare to advance.

This order reached the sick man as a bolt of insane cruelty. He got to his hands and knees with a freakish pain in his forehead and stared at his blurring rifle. "Take care of your weapon and your weapon will take care of you." He was disintegrating through his mouth and his anus. He had always known the day would come when he'd be incapacitated and the corps would demand that he stand up and walk, run, dig, stoop, aim and fire, or "close with the enemy."

Ashley was reluctant to give the order that meant abandoning hope of contact, but after waiting several minutes with the new sunlight shining hotly down on him where he sat, and after deciding that further delay and hope were unjustified, he gave the order and the line rose out of the sharp-bladed grass. They advanced in a line abreast. The ground here was level but the vegetation deepened, and not far ahead lay the beginning of the rise which was the slope of the mountain. In imagination he saw the baseplate of the enemy's mortar buried under two inches of loam and leaves. The sunlight was on his left cheek, the breeze in his eyes. Walking was less difficult than usual because his trousers weren't soaked with perspiration.

Four places to the right and sinking deeper into the grass with every step he saw a certain Lance Corporal Freeman with raised rifle, and wished he possessed the power to make him platoon sergeant; and not far to the left he could see the sick man staggering along.

The right wing was fast, and he slowed it with an arm signal just as they entered thicker vegetation which made each man an individ-

ual. It grew in tiers, with a tier of red-skinned vines to clog the
footing and a tier of heavy brush with waxen leaves to smother the
chest and a higher tier of small treetops to blind the eyes. The next
shift of vegetation would doubtless be to the impenetrable, since the
ground was rising. The idea of impenetrable vegetation was one
Ashley could never accept until he met the reality.

One step farther and he found himself on a trail. It was like a
bored conduit. It was so low and small it was like a trail for chimpan-
zees. He stooped down and followed it, which took him but little
off his direction. Something about this trail, its secretness, disturbed
and thrilled him. The sunlight was coming down in scattered shafts
through the entanglement. Looking back, he saw his radioman bent
double and holding the end of his antenna downward, while behind
the radioman he saw the medical corpsman with face thrusting and
mouth wide open.

At this moment came a sound of a kind so commonplace in his
experience that the first fraction of his response was to ignore it.
Moreover, it was just the sound he had given up all hope of hearing
—the sound he was dying for: a chopped report with that quality of
nasalness identifying a mortar. And while this sound is never very
loud, it seemed so close that his sinuses pulsed under his eyes with
the report. Rather than going faster, everything suddenly went
slower. His brain was rather infertile.

He fully understood that he had the advantage of knowing how
many rounds the enemy would fire, but if this was an advantage he
made no use of it.

He made no use of anything. He watched as the corpsman drew
his pistol. Ashley was terrified, with his inhalation of death in the air
like a gas, and he turned to face the empty trail in front of him, but
the second report came and brought a sudden end to his terror. The
enemy could put six or eight rounds in the air before the first landed,
and upon the second report Ashley reached back his hand. His
radioman came forward holding out the handset, but instead of this
Ashley turned and grasped the man's wrist and drew him close with
an intense force and whispered in his ear: "Tell the company . . ."

The man's face was completely transformed. He asked: "What?"

"They're going to be hit—quick."

Command and control. Fire and maneuver. "The commander
influences the course of the engagement through fire and maneu-

ver." But Ashley had as yet nothing to fire at, and he couldn't maneuver his troops without shouting. It was intoxicating chaos. He felt that he'd breathed it only a moment earlier, although it had been a month since his last contact. The same intoxicant gas was in his lungs. He released the safety on his weapon and set the selector on automatic (the word AUTO engraved in his eyes) and walked. He forgot to count the reports. He smelled the burned powder and walked into the smell.

He was taken by his shirt from behind.

"Sir, the company says—"

Whatever the company had to say couldn't possibly interest Ashley. He jerked loose of the man's grasp and left the trail by a screw tree, following, as he thought, the scent of the powder, and in a short moment following also, although he could hardly believe it, a voice.

"Ong, bok, dok, yak, bao . . ."

The smell of burned powder was a smell of his boyhood, and this voice blended ill with it.

When the mortar began firing it did not divert the sick man. His body was dehydrated and diseased, he had vomited all his water, his eyes functioned painfully through the salt, but he altered neither his direction nor his pace, but continued through the foliage, wanting only one thing: to fall, so he could lie on the ground with a clear conscience. He came to the trail and crossed it, glimpsing a fellow marine as he did so. He heard an automatic weapon firing, and still he kept walking. The noise was monstrously loud in his head. The sick man was wretched but he kept walking, understanding as never before the cruelty of what he heard. But the stooping through the bushes was worse than the noise.

Quite to his surprise, he suddenly stood at the edge of a little clearing with brush piles here and there, and saw a man in a black shirt and shorts on the other side, raising a short weapon. The sick man observed the backward slant of the cylinder at the gas port of this foreign weapon. The thing spat at him as if he were a stone in a quarry and this the drill. He was no stone. He was a sensing creature. The earth struck him sidelong, but having struck him such a painful blow, it now tabled him, and he gathered comfort from shock. After a gap he discovered how good it feels to stop trying.

Nothing amazed him because his mind was in an accepting mode. The clearing was turning, and he accepted even this. He accepted the blow the earth had struck. Lieutenant Ashley was firing with his weapon at his shoulder and all his teeth exposed, and his firing brought forth a gook scream (it couldn't have been an actual word but it was surely a gook sound); then Lieutenant Ashley, too, screamed, ordering the right wing to wheel, and perhaps the sick man's hearing was turned like his vision, for the lieutenant's voice seemed twisted, it seemed mad.

In a perspective of blood and salt the sick man saw Lieutenant Ashley drop to his knees and fire a burst of that hideous invisible stuff along the ground, while a black object sailed through the turning air from the gooks. The object, which the sick man recognized by rote as a grenade, hit the lieutenant on the shoulder, which surely hurt his bone. It bounced, and the lieutenant took no notice but fired again from a low and hardened body, while the sick man waited for the explosion; but it didn't explode. The lieutenant was up and in the center, firing and shouting or screaming, and then looking around with glutted eyes and firing another burst. At what? The lieutenant approached. It was his eyes the sick man stared at, but even these couldn't amaze him.

X

"All right, all right, god damn it, I'll *tell* her," said Vail as if some third party were nagging him. "But it's meaningless, there's no point in doing it, she'll think I'm bananas. What am I supposed to say, for Christ's sake? Am I supposed to write a special letter, devoted entirely to this terrible crime? Jesus *God!* 'Dear Kit—Prepare yourself. Don't read this standing up. I shot a fucking chicken!' Then once I say that, I obviously have to say it was weeks ago, months ago, it seems like years ago. First, murdered a chicken. Second, concealed the murder. My god, if I write a letter like that she'll divorce me. Anyway, I don't have time."

He looked at his watch and saw that he had about twenty minutes, time enough to open his footlocker, take out his tablet, write a letter and address an envelope, and leave it on the mosquito net above Captain Werthim's cot. The captain would mail it four days later, as he always mailed the letters Vail left behind when he went out on a "war." In short, he did have time.

He spread a rag out on his footlocker. He field-stripped his pistol, cleaned the grooves with a toothbrush, and wiped and sprayed the parts. He refrained from any articulated comment connecting his pistol and the chicken, and by so refraining confessed that same connection. "OK," he said, "this is the very gun." He started putting it back together and looked up in surprise.

"I can't tell her now," he exclaimed, "not after she sent this." And he touched his shirt pocket. In this pocket he kept—wrapped in a waterproof battery envelope—her latest letter. In his private vocabulary it was The Letter.

"She wrote me this," he thought, "and am I going to answer with some bullshit about a chicken?"

He cocked the pistol, held it next to his ear, and squeezed the trigger. Between the start of his squeeze and the snap of the hammer he could clearly hear the faint grinding of sand in the mechanism— to which he said: "Nothing's perfect." Someday he'd take it to an armorer for a real cleaning. He slapped in a loaded magazine and holstered the pistol, and touched his shirt pocket.

"A harelip, a harelip, a harelip," he thought. He had seen a young man who wobbled around An Tan, who had an awful harelip. The question was, do the lucky really know themselves? The afflicted do, because their afflictions "help" in forming the identity. But the lucky are turned loose.

Vail never thought of himself as good-looking, but he couldn't help knowing about his body—that it was good. It could regenerate itself, and had; he was stronger than ever. Being strong, he had a weak grasp of death. He classified it as a fact. He declared it to be inevitable. He could conceptualize, but he could not feel death— except rarely, as after the ambush, and then it faded.

He answered religious questions with the words: "I am going to die." He recognized too that Katherine was going to die. He had not yet applied the thought to Terry. From the fact of death he took, from this source he derived, all the value of life. Some men value their lives according to God's love, the measure of which is that he won't let them die. Vail and his wife valued their lives according to their conviction that they would die. If they faced death, they believed, they could face life. If you face it, you can value it. If you don't, you can't.

But when he saw the harelip, a wretched, wretched young man who also had a problem standing still, Vail thought it all through again.

He was healthy, strong, unafflicted. He lacked an affliction to focus his thoughts from time to time on death. In fact, his knowledge of death was only an abstraction. He didn't feel it the way he felt love, fear, or hunger. So—did he really know what he was doing? Did he secretly reject death, deny it?

"Nothing's perfect," he thought as he pulled out his "field marching pack." It had been under his cot, completely ready. He unstrapped it anyway and checked the contents, thinking:

"I forgot about it. It's as simple as that. And even if I had remembered I still wouldn't have mentioned it because it's meaningless, which is exactly the reason I forgot it. And don't tell me 'nothing is meaningless.' There are continua in Nature, like the spectrum, like irrational numbers, and somewhere at one end of some continuum there is something that doesn't mean a god damn thing. Like shooting a chicken. Jesus, will you let it alone? Anyway, I don't have time." He saw that he had ten minutes.

He opened the footlocker with the intention of putting away his pistol-cleaning implements, which he did, but he also took out his writing tablet, closed the locker and sat down on it, and opened the tablet on his knees—and wrote: "Dear Kit."

"What next?" he said.

He smoothed out the surface of the tablet and thought: "This might upset her. She's probably reading all kinds of crap about combat fatigue or shell shock or whatever they're calling it this time—"

There was something uneven under his hand. He smoothed the tablet again and encountered it again—something under the paper. Evidently he hadn't noticed it when the tablet had been thicker, but as he used the pages it came closer and closer to the surface. He lifted the pages and found, stuck between the last page and the cardboard backing, a folded sheet of newspaper. At first it meant absolutely nothing to him.

But as he unfolded it he began to feel a faint recollection—maybe he had put it here weeks ago, weeks or months.

It was a sheet of the *Pacific Stars & Stripes,* and he remembered that he'd written something on it, going right across the page, across pictures and headlines alike, with a ballpoint pen. He could see the lines running over the white spaces, but couldn't follow them through the heavy ink of the headlines and the darker portions of the pictures, so he got up and went to the door and tilted the page to the direct sunlight. He remembered that while writing he had wondered whether his "letter" would be legible.

The chief medical corpsman was going past the tent with the night's rat catch brimming over a bucket.

The chief saluted and said, "Good morning, Mr. Vail."

"Good morning, Chief. Got yourself some rats."

"Yes, sir."

Vail tilted the page and with difficulty but a rushing sense of recognition read:

"Dear Katherine—I am with two battalions of the Vietnamese Marine Corps. We spent last night on high ground where there was no water and as soon as we came down here—we are in a village—everyone started looking for water. I was filling my canteens at the well when I heard a terrific squealing. Some of the Vietnamese were chasing a pig between the houses. They cornered it against a house and caught it. One man cut its throat but it didn't bleed much, only a trickle, and another, while a man held it down, tramped on it with his heel. He was trying to crush its skull but he crushed its snout. All the while the squealing. They couldn't kill it so they began to butcher it alive because others were rushing up. The man who had stamped on the snout held on to a hoof and cut off a hind leg and hip. The pig's eyes had been bulging and mostly white, with very little black, but all at once they seemed almost normal, all black, and it watched the man take off its hindquarter."

He had run out of space. There was an arrow, and turning the sheet over, Vail read: "This happened in the village of Dong Tien on the morning of 25 May 1966."

He quickly folded the sheet of newspaper, addressed an envelope to his wife, inserted the "letter," sealed it, and lay it on top of the mosquito net at Captain Wertheim's cot. Then after filling his canteens from a jerry can at the door of the tent, and putting on his pistol belt, helmet, and pack, and grabbing his binoculars, he went hurriedly down the road between the rows of tents to a place where a jeep was waiting for him.

Mo Duc hill was a fine and lofty place for the flies. It was perhaps the only cone-shaped cesspool for many miles in any direction. The ARVN had built a latrine of bamboo webbing, with a tin roof upon which the rain played, and inside a sort of a trapdoor in the middle with a small hole exactly in its center. People got sick frequently, at both ends. Nobody really tried to hit the hole. The man who wasn't alert could discover, at night or even in broad daylight, that what he was walking in wasn't mud. The flies walked in the same thing before visiting the men at their meals.

But there was beauty to the east. The sea lay six kilometers away, across a verdant, fertile, poignant belt of rice paddies and villages —the villages visible from the hill as dark green ornaments scattered across the paddyland. Beyond the paddies and villages, lying like a parapet-wall along the coast, was a low, linear hill sheltering the plain from the sea.

And beauty to the west. A curving green mountain range, with its opening toward Mo Duc hill, sheltered another fertile plain with yet more dark green ornaments.

These are the names of the villages:

Van Ha

Lam Ha

Dam Thuy

Lam Thuong

Don Luong

Phuoc An

Phuoc Hoa

Phuoc Vinh

My Hung

Phuoc Thuan

They aren't famous. They are only some of the villages east and west of the hill. Like Mo Duc itself, which looks natural enough from a distance, the villages were less appealing at closer range. All were fortified by the VC.

When Vail arrived on the hill he didn't pay much attention to the trench circling the pinnacle, which his predecessor had said no sane man would take shelter in; or to the bunker, or the revetted howitzer positions. What Vail noticed was that the hill was a safe place, and this made him feel depressed, almost sick.

Why was it sickening? Because of a simple device dimly understood by Vail. It is a needle. If you are in a safe place—selecting targets, deciding which weapons and which fuses to employ, assigning the units to do the firing—if you are doing all this, if you are part of the "process," and safe, the needle will reach you. It will reach your spine, reach up into your bowels, into your nose, ears, eyes, and heart. It will go up a big vein in your leg. But the needle is only so long. You can escape it by going forward into combat. That was why safety was torment and combat was relief. It wasn't that Vail loved danger.

He threw his pack and helmet into a crawlway and went in search of the Army major he'd been told to report to. The crawlway was a two-foot space between the dirt top of an ARVN bunker and an aluminum roof designed to prevent the rain from dumping the

bunker on its inhabitants. The Army major was a U.S. "adviser" to
the ARVN. Vail had never met him.

Vail wandered around—past a flagpole and two slit-entrances to
the underground bunkers, and past the marine operations liaison
team (Vail and his four troopers were the supporting arms team)—
and looked down the slope into a cemetery where a Vietnamese woman was worshipping her ancestors by emptying her bowels.
Still wandering, more or less, he found a place to which he laid a
subtle kind of claim, and told his team to erect an antenna. While
this was being done Vail saw and saluted a U.S. Army major,
a shaggy scarecrow of a man whose named turned out to be
Perkins.

"Hey, Mr. Two Six," said Major Perkins.

The major asked Vail if he wanted to come to the pinnacle for a
second, so they started to wend their way through the guy wires and
antenna poles at the end of the aluminum roof. But they stopped,
almost together, when Major Perkins saw the ship.

She was gray and her mast was raked back. She made very little
smoke. She was almost motionless.

"Well . . . so . . . that's yours?" Major Perkins asked.

Vail said she was his. The two men stared as at an icon.

The line of her deck from this distance appeared to be in the water
at her stern, but it rose as it went forward toward the lifted bow.
Thus the form of the hull was a rising flying form, as suitable in its
way as the wing of a bird, and the impression was not of power but
of ease. Her superstructure, gun mounts, and raked mast didn't hurt
this impression. She was all grace and she led a self-sufficient existence.

"Well—can you come around this way for a sec?"

"Yes, sir."

They left Vail's "place" at the edge of the aluminum roof, where
Richie Rood was decrypting the ship's ammunition report and the
other three men were plucking and tightening down the guys, and
walked around the end of the bunker, partway up the slope to the
pinnacle. The major stopped and held out his black-haired hand
tentatively, indicating that his subject lay on the plain, but the words
weren't quite ready.

"Uh . . ."

With his dishevelment, abstraction, and caved-in physique he looked like an underpaid high school teacher who has just been assigned to coach the basketball team.

"Ah—you see right out there . . ."

His hand dropped and he said, "Shit," and unfolded a map, which he studied carefully, then referred again to the outspread plain.

"You see that vill . . . that, uh, Phuoc Luong?"

"No, sir."

"Well—to the right of the paddies in the middle, sort of. Coordinates . . ."

He bent to his map, read off the coordinates, and then glanced with patient brown eyes at Vail. In a few moments they were looking at the same village.

"Now do you see the church? You see the steeple?"

"Yes, I see it."

"OK, that's what I want you to see, is the steeple. You see the white steeple. Will you blow it down for me?"

"I could," said Vail, "but haven't you got a nice orphanage or hospital?"

"Well, you bastard!" exclaimed Major Perkins, as if they'd known each other for years, which indeed Vail almost felt they had. "Listen, I'm a Catholic, I guarantee I wouldn't ask you to blow down a real church, but that's all VC out there. They use that as an OP, you know. Every time the Arvin go anywhere out there Charlie has a guy up in the steeple who sees our people coming and puts out the word, and they adjust their mortar fire from up there and they ding at us whenever they please. Ding-ding-ding, some little bastard up there in the steeple."

Vail uncased his glasses and focused on the church. The glasses seemed to collect light and the church shone brilliantly in the dark green of the village canopy. Vail could see its peaked front, red tile roof, and white steeple.

The major watched Vail—watched him take away the glasses and squint and study, saw the negativism in his sunburned, more-than-equal face.

"Sir, I might expend thirty or forty rounds on that damn thing and never—"

"OK, OK."

"I could knock it down eventually, sir, but I'd hate to spend my ammo that way."

"Yes, Dick, OK, that's all right."

If Major Perkins was disappointed he smothered it in the energy of his dismissal of the subject, saying "No problem" and "No big thing" again and again as they were walking back—so often that Vail felt awkward.

They came down the slope, and as they passed under the guy lines Vail let the major precede him, so the major was first in rounding the end of the bunker.

And he stopped there so abruptly that Vail bumped him.

"Ick—holy Jesus, look at that thing now. It looks like the mechanical monster."

Vail looked and saw that the ship had moved so close to the beach that its hull and gun mounts were cut off from view by the linear hill. Only the superstructure and radars projected over the hill. The black-topped funnels were scarcely smoking. The polyglot modular superstructure and spiny top-hamper seemed to be waiting, not quite lifelessly, not quite blindly.

"Hey, Dick, I've got a hell of a target. I've got a lucrative—hey, Dick."

Major Perkins was speaking even as he emerged head and shoulders from a narrow slit in the earth which was the entrance to the bunker, whence a weak light came.

The major's sharp flashlight beam began probing.

Shutting his eyes against the light, Vail said: "Here I am, sir."

He heard the major's boots on the sandbag stairway and saw the swinging feet traversing the stony ground in the flashlight beam.

"Right here, sir."

The beam swung up and hit his eyes. He closed it out.

Major Perkins saw Vail sitting on a wooden box beside his radio operator, with a plastic-sheeted map spread over his knees, eyes closed patiently—no hat or helmet, a cigarette burning in one hand.

Major Perkins said, "The Harelip has got us one hell of a target."

"The Harelip?"

"Yes—he's an Arvin spook. He mixes right in. The VC think he's a peasant and the peasants think he's a VC."

"Is he a real harelip? He doesn't happen to walk with a sort of a wobble, does he?"

"Hell no—I mean I don't know. What difference does it make?"

"None."

" 'Harelip' is just his call sign. Maybe he is a real harelip, for all I know. Shit, I never saw him."

"Yes, sir. What's the target?"

Vail shone his red flashlight on his map, and Major Perkins squatted down and his long, slender red finger went directly to a place and tapped it thrice.

"Right there. Six eight four—five four eight. Right in these three or four little hooches."

"Yes, sir, that'll be fine for my range dispersion. What's the nature of the target?"

"Just a company—just an entire god blessed company, is all."

Vail put out the light.

"An entire company?"

"You bet your ass. The Harelip says they're asleep, all but three men on watch. He says they're not dug in, they're just in these flimsy little hooches. He says they're sleeping in the hooches and all over the yards on banana leaves, like cordwood. He says they just ate."

"He said 'cordwood'?"

"Hell no, I said that. He doesn't speak English. I said he was an Arvin."

"Yes, sir. Is this Harelip a liar?"

"He's no worse a liar than anybody else."

They were silent, and Major Perkins wondered why Vail was hesitating.

Vail again examined the map in the red glow. There were four houses at the foot of a gentle slope, facing the edge of a paddy field. It was quite a typical cluster of dwellings, such as he had often seen, smelled, and slept in himself. Particularly, the banana leaves summoned up a night when he had slept on a dozen of these beside a house; and the H&Is which he had programmed awakened a baby and made it cry. He remembered how providential it had seemed in the next day's rain that they could sit in the doorway and put the antenna right through the straw roof without causing a leak.

Major Perkins said, "I have no reason to think he's a liar. Maybe he's exaggerating a little bit. Major Lich seems to trust him."

"Are you in communication with him?"

"Intermittently."

"Can he adjust artillery?"

"Shit, I don't know. I could ask Major Lich."

"Rood," said Vail, "go ask."

Richie Rood got up in the dark without speaking and disappeared into the slit.

"Is he in a safe place?"

"Yes. He said he was moving back."

Rood returned. "Major Lich says the Harelip isn't an expert or anything, sir."

"OK," said Vail. "Where's the Double-E 8?"

Another of Vail's men on the periphery carried the telephone toward Vail, carefully drawing out the wire from a loose coil under the roof.

"Rood, you write this all down in your book."

"Yes, sir, I will."

Vail took the telephone in his left hand. He already had the radio in his right.

"Crank me up," he said.

Rood bent over the EE-8, the telephone connecting Vail to the artillery fire direction center at the bottom of the hill, and cranked the handle.

"Hey, Bob," said Vail into the telephone.

"Hey, pardner."

"Listen, Bob, better cock your cannon."

In the earpiece Vail heard his friend call out, "Fire mission," to the crew of the fire direction center; and had he not been otherwise absorbed he could have heard faintly the very same cry repeated a moment later among the gun crews in the soccer field at the bottom of the hill—for the night was damp, still, and thick, and sounds carried.

"All right, Dick, speak."

"Coordinates: six eight four—five four eight."

"Yep."

"Victor Charlie company."

"You're shitting me."

"Cannot adjust."

"Yep. Let's say a battery six?"

"Fine," Vail agreed. "This is at my command."

"Yep."

"I'm going to fire both you and the Navy, assuming you agree the target's worth it. It'll be 'time on target.' "

"OK."

"What's your time of flight, approximately?"

"Oh—I'll figure it exactly in a minute, but it'll be around forty seconds."

"All right," said Vail. "Remember, it's at my command. I'll lift that restriction after I give you the four-minute mark."

"OK, pardner. Who says there's a company out there?"

"Somebody called the Harelip," Vail said.

"U.S. or gook type?"

"He's Arvin, they tell me. Don't call me, I'll call you."

"Yep—all right."

"Mozart, Mozart," said Vail into his radio, "this is Alligator, over. Rood, did you write down the coordinates that I gave the artillery?"

"Yes, sir."

The ship responded. "Alligator, this is Mozart, over."

He said to Rood: "Read what I said."

"Six eight four—five four eight."

"Thank you, Rood. Mozart, this is Alligator, we'll use about sixty rounds in the next few minutes, HE, fuse quick."

"Roger, thank you."

"Major Perkins, would you be kind enough to tell the Harelip at your first opportunity that he's got to observe these rounds for us —if he can."

"Sure, I'll tell him."

"Thank you, sir. Mozart, this is Alligator. *Target number:* one six; *coordinates:* six eight four—five four eight; *height:* one zero meters. Victor Charlie company on the surface of the ground. Four guns, ten salvos, fire for effect using HE fuse quick. At my command. Cannot adjust."

Vail listened with care as the ship read this back, then continued: "Your read-back is correct. We will fire 'time on target' with Uncle Sugar artillery. Please give me a four-minute mark. I will transmit your four-minute mark to artillery. The mark you give me—"

He paused, wondering if the ship had ever fired a "time on target" mission. Its effectiveness depended on the precise simultaneity of the initial salvos of both the ship and the artillery battery.

"The mark you give me will mark four minutes until the impact of the first salvo. Therefore you will fire four minutes after the mark, less time of flight."

The ship said she understood.

Vail asked: "Are you ready to give me the four-minute mark?"

The ship said she was.

"Roger. Wait." Vail picked up the telephone and a man cranked it, unasked. "Say, Bob," said Vail.

"Yep."

"Are you ready for the mark?"

"Yes. Is the Navy?"

"Yes," said Vail. "Hang on now. Mozart, this is Alligator. I have the artillery on my other ear and we are ready for your mark."

"Ten . . . seconds," declared a sepulchral voice through the radio; and Vail repeated into the telephone:

"Ten."

"Five."

"Five."

"Four."

"Four."

"Three—two—one . . . mark."

And Vail at the same instant said: "Mark."

"Mozart," he resumed a second later, "I roger your mark. 'At my command' is lifted. Fire as instructed."

The ship responded: "Roger."

"Say, Bob."

"Yep."

" 'At my command' is lifted."

"OK. I'm going to make it a battery eight."

"OK, fine," said Vail.

The battery of six pieces multiplied by eight plus the ship's four guns multiplied by ten made a sum of eighty-eight. The silence that ensued differed from the silence that had preceded Vail's arrangements by the addition to it of this number, this abstraction: 88.

Into this silence the ship raspingly intruded with her final statement: "Gun-target line, two six niner degrees true. Ready five five."

Regulations required that Vail repeat this, but for some trivial reason, surely, in his psyche he preferred not to speak. He passed the handset to Rood and Rood spoke for him, the silence then reascending, carrying still its mathematical fact.

The time of flight of the ship's projectiles being, as she had reported, fifty-five seconds, she would fire at three minutes five seconds; and the artillery, being closer, would fire at approximately three minutes twenty seconds, so at precisely four minutes the initial salvos would arrive from their different sources together.

Vail stood up. He hadn't any idea how much time had passed. He half expected to see the sky turn white at this very minute. Standing, he was aware for the first time of a dark circle of figures around him.

"Rood, you call me if anything . . ."

"Yes, sir, I will."

"I'll just be down here."

He started walking. Some men stepped aside. He passed the weakly lighted slit of the bunker entrance and kept walking over the invisible ground until he was past the end of the bunker and had a clear view of the invisible west. He stopped, sensing perhaps by smell that he must be near the edge of the trench. He looked to the west and could see nothing; or else he saw or imagined the form of the mountains beyond the plain. Of the plain itself he saw nothing. He stood waiting, and the night breeze was warm, too warm.

There were voices in his mind. These were the voices of intelligences which could never have come to life had he been elsewhere: had he been down there, for instance, where the Harelip was; or on the northern mountain where Sergeant Hackman was lying with a four-man recon team or on the southern where Mush Head lay in equal silence with another. But here in the safety of Mo Duc hill they came to life and found voice in the special fertile atmosphere of his mind when he was *safe,* and doing this "work." So strongly did he detest this safety that he was uncertain whether the smell he smelled was before his feet or in his mind, like the voices.

But he was also aware with the whole energy of his conscious mentality of the abstraction "88" in the night, which it seemed to him he alone had put there, and all these others executing his decisions—eighty-eight projectiles about to be fired having a certain kind of force, on the mind and on the night, which their firing cannot exceed.

Still the voices were rather lively in his mind.

He whispered: "God damn it, what a stink."

The flashing of the ship's guns, a bright white light palely imbued with chartreuse, commenced on his right. She must have moved slightly seaward, because what he was witnessing was the direct flash of her guns and not only the upward refraction of the light into the atmosphere. After the first series there was a halt and a renewal of blackness, except for the lingering dots in his eyes, and then a second bright series. All was perfectly soundless.

There was an inexplicable eruption of dim light in the zenith. But he understood almost immediately that this was the artillery light; and, at the same instant as this realization, there came to him the collected blasts of the artillery pieces and the naval guns all at once. The sounds made a stack—then silence like an interval between pain waves; and next the high penetrating reports of the ship's second series even as he saw the flashing of her third.

So he turned toward the target, which he could not see but he could imagine. But in the extraordinary vividness of his imagination at that moment there wasn't a single picture; his thinking was abstract, there was rather an intense expectation, a wish almost unendurable, that a connection be made between the concept "target" and the audibly streaking projectiles in the sky overhead.

This wish was painful. The pain was not of any sharp kind but of a smothering kind.

The artillery light pulsed again to the zenith and the ship rapped out its black noise, and then there was light over the target which took the form of white spasms in the layer of mist that overlay the target; for it was this low blanket of mist which seemed to be the place (an illusion) where all the punishment was inflicted. Indeed, he saw only one of the orange flashes at ground level, and he wasn't certain even of this one; all the rest was the quivering dispersal of the light through the long layer of mist.

There was now a lengthy confusion of sounds and white light— of the guns and howitzers speaking and the projectiles sliding through the air and of their explosions on the plain, and of flashes from three sources; which all subsided with a sinister graduation until the end came with a quivering of light on the plain that was partially smothered in the smoke and earth in the air.

"Hoo-wee!"

Vail turned and saw there were several men behind him.

"Ick—holy shit." That was Major Perkins.

"It was on, wasn't it, sir?" said another voice.

Vail, not recognizing this voice, assumed he wasn't addressed, and started back.

He heard Major Perkins say, "You bet your ass."

Richie Rood, sitting cross-legged on the bare ground at Vail's "place"—by the radio, the EE-8, the wooden box—writing in the report folder by the light of a red flashlight, looked up with shadows reaching up toward his eyes.

"Sir, she says 'rounds complete' and she would like an assessment."

"Tell her, 'Record as Target Number One Six, your rounds were in the general area of the target, detailed assessment not yet available.' "

Vail sat down on his box, his hand making the habitual semiconscious motion of touching his wife's letter. Richie Rood transmitted the message. Major Perkins came, Vail stood, they conversed. The major said it was a beautiful idea beautifully done, meaning the simultaneous use of two supporting units on the same target, and Vail said that in the particular circumstances and given the fact that the greatest number of casualties are "obtained" in the first thirty seconds—and so on and so on, explaining his decisions. The major went into the slit and Vail again sat down, his hand making its customary motion to his shirt.

"Rood, would you please check all our teams."

"Yes, sir, I will," answered Rood, and he began calling the teams.

Vail had seven teams in the field: Hackman's, Mush Head's, one with each of the four rifle companies of the infantry battalion, and one with the battalion command group. While Rood was calling all these Vail sat leaning on his elbows.

His imagination spread a scene before him and punctuated it with cries of pain and calls for help. There was of course no way to judge the veracity of such a picture. "The whole 88 might have been a waste," he said to himself, meaning a waste of ammunition. But his imagination continued to embellish the scene and make it more terrible. And Vail stared, until he exclaimed in anger, "For Christ's sake!" and tried to dismiss it.

But something unexpected happened. A certain discrete faculty of his mind—one that worked rationally and served him as a soldier—observing the scene, connected it with the enemy's custom of "policing the battlefield," or picking up and removing his bodies after such a strike as this. The idea was: if you get such a target again make a strike, wait five minutes, and make another.

Vail stood up. He checked the side pockets of his trousers for rations, but there were none; but then, his impulse of hunger passing as quickly as it had come, he stood with arms across his chest and stared out toward the ship. Black night, breeze.

"Sir, they all report Alfa Sierra."

"OK, OK, good, Rood, thanks."

He walked more or less blindly for a few paces along the edge of the aluminum roof till he came to the operations people.

"Is it quiet?"

"Yes, sir. Did you get some?"

"I don't know yet," Vail said. "Probably some. May I talk to Bravo Company?"

"Sure, Lieutenant."

A radio handset appeared before his chest. He took it, fumbling for a second in the dark, compressed the switch, and said, "Bravo, this is Alligator."

"This is Bravo, go."

"May I speak with Bravo Six, please?"

"This is Bravo Six."

"I mean Bravo Six Actual," said Vail.

So, after a moment, he heard the familiar and confident voice of John Ashley: "This is Bravo Six Actual." He was now company commander, Dip-shit having gone back to "the world."

Vail was extremely happy, unaccountably happy, at hearing this voice. He said, "Bravo Six, this is Alligator Two Six. Greetings from the cesspool."

They conversed. Vail's happiness grew intenser, and evidently Ashley shared it. But when he had finished the conversation, which was necessarily short because unofficial, he asked himself: "Why am I so overjoyed to talk with that bastard?"

"Oh, here you are," said Major Perkins.

"Yes, sir."

"Well, you really hit it. The Harelip says . . . he went right in and helped police the place up—"

"No shit."

"Yes. He did. Here it is."

The major held his light on a piece of paper on which he had copied the essentials of the Harelip's report. It said thirty-one killed and "many" wounded.

Vail took the paper.

As Vail left him without a word, taking the sheet of paper, Major Perkins thought Vail's minimal observation of the distinctions of rank was getting too minimal.

Vail thought: "Why take the paper? Can't you remember 'thirty-one' and 'many'?"

"Rood," said Vail, "call the ship and tell her she gets credit for fifteen killed. Michaelson, call the artillery on the Double-E 8 and tell Captain Dorsen he gets credit for sixteen killed."

Vail had to crawl on his hands and knees for a short distance to reach the level place directly under the peak of the aluminum roof. He spread his shelter-half, brushed some sand from it, and lay down on it without undressing. He was on his back with his head resting on his rolled-up extra pair of trousers. There was an area of diminished darkness on the right which showed where the edge of the roof was. He could hear, just barely, the voice of Major Lich, which was slow and curved in English and quick in his native language. It was quick now. He could also hear the murmur of a series of exchanges between Rood and Michaelson, exhibiting that difference of tone which an officer's departure always makes.

It seemed that Vail wasn't tired. It seemed that even if he was somewhat tired he wasn't going to sleep. Although his legs ached, he was far too alive with a rhinestone sort of life.

Some time later he heard his name called, and looking at the luminous dial of his watch, he was surprised to see it was past two o'clock.

"Yes?"

"Sir," came the voice of one of his new men, "Major Perkins wants you."

He lay there staring upward, thinking: "Major Perkins, Major Perkins, who in the hell is Major Perkins?"

He checked his big pockets for his flashlight and map and touched his shirt pocket where the letter was and began crawling out, and was nearly out before he remembered who Major Perkins was.

"The Harelip has got us another target."

"Yes, sir, that's good, I suppose he followed a remnant of his first target."

"That's just what he did. He's got a platoon, at this location, here, he says it includes a sapper squad, he says there are three officers with it."

"Fine. Fine. Listen, Major . . ."

The voice Major Perkins heard was a controlled, close voice.

". . . let me ask you . . ."

"What? Go ahead."

"Are you still in communication with him?"

"Yes, I think. We were a minute ago."

"You tell him, sir—tell him to stay away from the target area afterward."

"All right."

"We'll run a sort of a two-part invention this time."

When during the silence after the four-minute mark Vail recalled using this musical term, "two-part invention," he was at a loss to explain where it came from; unless from a letter of Katherine's of a long time ago, when she spoke of harpsichord music.

"OK, so I'll tell him to stay away because there'll be a second fire for effect after the first."

"Right, sir."

Major Perkins started to leave, but Vail said:

"Sir—ask him please to tell us if the rounds are on target."

"OK."

"And, sir, if he calls during the mission please ascertain whether he's giving you an adjustment or a sensing."

The major said, "OK," again, stepped from the darkness to the weak light, and went down the slit.

Vail set about the creation of the two-part invention. He arranged everything as before except that the artillery battery, after completing its fire for effect, would not wipe the data from the guns but would be prepared to fire a battery three, using either the same data or new, if an adjustment was forthcoming from the Harelip.

The ship, after her fire for effect, would allow her computer to go on generating a solution. The solution during this period would flow from the computer to the guns. The guns would continue their motion in compensation for the gentle roll and pitch of the deck in the serene seas of that night, aiming always at the place where the computer determined the target to be, with due allowance for wind, humidity, temperature of the air, temperature of the propellant, range, elevation, air density, roll, pitch, drift, bore erosion, parallax.

The sailors in the gun mounts during these minutes did not experience the silence which was elsewhere so interesting, because the flow of gun train and gun elevation orders from the computer translated in jerks of the mount. The cool hands took these jerks and lurches with no greater show than the constant though varying motion of the ship in the sea. But the new men felt the jerks, some of them, to the core of their brains. Each jerk was accomplished with a mechanico-electric scream. The interior of a gun mount of a ship at sea could be the most mechanical environment in which men function. It is surely more so than a space capsule, where things float around. Here the light is red, there is no ventilation, the noise is either deafening or eerie—the wheeling of the drive motors—and the men never know when they'll be jerked. Nor do they know, except rarely, where they're shooting or why.

Vail watched the trembling of the final light in the pall over the target and turned quickly, although there wasn't any hurry, and went to the slit. Here he first squatted like a peasant, then stood, and stared into the slit at the dark sandbag wall, waited, and listened. No one in the bunker was speaking. Approximately a minute had passed since the last salvo of the first fire for effect.

It was a situation of engaging simplicity, whose factors were these: when if ever would the Harelip call? When if ever would the enemy start policing up the bodies? How seriously would the ship's solution deteriorate in three, four, or five minutes?

Vail resumed his peasant posture with his arms on his knees and the cigarette convenient to his mouth. He decided to wait thirty seconds more, and was astonished at the silence all around him.

He stood up. Everything dissolved in his decision. He went to his place, sat on the box, discarded his cigarette, took the telephone in one hand and radio in the other, and said:

"Crank me up."

A trooper cranked the EE-8.

Vail said: "Hey, Bob."

"Yep."

"Are you ready for a three-minute mark?"

"Sure. OK. Same data?"

"Same data. Hold on. Mozart, this is Alligator. Are you ready to give a three-minute mark?"

They established a mark, and another number was in the night. This was 38.

Something urged Vail to cock his pistol, put the muzzle in his mouth, and fire it. He disobeyed. With "38" in the black atmosphere all around him, he went to the place by the trench where he could see the target area when the flashes should reveal it. Standing here he recognized the urge of the pistol as "not serious," which is to say there was no danger he would obey it. It was the result solely of his safety, which was an aberrant condition. The needle searched him. A picture kept appearing of himself opening his mouth to an absurd width and putting in the pistol; his eyes were also opened, almost bulging, and he had curled his lower lip over his teeth to keep the pistol from grating on their edges. It is no crime to shoot a chicken.

The second part of the two-part invention now commenced with white-chartreuse flashes at sea, and all its events both of sound and light ran their appointed course; after which Vail waited with unusual anxiety for the Harelip's assessment. Could he believe the Harelip? When finally it came it reported nine dead and "many" wounded, including two officers, one of whom would die.

Vail thought: "Loss of blood."

He assigned four dead to the credit of the artillery and five to the ship.

"The big Two Six, I presume." The words came across the trench in the clear, carrying voice of John Ashley, who held up a hand in greeting even as he lifted a foot to embark on a perilous crossing. The bridge over the trench was nothing but a log. There was a bamboo handrail, but Ashley disdained it.

Vail, who was shaving by a metal mirror jammed into a crack in the flagpole, had known his brother-in-law would be coming to the meeting but hadn't expected him this soon. He was glad to see him. Here was a man intimately related to Katherine, who had set eyes on her and on Terry living their present life, who knew things about Katherine that Vail did not know; who had known the legendary father. Here, to be honest about it, was her brother. Vail shouted hello and went on shaving.

He was naked to the waist. The ground around his feet was spattered with shaving suds, but the water in his helmet was clear. It was also hot. The naval gunfire shaving-water can was kept in the sun and the drinking-water can under the aluminum roof. By this system the one was always kept hot and the other warm. The muscle in his right arm stirred as if it could do this tiresome job in its sleep. One leg of his trousers was bloused at the boot top in correct Marine Corps style, and the other hung loose where he'd scratched an insect bite till it bled.

The ocean was a tilted plane fading eastward. The ship had gone to rendezvous with an ammunition carrier and wouldn't return for some hours. It is surprising how quickly a ship disappears in a sea so vast.

He glanced from Ashley to the mirror and back, and called: "If you fall in, John, there's no shower around here." It was an awkward thing to say, and he felt its awkwardness, but Ashley's walk over the vile trench seemed to call for some comment.

He bent over his helmet to rinse his face and ears, and drew several handfuls of water across the back of his neck. He stood up with water running down his chest and back, and there was Ashley —with tightly strapped pack, bloused trousers, tipped helmet, muddy boots, and a streak of mud melting in the sweat on his face. He was smiling and his eyes were like two rare blue jewels.

They approached each other steadily. Vail's right hand was out and slightly to his right. Ashley of course never forgot how big Vail was, but each time he saw him it was a kind of surprise. Vail's forearms and head (not his body) were tanned—a farmer's suntan. There was a dark sun-tanned V pointing down his chest, disappearing in the hair. The chest and thick shoulders at the level of Ashley's eye, the he-man swing and crack with which his hand arrived in Ashley's, all constituted Vail's signature to Ashley.

"I tried to call you in the Land of Sand," Ashley said, "but that god damn phone system is so god damn Number Ten—"

"I tried to call you too, as soon as I heard you'd joined the regiment," Vail replied.

They stopped at the flagpole, and Vail put on his shirt and replaced the liner in his helmet, having dumped his water. The limp ensign of Vietnam Cong Hoa dangled its yellow and red bars over their heads. While Vail gathered his toilet articles from the cement base of the pole Ashley, in a derisive circuit, surveyed the fence and gate, the latrine, aluminum roof, tents of the ARVN, howitzer pits, and stacked ammunition. The howitzer ammunition was stacked in the open, which elicited a snort of incredulity and scorn from

Ashley. Three ARVN soldiers walked by in their scale-model
utility uniforms, with hip pockets big enough to hold a cigarette
pack.

Ashley said: "I'd like to see the skeleton of one of these little
bastards." After a second he added: "We're both exaggerating,
right?"

"Exaggerating what?"

"I didn't really *try* to reach you," declared Ashley. "I made a
token call and this snuffy on the line said, 'Working, working,' so
I hung up and never gave it another thought. I was fucking busy."
He smiled down at Vail, and followed his face upward as Vail rose
and looked inquisitively at him, and zipped his shaving kit. It was
perhaps the closest look Vail had ever bent on Ashley.

Vail said: "Major Lich has invited us for tea."

"Shit."

"His tea," said Vail, "is made by Haig & Haig."

"No shit."

They went into a slit and down the sandbag stairs, and along a
corridor as wide as their shoulders. After two turns they came to
Major Lich's principality, a little rectangle with red earth walls stud-
ded with stones, and pallet flooring. There was a radio and the code
and cipher books associated with it, two upright steel cabinets, a steel
closet and a bunk, and a table and three chairs.

"Enough chairs!" said Lich, greeting them and dismissing the
radioman in the same motion.

Ashley said he hadn't sat in a chair for two weeks.

"Then luxury," invited Lich with another gesture.

He produced a bottle of Pinch and shouted in Vietnamese,
smiled, invited Vail to sit as well, and said: "One minute, gentle-
men."

Major Lich had attended artillery school at Fort Sill, but Vail had
only a vague idea how far his English went.

Lich's cowboy came in with teacups and put them on the table.
Lich dismissed him, and Ashley said:

"No booze for the cowboy."

"No," agreed Lich amiably.

They drank, and Lich said to Ashley: "You are with?"

"Bravo Company."

"He's the new skipper of Bravo Company," said Vail.

"A lieutenant skipper," mused Lich, with a glance at Ashley's single silver bar. "A smart successful boy, am I right?"

"Not really."

"Yes," said Vail.

"Don't I wish," Ashley put in, a little roughly.

"For me, this war, many years."

Neither of the Americans said anything to that.

After a moment Major Lich added: "A smart successful boy, I am, past tense." Lich's smile was the same color as his skin. He displayed it now and said: "Smart successful too," indicating Vail.

"Hey yes, man, what about that? I hear you really gave the bastards their iron ration."

Vail had previously thought: "The father who ran the two-part invention wishes to congratulate his daughter on receiving fifty cents from the tooth fairy. Is he allowed?" The residuum of that thought, its smell, passed through him now.

"I'm just doing what anybody would do," Vail said.

"Like hell you are," retorted his wife's brother. " 'Anybody' would fuck it up. You're doing a first-class job, is what I hear. You're the only one getting any VC, do you know that?"

Major Lich rocked a bit on his heels and assumed the attitude of a man about to make a comment. As if summing up a long and complex discussion, he said: "Big guns, only way."

Ashley said: "Sometimes. I was being pursued one time a couple of weeks ago and I had to keep going because that was the order, but it looked like I was running. That really frosted my nuts. I had a naval gunfire type with me named Stilwell. Do you know him?"

"Yes. Mike Stilwell."

"Oh yes," Lich put in politely.

"Well, Stilwell said, 'Listen, Skipper, if you'll stop for just a second I'll chew up those fuckers,' so I stopped. We were on a hill and all the troops could look down where we'd been. Stilwell called his ship—it was a rocket ship, 'Professor X-ray'—and it was just as if a thousand bombs planted in the ground all started blowing. This Stilwell said, 'How was that?' The troops were whooping like wild men. The Navy is a lot of pussies, of course, but that day there were some marines who changed their minds. But it's just an area weapon, isn't it," he added.

"Rockets are," Vail assented.

"I mean all naval gunfire."

"No. You can use it against a point target, but a good deal depends on the slope and vertical face. Is that right, Major?" he added, hoping to bring Lich in.

"But it's mainly an area weapon," Ashley persisted, without a glance at Major Lich.

"All right, 'mainly.' "

"What I detest," said Ashley, "what I *detest* is the whole philosophy of massive application of firepower."

"I doubt that you do. Or would you prefer a massive application of manpower? For example, your own men."

Major Lich apologized and interrupted. He said he would have to excuse himself now. He had to prepare the meeting room. Vail wondered what such preparation could consist of. The major left the bottle on the table, and showed Vail how his closet door locked when closed. He shook hands and left. He had not sat down and had drunk only a teaspoonful of whisky.

Vail said: "You scared him off with your war story."

To which Ashley replied: " 'Big guns, only way' bullshit. Big guns wrong way. Do you want any more booze?"

Vail did not.

"Then let's put it away now," Ashley suggested, and got up to do it himself.

Their eyes met for a second. Vail supposed Ashley had a right to be cautious, with his battalion commander expected in the bunker in a few minutes. Ashley didn't attempt to defend himself against the surmise Vail had so obviously made. He sat opposite Vail, put a cigar on the table and cut it in half, and said: "You can't split a cigar three ways." Then he lighted up (so did Vail) and said: "Are you ready for this? I've got a theory."

"I suppose I'm going to hear it whether I'm ready or not?"

"Because it's important."

"I see. An important theory."

"It explains your life. Pardon my immodesty. My life too."

"Is that all?"

"It explains," said Ashley, "why it's so easy to kill."

"In that case it doesn't explain anything."

"Look, why pretend? Just to go along with what 'everybody knows'? Just to go along with convention? We grit our teeth and do our duty like men, and all that shit? Nobody talks about it. When they do talk about it they make a big mystery, a religion of it. 'Grit your teeth, be a man, do your duty, don't talk.' But look around. Does it really seem like such a big deal? Does it really seem all that impossible?"

"Nobody said it was impossible," said Vail.

"The marvel is that people don't do more of it. Wait'll you hear the theory. You'll see that every item I've identified makes it easier. Nothing stands in the way." Ashley smiled again and repeated: "Nothing."

Leaning back and dragging on his half of the cigar, with his helmet off and sweat darkening his blond hair, grenades hanging from his suspenders, his eyes bright—his face ruddy and healthy yet somehow suggesting exhaustion—Ashley set forth his theory.

"I call it 'Near and Far.' You'll see why in a minute. All right, it starts with a division of the world in the most fundamental way. There's the part you're aware of and the part you're not. It's an imperfect division. Awareness shifts and moves around in the world, I know that. The point is that the division sharpens, and approaches perfection, in a firefight. I would say, and you would say, and everybody with combat experience would say that in a firefight nothing else exists. For that period of time the world is perfectly divided, and the only world you know or care about is the action.

"OK. No strings, nothing irrelevant, a self-contained world, with a man in it. The man is in the action. He isn't simultaneously learning sportsmanship in his high school gym class or wandering the stacks of some library or touching some girl's tit. It isn't really accurate to say everything else has been obliterated; it would be more accurate to say everything else never existed.

"Within this action there is another division. It is divided between marines and enemy. Nothing could be clearer and nothing is ever more powerful. If you live to be a hundred you carry this to your grave—you were in a firefight and there was your side and the enemy. This division is two things, two forces: it is a separation from the enemy, first, and it drives you deeper into your side, second—deeper into the Corps, so to speak. OK? Have I said anything stupid yet?"

"Please go on," said Vail.

"We know who we are, but who is the enemy?" Ashley continued. "We are 'our side.' Each one of us depends on the others. Something happens to our feelings about each other—comrades! A funny European word. It's embarrassing to talk about it, but it happens. But who are those—subhumans—on the other side of the divide? How do we define those apes, those bipeds, those vermin? They are the fucking enemy who, one, will kill marines; two, are trying at this very minute to kill marines; three, have already killed marines.

"That's enough right there, but there's more to the enemy's definition that makes it even easier. He's a totalitarian, a communist, a terrorist. And he's a digit in the body count, a mere statistic. A difference of race helps but isn't essential. Don't the Vietnamese kill each other? Didn't the Spanish and the Russians? The anarchists and communists in Spain killed priests and nuns because they were 'the church,' and the Falangists killed anarchists and communists because they represented anarchism, communism, and degeneracy.

"I'm not evaluating anything, you understand," Ashley interposed. "I'm just describing reality. I'm making my contribution to the scientific understanding of human nature. You didn't laugh. OK, here's 'Near and Far.' This is the best part.

"I call a man *near* if he can reach me with his personal weapon. If he can't he's *far*. All right, if he's near he's going to kill me. He's going to kill Corporal Daws, or Hagans or Serico or somebody; a marine. And I can kill such an enemy without so much as a flicker. So can you. If he's far away he has the advantage for the theory of being still the enemy—although he's not a present danger, he is still the enemy—and besides that, I can't see his face; his limping, his glaucoma, his malnutrition, his dirty hands, his haircut—none of it. I can't hear him if he screams. And the summary of it is that he's just as easy to kill whether near or far.

"There are other items. There are probably some I haven't thought of. There is the exhilaration of conflict. There is fear, if you happen to feel it, which also makes a man act—it doesn't only paralyze, it also opens the way to action. There's the game atmosphere, as if it were a complicated game with certain moves prescribed under certain conditions. When the conditions emerge you make the move whether you want to or not. There's the fact that our whole purpose is to exterminate the enemy, to convert people into statistics. There's the fact too that a man who risks his own life, whose life is in the balance, feels entitled to take his enemy's. There are probably other influences that I haven't thought of. But everything I've found is an influence in one direction. There are no contrary influences. This whole business, this theory or whatever it is, I mean the things the theory describes—all these things constitute the most important, the most essential and elementary part of military technology. This is the only modular assembly that is absolutely essential, without which all the rest would never work. I know the facts. I experienced the facts first, you see, and then constructed the theory as an explanation. I observed. I didn't invent anything. Furthermore, this applies to practically everybody. You take any slob at home, any clerk, and bring him over and he'll prove it. You take a lawyer—he's been merging corporations or divorcing people—wow, man, that is living. Bring him over here. At home he feels bad if he runs over a dog with his car. Bring him here and put him into the process and just watch him.

"Take a trooper armed with a flamethrower. Let's say he's approaching a cave. He knows the gooks are inside but they won't come out, and say they're armed—we'd probably throw tear gas in, but this is just a hypothetical example. Let's say there's been a hell of a fight going on. The trooper shoots a tongue into the cave. He can't see anyone's face. If he wants to he can rationalize it: 'I'm not burning these bastards, I'm exhausting the oxygen.' That was far. All right, let's say that as he approaches the cave a gook comes out carrying a rifle. The trooper cooks him. 'Near and Far.' "

Vail didn't hear every sentence. From time to time, rather, he listened to an echo. It was himself saying to no one in particular what he had in fact said to Terry. "If I'm a good and strong man, I will go back."

At the meeting the commanders of the ARVN battalion and the U.S. Marine Corps battalion asked Vail whether he thought he should prep the vill.

Vail stood up. He said it was a fortified vill, and that everyone in the room knew that. Everyone nodded; if the sun rose in the east this village was fortified. Vail was no orator but he was sophisticated enough to pause for a second or two just at this point.

He said that when the marine line advanced on the vill the VC would all run and disperse; or the main body would run, leaving a rear guard to harass the advancing marines with sniper fire, probably just rifle fire; or the VC would resist with all they had, to hold the marines in the open paddies as long as they could, to kill as many marines as they could. Vail apologized for taking so long to reach his point. He said he wasn't quite there yet. (Luckily for him, his reputation had preceded him into the meeting.)

He then said there was only one way to find out what the VC would do, and that was to march a bunch of marines toward the vill. If the VC all ran, the marines would have a walk in the sun, and no casualties. If the VC assigned a rear guard to slow the marine advance while the main body dispersed, "a few" marines would be hit by rifle fire. If the VC commander chose to pitch it, he would await his best moment, probably when the marines were in close range, and open up with his machine guns and mortars. "Many" marines would be hit.

In all three cases, Vail said, the noncombatant villagers, if there were any, would take early alarm and get in their shelters.

He said that in his experience, which he characterized as "limited but adequate," an uncovered advance on a fortified site was not a reasonable undertaking. It was a gamble against odds that the VC would all run. In fact, the pattern of VC activity in the district had been to seek contact, on advantageous terms, to wound and kill as many marines and ARVN as possible.

As he spoke Vail saw that they were listening. Nobody seemed impatient or irked that a subordinate officer should take up their time this way. Perhaps he was saying what many of them thought. He was emboldened to comment that our side wasn't the only one following a strategy of attrition. He did not go so far as to say, although he believed, that to march the marines toward the vill without benefit of covering fire was to trifle with their lives. He concluded: "I recommend a preparation fire, and a heavy one."

The ARVN commander, who was providing a blocking (not an advancing) force and whose troops therefore weren't at hazard, deferred to the marine commander. This man thought for a long time, and no one in the room, certainly not Vail, envied him.

At length he said he understood the Rules of Engagement to allow a prep fire in these circumstances. But he said that anybody who read the Rules knew their intention was to minimize civilian casualties. Then he was silent again for perhaps another minute, his eyes flitting back and forth across the overhead timbers.

He said: "There'll be no prep fire, but, Dick, I want that ship on a hair trigger."

It was dark when Vail and Ashley came out of the slit. Ashley had to get back to his company, which was spread out for the night around the marine artillery battery at the bottom of the hill, between the cemetery and the highway. They stood by the flagpole till Ashley could see his way.

Vail said: "You better use the handrail this time."

"Don't worry. You're right, of course," Ashley said, "they all know you're right, even the colonel, but I'm glad you lost."

"I thought you might be."

"I don't want a prep fire, I want contact," Ashley declared, and Vail said:

"I know."

"What have I got a company for? I've got this great, responsive, resilient *instrument*—OK, let's use it. Shit, I didn't come over here to hike."

Vail let a moment pass, then asked: "You're not going down alone, are you? I'll get some troopers to go along with you."

"No, no," said Ashley, "I've got a squad," and he called into the darkness, "Corporal Daws!"

A patient, confident, probably black voice replied from across the trench: "We're waiting, Skipper."

"But you know, right or wrong, all this reasoning and explaining and justifying is bullshit—you know that, don't you? I mean the explanation is purely institutional. I've got my company, and because I've got it I want to use it. You've got your ship, and the fucker goes boom, so you want to blow the shit out of somebody with it. Isn't that why you came back? And as I say, it's so easy."

"Dearest Richard—

"The nicest man was on television just now talking about 'acceptable losses' and oh, what a pity you missed him, you would have agreed with him so profoundly. He was just the handsomest most wonderful smiling thoughtful gravely reasonable Wildroot Cream Oil pragmatist you ever saw, and he spoke with such patrician restraint, implying—of course he didn't say such a thing straight out —implying that a policy is not a self-sustaining creation at all but is sustained by 'acceptable losses.' And I inferred—of course he didn't say this either, but being a pragmatist myself I inferred that unacceptable losses shatter and poison a policy, which would be wicked and unfortunate. But do you know, Richard, I don't think his wife, his child, his dog, or his anal biopsy are included in the acceptable losses. If we must steel ourselves as a nation against the loss of an anal biopsy it will have to be somebody else's. This is mere sarcasm (and you would say it isn't *relevant*) but why is it, Richard, that the people who believe absolutely in the sanctity of life are always the powerless? Why is it that no one with any responsibility believes that life is sacred? Is it like the juries trying capital offenders—if you don't believe in capital punishment you aren't allowed on the jury? Or is it this way, that we will certify the sanctity of some people's lives in some circumstances but not everyone's life everywhere? But you know if everyone's life isn't sacred then no one's is. Isn't that an amusingly antique opinion, a relic of a bygone time? What is more antithetical to me—this is a confession and perhaps a perilous one—is the person *who is willing* to include himself, or his own, in the 'acceptable losses' or to hazard their inclusion.

"Don't retaliate—I'm too miserably sick. I've been sick with a virus and have spent most of the last several days in bed, five days to be precise, and do you know what this illness does to me? It gives me an almost religious sensitivity and a very affecting, humane perspective. This always happens when I'm sick. It is like—in a way it is like our living apart. That too gives me a definite pang which lasts till we are together—and besides my famous self-confessed 'reservoir of sensuality'—in which I beg you to make waves on your return —it also gives me—our separation and my singleness give me—I am hesitating, my pen is 2 inches above the paper—it gives me a different and keener life, with a slow-burning joy in contemplating you (and you never ruin your image with curses or dictatorial conduct) —a life which *educates* me, and from which I plead will you release me?

"I had decided that sensuality, as I know it, is not gross, is fine; is humane, kindly, charitable, or could be so. With that opinion recently in my head I began reading Tacitus when my illness relented, and I unluckily came across this—that for the gratification of his *sensuality* the emperor Tiberius would send out slaves searching the countryside for objects for his lust. Tacitus says Tiberius in-

dulged in depravities with these *objects* for which new names had to
be invented, but he doesn't give the names. And these objects, if I
am reading it correctly, were young boys and girls and children. And
evidently Tiberius gave orders—we would say 'specifications'—as to
their physical *and social* characteristics. The slaves not only found
these boys and girls and tore them from their parents but used them
themselves. Then the emperor used them, and I asked myself, who
used them next?"

After this sentence her handwriting changed. Vail was sensitive to
such changes because to him her letters were not only their content.
They were also pieces of unconscious handicraft, and the most intimate aspect of this was her handwriting. His flashlight began failing,
but when shaken in a certain way it burned brighter. Several heavy
raindrops fell with tympanic noise on the metal above his face, and
he heard them. His head ached unsteadily behind his eyes. Her
writing henceforth was smaller and more uniform.

"Dearest—little Julie O'Connor is dead. I had put this letter down
and was sleeping when Terry brought the mail to my bed. There was
a letter from you, which I saved till last (I still haven't opened it; that
was this afternoon—this is night), and one from Mrs. O'Connor—
Carolyn. She said her daughter had died of leukemia, and all the
time we were neighbors in Washington and the girls played together
I never knew Julie had leukemia, yet she must have had it even then.
I remember she was not very willing, and often unwell, and for that
reason Terry wasn't greatly interested in her. Do you remember the
mouse school?

"Without realizing how weak I was I dressed immediately, and
when I got to the end of the lane the car wouldn't start, from being
idle five days, so I walked to the Willoughbys', stopping several
times to breathe. Thank heaven it was a warm afternoon. Then
before telephoning I had to rest a minute—Mrs. Willoughby is so
incredibly kind—how can there be people like her on this earth? I
called Washington and Carolyn was very steady—she was, I think I
should say, extremely steady, by which I mean she nearly shook.

"Julie was dead; had died two weeks ago yesterday. They and
their doctor had discussed whether it was kind to prolong her suffering further and whether it was possible to do otherwise, and after
a time they saw it from Julie's standpoint exclusively and extin-
guished their own hopes and thought only of Julie. Carolyn inter-

rupted herself and thanked me for calling. She said she had hoped I'd call. She wanted to hear my voice. I nearly broke down at that. Then she went on and told me more than I wanted to know, especially about how Julie went bald and they gave her a wig. She went faster than most leukemia patients but was helpless and drug-extended longer than many, so Carolyn said.

"You know, Carolyn had been a lapsed Catholic. (She told me all this.) But during the girl's illness she said she slowly realized that this death approaching could not be real. This girl—you remember her face—she said, could not be dying *absolutely*. Why have I forgotten exactly what she said? It was just a few hours ago that we talked.— I have just put Terry in bed and read her a story and now I remember. She said an innocent and lovely and kindhearted child such as Julie could not be simply suffocated. She couldn't deny the suffering but she denied the end. There must be life after death, she said, and these are the words I was trying to remember, 'because nothing else makes sense.' I was on the verge of saying I'd agree if she took out the 'else.'

"Dearest, do you know what I've read?—a newspaper article telling how many children died in New York City in the first half of this year by falling out of windows. This is called a social and human problem. The same reporter tells how many were beaten to death by their parents.

"Just before my illness I was shopping in the supermarket where they pipe in music to spend your money by and hark, out of the walls comes Bing Crosby softly mooing 'May the good Lord bless and keep you,' which of course is *not very sophisticated*, but, Richard, when I think of this in my present state of mind and body it almost strikes me down—for if 'the good Lord' doesn't bless us who blesses us? Where else did our sanctity come from if not God? And if we recognize our past religion as a myth are we greater because we have gotten, as you would say, an atom of the truth, or lesser because we gave our sanctity for the atom? If it is better to know the truth (as I tell myself it has to be) —suppose the truth degrades us. If we were ignorant in former times, suppose we were noble. And Julie O'Connor's wig is in the atom. I know it was in the 'ignorance' as well— but you see, we have now in our possession this wretched atom which, if it were anything else but the truth, we should despise.

"Dick, do you believe our solitude is noble? If so we must look

to ourselves. We look to ourselves and we see napalm. We see the
Nazi apparatus. I only ask, is life sacred? This is an undergraduate
question I admit but do you know, I think most people grow up and
adopt attitudes and biases but never truly answer the undergraduate
questions. Last fall I was walking in the woods on what they call a
side hill when I came to a stone wall, a very carefully made one. This
meant that the land had once been cleared by a man, an ax, a saw,
and a team of oxen. I think it must have been pasture or hay land
because in those days they cut hay on hills. This man, I felt, had one
life—as if he had one dollar which he could spend as he chose, but
only once, and he put his dollar down as if to say, I'll put my dollar
on this land, and having cleared and farmed the place he died,
naturally, and now the beech trees are a foot thick in his so-called
field. I know you'll say what's the harm? I know you'll say I am
confusing the sacred with the everlasting, and if that is confusion I
am confused. But listen—Dick—I insist, this is not essential. Not
important. But what about the law of the Romans that if a slave
murdered his master all the slaves in the man's ownership were to
be executed? What about the trial of Servilia by the Senate, who was
'given her choice of death' because she had consulted an astrologer
about her father's safety? The Roman soldiers, as Tacitus says, 'glut-
ting themselves on the Germans' blood'—'the slaughter lasted until
nightfall'—'he opened his veins'—'he divided the arteries of his
arms'—'she applied a knife ineffectually to her breast and throat
until a blow from the centurion drove it through'—through her
throat?

  "You know how I hate the Romans, Richard, so why do I read
this horrid stuff? Only for the sake of the continuity, dearest, for this
is the continuity of history and not only of history but of our life;
and because I believe it is the truth, and I am fond of the truth too.

  "Did I ever rave to you about the Melian massacre? The island
of Melos refused subjugation by Athens, the Melians saying their
city was free and would not willingly become part of the Athenian
empire, so it was voted in the Assembly at Athens that the Melian
men be killed (that is, all the men) and the women and children
enslaved. This wasn't done in the aftermath of battle (although there
had been a siege) but in the Assembly after debate. It wasn't done
by Huns, Gauls, African savages, Mongols, Visigoths, or even Romans but by the free men of Athens, the audience of Sophocles,

Aristophanes, and Euripides. But I confess all the butchered and enslaved melt into the idea of Julie O'Conner gone bald—and Carolyn told me that she and her husband explained to Julie what a wig was, after she'd been wearing a cap for some time, and asked if she'd like one, and the girl said she wanted a red one. Carolyn said her husband objected ('gently') to the child and said she had been a blonde so she ought to have a blonde one, it would look nicer, but the girl grew sad. They gave her a red one. She had none of the coloring of a redhead. She must have looked—I fixed on the unsubstantiated idea that this wig was her last present. My mind treats it as 'her last present.'

"Something else had got stuck in my head—that Sophocles owned an arms factory; and I even felt sick with the thought: 'The writer of *Antigone* manufactured swords.' I had to investigate this and I went wallowing through my books and found, thank God, that it was not he but his father who had an armor factory. But you see how ready we are (I am) to embrace a detestable paradox almost with lust. We are so imbued in this filthy age with paradoxes, impurities, and *chaos* that we see them (I see them) even where they don't exist. But this is no paradox, this is pure. Outside the citadel of Mycenae there is a ravine, a deep jagged gorge, called Chaos Ravine. How many female infants and defective male ones do you suppose were cast into this *chaos?*

"Dick, I only ask, is life sacred? I write this to you because you are my friend and husband and also out of fear, in a way, because, forgive me, you seem to be willing to kill. If you can take life, how can it be sacred?"

Early in the morning while there was still mist in the valley the VC opened up on Ashley's company as it moved toward the village. Vail sent a warning to the ship in these words: "Alligator Bravo is in disadvantageous contact. Please stand by to assist." Then, taking a radio and Richie Rood, he went to the pinnacle and listened to the rattling of the fight through the mist. A person, separate from himself but within, observed how little he required: a map, a radio, and a reason.

The thinning mist revealed troopers of the blocking force to the left of the objective village, and the village itself. Vail still couldn't see Ashley's men, but he talked with his Bravo Company spotter, who said two marines had been killed and three or four wounded.

The battalion commander halted Ashley in the fields and called Vail.

Vail specified four guns in adjustment. The first salvo of four projectiles struck in the rice paddies, the fertility of the soil showing in the blackness of the eruptions. He saw some people running toward the village. In a countryside where everybody wears pants it is difficult to tell sex at a distance and equally difficult to distinguish farm tools from rifles, but in this instance it made no difference anyway.

Speed was imperative, and Vail made no attempt to bracket the target but moved in a single step from his first sensing to the village. This salvo of four threw up its variegated evidence from a place deeper in the village than Vail had hoped; he wanted, as the optimum, salvos straddling its edge; but failing this, and the time being tense, he accepted what he had as good enough, and laid down a fire for effect of four guns, four salvos.

During the delivery of these sixteen projectiles, which rushed with a soft rippling over his head, he surveyed the whole of the target and decided on his next adjustment. He would move the fall of shot some distance to the right, enfilading the edge of the village facing Ashley, and doubtless benefiting Ashley more by firing on this line than on any other.

This being accomplished with efficiency, both in the adjustment and the rapidity of the fire, he stepped in single four-gun salvos up and down the length of the tree line facing Ashley. He was assuming the enemy's firing positions were at or very near the line, which was the edge. In this way he expended thirty-six rounds on the line. The fusillade in the valley, he imagined, was diminished. He concentrated his fire then on a slight promontory of betel palms and houses projecting a few yards into the paddies, and expended sixteen rounds. Then, the smoke and dirt being troublesome, he went in a single shift to the other side of the village and laid down two eight-round fires for effect around a junction of pathways. Then moving farther, going again by single salvos of four guns each, he stepped here and there at random, with some concentration around the masonry structures and less around the mud and grass.

He ascertained by radio from his spotter with Bravo that the promontory was, as he had suspected, the location of an enemy automatic weapon or weapons, so he returned there and gave it such punishment as seemed reasonable, then doubled the number, then commenced a second excursion up and down the right edge of the village, going by fifty-yard steps with single salvos of four guns each. The smoke and dirt so accumulated that he could no longer see this edge, so he shifted to the center of the most distant edge, and walked back toward the nearest, in staggering shifts to the left and right; then he checked fire.

The ship silenced herself and reported:

"I am in check fire."

There was quite a silence, and a lethargic clearing of the smoke.

Vail called battalion and suggested that the preparation was adequate. Upon the battalion commander's affirmation, he told the ship the mission was ended.

Aboard the ship the gun crews relaxed. In the valley Bravo Company stood up, looked, and advanced out of the mist toward the smoke. And on the pinnacle a cleavage widened in Vail's soul, called Chaos Ravine. And the figures that had run across the paddies, across the lenses of his binoculars and of his eyes, and across his soul, disappeared in it. At the bottom the torrent was blood; the rocks of its sides were limbs. It was wide and getting wider, deep and getting deeper.

XI

V ail met his death in this way:
He stayed on Mo Duc hill for three more weeks, and the slaughter never ceased. During this time he ruled himself by his intellect. He fixed on the idea that he was a soldier whose mission was to save American lives by offensive and defensive measures. He was clear enough to see that this reduced him to his duty. There was contamination in this "duty," but to abandon the marines would be an abomination, and never to have come to their side worse still. He was more conscious of the contamination of his acts than of their virtue; while the men of the companies he served saw the virtue and not the contamination. The rapid piling up of statistics, first in two digits and finally in three, had the merciful effect of dulling his appreciation of their meaning. He did not believe in absolution, but having grown up in a Christian ambience, he knew what it was. He did not believe that sins are washed away by magic, forgetting, or the blood of a Lamb. He believed that some men assimilate their contamination and some are destroyed by it. He believed that our acts stay in us.

When offered a place of safety, Vail chose the chance of death. Who wouldn't? What was being offered was a job on the division staff, where the paper war, the pen and ink war, the bowing and scraping war, the coffee cup and air conditioning war raged without mercy even on Sundays. This offer was made by the colonel of artillery, who summoned Vail immediately on Vail's return to garrison from Mo Duc.

It was characteristic of this colonel to summon a subordinate officer, who had been in the field five weeks, without giving him time to eat, wash, or rest. It was night. Vail got Rood and borrowed a jeep and traveled the two miles from the infantry command post where he lived to the colonel's tent at the artillery command post.

His jeep was stopped en route by a sentry, who pointed a flashlight in his face.

Vail said: "Take that god damn light away."

"I have to see who it is, Captain," answered the sentry.

Vail was on the point of doing something irrational when Richie Rood drove on, before the sentry had given permission, but the sentry was cowed.

The colonel's tent was lighted by an electric bulb. It had an interior heat wall of soft white canvas.

"You know I have a policy, Mr. Vail—sit down."

Vail sat. He detested this sedentary lieutenant colonel because the man always talked and acted as if artillery were the Queen of the May. That it existed to help the infantry he never admitted, and perhaps didn't know.

"You know I have a policy that no man with less than thirty days left on his tour is required to go to the field."

"Yes, sir."

"You have five or six weeks left before you go home."

"That's correct, sir."

"And I have a requirement here from division for a naval gunfire officer for the division staff, and if you want the job it's yours."

"No, sir, thank you, I don't want it."

"Nice job. Division FSCC, air conditioning, nice club, good mess, girls, nice PX."

Vail declined again, and it was evident the colonel might force him. On perceiving this he became frightened, and he prevented his jaw and mouth from breaking out in a babyish trembling only with the utmost difficulty. For the prospect of taking shelter was unbearable. Death or the chance of death he could face; not the needle.

He scanned the argument that at division he wouldn't really be a part of the "process" except abstractly; farther than far; but it didn't work.

The colonel relented, seemed human for a minute, and said: "I wouldn't like the Puzzle Palace myself."

Vail departed trembling with relief and nervous elation. The sentry stopped the jeep. Richie Rood brought it to a halt with a jerk that flopped him forward.

The sentry pointed the light. Vail's eyes went to it, submitting to the pain of it, and for a second there seemed to be nothing left in the universe but this radiating light; and in the light he saw himself pointing the pistol in his mouth. There was a tinge of comedy because his mouth and eyes were open so wide.

"Stop entertaining yourself," he thought. And a minute later as the jeep went tearing through the dark along a dirt road: "If you don't tell her about the chicken she'll never know who you really are." And later: "The chicken tells *who I am?* Cut it out—ridiculous!"

Going to the shower the next afternoon, barefoot over the hot sand, he listened to the chugging of the water pump and heater as he approached the boarded enclosure. The men waiting on the dry boards scarcely talked. When the water sprayed forth they swarmed under the horizontal pipes and quietly came to life, first with complaints about the temperature of the water and then with shouts and derisive laughter and all kinds of personal abuse. All these men—some had been at Mo Duc and others were rear-echelon "poags"—all, the shouting, the whooping, and the quiet ones, as they soaped themselves and looked with darting or mocking eyes and bent their bodies beneath the streaming water, all seemed harmless and vulnerable. As Vail washed his body clean, seeing the vulnerability of even the strongest and the strength of even the most vulnerable, he perceived their sacredness. As Boethius says, the mind not only receives an impression as sand takes a footprint but reaches out to seize an idea. In this fashion Vail thought that these bodies and these lives were sacred too.

Not much later the regimental staff was assembled in a tent and various specialties were asked how they could support a certain scheme of maneuver, and thus in the course of a three-hour meeting the proposed scheme was modified and simplified and a new operation set in train. Vail made suggestions whose effect was to increase the target-acquisition capability of the maneuver units, and his suggestions were received as excellent and novel and were incorporated into the plan.

The point of departure was Pussy Corner. The whores came to the

edge of the road in the dawn to wave farewell to their steady custom-
ers, and giggle their destroyed teenage giggles.

Then, having organized itself by the confusion and curses of sleep-
less men, the convoy entered the highway to its full length of a
thousand meters and ran south through the dust of its own passage,
stirring sound waves across the rice lands, until presently it halted
eight kilometers south of Quang Ngai while the scouts found a way
around a blown bridge.

The vehicles of the convoy—trucks, tanks, Ontos, howitzers, and
radio jeeps—moved by fits, in steps of a few dozen yards, and paused
for a few minutes, a detour having been found around the blown
bridge. There was a deep ford by a sugar field. Vail and Richie Rood
were in a radio jeep whose value to the government was $135,000.
He knew the price because his signature appeared on the account-
ability sheet. In theory he could converse with the whole Western
Pacific on this contrivance, but in fact he was unable to reach the
only ship he needed to reach. He tried repeatedly, and repeatedly
failed.

Vail and Richie Rood came to the ford, and this was a place he
would have remembered. The depth showed in the delicacy of the
white lace on the ripples; but the rest of the stream was brown,
turbulent, and cool, and severed the trail without effort or trace. On
this side a steep muddy track led down into the stream, and on the
other it led out to a green field of sugar. On this side were rushes
and trees and a low cemetery wall, and a bamboo woods—on which
each vehicle turned its back as it descended. The larger vehicles
crossed unaided, but the smaller got stuck in the middle, whence
they were winched across by a truck braced with wheel blocks on
the far bank.

They went down the track partly sliding. Vail raised his feet and
propped them on the dashboard as the jeep entered the water like
an uncertain turtle. The water didn't come in in any great amount.
It rose truculently all around the wheels and threatened the sides as
the jeep bounced over the rocks on the bottom, and finally halted
against a stone which visibly swelled the water.

Vail waded through the knee-high current to fetch the cable from
the winch. He came to the winch and took the cable in his hand.
Then all his senses signaled catastrophe, and turning, he saw and felt
upon his face a black and red burst on the roof of his jeep. After this

burst, which he did not hear in the ordinary sense, there was a continuing tone in his head like a held screech.

There was some spray falling in the air, and the remnants of the burst. He himself was hurt in some way. He thought he saw Richie Rood with a colorless substance flowing like lava from his mouth, and he heard a voice (his own) shout: "Hey, Rood," though he could barely hear it through the tone. On former occasions of this same general kind he had discovered that his pistol was in his hand, firing at something. This time no such thing happened.

There was firing all around him, including machine guns—he thought it was mostly friendly. But in truth he made no analysis. He wanted to help Rood. He lunged into the stream and in his final steps seemed to remember that on seeing Rood, if he had seen him, he had seen no eyes, nor any sockets either; but this was perhaps confusion. He saw Richie Rood's arm and hand pointing out and the fingers dangling in the stream. An uncontainable emotion, a panic of love, made him shout again, but not exactly in English, and just as he would have reached the jeep he realized he was in another burst. And something took him by surprise, and there was time for his intellect to perceive it. The shock, the heat, the feeling that all his face was ripped, the push, the sudden asphyxia, none of these was really unbelievable. The surprise was how they all came together at once. This was the last addition to his knowledge of the world.

There may be victory "at the end of the tunnel" for some; perhaps only survival; there is never light.

Katherine's hair touched her shoulders again, for her husband's sake. And so was every other effect of her ascetic self-consciousness fast fading in her anticipation of his coming back. There had been a time in the depth of her sequestration when she'd thought that even waiting would be a joy during the last month, and it was half true.

She had deepened her studies of Greece. But in comparing translations of Euripides and seeing their grotesque differences, she began to realize how specious her appreciation must be so long as she read translations, and she asked: "Shouldn't I learn Greek?" She asked this very tentatively, for it seemed a great undertaking.

She pinned up her hair, bathed, dressed in fresh Levi's and a closely fitting blouse, and taking her blue jacket from a peg, she walked down the road toward the Willoughbys' with Yuk racing ahead.

It was a cool sunless day in a damp summer. Mr. Willoughby was taking his second cutting of hay, and she could hear the clattering of his old sickle bar coming from the hayfield where they had waited under the hemlocks for the deer.

She went around the edge of the dooryard, avoiding the mud. In her mailbox she found a single pristine letter. The border was red and blue and it bore Richard's hand, and his address and the word FREE where the stamp would be. It was at once a familiar and a valued object. She put it in the pocket of her jacket. These letters, although sometimes acts of love, were more often the intercourse of friendship.

Walking back, she heard a car overtaking her, a happening so rare on this road, which hadn't gone anywhere for half a century, that she turned to see it, surmising it was somebody lost. But the car was gray and the driver was a sailor, whose white hat was the first thing she saw; and as she stepped backward off the right side of the road, the car passed, and she exchanged a glance with a naval officer. She watched the car go before her up the road, raising no dust though it was July. It turned at her lane, but since there was no other route, the question was, would it turn around and go back or was it intended for her lane?

She hesitated, and Yuk, who had been undecided whether to give chase, returned to her and awaited her initiative in such a puzzling situation.

Seeing that the gray car did not return, she composed her mind and began to walk, permitting herself but one comment, which was on the black lettering and the serial number on the trunk lid, the car having no license plate. She said: "Must everything in the country have a number?" And she walked after the car.

It was parked at the turnaround, and the sailor was inside. She went by and started up the path through the birches, whereon Yuk set up a strenuous idiotic barking and danced forward and back until she said,

"Oh shut up, Yuk."

But the dog forced her to repeat herself, and it was this which put a narrow crack in her composure even before she looked up to see the naval officer standing on her porch looking down at her, or heard his question, whether she was Mrs. Vail.

"I not only am, I always will be Mrs. Vail," she thought; and said aloud: "Yes."

He was Lieutenant Commander something.

She hardly saw his uniform and did not see his face at all, but she caught the rank. Richard had said all lieutenant commanders were soft in the head. She forgot the reason, but Richard declared that even good men went bad on promotion to that rank.

Inside she took off her jacket, and the officer could not but see her excellence.

She said: "You have to be gone before my daughter comes."

Every repetitious governmental event has a form, and this is the form of this event.

The Casualty Assistance Call Officer (CACO) does not speculate. He tells the primary next of kin (NOK) only what is known of the death, that a telegram will confirm his verbally furnished information, and that a letter from the commanding officer of the deceased service member may amplify upon it. If the NOK desires to relinquish control of the remains to another person the CACO obtains a written statement to this effect, which he air-mails to the appropriate authority. After the initial notification the CACO does not leave the NOK alone. He assists her in telephoning a friend or relative and remains with her until the arrival of the friend or relative. However, there is no way to publish absolute guidelines for personal notifications of this sort, and the CACO must be prepared to deal with any situation as it arises, for example an NOK who insists she does not want a friend, relative, or clergyman.

In the full performance of his duty the CACO will thoroughly cover the rights, privileges, and options of the NOK in these areas: burial allowance/reimbursements, government headstone, memorial flag, military honors, military funeral with firing squad and/or bugler, arrears of pay, death gratuity, personal effects of the deceased service member, decorations and awards, transportation for dependents and household goods, insurance, social security, uniformed services identification and privilege card, hospital and medical care, exchange and commissary privileges, Navy Relief Society aid, and other appropriate assistance.

Every element of this is not accomplished, of course, in the initial visit of the CACO, but a start is made.

There was a piece of meat thawing on the counter. In her wandering about the empty house she picked it up (it was the last steak from Mr. Willoughby's deer), testing whether it was thawed. She put on her jacket, intending to go out, and then forgot the intention.

She saw Richard running toward a marine, some new Bishop, and a sob broke through her throat.

She started to say his name, but the power that convulsed her permitted no such privilege. It shook and doubled her body as if it would shake out her life. It clamped into her throat with a familiar pain. It gave her no time to breathe.

She sat at the kitchen table and knew exactly where she was. She saw where Richard had sat the night the snowflakes beat on the window around his head. She pushed a cup and saucer aside with her forearm, and took a deep breath. She imagined that the lieutenant commander still sat at the table and said: "He was going to the assistance of a wounded man."

She saw that image again. The sobs smote her again and brought an awful pain to her throat, and no liberation. She couldn't resist, but there was nothing to surrender. Then she got another chance and pulled in one single rippling breath, and then came a series of sharp, hard contractions in her throat. She gave voice for the first time, to release the pain, but the sounds she made were mere inarticulate cries. She couldn't say "Richard" until much later, when she sat quietly staring out the window at the green leaves of the maples.

She prepared herself, because she wanted to speak. Very carefully she said: "Richard. My beloved."

She went down the lane to meet Terry, and knew the girl was coming when Yuk ran eagerly ahead with the imminent meeting visible in her ears. There were the sounds of their greeting and then the dog returned and Terry came into sight at the turning, after her trip to town with Mrs. Willoughby.

Katherine said: "Terry, go change into your old clothes and we'll help the Willoughbys milk."

The girl exclaimed her happiness and ran past Katherine toward the house. She had a new pin on her jacket. It was white, the size of a half-dollar, with red letters, and it said: "I go to the dentist."

Katherine lay down among the pines, her body making no search for comfort on the ground. She felt the cold in her shoulders and her back. "Is the heat leaving, or is the cold coming into my body?"

When she was newly married she had discovered how congruent their bodies were. She rolled over in their bed and pressed against his back, finding how perfectly her body could be joined to his if she lifted her knees against his bent legs—how humorously parallel their bodies were when both lay on the same side. In a spirit of experimentation she rolled over and her sleeping husband followed, and she felt with joy that he lifted his knees against her. This friendship, as she called it, was an aspect of her marriage she hadn't foreseen. She had thought: "It's right to be married."

They went to the Willoughbys' and were given the job they liked best, which was feeding the calves. Terry entered a pen warily because she had once spilled a pail of milk when the excited calves pressed upon her, and choosing "Treckie," she squatted down, holding the pail by the brim and tilting it for Treckie, and defending it against the others; all the while saying, "Is it good, Treckie, do you like it, girl?" and other pet talk, mimicking adults. She no longer stammered. Katherine fed a black calf. The calf thrust its big head in the pail right against her hands, where she held the brim, and drank without pause; and its eye trembled against Katherine's knuckle.

She asked herself: "Shall I open the letter?"

XII

Katherine woke in the night amid a sense of well-being. Her body was suffused with a good feeling, but it wasn't just her body. She sat up in bed, by the open window at the peak of the roof, listened to the wind, and discovered that it too had a good feeling. It made a clean, free sound. She looked at the radium-lit hands of her watch: 2 A.M. and ready to bound out and "meet the day," except there was no day to meet. What was this vague happiness? A dream, she presumed, which had escaped her mind, still lingered in her body. She touched the boards with her bare feet and walked around the end of Terry's bed and listened with incipient maternal concern to the child's stertorous breathing. Was Terry catching cold? Katherine went to the railing at the front of the loft and looked down on the living room, full of shadows and half-imagined shapes, and descended the stairs.

She turned on the bathroom light, squinted her eyes against it, and hesitated. She had perhaps heard a sound. Perhaps from the daybed. Was Ella here? What month was it? Turning, she caught the approach of a large, tall figure into the light. With her eyes still defending themselves against the bathroom light, she saw a white-haired, very old woman in a long gray gown, and immediately recognized Mrs. Willoughby, who said: "Are you all right?" and Katherine thought: "Of course I'm all right."

Before she had time to ask why Mrs. Willoughby was here she remembered the answer, and there came a moment without up or down, without a plane, and the floor struck her.

She was cold, she was wet. That which could not happen had happened. That which could not be true was true. Everything else wobbled, this truth was steady. Everything else coruscated, this one light shone steadily. Shone, burned, but had nothing to do with her.

Mrs. Willoughby held Katherine's head in her lap and applied an ice pack gently, and nothing hurt. There had been a noise, a bang, and then a tone like a held screech, but it was gone. She thought: "An old, old woman who can still sit on the floor cross-legged."

Katherine and Terry went around holding each other. They all but dressed each other. They ate breakfast holding hands. Terry hadn't cried yet, and her eyes looked dry as sand. She looked at her mother every once in a while simply to see where she was headed.

Katherine felt a pressure of anxiety to get the funeral over with. Once she knew she wanted this, the prerequisites clicked into sequence in her head. First, locate Dick's father. Second, tell the lieutenant commander where to send the body. For body she said "casket." Third, order plane tickets for herself and Terry. Dick always said there was no point in calling his father after 10 A.M. even if you could find him, so they went to the Willoughbys' house immediately after cleaning up the breakfast dishes. Mrs. Willoughby, who had driven tractors when tractors were hard to drive, drove Katherine's jeep station wagon, and Terry sat on Katherine's lap.

Dick understood his father's history thus: Mr. Vail was a technical man, a mining engineer, with a humanistic mind. The questions he could not answer about life, death, and meaning tormented and would have tortured him, save for drink. His fertile mind bred the questions and rejected all answers. By drinking for about thirty years to escape the questions that his mind threw up, he coarsened and dulled and dimmed his mind, and made it unable to throw up questions. Richard believed this was intentionally done, because his father was so intelligent. Intentional or not, by a conscious and sustained program Mr. Vail put out his own lamps and had been moving about in a shadow world for many years.

Doing as Dick had done, Katherine called Mr. Vail's last number (disconnected), then the mining company's pension office in White Pine, then the Elks Club in Iron Mountain, in the Upper Peninsula of Michigan. From the Elks she received two numbers, and on the second call heard herself telling her father-in-law that his son was dead. He exclaimed and exclaimed and exclaimed, and his sorrow upset Katherine, and frightened her. Now he would surely get drunk and fall down the stairs or walk in front of a car.

Terry sobbed on the flight from Boston to Detroit, all the way. She was unaware of the stewardess and the kindly man on her right. She leaned against her mother's side and sobbed, her face red and her knuckles white, and she said: "Now we can't touch him." Katherine insisted they could. "We can always touch him and love him," she said, but Terry sobbed and shook her head against Katherine's ribs. She didn't stop till the plane touched down at Detroit, and she started again when they took off in a smaller plane for Iron Mountain.

The funeral was ghastly and crude, and the eulogy presumptuous. Above all Katherine felt a falseness in the whole proceeding. Nothing that was done was necessary. Whatever was necessary, and she didn't know what that might be, wasn't done. The burial had a forgivable melodramatic dignity. Katherine kept observing Mr. Vail at her side, and found she loved him. She hoped Dick was wrong when he said this old man had hastened his wife's death by depriving her of all hope, by preferring alcohol and in that way evading and ultimately abandoning her.

A member of Congress who happened to be in town attended the burial ceremony. His home secretary had informed him that a graduate of the local high school who had been killed in Vietnam would be buried colorfully at Hillcrest. The home secretary obtained an invitation for the member of Congress from Mr. Vail late one afternoon. The member of Congress was photographed in front of the honor guard, bowing his head as they fired their salute. When the service and ceremony ended the member of Congress said: "May I offer my sincere condolences to the widow," and Katherine walked on by. She wasn't snubbing him; she just didn't react to the word widow.

She was thinking Mr. Vail had liked the salute, and she took his arm.

Where an American goes to high school, there is his home. So on that principle this was Richard's home. It seemed remote, boreal, and hard. The people must either toil like slaves or loaf on welfare. "We are his true home," she thought, meaning herself and Terry, but she wasn't so sure. For many years afterward, until his death, she pictured Mr. Vail at the Elks Club, his position marginally improved because his son had died in the Vietnam war.

She wrote to Dick's half-sister in California, saying how glad she was they had finally met, and thanking her for various kindnesses during the three days in Iron Mountain. The woman replied that her door was always open and said: "I am in love with your sweet adorable daughter." Katherine thought: "So am I."

Now came Mr. Willoughby with a proposal. There had been so much rain so well spaced out between days of sun, and he had spread so much manure last fall and early winter, that he planned to take a third cutting of hay on two of his fields. He reported this plainly as a rare phenomenon, verging on the remarkable. Did she want to drive a tractor and a truck? She would drive the tractor pulling the hay conditioner while he cut, and later the truck when they gathered bales. Katherine asked what a hay conditioner was. He rolled the knuckles of both hands together like gears and said: "Squeezes the juice out. All you do is pull it." She hesitated, and Mr. Willoughby added: "It does make a noise." Katherine declared the noise wouldn't bother her, and so joined the historic crew that took a third cutting of hay in a single summer from Mr. Willoughby's fields for the first time in two generations; and perhaps ever.

They worked between milkings, from about 9:30 A.M. till about 3:30 P.M., and broke for lunch. They were Willoughby, driving the tractor with the sickle bar; Katherine, with the tractor pulling the hay conditioner; and later when the bales had been made two high school boys named Sam Crillis and Sam Pettingill, the "two Sams." Terry spent the mornings helping Mrs. Willoughby make lunch, and during the trucking phase rode in the cab beside her mother in the afternoons.

Katherine began to notice how every myth came true.

The first day was windy but brutally hot, and Mrs. Willoughby marched to the edge of the field carrying a straw hat with a ribbon and ordered Katherine to halt her machine and put it on. So Katherine, wearing jeans and a light red-checked shirt, drove a Ford tractor around the Willoughbys' steeply sloping field while a hot wind whipped at the straw hat, securely fastened by a red ribbon under her chin.

She followed at some distance behind the chattering old sickle bar, looking now at Mr. Willoughby's narrow, bent back and reflecting on how long he had lived, and now at the green hills with their tawny lace of dried June grass rising around the field. She watched the hay fall at the approach of the sickle bar as it slid invisibly along the ground to the right of Mr. Willoughby's tractor. And that evening she listened to Mr. Willoughby tell how he'd once cut the legs off a fawn hiding in the grass.

After the boys joined up Mrs. Willoughby made two pies a day. The noon meal was always a feast. There was always meat, potatoes, a vegetable from Mrs. Willoughby's garden, salad, and pie. They ate in the dining room because the kitchen was too hot, and went over the carpet in stocking feet. After the meal they put their shoes or boots back on and sat under the willow by the dooryard drinking ice water. The willow had been trimmed high, and made a canopy that held off the sun and let the breeze glide through. The boys carried Terry piggyback, and she whipped them with a willow switch and made them buck.

Late one afternoon the wind rose as the sky closed in and grew dark, a dark indigo, and the maples bordering the field on three sides lifted their leaves to expose the silver undersides. A half dozen leaden drops hit the hood and windshield of the truck. Katherine looked down the row and estimated that twenty or thirty bales still lay on the ground, and she had something close to a full load in back.

The boys began to scamper and Willoughby to shuffle as if on hot coals. He forked a bale and waved her down the row, and more drops beat against the dull glass and hissed on the hood. She kept moving. Looking at her side mirror, she saw Willoughby make a fulcrum of his knee and lever the bale up and pitch it over the side into the truck. And she kept moving as the two Sams went whooping down the row dragging the bales into a line, lifting them to shoulder height in one motion (they didn't use forks) and pitching them up in another.

"Quicker!" Mr. Willoughby called, and hobbled ahead. The rain came quicker too. The wind increased, the light fell, and the hood of the old Chevrolet started steaming. Katherine speeded up and felt she was driving the three workers unmercifully, pulling them along by the speed she maintained as the thirty-year-old Chevy whined along in first gear. But Mr. Willoughby loped ahead with his fork, saying, "Quicker!" She kept track of the boys in the mirror and never slowed down, even when she saw a bale in the air and was sure it had fallen short. Now the rain came flying down and enveloped the cab. Terry knelt in the middle of the seat, propped one hand against the dash, and operated the windshield wiper with the other, and Katherine cried out with delight: "How did you know that?" The girl said Mr. Willoughby had shown her that a long time ago.

As the girl flipped the lever back and forth Katherine glimpsed her rapt face and said, "Miss Theresa Mugwump Vail." Terry kept at the lever.

The three figures struggled in the wind-driven rain, one of the Sams approaching with a bale in each hand and his face contorted against the downpour. He swung the first bale up without putting the other down, which Katherine wouldn't have thought possible, then sent the last bale sailing over the rails and jumped onto the running board beside her. The right door opened and Mr. Willoughby slid in in half his usual time. The other Sam jumped onto the right running board. Katherine turned a great downhill loop under the maple branches and headed the massive lumbering load toward the barn. She didn't dare shift to second even though the rain was now a solid wall, because the field was too rough and the slope too steep.

At the creek she had to execute a sharp turn to approach the ford at a right angle. The ford itself she crept through, rocking from side to side over the stones. A bale slid off, and Willoughby, on being told of this by the Sam on the right side, said: "Leave it. Get to the bahn."

The grass on this side of the creek was smoother, and Katherine revved up in first and clanged the old gears into second, and the rain whipped down, and the Sams turned their backs to it.

She coasted into the dark cave of the barn. The sound of the storm leaped away and hovered at roof height, where it changed instantly to a benign and distant drumming.

The rain slackened but went on. Katherine shivered as she stood at her stove breaking eggs into a skillet to make an easy meal. Terry sat in a chair swinging her legs and staring at nothing. Katherine still shivered after they had eaten their eggs, toast, and raw carrots. She put on her blue jacket, listening to the letter crinkle in the pocket, and brought in two armloads of logs from the porch. As she laid the fire and stacked the extra logs by the hearth she examined each log for scars where the wedge had been driven in. Finding such a scar, she looked closely at it and ran her fingertips back and forth across its surface.

Then came a plague of decisions. The principal of the school asked whether she intended to enroll Terry for the fall semester, and she put him off. On the same day the accountant at the ski resort telephoned while she was in the fields with Mr. Willoughby and the two Sams. She returned his call at lunch, expecting to be offered the job she had held last winter and not knowing how to answer. Instead he asked if she would drive over to discuss a different job. She tried to put him off, but he pressed, and she said: "You'll have to give me a few days, Ed. My husband has been killed in Vietnam." The accountant of course was stunned, and she knew he was, but it didn't seem to matter any more than anything else. She thought: "You might as well say it." Next Mr. Willoughby decided to take a third cutting from yet another field. Did she want to help? Yes she did— and she silently estimated her earnings at $1.75 an hour. Having made this commitment, she found herself in a fix when a call came from Washington about the apartment. She had sublet the place to a friend of Richard's from the oceanography office. This man and his bride now asked if they could take up the lease, which was due to expire at the end of September. And would she sell any of her furniture—for instance her couch and coffee table and the lamp with the brass shaft? They needed an answer on the first question by the end of August, on the second at her convenience. She asked for a few days.

She spent those days in the fields. Now she would put on gloves, climb down from the truck, and drag bales to it and boost them with her thigh and pitch them into the back. She tried Mr. Willoughby's pitchfork technique, but couldn't get the knack of it, or wasn't strong enough. Her arms and back grew sore.

She almost certainly had to go to Washington—but having given her promise to Mr. Willoughby, she couldn't leave before they finished haying, and rain was delaying the work. The Willoughbys were ingenious at finding things they "needed" her to do, and she marked this ingenuity and was so touched by it she almost cried. But it began to look as if the haying would stretch out to Labor Day. She didn't fancy Terry missing the first few days of school—although it didn't really matter—nor did she want to leave her alone, even with the Willoughbys—although that might be all right.

Then she observed that the first decision was already made. Terry would go to school here, at least in the beginning, because—where else could they live? She telephoned the principal.

Then she thought: "Now comes the hard part." But it wasn't so. The second decision was made too. It was obvious she'd sooner live in hell than Washington *at this moment in history*. Her mind recoiled from the task of formulating her reason. She simply knew she couldn't live there "now." She told the couple they were welcome to the lease—and she'd call later about the furniture.

The next decision, surely, would be difficult. But no, merely unpleasant. She started by recollecting that she had not informed Terry of the death of her playmate Julie O'Connor. She affirmed now that Terry must be kept in this state of ignorance. But she, Katherine, must see and wanted to see Julie's mother, Carolyn, when she went to Washington. "So that's that," she said. And she said to Terry: "Dear, I have to go to Washington to put our furniture in storage."

"What do you mean?"

"Oh—storage . . ." She hadn't expected quite this turn. "I'll tell some men to put it in a warehouse where it'll be safe. When we want it again we'll write a letter and they'll send it to us."

"They'll send it here?"

"They'll send it—wherever we are," said Katherine.

Terry looked away, and Katherine let the conversation lapse without reaching the main point.

She came to it the next day. "Terry, babe—when I go to Washington you'll stay with the Willoughbys and sleep in the room across the hall from their bedroom. You know the one?"

Terry nodded.

"I'll call every night."

The girl said: "I want to go with you"—giving a little stress to the word "you."

"Babe—you can't. You have to go to school."

Terry said nothing for a while, then looked directly at Katherine with her eyes like Richard's and suggested she go to school in Washington for the duration of Katherine's visit there. "I could go to school with Julie," she added.

"Julie doesn't live there anymore," Katherine said.

"Where does she live?"

"She moved away."

"Can I really leave her?" Katherine thought. The only other choice, since she had to go, was to take the child and stay in a motel and skip the visit to Carolyn O'Connor. "No," she said, "damn it," and after a few minutes said again, "Damn it."

But in spite of the "damn its" her logical apparatus stacked it all up into a straight pillar. Washington was a contamination zone. This place was clean, elemental, and the Willoughbys loved Terry. So Katherine and Terry would stay here for the time being. But she must see to the furniture—and she must see Carolyn O'Connor, whose daughter had been taken by leukemia. "I have to see Carolyn," she thought.

She said to Terry: "Miss Mugwump, here's how it will be. It won't be so bad. You'll go to school one day while I'm driving to Washington. You'll come home and help Mr. Willoughby with the evening milking. He'll want you to feed the calves. We'll be apart that night but I'll call you, and you'll sleep right across the hall from the Willoughbys. The next day you'll go to school and I'll be taking care of our furniture. We'll be apart that night too—but I'll call you. And on the third day I'll be driving back while you're in school, and we'll be together that night. OK? I'll just be gone two nights."

Terry went to the kitchen and got a big grocery sack and began putting in it her toothbrush, underwear, jeans, dresses, and a couple of books.

"I'm not leaving now," Kit said when she grasped what the child was doing.

But until she did leave Terry lived out of this sack.

Before heading south Katherine stopped at the ski resort and listened first to the accountant's awkward expressions of sympathy and then to his deftly organized proposal of a full-time job.

She was familiar, he said, with the revenue sources. These were the hotel, condominium rental commissions, the restaurant and bar, the gift shop, ski and equipment rentals and sales, lift tickets, lesson fees, and the rental of two nearby business properties.

He, the accountant, had persuaded the partners that he needed an "executive assistant"—because of the diversity of the revenue sources and the accounts payable and receivable associated with them, because volume and payroll were growing, and because of the trouble one always has with nonprofessional part-time help. "You would supervise the part-time bookkeepers," he said, "do all the buying for the gift shop, run the NCR machine"—this machine was known to the part-timers as Thor—"and help me in every way. Too much money slipped through our fingers last season. This year we tighten up the whole operation."

She asked for a week—and began her drive to Washington with a nightmarish vision of Thor rejecting her entries.

It was dark when she cruised by the apartment. She went around the block and passed by again, looking at the door, the courtyard, the lighted windows on the third floor. She looked at the window where she had stood while she watched Terry cross the courtyard carrying Crackpot, and remembered how the cat had batted at Terry's hair. Katherine circled the block again, saw the windows again, and slowed as she passed the playground next to the building. Of course there was nobody in it at this hour, though it was lighted.

She drove to the O'Connors' and began looking for a parking place, and had such bad luck and drove around so many familiar blocks that she began to have that "cruising" feeling, as if she were out looking for Crackpot.

She entered the lighted vestibule of the O'Connors' building, put down her bag, and pushed their buzzer, and an attenuated voice came through the speaker box: "Katherine? Is that you?"

"Yes, Carolyn," she said, and her own voice sounded attenuated.

The lock release buzzed, and she pulled open the inner door and went to the elevator, which stood open. She stepped in and punched *8,* and as the doors closed she saw her bag where she'd left it in the vestibule. This didn't irritate her. She carried the image of the bag, stranded between the two glass doors, up to the eighth floor and back down to the ground floor again. She contrived to prop the inner vestibule door open with her foot and reach out and grasp, just barely, a strap on her bag, and pull it to her. She found the elevator doors had closed. The number board showed *8.* She pushed the *Up* button and waited, holding her bag, and she watched each number light up as the car descended.

The doors parted and she faced Mike O'Connor, Carolyn's husband.

"Are you all right?" he asked.

"Yes, I'm sorry, Mike. I forgot my bag and had to come back down for it. I'm fine."

Katherine had all but forgotten Mike.

As the doors closed he reached out for her bag, which she surrendered, and with his other hand he patted her, or gently slapped her on the shoulder. She looked into his eyes and, in a way, recognized him—remembered his blue Irish eyes. She felt his hand again clapping her on the shoulder in that strange way. They were deep into each other's eyes. He tried to speak—it might have been "I'm—" He closed his mouth and smiled as if acknowledging how foolish he'd been to try. There was such suffering in his smile that Katherine couldn't bear to look at it. She shut her eyes and violently embraced him. They twisted silently for a few seconds as if suspended from a chain. Then she was pretty certain the words he choked out were "Bless you, Katherine," and she thought: "He hardly knows me." She said: "I'm so sorry, Mike." She spoke clearly. But a second later, as they twisted slowly from side to side, she heard a ghastly noise —as she thought of Julie O'Connor's wig and of the smooth skull beneath it. She knew this noise came from her own throat and "knew" she could stop it, and she thought: "Stop!" But a noise even more ghastly and even less intelligent burst out of her throat, and she began trembling, and seized Mike even harder. She still wanted to stop. She felt his arms tighten around her back, and relying perhaps on the force of this embrace, she yielded just slightly to the force within—and it took its advantage. She might have held it back had Mike not patted her again on the shoulder and said, "Bless you, Katherine." But he did this, and for some reason she thought of Julie's head. The membrane of her restraint burst.

When the elevator doors opened at the eighth floor Carolyn O'-Connor helped her husband lead Katherine into the apartment, and they put her on the couch and put a blanket on her and sat with her in turns throughout the night.

In the morning Katherine felt as if she'd been beaten with a telephone pole, and had never slept and never would sleep. Her abdominal muscles were tender after so much crying. Her brain too felt hypersensitive to any motion of her limbs or body, as if a psychopathic force had passed through and ravaged it. She kept her eyes closed—even though she remembered she had a 10 A.M. appointment with the movers. She didn't know what time it was. She did know that Richard was dead. In her crying there had been a stimulus to her memory of the night she learned Richard would recover from his wounds. This crying perhaps bore a certain similarity to that—

at least her abdominal muscles hurt now as they had hurt then. But the aftermath was quite different. She lay now in the aftermath, thinking for the hundredth time: "He's really dead." The sentence retained its meaning through all these repetitions. It was the woman who uttered the sentence whose meaning from time to time seemed to fade.

She opened her eyes and saw the O'Connors' three-year-old son, Patrick, sitting on a little wooden chair beside her like a sentinel. She said, "Hello, Patrick," and the boy got up and ran to the kitchen.

Katherine realized with a bolt of horror that she hadn't telephoned Terry. She threw back the blanket—unconscious alike of her sore muscles and the fact that she was still in yesterday's clothes—and was on her feet when Carolyn and little Patrick appeared.

Carolyn looked very alarmed and seemed bent on calming her.

Katherine asked: "What time is it?" and on being told it was about nine she groaned and went to the phone. She got the number of Terry's school and telephoned it—but they couldn't call Terry to the phone except in a "dire emergency," the secretary said, because the second-graders were taking their "reading diagnostics." Katherine arranged to call at lunchtime. She hung up the phone and took Carolyn's hand and kissed it, and held it for quite some time.

Katherine showered, but she wanted neither breakfast nor coffee. She walked to her apartment, met the bride, and vacillated. The woman was offering good money for, as it turned out, five pieces of living room furniture. But did Katherine need the money? She hadn't received her first Navy check yet but assumed it would be adequate. And the pieces under discussion were just those she'd need if she ever reestablished a household, even a reduced one. "Am I going to live in the woods all my life?" she asked. But the movers were on their way and she must decide. She looked out the window into the courtyard and saw three black men with canvas straps over their shoulders. One pushed a hand truck. She turned back to the woman and said: "I'm sorry. No."

The movers didn't want to do it room by room, they had some other organizing principle in mind, but the women knew no other way to make sure they took only what was Katherine's and left the rest. So there was a little discussion with the top man, which Katherine left to the other woman, who seemed unduly worried lest her possessions be carried out the door with Katherine's.

Katherine watched the artifacts of daily life as they went out one by one—Terry's bed, the bed that had been hers and Richard's, the sofa, the lamps, boxes of pots, pans, and dishes, and books. She had never realized she owned so much or needed so little. She gave Richard's clothes to the movers.

The work was still proceeding at noon, when she telephoned New Hampshire. Terry was in the school office waiting for her call. "Dearest," said Katherine, "I'm terribly terribly sorry I didn't call last night," and Terry said it was OK. Katherine said she had forgotten and Terry said it was OK. Then after some hesitation, weighing the risks, Katherine said: "I forgot because I was crying so hard," and Terry said it was OK. When she hung up the phone, the top man confronted her with his inventory sheets, which she had to sign, and his notes on the various scars and scratches on her furniture, which she had to initial. She left five dollars on the kitchen counter to pay for the telephone call, and walked down the stairs and across the courtyard with tears in her eyes. She felt faint, and stopped at the playground to sit on a bench. The place was full of kids and mothers. She panicked at the sudden thought of encountering someone she knew, and got up and walked on. She thought: "You forgot Terry —for God's sake!"

That night she and Terry talked on the telephone for a long time about the reading test, a new girl in school, and Terry's bed and bureau. Katherine assured her these were safely stored away. She promised to be home before bedtime tomorrow night.

Mike O'Connor sagged with exhaustion, and went to bed not long after his little son, Patrick, did. Before he left the kitchen, where his wife and Katherine sat over coffee, he kissed Katherine's forehead and smiled at her. She said, "Bless you too," and he smiled and left the room.

Carolyn O'Connor waited till a door clicked shut at the far end of the apartment. "It's harder for him," she said softly.

"I see," said Kit.

"Not that he loved her more. I loved her with all my heart. But a father's love for his little girl—pierces. I'm tempted to say it's a greater love. All that stops me really is that I ask, how could any love be greater than mine? So if not greater, different."

"Yes," Kit said.

"Different from our love for our daughters. This has taken me a long time to understand. For the longest time I believed it was harder for him because of something in *him,* because of his character, you know? A lower degree of resilience. That he was too fine, too delicate in his soul for the shocks of this world. Then too, he has no faith. I searched for the reason in him, but I was searching in the wrong place."

Carolyn O'Connor paused, raised her brows, and asked: "Can you take this?"

"Yes. Please go on."

"Because it's as true of your husband as of mine."

"Please go on," Katherine repeated, in a different tone.

"I'm butting my nose in."

"Please go on, Carolyn."

"A father," Carolyn said, "loves his daughter forever as we love a baby at our breast. I mean with that same excruciating sense of the precariousness of its existence. Everybody says 'vulnerability' these days, but it's beyond that—so far beyond I can't say it. It isn't simply a love that depends on the baby's vulnerability. I call it 'piercing' love and let it go at that.

"When a girl grows we can grow with her. We've been there, been through it before, and go through it with her. We can ultimately be women together. The father can't. He sees her grow, and he may *know* that now she's five or six or twenty, but the quality of his love never changes. Something in him still cries out on her behalf just as it did when she was at the most precarious stage of her life. It was that way with my Mike and my Julie, and it was that way with Dick and Terry. I saw it."

XIII

The colors that autumn had no meaning or effect. All their brilliance was a mere sensation in the eye or brain. It was equally pointless to recall the "meaning" of last year's colors, the so-called beauty, because all the colors of last year dissolved into the red seeping into the green of Bishop's hat. There was a color that meant something. But exactly what? It meant something false. It was a true color but a false meaning.

True in that it meant the blood of the marine. False in that Richard hadn't gone back for Bishop, who was dead, but for "Western Civilization." He denied it, of course, but who can admit that an abstraction is more important to him than his own child?

Driving home from work amid these sensational colors, which rose with the hills on every side, she stopped in a village where she wasn't known. She pushed a cart up and down the aisles of a grocery store, buying food she did not want to eat. She opened a box of eggs to see if any were broken. It nauseated her to imagine putting the agglutinated contents of those round white shells down her throat.

Who did Terry have now? A thousand miles away one grandparent, if she got to him before 10 A.M. Several great-uncles and great-aunts in Chicago who had seen her as a baby, and several aunts, uncles, and cousins who had never seen her. An aunt (Richard's half sister) in California, and the aunt's children: three thousand miles away. The Willoughbys. "And her mother," Kit said.

She pushed the trembling wire cart across the parking lot to her jeep, and crowded the grocery sacks together on the floor in front of the passenger seat. She glanced automatically up at the vivid orange of a mountainside. She intended to open the letter when she got home.

Keeping it any longer—keeping it this long was a sickly pretense. "Everything is as it was." No—nothing is as it was. Living in the same place and in the same anticipation, saving a letter—"I have an unopened letter"—disgusting!

The jeep was a most eager machine, starting at a touch. It was a good engine encumbered by a body of rust and wreckage. She followed the paved road along the Second Branch, then took the dirt road up through Happy Hollow, then the lesser dirt road past her father's place and on to the Willoughbys'.

She was entering the barn when Mrs. Willoughby called her name and came across the dooryard from the house carrying a package.

Katherine lived in a bubble. The entire nation was obsessed, polarized, rent, and confounded by the war, but nobody at the office and the ski resort ever mentioned it in her hearing. She had learned only this afternoon and by accident that the accountant's son was to be drafted next week; the accountant himself hadn't said a word to her. Here came the package to penetrate the bubble. It was cardboard, and about eighteen inches square, and it didn't surprise her. It was obviously Richard's stuff.

She thanked Mrs. Willoughby and put it in the back of the jeep, where Terry wouldn't see it.

It wasn't very heavy. Probably a few paperbound books, his shaving kit, his billfold, containing her picture and the picture of the daughter he loved with a "piercing" love. "Something in him still cries out on her behalf just as it did when she was at the most precarious stage of her life. . . . 'Piercing' love. . . . A father loves his daughter forever as we love a baby at our breast." There was a blanket in the back of the jeep, the dog's bed, and she threw it over the box.

That night after Terry had fallen asleep, she put on her blue jacket. The letter still crinkled in the pocket, but not as crisply. Guided by the moonlight, she went down the path through the birches and fetched the box out of the jeep and carried it to the cabin. The birches were still in leaf, but some of the moonlight reached their slender white trunks. She stopped and looked at the grove.

She saved the box—didn't open it—hid it in the back of the broom closet in the kitchen.

"Open it, you fool.

"No, no, the letter is enough for one night."

She hung her jacket on a hook, poured a glass of Burgundy, and sat at the kitchen table and looked at the letter for the first time since the day it came.

"If you don't open the box," she thought, "you will simply substitute it for the letter. You'll have made no progress.

"Ah, well, I'm lucky the box came today.

"Why, if you don't open it?

"I'll open the letter.

"And the box. Do it."

She took a sip of wine and noticed the postmark. It was an out-of-sequence letter, postmarked some six weeks before he was killed. Leaving it on the table, in the light, she stole up to the loft and silently drew her letter box from under her bed and took it down to the kitchen. She sipped her wine and went through the final inch or two of the letter box, reading postmarks and ascertaining that the letter now lying unopened before her had been mailed before the last five in the box.

She stared at the red and blue edges of the envelopes standing upright in her letter box, and at the unopened envelope with her name in the center, Richard's in the top left corner, and the word FREE in the top right.

She thought: "I'll put it in the letter box—in proper sequence. I'll never open it."

She had made a habit of putting out-of-sequence letters in proper order. This was wrong for her consciousness but right for his.

She took scissors and snipped the envelope open, and was baffled at first. There seemed to be no letter, only a half-sheet of yellowed newspaper. One side had been scrawled over with wavy lines, which she took to be a crossing-out of that side. So she turned the sheet over, and found another wavy line in blue ballpoint ink. But this line was legible. It said: "This happened in the village of Dong Tien on the morning of 25 May 1966." She flipped the paper and turned it first one way, then another, till the wavy lines revealed themselves as Richard's script. She read with difficulty, tilting the paper to let the light strike the ink as it passed through the heavy black type of the headlines and the black portions of the photographs. She saw the men chasing the pig. She witnessed the pig witnessing its own dismemberment. She followed an arrow which seemed to suggest she turn the sheet over, and she again read: "This happened in the village of Dong Tien on the morning of 25 May 1966."

She put the paper down, and stared away, and thought for a moment, and then said: "So what? You cared more about this damn pig than you did about your daughter."

"What matters?" she asked, and saw her mistake right away. That was the wrong question; it wasn't rigorous enough. The right question was: "What's imperative?" In the interval between autumn and the first snow, in the season between seasons, when the daylight was gray and the land naked, and the message was barrenness, she discovered this question. When she asked it she drove away the confusion and stopped the maelstrom. "What is imperative?" she repeated, because she knew the answer.

She wrote three letters to her Polish relatives in Chicago—one to Uncle Casey and Aunt Marya and one each to Aunt Loretta and Aunt Harriet. She had set her hopes on Casey and Marya, but she mustn't slight the other two—hence the three letters. What she wanted was to spend Christmas with Casey and Marya.

Terry must have a family. Everything else moved back. While struggling to master Thor and to keep the right numbers pumping through the accounting office at the ski resort, she often thought of getting a job in the library at Dartmouth, or an administrative job at the college, where she still knew some of the faculty. She could see herself staying there a long time. "I'd be free to walk in the woods on Saturday and Sunday," she thought, "as before." But no such plan was "imperative," and anyway she hadn't walked in the woods since—"Just *since,*" she said, and added with deliberation, "Fuck that." As for learning Greek, what a joke! She declared: "You can't live in paradise forever, and nothing is as it was. I did love this place once."

But Terry must have a family. "I mean," Kit added carefully, "Terry must have her own family, because that's what they are."

"I could live anywhere and what would it matter?" Uniformity and flatness. "But Terry must have her own family." Therefore Chicago.

City of unmitigated ugliness. Crumbling stucco, vertical slums, horizontal corridors rancid with urine, garages with interminable

corkscrew ramps, sixty stories of smooth steel and glass, all antihu-
man. But humanity did concentrate and thrive there, and the relatives all lived there.

Katherine had a plan—not simply a hope. They would move to
Chicago in June, at the end of the school year. This was decided,
fixed. But she wanted Terry to feel good about the move, not to feel
only that she was leaving here but that she was returning there. So
Terry must meet her cousins, Uncle Casey must take her for a ride
on the el, Aunt Marya must be seen knitting, cooking, and dressing
for church. Then leaving her schoolmates and the Willoughbys
wouldn't be quite so bad for Terry.

"Ed, you may not like this but I'll have to take a week off at
Christmas."

"You're not serious," said the accountant.

"Yes. I'm sorry. I know it's a bad time."

"It's the start of the season, the first blowout. It's chaos. Quick
turnover—mobs of college kids—and Family Week. And you've
already promised time off to three of the part-timers."

"That was before I decided. I really am sorry."

"Jesus, Kate, you're supposed to be responsible."

"I am responsible," she said.

They left three days before Christmas, after putting Crackpot in
the barn and chaining Yuk in a vacant calf pen.

"I'm sorry, Yuk," she said, "I'm sorry."

The dog danced and yipped and couldn't believe it, and howled.
Katherine slammed the barn door on the howls. The Willoughbys waved from their porch, and Terry shouted, "Merry Christmas!"

They drove down the winding white roads toward the valley.

Terry asked: "Is Daddy in heaven?"

"Oh—that's a hard question," said Kit.

"Winnie said he is."

"Who is Winnie? You've never mentioned anyone named Winnie."

"She's a girl. Her mother said Daddy's in heaven."

"Said your daddy is?"

"Yes. Is he?" Terry was getting impatient.

"No," said Kit, "I don't believe he is."

Terry said: "Good people go there."

"There are some things we do not know, but only believe," said Katherine. "I'll tell you what I know, and what I believe."

They passed through a covered bridge, and she thought: "Good Lord, a covered bridge this morning and O'Hare this afternoon."

"Will it be true?" Terry asked.

"You mean will what I tell you be true?"

"Yes. Winnie says—"

"Winnie doesn't know. Her mother doesn't know. Those people *think* they know, which is called believing."

Katherine then proceeded as if Terry had said: "Well, are they right or wrong?"

"I do not *believe* there is a heaven," Katherine said, "a paradise, a wonderful place where good people go after they die. Winnie's mother evidently believes it. I do not. If there is no such place, Daddy cannot be there."

"OK," said Terry.

"Now wait," said the mother.

They had reached the paved highway. As she brought the jeep to a halt at the stop sign, the snow of their passage swirled over them and across the road ahead.

"I know," continued Katherine, turning to the child—who did not turn to her—"that Daddy lives in our hearts."

And during the flight to O'Hare the child thought: "He lives in our hearts," and felt all right. She imagined that a place named Chicago would have palm trees, and she pictured Uncle Casey and Aunt Marya's house as a white edifice set at the end of a drive through palms. Inside there was a Christmas tree, and scattered under the tree were the presents she and her mother had wrapped and mailed ahead—plus a doll and horses.

Katherine was thinking: "I am not going to feel guilty about a necessary lie, especially one that's literally true. He does live in our hearts. What was I supposed to say, that he lives in our hearts but we didn't live in his? That he had no room? If she needs a family she needs a father of the only kind she can ever have, a memory of a 'good and strong' man and the myth that he loved her 'piercingly.' God! If we had lived in his heart he'd be alive today, and we'd have our family, the three of us. And that would be what? That 'family' would be what?"

On the day after Christmas she borrowed Uncle Casey's car and drove to her old neighborhood. At first she thought her high school had been converted to a prison. The larger ground-floor windows were bricked up and the smaller ones covered with wire screens. There were screens likewise on the second- and third-floor windows, and a chain link fence around the entire grounds. The door she used to go in by was chained. She walked along her old path, which had been a brown track through the grass and was now a spreading sea of frozen mud, and came to a basketball court carpeted with the crystalline green of a thousand broken Coke bottles. Jars of yellow and red paint had been flung against the brick walls of the building, and the whole place looked consumed, as if fifty thousand malevolent people had swarmed over it for fifty years.

Of the two apartment buildings where she had lived with her mother and John, the first had suffered the same kind of abuse, with the same kind of result. The entire street, in fact, was unrecognizable, except that now and again she saw a familiar facade or cornice —at which times her heart leaped with recognition and pain. The second building was unchanged, remarkably so, but the street felt different. It was still clean and still a place where families could live, but now the families were Hispanic and Katherine was an alien.

She returned to Casey and Marya's thinking: "So that's gone too."

Ella called that night, having obtained the number from the Willoughbys, and wished Katherine a Merry Christmas and a Happy New Year. Katherine thought: "I should have called her." Ella said John would be home in March and a civilian in July, and a law student in September.

That night as Katherine pondered, sitting in bed with the reading lamp on and Terry sleeping beside her, she thought: "Excellent. Just the qualifications for a lawyer. He has a gift for analysis, and no values."

She relived the moment when she had pressed Terry's hand flat against Richard's back. She thought: "He certainly isn't 'warm and strong' now. I could say he's *cold* and quite *without strength,* but actually, to be physical about it, he's beyond cold. I could say he's *without temperature* and without strength. But what an odd little paradox—not without power. If strength is the ability to control one's self, and power the ability to control or affect others, then we have here a man who has lost all strength but still possesses power. Like a martyr or saint or hero, in that one respect, at least."

She mused for a while on this "paradox" and at length clarified it in these terms: "A man who cannot lift a pebble or blink an eye has power."

As the winter proceeded she found that her work wasn't boring. The people in the office kept the bubble tightly affixed over her, but she rather approved of this, having no wish or need to talk about the war. She didn't like all her co-workers but she observed them all, and two or three of the women she liked very well indeed. Going to work meant motion, it meant that she looked at others and others looked at her, it meant power over Thor's power over numbers. The mighty Thor did exactly what she bade him do. Not knowing how he did it simply meant that hers was a raw and arbitrary kind of power.

She noticed that some of the ski instructors, when they came to the office for their paychecks, noticed her. From her skin to the innermost cell of her body she was asexual. But the notice of this rather numerous band of athletes, or of its elite members, was something she was willing to accept. "It's all right if they look at me," she thought. "They're men, after all, they can't help it. They aren't offending me. I don't want to be ugly, or a hermit. And I am nobody's wife."

She enrolled Terry in the Saturday morning ski classes, which were free to the staff and their children, and made up on Saturday mornings the hours of work she missed by going home early on weekday afternoons to meet Terry. She wanted to be there to meet Terry. The Saturday hours allowed Ed, the accountant, to declare Katherine a full-time employee at last and to confer on her the fringe benefits, such as hospitalization insurance, that went with this status. Katherine had said, "I don't need the benefits, Ed, I have Navy benefits," but Ed conferred them anyway, beaming magnanimity all over the place. Whereas Katherine's only purpose was to have a reason to be in the office on Saturday mornings when the rest of the staff was not. In the solitude of the office, a chamber of space and stillness at the center of the resort's activities, she would send Thor whirring and blinking through his paces. When she tired of that she would add a few random columns from the restaurant receipts or the pro shop. And then brew coffee. And then venture out into the fleshpot universe of the resort and walk to the great glass wall and search the beginners' slope for Terry, and having found her, stroll back to the quiet, empty space, which smelled now of fresh coffee, and close the door behind her.

"You'd expect men to be morally superior," she thought. A man, after all, couldn't make love unless aroused. A woman could do so in a state of total passivity, even antipathy. "By 'make love' I mean the so-called act of love," she said, "or the act of so-called love. The act of surrender and commitment." A man could enter into this only when his body, by rites beyond his control, enabled him. He was spontaneous or he was nothing. A woman could apply a minute amount of lubricant in secret and fake it all from that moment on.

"But in fact men are not morally superior," she thought, "at least not on this ground, because their spontaneity isn't noble. These 'rites beyond their control' are simply the biological expression of their promiscuity, their essential indifference. There is no commitment involved, for them. They are always busy living up to their stereotype."

With speculations such as these she passed the morning instructing Thor.

"Casey doesn't count," she said as an afterthought, because she loved Uncle Casey and he loved Terry. He had told Kit in confidence that he would give Terry a bicycle when they moved to Chicago in June. Terry had had only a tricycle in Washington, and there being no place to ride near the cabin, she had reached the middle of the second grade without learning. "Well, she'll know how to ski," thought Katherine.

When the lesson ended the mother and daughter ate lunch by the glass wall, where Kit and Ella had talked, and watched the skiers taking their thrills and pleasures against the side of the mountain.

Katherine was on the point of deciding which of the intructors was the most appealing, and she had cut the field to three. The emphatically masculine one wasn't the brightest; he was also very young. The bright one was a trifle too well oiled in the joints, and supercilious, as if he presumed, insisted on a social gulf (to his own disadvantage) where Katherine felt none. And the best-looking one knew it. In their bodies they were superb, all three, and that was another complication. It was not an easy judgment.

Her deliberations came to a halt one Saturday morning when the head of the ski school, the dean of this faculty of Adonises, came into the office and asked for a cup of coffee. Her first thought was that any sign of interest from him would drive the others away—and he was well into his forties. And yet—he could have posed as the king of Norway, with his yellow hair, blue eyes, bronzed skin, and alert features, with his slim, erect dignity.

He must have seen her hesitate, because he said quickly: "Maybe you haff—none."

But the pot was in plain sight, and it drew the eyes of both like a magnet.

They talked easily for half an hour—perhaps more. He disclosed nothing except that he could be charming, and she disclosed less.

He came again the following Saturday, and things went along in the same path. He came again on the Saturday after that, and Katherine thought that at this rate the snow would melt off the mountain before they reached an understanding. She was now ready. She had said to herself: "It won't be so bad. I probably won't feel a thing."

She thought of Ella and of her brother, John, as a lawyer, and she crafted a feeble witticism out of the word *law,* seeing it as an acronym for League of Abandoned Women. She saw Ella's fingers entwined in the grass and the sun beating on her perfect, perfect body. She said to herself: "Surely I'm undervaluing John," and added the next minute: "Surely I'm not." John was the man who put the words "I am unnecessary" in Ella's mouth. John was the man who said Dick would earn wages, not money. It was a true statement, of course. And John was the man who would now set out to earn money as a lawyer. She wished she could love John or at least feel a fraternal bond of a kind that didn't shame her, and she wished she knew whether her shame about John was or was not shameful in itself. "Am I so much better?" These were the words he put in her mouth. "If he's my brother, how good can I be?"

One thing she did affirm: she was guiltless toward Richard. "I do not feel guilty because I have no guilt," she said. "I never deceived him, never betrayed him," and she refrained from adding "until now," although the phrase suggested itself. But that was a mere flourish, merely an instinct for self-dramatization. There could be no deception where there was no one to deceive, and no betrayal where there was no compact.

Lars had a room with a splendid view of the mountain. He kept a pair of binoculars on the windowsill.

"Are your eyes good?" he asked.

"Yes."

"Twenty-twenty? Perfect eyes?"

"Probably," she said.

He adjusted both lenses to zero and then crouched just a little, assessing her face, and closed the angle of the glasses slightly, and handed them to her. They were perfectly adjusted, and she located Terry through them in a few seconds. The child, dressed in a new red snowsuit and white stocking cap, stood on the edge of a group of children surrounding their instructor at the bottom of the beginners' hill. Katherine swept to the top of the mountain and along the ridgeline. It was a sunless, not very clear day, and the woods were dark and vague along the skyline. She followed the ridge as far as she could, till she had all but forgotten that ski runs existed below, then searched again for Terry. And naturally, Terry still stood outside the group of children. No amount of luck or magnification would ever display to Katherine's eyes an image of Terry boldly in the center of a group of children, claiming her share of the instructor's attention.

Katherine handed back the glasses.

Lars took them but did not look out the window. He looked into Katherine's face and asked: "Does your little girl like to ski?"

"I think she likes it well enough."

"But she does not love to ski?" He spoke with a mongrelized accent and intonation, which he apologetically called his Swiss accent.

"She doesn't love it but she is trying to learn," said Katherine.

"Do not force a child," he said. "Forgive me because I cannot speak in degrees, I can only say in the hard clear words, do not force her. I have taught children."

And Katherine thought, "What am I doing here?"

Her prepared answer was that she was a free, unmarried woman —capable, presumably, of counterfeiting passion or at least pleasure. The question was, why? Why must Terry stand shivering on the fringe of a group of children, where perhaps she couldn't even hear the instructor's words, so that Katherine could seat herself on this strange bed and remove her shoes? But Katherine clung to the conviction that there was a cruel rationale in it, and to the belief that she could stand it.

A few weeks ago, when the snow had piled knee high and drifted over the top wire on some of the fences, she had borrowed Mr. Willoughby's snowshoes and gone out for release. Instead of release she encountered another paradox.

There was only one reason to defend the West. It was the reverence in the West for the individual, the value in the West of the human being. The West values a single soul. So what did Richard do? "He left the single soul he should have valued most. He abandoned the only soul he had an absolute duty to nurture." She remembered when she had said something like "Good God, Richard, do you love us?" And of course he had answered yes.

She put her hands on Lars's shoulders and she almost said: "You're so warm and strong." For whose entertainment would she have uttered such a loathsome irony? For her own?

She remembered the elliptical copse of birches halfway up the mountainside, and how John and Ella had skied down in such lovely curving harmony.

She became aware that Lars was sitting up, and that he had spoken. She looked at him, saw him push back his king of Norway hair. He had said: "Are you sure?" And he looked grave, and uncertain.

Katherine reached up and laced her fingers gently behind his neck, and drew his face down toward her breast, and thought of an adolescent fantasy in which, many years before she had ever known a lover, she had signaled her tender understanding in just this way.

Lars's gentleness surpassed her own. She thought at first it was mere technique from a citizen of the world (rather the skiing world) who had gone from Norway to Switzerland to France, whose speech seemed to carry the accents of a worn cynicism. "If this is technique," she thought, "who knows what might happen?" And she didn't pause to ask what that meant.

Every time she moved her body, however slightly, she saw Ella lying in the hollow, her arms overhead, fingers twisting in the grass, and her left breast slowly flattening against the blanket. "He'll let her work," she thought, "and pay the bills through law school, and when she can hold a pencil under her breast he'll divorce her."

Lars said something friendly or reassuring. Such at least was the timbre of it—she missed the words. It did seem possible now that she'd been wrong in believing she wouldn't feel a thing.

"Lars," she said, "you're a very gentle man."

He replied, strangely, "Let us hope so."

Katherine didn't know what this meant, if anything, and let it go.

"If Richard went back for the marines," she thought, "if they were the reason—" But she didn't follow through; she was tired of following through.

There was in Lars's "technique" something that suggested a want of the necessary confidence, so she sought out his eyes and smiled at him, and instilled confidence by touching him. He did seem to be a conscientious as well as a gentle man. His body was different from Richard's—smaller, the muscles smaller and neater, and of course Lars was much older. This was evident she knew not how. Half the mystery of Richard was never knowing when he would aggress.

Lars elicited from her dried-up soul a drop of happiness; a little surprise.

He said: "The maiden awakens," and kissed her.

This hurt or dismayed her somewhat, because a kiss is so much more intimate than it seems. But she didn't recoil or withdraw; she touched him again, and was consciously tender, considerate, and deft. She felt she owed him all her deftness, and she allowed him to kiss her.

Whether he was Lars or Richard her hand could scarcely tell. She saw dead soldiers sprawled on a tank, and the tread of their boots. Her mind added details that had never been in the photograph. The hand of one man hung down, and his fingers were pointed delicately, as in a painting by Michelangelo. "This is a trick, this is an artistic trick of the imagination to make him seem alive," she thought, and her heart contracted with love of the dead soldiers. And she saw Terry standing in the snow, her dark "Richard's" eyes fixed on the ski instructor. Katherine let herself do what she felt a desire to do, which was cry out—and she thought: "For whose benefit did you make that noise?"

When her body began to recognize Lars—as it had recognized the sun when she lay beside Ella in the hollow—she forgot to challenge her sincerity; and she didn't ask for whose benefit these changes were occurring.

When her body abandoned her she thought, "Here's one power Richard doesn't have." And as the ecstasy continued past all reasonable duration she said to herself: "This doesn't mean I'm with Lars. It means I'm alone."

"Did you enjoy your skiing lesson?" Katherine asked.

They were sitting in bed, side by side with a pile of blankets on their legs. The night had turned extremely cold and Katherine was wearing a heavy flannel shirt. She had bought a small lamp for Terry's side of the bed, since it was their habit now to read in bed together and even sleep together on cold nights. Terry was reading something called *Dog Heroes,* and Katherine had been struggling with a note to Lars. Terry said the skiing lesson had been OK.

"By that do you mean you don't like your skiing lessons?" Katherine asked.

"Oh—they're OK," the girl replied.

"You know, you don't *have* to take the lessons," the mother said.

Getting no immediate answer, Katherine returned to her writing, and suddenly it came clear. She would omit everything superfluous or embarrassing. She would throw out the too-precious idea of asking his "forgiveness" for having "used" him as an "instrument," and all such poetics. She took a blank sheet and wrote effortlessly: "Dear Lars—You were selfless and kind"—she added mentally, "not to say magnificent"—"and to say that I thank you is scarcely enough, but is all I can do. Forgive me, I cannot speak in degrees. I can only say I thank you, and that I will always remember your kindness.—Katherine."

"Now, Miss Theresa Mugwump Vail," she said, "may I interrupt your reading once more?"

"No-no-no—just a minute," the girl replied, holding up one hand and reading on intently, and Katherine took up her question only after the child closed her book.

"Do you want to stop taking skiing lessons?" Katherine asked.

"Well—I like it—sort of."

"You may keep taking the lessons if you want," Katherine said. "If you want to stop, I will ask my boss if I can change my schedule. I could stop working Saturday mornings, in which case I would work an hour longer on school days. That would mean I couldn't meet you after school."

"But you could come to milking?"

"Yes. I could meet you in the barn while you helped Mr. Willoughby with the evening milking."

"OK," said Terry.

"OK," said the mother.

"Did Daddy like to ski?"

"Actually, Daddy liked cross-country skiing," Katherine said, and explained the difference between that and downhill skiing. "But what he really liked," she said, "was snowshoeing. Daddy loved to go out in the woods on snowshoes and walk all day long, because on snowshoes you go where nobody else can go."

"Can Yuk go?"

"Oh yes, of course, a dog can go anywhere."

"She couldn't go to Chicago."

"The next time we go to Chicago," said Katherine, "we'll take Yuk."

Katherine produced the L. L. Bean mail-order catalogue, and they studied and discussed the various designs of snowshoe.

"They have children's ones," Terry said tentatively.

"You see, babe, if you had a pair of these you wouldn't sink in the snow. You could walk right over the top," said Katherine.

She winced at the price but ordered a pair for Terry. Putting the two envelopes in the mailbox the next morning, she had a feeling of exhilaration.

"The great Toad, the daring Toad!" Katherine exclaimed, and took her daughter's hand. They had been reading "The Further Adventures of Toad" in *The Wind in the Willows*.

"See, he doesn't *mean* to be bad," Terry said eagerly, "but he can't help himself. When he sees a motorcar he just steals it! And he drove it into the horse pond!"

"The great wonderful reckless Toad!" said Kit, thinking: "What the hell has come over me?"

XIV

S he didn't intend to attach any great importance to the box. Indeed, her intention was to give it minimal importance. Barring the chance that Richard had kept a journal, and he was not a writing man, or had written another letter never mailed, there could be nothing much in it. The box was depressing. It lacked the sacred dignity of an urn of his ashes, yet it made a claim as if it were exactly that. But what could it contain? There would be some or all of her letters, his paperback books, those he hadn't read or given away, his wallet and shaving kit, and probably a flashlight or some other utilitarian object or two. Imagining these things was not pleasant, and she had no desire to finger and fondle them. If she did, a malign god would grab her throat in his steel claw and start crushing her windpipe, and she would cry, her throat and stomach and back muscles would ache, and she'd be back again where she dreaded being.

Her present situation was difficult enough. "Not terrible," she said aloud. She knew what terrible was, and this wasn't it. She was harried. She had begun looking at the help-wanted ads in the Sunday papers, just to collect ideas, and there were none she wished to collect. And she didn't know where they'd live when they got to Chicago. Aunt Marya and Uncle Casey had offered a room while they searched for an apartment, but where were they to search? In what school district? How much rent could she pay? Must she be on a CTA line? Would there be friends for Terry close by? Suddenly Terry had a friend right here, Winnie Smallwood—"And now I've got to tear her away."

"Oh damn, I hadn't thought of that," she said a minute later. "Will they accept a dog and a cat?"—meaning her prospective landlords, whoever they might be.

The help-wanted ads were a lesson in something. Here were thousands upon thousands of jobs spread across the pages Sunday after Sunday, and not one she wanted. For a time she contemplated studying philosophy seriously, meaning graduate school, followed presumably by a career in teaching and writing esoteric articles. But the universities were becoming so politicized, and she was so uncertain what her position would be—and then, was she humble enough to accept tutelage? Could she strive for high marks and praise, knowing her career depended on them? She recognized in these objections the signs of a fundamental dubiety about the whole idea.

She began to read some of the Greek plays she loved, and risked her equilibrium by opening *Antigone,* because she had to make herself strong sooner or later. Five pages into the play she stumbled over the line: "Of this I am sure—our country is our life." Katherine put the book down, dislodged the cat from her lap, and began pacing.

Over the winter and spring an emptiness had accumulated within her, to heal the edges of her wound. The wound was still there, healed; the emptiness was still there, separating the edges of the wound. One detail at a time, she had begun to see that the war was still going on, and the focus of her thoughts moved from what the war had done to Richard toward what it was doing to the country. She didn't agree, she herself would never say "our country is our life," but she knew what it meant, and assented to it this far—that the war was doing to her something very like what it was doing to the country. What the essence of this was she didn't know. Among its symptoms were that she was more accepting of the artificial categories purveyed by journalism, that politics and policy were everywhere, and that daily life was charged with facile concepts in strategy and history. And hardly anyone admitted to a flicker of a doubt about anything. She built up the fire and sat down again with her volume of Sophocles, and read on the very next page: "Alive or dead, the faithful servant of his country shall be rewarded."

She slammed the book shut, called the dog, and went out into the night for a walk.

She already knew, but each week added fresh evidence that neither Richard nor any other veteran of this war would get his "reward." They would not be absolved; they would not be made whole.

She opened the door of the broom closet on a chilly night at the end of May. She had waited for a cold night so she could build a fire, perhaps her last, and dispose of every magazine, paper, junk book, and unnecessary box and bag in the place before beginning the main work of packing for Chicago. Much had already gone up the chimney when she reached up and took the box of Richard's personal effects down from the shelf. She was hot and sweating, and her heart was beating from the work. She put the box on the kitchen table under the suspended lamp and looked at it without emotion—yet she could feel her heart bulging in fast, frantic beats inside her chest. But no emotion; none. She stood there, a vacant woman with a frenzied heart. She went to the bathroom, seeing the box on the kitchen table all the while. Having completed her errand, she rinsed her face and looked at herself in the mirror, thinking: "Richard loved this face!" She got a knife from a drawer, slit the box, and sat down to examine its contents.

Here on the table before her, finally, were the things she had expected to see, plus an envelope with her name typed on the front. She opened this and unfolded an inventory sheet signed by a Lieutenant Michael Wozniak (she remarked the Polish name), "Assistant S-1," whatever that might be. At the bottom Lieutenant Wozniak had written: "The abovelisted items represent the entire contents of Lt. Vail's footlocker less government property and worn out clothing. We also included the contents of his pockets at the time of arrival at C-Med." And Katherine did find a brown paper bag stapled shut and labeled CONTENTS OF POCKETS, with Richard's name, rank, and service number. It was the size of a child's lunch bag and was virtually weightless. She looked at the whole array, at the packet of her letters, the razor, the photograph folder, the pencils, writing tablet, memo books, and sheath knife (the one Richard took to Antarctica while she was carrying Terry)—and she picked up a green, pocket-sized memo book.

Paging through it, she found entries of two kinds—sets of letters and numbers that were apparently a code, and large, awkward, but careful entries in pencil, which she surmised had been made in poor light. These latter were evidently in English, but so pervaded by jargon and abbreviations, and so full of numbers, that she couldn't guess what they were about. But the hand was Richard's, and she felt as if he had passed outside her window.

She took the packet of her letters to the fire and threw it in, then returned and stared indecisively at the rest—and puzzled over the memo book again. As she went deeper into it she came across several pages in somebody else's hand, and this person had written out some terms Richard abbreviated, including "Night Defensive Fires" and "Harassment and Interdiction Fires." Going backward, she found that many of Richard's entries were headed "NDF" and "H&Is." She took the book to the fire and threw it in.

She put his razor, sheath knife, and flashlight to one side for Mr. Willoughby. She took the photograph folder, containing her picture and Terry's, to the desk in the living room and put it in a drawer.

The writing tablet had a white cover showing the Marine Corps emblem and the motto "Semper Fidelis." She riffled through the few pages still in the tablet and concluded they were all blank, and she was on her way to the fire when she thought it might be possible to bring out the impression of whatever he had written last by sweeping across the first blank page with charcoal or soft pencil. She rummaged in her desk for the charcoal she had used to make gravestone rubbings, and returned to the kitchen table and opened the tablet.

The first page wasn't quite blank. On the top line he had written a date—the day before he was killed—and on the second: "Dear Kit —Yes—"

She now turned every page carefully. There were only six left, and all were blank, nor was there anything written on the front or back cover.

"Yes," she thought.

She wondered now whether in any of the letters burning a few feet away she had asked, do you still love me? and whether this was his answer. Did he have a premonition of death and intend to write this single word, and nothing more, and to leave it for her to find exactly as she had found it? He might indeed have foreseen his death. "But he would have said 'Yes I love you,' not some mysterious monosyllable. He didn't deal in theatrics." She looked at the word again, and it kept repeating itself in her brain—"Yes"—meaninglessly.

"He was starting a letter," she said, "and was interrupted—he had to get ready—"

She felt a catch in her throat, and put the tablet down and closed its cover—which she couldn't do without seeing "Semper Fidelis." Tears started in her eyes, but she took control of herself by saying:

"It does not mean 'Yes I love you.' It is a word whose meaning I do not know."

She decided to finish her business as quickly as possible, and she opened the little bag labeled CONTENTS OF POCKETS. Here was a thin wallet with a stenciled card inside. "Official military identification cards removed in accordance with III MAF order . . ." and a long number which had the bracing effect of arousing her antipathy. What remained in the wallet were a few dollars in Military Payment Certificates and Vietnamese dong, a laminated card with another set of numbers in Richard's hand, and a printed card giving the symptoms and treatment for heatstroke and heat exhaustion. There was a pocket knife, and there was a letter.

The letter had been folded double. It was very delicate and worn, and judging from the texture had been soaked through, perhaps more than once; and judging from the color, once in blood. She unfolded the envelope, and the scarcely legible writing on the front was her own. A little cascade of dark powder ran down the crease.

To touch the letter was to risk destroying it, but she parted the envelope and lifted it out, and spread its remains flat on the tabletop. It was disintegrated along the folds, and much of what she had written was effaced. She knew without reading which letter it was, but she lifted the pages one by one until she reached the question: "Is life sacred?"—obliterated almost, but plain enough to the eye of the one who asked it.

She opened his writing tablet, removed the first sheet, and placed it beside the letter.

Katherine put on her blue jacket. She called the dog and went outside, but the night was so dark she kept stumbling and going off the path and lane into pine branches, and she wasn't willing to wait for her night vision—so she came back into the cabin. Still wearing her jacket, her face flushed and her hair disturbed by the wind, she stood looking down at her question and his answer.

"Or what I think is his answer," she said to herself in an admonitory tone.

She removed the jacket—she was wearing jeans and a sweat shirt—and looked again.

"Certainly if you place the word 'Yes' beside the question they appear to connect," she said, still in her skeptical vein, "but what you're seeing is simply the physical proximity you yourself created.

I could write 'Is the earth flat?' and put it in the same place—and by the same procedure I would have a professional geologist saying it was."

Now she looked again at the letter and envelope, particularly the dried blood. She moistened her fingertips, picked up some of the powder, and licked it.

She said slowly: "If 'Yes' is his answer, he must have been in agony." And a moment later: "If 'Yes' is his answer and yet he continued—continued to fight—let's call it *fight*—" Her eyes filled with tears, but she wiped them and sat down and began writing in Richard's tablet with Richard's pen.

"I will use the razor of the written word. I fool myself too often in the privacy of the mind, but if I write, then the sentences that track will declare my meaning and those that don't will declare that I have no meaning.

"I profess the sanctity of life. Further, I challenged my husband from my cloister to say whether in the midst of battle he held life sacred too. I wish I had not. I reaffirm my belief that life is sacred but wish I had not added to my husband's burden.

"I wonder why I did so. I see the possibility that I was continuing by unfair means the debate we had over his going back. If I did this, what I did is despicable. I was charging him with self-contradiction. I believed all along and believe now that he held life sacred in the same way as I, yet I condemned him as 'willing to kill.' But I never said, at least I don't recall ever having said honestly: 'Life is sacred.' Instead I asked the rhetorical question: 'Is life sacred?' I was evading something, I hope not maliciously. What was I evading?"

She looked at the objects scattered on the table. She got up and brewed tea, and built up the fire, for the house was getting cold. She threw the empty box and the inventory sheet into the fire, and stood over the table drinking her tea and reading what she had written.

"I evaded my own self-contradiction, because I too am willing to kill. Not that I ever could, except perhaps in defense of Richard or Terry. But willing in that I believe in the just war. He thinks this one is just and I do not. That is a deep, terrible difference between husband and wife, but it doesn't make me a pacifist. And as I regard pacifism as the abdication of ethical responsibility, I had no warrant to taunt him with the sanctity of life. If Richard was inconsistent, so was I. We held life sacred, and we admitted war into our moral universe.''

She picked up the stenciled card that had been inserted in his wallet and read it again: "Official military identification cards removed in accordance with III MAF order No. . . ." She flipped it back toward the wallet. She had no idea what III MAF was, and didn't want to know.

"I abhor and abominate this awful war because I cannot believe in its necessity. If it is not necessary it is not just." She thought out three definitions of "necessary," but that was a path she didn't go down. She continued: "Richard went back, I think, because he was devoted to the marines, but he also believed in the necessity and justice of the war. He believed human beings make their own souls, or participate in the making. He said as much in speaking of his father's 'crime' against himself. And he therefore believed in freedom." A moment later she added: "He believed in the sacredness of life but also in the sacredness of freedom.

"I wish he had been slightly more political and talkative. I could then be firmer in my conviction that he did believe 'our country is our life' in this sense: that a totalitarian government smothers or tries to smother the human spirit, but in a free country the human spirit has a chance.

"Richard, I believe that too. When you died I was blinded with pain, and I said, 'His ideas are more real to him than Terry and I.' I would now say, perhaps with equal pain, 'He refuses to surrender his ideas for us.' No—the pain would be less. My beloved, forgive me for trying to forgive you. Whatever power of absolution I possess I now exercise for you, and bless you with my love."

She slept soundly and late, awakening to find that Terry had taken herself off to school. The cat sat on the kitchen table taking the sun. Yuk was stretched out like the dead on the cool bricks of the hearth. Katherine breakfasted, drank a cup of coffee, and then read what she had written.

"Move it, Yuk. I'm sorry, sweetheart," she said, and the dog lugged her bones off the hearth as if they weighed a ton.

Katherine sat on her heels and raked clear some embers, and set the corner of the tablet aflame.

Katherine drove slowly through the short pines and stopped at the top of the scrabble. The cat was safely in his cage in the back seat. Yuk was suspicious of being leashed while in the car, a most unusual restriction, and commenced her protest as the mother and daughter got out and slammed their doors. Katherine didn't waste her breath admonishing the dog, but took Terry's hand, and the two began walking up the tractor path through the woods. It was about a ten-minute walk to the open place where Richard had split the logs.

The woods were cool. The open place, with the great stump in the center that Richard had used as a splitting block, was hot and brilliant with the early summer sun.

The old stump was scarred by awl and wedge, and split by age. Katherine poked a stick into one of the splits to test its depth, and couldn't find the bottom. She took off her wedding ring, a plain gold band, glanced briefly at Terry, and dropped it into the stump. The girl, watching this with intense, reverent eyes, attempted to look into the crack to see the ring. She put her finger in, but it would go only to the second knuckle. She took from the pocket of her shorts a gold Thai dancer that Richard had sent her from Bangkok, when he took five days' leave there. The dancer's lower body was a fish's, and was sharply curved; her upper body curved with a stylized loveliness toward the finned tail, and her hands reached lightly up. Terry dropped her into the same split.

When they returned to the car Yuk all but barked the windows out. Crackpot screeched his rage. And the car itself set up a tinkling, crashing cacophony as Katherine sped down the scrabble. Katherine was resolved there'd be no tears at the Willoughbys', where they had to leave their keys, but this had perhaps been an unrealistic hope. She drove at a reasonable, resolute speed past her father's farm and down the dirt road winding down toward the valley. The timbers let out a clangorous roar as she sped through the covered bridge.